alphar

GODLESS

A NOVEL BY
DREW STEPEK

ALPHAR PUBLISHING, Burbank, Ca

LIBRARY OF CONGRESS CATALOGING IN PUBLICATION DATA
Stepek, Drew
GODLESS
1 Title
ISBN 09786024-9-8
ISBN 978-09786024-9-9 (at 13 digit)

Hardcover edition Published June 2006 by ALPHAR
ISBN # 09786024-9-8

Soft Cover edition to be published November 15, 2006, by ALPHAR
ISBN # 978-09786024-9-9
PRICE: US: $15.95
UK $9.95

Editing: Charlene Rashcow, Jon Adcox, Bobbie Christmas
www.godless.com

For Charlie

FROM THE AUTHOR

My friends and family have told me for almost twelve years now that bulimia and alcoholism are eventually going to catch up with me. Even though I understand their concern and their love, I didn't begin to come to terms, or at least try to come to terms, with that reality until recently.

Not long ago, I returned to Los Angeles from a college friend's bachelor party in Las Vegas. The debauchery was everything I expected. From what I remember, it was a nice time. What I didn't expect was the strange new feeling I returned with. It wasn't any kind of catharsis or revelation about my self-destruction or any kind of bright idea that maybe I'm getting too old to be treating myself that way. That shit is for reborns and guilty assholes. I'm not hurting anyone. What the fuck do I have to feel guilty about? Rather, I returned with a feeling in my chest that I hadn't felt before. My lungs were clenched and I found it extremely painful to eat. I thought maybe I was going to feel that way forever, that maybe I had either finally blown my heart or torn my esophagus beyond repair. I guessed that the twelve years of self-induced vomiting was finally taking its toll. I spent three days feeling like someone hammered a bunch of rusty nails in my chest whenever I ate, drank, or smoked. Three days, that's nothing, right? When you fear for twelve years something is going to happen, three days seems like the final stretch and the end of the line.

The next day, after I was positive it was some fluke—maybe an old college chum sat on my chest while I was passed out—I returned to the bathroom. I threw up, and I didn't even think twice about it. I told myself that I had once again triumphed over the laws of the digestive process.

That instance is important to the story you are about to read, because it's real. *GODLESS*, although filled with fictional settings and fictional characters, comes from someone who knows what alcoholism and bulimia are and how deadly they can be when mixed together for a long time. I'm not preaching. I would never preach about this. I have nothing to say that would make you change your mind. I refuse to change.

The closest I came to overcoming my mess was when I spent some time in a hospital. Even then, I decided that my primary objective was to get the fuck out of there by cheating the system and lying.

I'm lost, and I've lost so much because I've failed to recognize. I've lost friends, loves of my life, and pieces of my former self. Everything fades away every time I enter the restroom with the purpose of throwing up. I can't blame anyone, and I can't listen to anyone. It's all a fucking void. For those three days, though, I felt the gears of mortality and the price I will eventually have to pay for my refusal to change. Did I find God? Did I want to live so strongly that I found a higher power? No. I found myself right back where I started.

Our society is godless. We sit on our thrones, point our fingers at each other, and yell obscenities so we can have bragging rights to play and pray for the winning team. We throw sticks, stones, knives, and bullets at each other so we can pound our chests to flaunt our strength and allegiance. We love to see others in pain, because it makes our lives seem better by comparison. We masturbate on our successes, because we think we have triumphed over evil. We don't care what anyone else has to say, and why should we? When it is important to speak, we don't say anything, because we can't admit when we are wrong. Is this why your god put us here? Is your mission in life to brag about your personal eternal bliss and wipe your ass with the convictions of others?

In our quest to find the meaning of life, to justify why we are alive, we chose sides and criticized our childhood playmates for accepting a higher power we didn't agree with. They were perfectly acceptable before they decided they wanted something other than the misery we stew in every day. We create antagonists in our minds rather than realizing how similar we all are. We misjudge helping hands as adversaries and good deeds as selfish acts. There isn't anything wrong with thinking differently, but there is something wrong with thinking that you're better than anyone else. I don't consider myself a prophet for profit or a martyr for barter; I'm just sad at the way we look at each other. As a race, as living, thinking, functioning beings, we should all be fucking ashamed.

Isn't that what it has come to? Do you sleep soundly at night knowing that the faithless vagrants on your street, in your alley, in your garbage, can do nothing more that hallucinate about collecting welfare faith? If they could manage to get roofs over their heads to block God out, don't you think they would?

Not everyone can be classified as a fuck up or an invalid either; some people have just lost their way and their will to live. Can you blame them? I'm not a saint or a champion of human justice; I ignore the cries of the street urchins just as much as you do; however, I am willing to recognize that something is wrong.

What do you see when you look at the dysfunctional mayhem we've created? Do you think someone upstairs cares about our misfortune? Are we led like cattle to a slaughterhouse because we are indeed imperfect? Are we alive because we need to fulfill the wishes of someone else? Have you ever stopped to shake hands with people who are different from you rather than snickering at them because you can't understand their beliefs?

Do you care that kids bring guns to school or that others choose death rather than life? Of course you do, but aren't you glad they aren't your kids? Do you honestly think that your god, whom you have never seen or spoken with, is better than your neighbor's? Somehow, I believe the comfort of a higher power is obscured behind opposing jerseys and defending goals. Sure, things were like that from the beginning, but it has gotten much worse, even as we are told that we have grown wiser.

It seems all too easy to poke fun at religion or scrutinize it because we have lost track of who we are. My intentions aren't to demean or lessen the effect of religion or the positive lessons to be learned from it. I don't look down on people because of what they believe. As a matter of fact, I envy them for having the power to see something I can't. In my world, one shocked by reality, I can't accept that I was created by anyone other than my parents. I can speak with them, and they can give me advice. They are tangible. They are my gods, because they guided me as best they could. They are my gods because they were the first people I listened to or thought about when I was born.

Life is a miracle. It should be accepted as that and cherished. Your pain isn't going to go away if you believe in anything in particular. Choosing a doctrine because someone regards it ethical isn't going to grant you a permanent invitation to the game. The game will never end, and the pursuit of happiness, acceptance, and dreams will never go away. Everyone does have the right to find happiness.

I can't apologize for all the mistakes of the world and its inhabitants. I can't justify bad things. I can't mop up your tears and tuck you in at night. I don't want to. I can't apologize for the way that I feel. I hope you're right, and someone else is caring for us, watching us. The world would be safer if someone cared enough to tell us how wrong we are. I can, however, apologize for my mistakes. I hope someone, somewhere, someday, will understand why and where all of my pain and hatred come from.

Every day of my life, as I attempt to put the puzzle pieces together, I end up back where I started, asking myself four questions.

Do I know who I am?

I mean, really know who I am?

Do I know where I come from?

Do I know where I'm going?

Be true to yourself and respect other people. Most importantly, don't ever leave any words unsaid, even if you think other people aren't listening.

Drew Stepek

BOOK ONE

NAZARETH

"They said with one accord that I got drunk oftener than was necessary and that I was wild and Godless, idle, lecherous and a disconnected and unsettled rover."

Samuel Langhorn Clemens

CHAPTER ONE

Some things are best left unsaid.

"You go to school with my stepdaughter, don't ya, boy?" It was difficult to hear Rick Conroy, the owner of the AutoRX, over the cranking of ratchets and humming of nut drills. He was talking about my friend Lori Conroy. He wiped grease and piss off his forearm and started writing up my paperwork. Not realizing it, he licked his pen and got a glob of ink all over the side of his blistered lips.

Conroy's skinny frame hunched over. The grease dripped down his face.

"Yeah, I know her."

"I thought so. I seen ya around her all the time. What's your name? Deece?"

"My name's D. Lori and I hang out." He didn't answer, so I kept talking. "I've known her since you all moved here when I was in grade school." Trying to take my attention away from Conroy's lazy eye, I looked up at the clock behind him, where a bikini-clad model was holding a mug that said, "Time for a beer." The model's non-existent head was the clock face. I attempted to speed the conversation along, as his eye was making me uncomfortable and my shoes were swimming in crusty rags. My friend Freddy Brubaker would be waiting for me at our high school homecoming game in a few hours. "So what's the damage, Mr. Conroy?"

A huge thud rang out in the garage area. Deteriorated plaster and dust snowed from the ceiling and a makeshift shelf of die-cast racing cars behind the register collapsed. "Oh shit!" I screamed, hoping the disaster didn't involve my car.

Conroy spun around. "What the hell's goin' on back there?"

"Nothin', boss, just dropped a fender," came a voice from the garage.

"Be more careful, ya fucking invalids." Mr. Conroy turned back to me and slapped me on the shoulder. "There goes your car." He laughed, but it wasn't a warm or mirthful sound. "Just jokes, boy."

"Hilarious." I looked down at my watch. It seemed like a safer place than trying to choose which of Conroy's eyes to make contact with. I tried to look at his sleeves-optional T-shirt that said "Muff Diver" across the front, but I could feel the wandering eye hovering. "So, what do I owe you?"

Conroy drummed the pen a few times on the paperwork and tapped away on his calculator. Then he ran his blackened hands through his hair plugs. He tore off the receipt and looked at it. Defeated, he chucked his first estimate by the trash, the cemetery of all his mathematic mistakes over the past year. Crumbled up paper littered the corner of the register.

"You ever poke her?"

"Huh?"

"You ever poke Lori? I know all you kids are fuckin'."

A year earlier, I would have jumped at the chance to have sex with Lori. She had it all—big full lips, dirty little eyes and a slight gap between her two front teeth. However, something was wrong with her and the distance that she was keeping from her close friends was reflected in the thirty pounds she had dropped over the summer.

He paused and smirked. "Come on son, you can tell me; she ain't mine by blood."

I sighed and closed my eyes for a second. "Can you please just give me my bill so I can pay it? Jesus Christ, Mr. Conroy, all I had done was the oil."

Lunging forward, he snatched me by the collar. I turned my head. "Don't you take the Lord's name in vain, boy. If I find out you're fuckin' my daughter, I'll beat your sack through your throat." He put his fist under my chin. I didn't answer; I just looked at him with cold eyes, waiting. "Don't get smart. What's the matter? Did your daddy get canned from the mill like all these other poor bastards? Are times tough? Not for me, ya little prick. Even your poor ass has to get around somehow."

"Relax! I'm not having sex with your *stepdaughter*." I shook away his grip. "I just need my car so I can go to the homecoming game."

The eye glanced at me one last time and he pointed his finger at me. Shaking his head, he retracted whatever thought passed through his mind. "Homecoming game. Yeah right, they ain't gonna never win in this town." He strutted back toward the garage, flipping the pen backward that left an ink-stained money shot on his mouth. "Jose, get your Spic ass up here and do this little shit's paperwork."

I thought my town was shit, and my conversation with Rick Conroy at AutoRX backed me up. It was poor and dying. If I stayed there, I would most likely die, too. I wanted out so bad that I met my mailman every day after school, anticipating my college acceptance letter. Every day. It never came.

I paid Jose and he drove my car around for me.

"Have a good time at the homecoming game. Go Badgers."

"Here you go, Jose." I gave him a couple of bucks for his trouble and got in my car. "Go-fucking-badgers."

The smell of oil still burned in my engine, making me sick. That fucker Conroy hadn't done shit to my car. The smell inside, though, was better than the stench I would suck in by rolling down my windows. The paper mill upwind shut down about nine months before, leaving most of our town, including my workaholic father, unemployed. Its closing, however, didn't rid the area of the pulp-burning stench, punctuated by the odor of dead animals. The combination smelled something like the aftermath of a bombed sweatshop. Most of the wildlife was killed drinking the foulness that filled the water. I stumbled on carcasses frequently.

In one respect, though, I guess I could thank that paper mill. It gave me the resources to fill out the paperwork necessary for a scholarship. I'm not an environmentalist, so, forty some-odd years of toxins from the mill didn't seem to affect or bother me nearly as much as their absence had destroyed the town and its people.

I drove through the town and observed its decline. You'd think that on homecoming weekend there would be banners and signs welcoming home the alumni. But in my town, there were two kinds of alumni: those who never left and those who never wanted to come back. I wanted to be one of the latter.

I drove by the few storefronts that were still in business. The wooden signs hung on by one nail, and the burned out neon signs were indecipherable. The only store that still had a neon sign intact was Rick Conroy's AutoRX. "Get In Check." It boomed in my rearview mirror. "Get Auto RX."

Over the summer, Lori and I used to break into her stepfather's garage and drink. Every time before we left, we'd cut the circuit breaker and shut down the pulsating sign. We figured we were doing the town a favor.

No store stayed open after five. What was the use? Nobody had any money to buy anything. Most of the stoplights were malfunctioning in the center of town, but I always stopped, whether it was working or not. At a flashing red light I saw the town barber, Remy Woolfe, sharing a forty with a loiterer.

"Hey, D," he waved, jogging up next to my car. "Need a haircut?"

I held my breath and rolled down my window. "Sorry, I'm a hippie this year, Mr. Woolfe." I nodded back at his companion. "I think you might want to cut your buddy off." The barber turned around to see his loiterer dropping a deuce in the alley next to the shop. The bum's uncircumcised cock dribbled into a pile of trash. Woolfe ran back to the shop and started chasing his pal down an alley with a broom. Shit streamed down the man's leg as he scrambled to pull up his pants.

Driving by the homes proved even more depressing than driving through the center of town. Rather than having space between them, they were all sewn together by discarded appliances and the rest of the shit in the yards. I stopped at one of the homes. I knew my mom was looking for a filter for her dryer and I actually saw a dryer that looked like ours.

A woman came to the door with a baby attached to her tit. "Yeah?" She coughed.

"Can I look at your dryer?" I said, averting my eyes from her boobs. "My mom is looking for a filter."

"You getting a good look, kid?" I must not have looked away quickly enough.

"Sorry, I wanted to know about the dryer." The door slammed shut. It turned out to be the wrong model anyway.

"Thanks. Wrong dryer. I don't need any milk. Shit." Too busy trying to be a smartass, I got tangled in boob lady's fence. Wrapping and covering almost every other inch of the town was "the virus vine." In our part of the country, people called the uncontrollable kudzu weed the virus vine. Kudzu spread, covered, and swallowed our town, eliminating it and all of its value from the face of the earth. It grew on houses. It grew on phone lines. If you left your car unattended long enough, it grew on your car. Maybe the town was best that way, unseen, unsaid, and unnoticed.

Before I went home, I met my pal the mailman. Nothing. No ticket out, once again. Then I changed out of the shirt that Rick Conroy stained with oil when he threatened to knock my nuts through my throat. Looking a little better, I left the house. I had to make my afternoon stop at Nazareth.

You see I'd discovered a way to cleanse myself of the confines of prom dates, football pep rallies, and lame tri-screen-enhanced motivational speeches in an auditorium. The latter interested me the least. Although the intention seemed honorable, those presentations were always M.C.-ed by some hack ex-cop who had evidently honed his audio/visual skills rather than his filling-out-retirement-paperwork skills. Besides, I didn't believe these "Drink, Drive, Die" speeches were what George Lucas envisioned when he created THX. Instead of indulging in the lackluster rah-rah of high school life, I chose to pay my respects to a tree.

"Paying my respects to a tree" wasn't slang for getting high or anything like that. The tree offered a place where I could write, think, and be alone.

The tree stood at the center of my Nirvana. I never understood how it grew from the tainted soil of my town. Standing about thirty-feet, the tree, which I jokingly dubbed Nazareth, nestled on the side of a bog bank contaminated by the atrocities of the paper mill.

Quite a persistent old bastard, the tree had been there for as long as I could remember. It had two extended limbs that sprouted out, reaching eternally for some sort of hope. The shaft displayed the agony of a martyr's face: twisted, torn, and weathered. Brought to the tree by the moisture from the venomous swamp were thousands of gnats and marsh bugs that sucked at its tears of sap. Although the oak was a landmark, its beauty never stopped me from "baptizing" it after a good night of writing and a few too many beers. When I was about five, this scumbag neighborhood kid Tommy Horton took a piss on me when we were out catching toads by the mill. I guess pissing on the Nazareth was my revenge.

A behemoth from top to bottom, the tree wasn't going anywhere. The base was so thick and soundly embedded in the ground that even the swampy muck that sucked the life out of most seedlings was pissed back down into the bog.

"Hey fucker." I tapped at the base of Nazareth and sat down to write about my confrontation with Rick Conroy before I went to the game. To avoid having to change my clothes again, I brought a bleacher seat with me every time I visited Nazareth. It was better than walking around with sludge on my ass, and having to explain that I didn't shit myself. Usually, I sat with my back against the tree. This method produced the best results for writing. Sometimes, though, I sat in front, admiring it. These writings usually turned out to be kind of pussy.

I never brought anyone to the tree, except for one time when Lori and I had been out throwing apples at cars. We had accidentally nailed a cop car and needed a place to hide. Since we didn't want to risk breaking and entering the Auto RX, I took her to my place. She wasn't so skinny then.

CHAPTER TWO

The wind that homecoming night smelled like burnt embers as it breezed through town, fighting away the always-lurking stench of the old paper mill. The fall of my last year of high school wasn't an Indian summer. Quite the contrary, the weather was bitterly cold.

That night our team delighted us with the homecoming football game. The cheerleaders were so cold that not even their team spirit and mascot-blessed sweaters could help them avoid the crowd heckling them. The home team fans were no better off because seating was scarce. In the center of the bleachers was a giant hole that we called "the shit pit." During the final game of the previous season, some idiot kid doused the termite infested seating with kerosene before the game and lit the center on fire. I think he'd played on the golf team and had decided to protest the sale of the local golf course to a waste disposal company.

Outside the field, I met up with Freddy Brubaker, bundled up and tribally face-painted red and black, the school colors. In a furry-hooded winter coat, the blushed, scrawny Freddy looked like an order of cotton candy. From under the coat, part of his straight, brown hair fell in his eyes.

He shot me a shaka. "What up, D?" Then, he made an idiotic face like he was cool.

"Nice shaka, fag. Did your small ass go surfing in the toilet this morning? There is nothing going on. Absolutely nothing."

"I think we're gonna win this year. Don't you?" He laughed, and we headed out to the game to cheer on the team. Even though there wasn't anything to cheer for. We were the weakest and smallest team in our conference. Our homecoming rival blasted through our rag-tag bunch of maybe-they-should-have-played-soccer contestants and left them for the over-worked janitorial staff to clean up. The homecoming game, like every other game, wasn't much of a contest. We hadn't beaten our rivals in more than twenty years. We lost 45-3. As in every game that season, the golf team rooted from the opposing team's bleachers.

Luckily, our field goal kicker, Jim "Launch" Lonchar's day job was playing soccer. As the team's only asset, he helped save a little bit of face.

Nothing felt worse than losing our homecoming game every year, but that year it didn't seem to faze football fanatic Freddy. The primetime feel of bright lights and shiny helmets impressed him, but he insisted he could never play the game, because of his inability to concentrate. I'm sure Freddie's setback had nothing to do with the fact that the kid stood five foot six on his tiptoes and weighed a buck twenty.

I'd known Freddy almost my entire life. We grew up directly across the street from each other. He was rich, at least by our town standards. His father, Buck Brubaker, had made some sound investments years before the mill closed, and his mother, Trudy, came from old money. The youngest of four Brubaker boys—Billy, Timmy, Tommy, and Freddy consecutively—he wasn't the brightest kid I knew. He spent much of his early life juiced up on Ritalin to control his outbursts of hyperactivity. Also plagued with ADD, he spent his school time in those "special" classes; still, all of his birthright setbacks never stunted his optimism.

As my closest friend, Freddy always spotted me when I was low on cash. I wasn't making much money cleaning up at the local bookstore. The money aside, I loved him like a brother. As small and as silly as he was, Freddy always stood up for me in any situation.

"Hey, man, you're not going to believe the news I got today." We jumped into his overly lifted Jeep CJ-7. He popped the clutch to take off, and kicked his theme song, "Stigmata" by Ministry, into the CD player. The thundering drums and stinging vocals of one of the evilest songs in history blared out of his swass five-speaker system. He raised his hand for a high-five. "I got into State early admission. I'm out of here, kid."

It looked like Freddy was to be the first to escape. I changed the subject.

"Don't worry about me. I should be fine working at the tollbooth on the Bay Bridge. Maybe I'll hook you up some time." Bringing snacks and drinks to my mailman, helping luck along, were in vain.

"And check this out, bro." He reached into his center console, and he made a real face. It was one of pride. His little eyes blinked and his perfect teeth sparkled. "Look what my old man got me. He opened the letter before I got home from school today." Like pulling a sword from a stone, he flipped the object out of his pocket, and shined it off the interior lights of his Jeep. Freddy showed me the one gift from his hard-ass father that wasn't a token of his wealth, at least to Freddy. It was a Mont Blanc pen. He didn't care about the price, maybe because he didn't realize it was worth more than I made in a month. He just cared about what the pen, with his name engraved on it, symbolized. I wanted to grab it from him and throw it out of the plastic windows of the jeep. Jesus, Freddy, I thought, it's fucking freezing out; would it kill you to put the hardtop on your truck?

Freddy had been pinned as an underachiever and a dunce by ignorant teachers most of his life, so the gift truly reflected his rising above the expectations. To me, he'd just gotten lucky. His dad probably bought Freddy's way into State.

Shit.

"Dude, this pen can write on anything," he began, "and according to the little manual, it's indestructible." He complemented his ridiculous sports-fan outfit by placing his trophy in his front shirt pocket.

I said the unthinkable. "Oh, so you can read, Freddy?" I don't really know why I said it. I just kind of fired it out, out of spite and jealousy.

He downshifted the jeep and cut off another car. Then, he lifted his ass and lofted a fart my way. "What the hell is that supposed to mean? I haven't seen any acceptance letter for you yet, pal." He gripped onto the pen.

Realizing I'd been an ass and managing to care, I tried to salvage the conversation, as well as our friendship. "No, man. I didn't mean to say that. Shit. God, Freddy your ass reeks." I blew the gas back at him with my gloves and got back to my apology. "I just want to get out of here. I hate this place. I'm starting to hate myself for being here."

He didn't answer, so I kept talking. "Life doesn't revolve around an old, abandoned paper mill. The desperate assholes in this town, they really believe it's going to reopen. I only write on paper. I don't give a fuck where it comes from."

"Whoa! Fair enough, dickhead. Don't worry, D; your letter will come." He gave me a shadow boxer duck and punch and blew through a red light.

I looked away from him, back out the window at the dead town. "Thanks. I'm an ass. Where are we going, anyway?"

"I don't know. A few of the football players are having a party. It's probably to honor Lonchar for putting some numbers on the board." That was Freddy's way of dressing up shit with a cherry, a skill he had mastered. Like how he didn't really see himself as a slow learner. He saw the teachers as moving too fast. "Hey, man, what's up with Lori's step dad and the Christmas lights?"

At first I didn't want to discuss it because of my conversation with Rick Conroy earlier that day. I didn't see Lori at the game. I guessed she had learned to accept losing. Freddy didn't know that though, and took my silence as an invitation to keep talking.

"Check it. It's the middle of fucking October, and he's already building a shrine to the baby Jesus. First one to get them up every year. Last one to take them down." As we drove by Lori's house, I looked out the plastic Jeep window—now icing up—and saw Rick Conroy, whistling away and lacing the house with bright flashing lights. The guy couldn't have looked happier. After the paper mill closed, the locals did anything they could to raise their spirits and keep them busy.

All the Christmas cheer in the world didn't justify the shitty things he said about Lori.

"I don't know," I said at last. "Lori has kind of a strange family. She's a little messed up." I knew her well, but I didn't have a clue to the motivation behind her stepfather's holiday excitement.

"You're telling me. When was the last time that twig had a burger? She needs to get with it." He laughed. "Maybe she fasts all year and feasts on Christmas."

"Fuck off, Freddy. I think there's more to it than that." I knew Lori had eating problems, and I didn't think it was any of Freddy's business.

"What's gotten into you tonight?" He said. "Shit, the girl gives you the Heisman one night when you try to tag her and it's my fault. You're being a dick."

I squirted a gleek of spit in his eye. "I never tried to tag her, Freddy. She's a good friend of mine and I'm worried about her. You used to be friends with Lori, too."

"Not anymore." Freddy got pissy over the summer whenever I decided to spend nights kicking around with Lori. He felt that I had some deep love for her. I always thought that he liked her.

After driving around for close to an hour, Freddy and I ended up parking at McDonald's, the usual meeting place for all the anxious seniors looking for the locale of the night's festivities.

"Hey, Freddy, you fucking little bitch," yelled Lonchar. "I heard about State. You outta here, boyeeeeeee!"

"Nice field goal, Launch. Maybe I can talk to the State football coach." He nudged the kicking champ in the ribs.

Lonchar buffed his knuckles on his jersey. "Football! I want to play soccer!" They both shared a laugh. As much as Lonchar joked, his part-time football career paid fairly well. An entourage of star-struck girls surrounded the field goal hero. If I didn't know any better, I'd have sworn that Lonchar had just won the Super Bowl and signed a seven-figure commercial deal with McDonald's. I knew his parents could never afford to send him to college. As far as his grades were concerned, maybe it was a good night for him to be The Man. "Hey, boys, Dodge is having a jammie at his house. Parents are gone. Two kegs. Pick your poison."

"Sounds good, man. We'll catch you there," I said as we headed out of the parking lot. Both Freddy and I anticipated a messy night.

Freddy pursed his lips, "Hey man. I didn't get anything to eat before the game. Can we stop at the doughnut shop and pick up a snack? I don't wanna get too wasted."

I looked at Freddy and I couldn't think of anything worse

than doughnuts and beer for a hyperactive kid having the most exciting night of his life. But I just shrugged. "You're drivin'."

We pulled in front of the doughnut shop, and I kept thinking about the horrible thing I'd said to him. I hoped he had forgiven me.

"Do you want to come in, D? Maybe you can get something."

"Yeah, that's cool." I'd come to terms with the fact that I would be babysitting a drunken maniac that night. It didn't bother me; I owed it to him.

On our way into Al's Do-Nuts, we noticed an unfamiliar, aggro kid ranting nervously at passersby and screaming into the payphone. He had a bushy home-sculpted Mohawk pulled into a ponytail—the kind of haircut we called "The Bolt"—a cheap pleather jacket, and sweat beading up on his Cro-Magnon brow. The guy's face looked more like it was covered in scales than skin. We passed him; he gave us a once over and remained fully tuned into his conversation. I'd never seen the kid before so I assumed he was passing through, probably picking up a package from one of the unemployed town folk striving to make ends meet. Judging from his sunken black eyes and beyond-pasty skin, the only place he would qualify as a familiar face was a cockfight in Kentucky.

"Take note, young Freddy," I said as the glass door closed behind us. "Butane is not a proper inhalant when mixed with crank."

"Ya think? That kid needs some booger sugar about as much as I do right now." He laughed and shuffled through his pockets and we entered Al's to the ringing, distorted doorbell. "Hey, D, order me a bear claw, a honey glazed, and a couple of the gross old ones to throw at people at Dodger's house. I left my dinero in the car."

"Cool, I'll be inside," I said as he turned around and headed back out. Al's wasn't any different than any other brightly lit doughnut shop in town. It seemed like a great place for homeless people to sit and sip away on a small cup of coffee for a few hours to stay warm.

"Hey, Barry. What up?" The doughnut man of the night was our football team's ex all-star running back Barry Denn. I pointed to a framed photograph behind him. "Employee of the month, huh?" The picture was of Barry in his Al's uniform smiling. Some time during his night shift, Barry rolled up a napkin and pasted it onto his mouth like a blunt.

"What up, D?" He returned. "Deed mine boys sing redemption tonight?" A funny thing about Barry was that after his junior year he began speaking like a Rastafarian. He told everyone he was born in Jamaica and moved to America at a young age. If you didn't know any better, you'd swear he was the long lost descendant of Bob Marley, Peter Tosh, Bunny Wailer, and Jah himself. As a matter of fact, he always wore a ring that was rumored to have belonged to Marcus Garvey: the father of Black Nationalism. I suspected his birth records would tell a different story and that the whole charade was an excuse to smoke weed. Besides, I knew Barry before he grew his high top fade into dreadlocks and traded his dookie chain in for a leather necklace with a red, yellow and green African medallion.

"Take a guess who won, Barry."

"I and I did not think so. I saw you out by dat old swamp again today. Why you go dere? It smells."

The feeling of my hidden place being exposed crawled around on my tongue. "I don't know. It's away from this shit. The smell there seems better than the smell of the rest of this dead city."

"Gotcha. Any partying going on later?"

Barry was the one great hope our football team ever had of winning a homecoming game; however, after one article too many in the local newspaper about the great Barry Denn, he dropped out after his junior year and tried to go pro. It didn't work out the way he expected. After that, he took some night classes and successfully completed his G.E.D. Unlike most ex-sports heroes who still lusted for the glory years, he tried not to talk about the past. The rest was doughnut history.

"Yeah, Dodge and those clowns are having a party. Can you grab me a bear claw, a honey glazed, and a couple of those old heinous ones?"

"Is done." He flicked open a bag and masterfully juggled the doughnuts into the bag. Something caught his attention. "Ey, D, looks like Freddy's havin' some trouble with dat ragamuffin."

I'd forgotten about the living dead lingering outside, so at first I didn't register Barry's comment. Nonetheless, before I could turn around, the bell signaled that Freddy was already on his way in. As usual, he was all smiles.

"What was that all about?" I asked.

"That freak just wanted to borrow my pen to write down a number." Freddy didn't even seem to think twice about lending his trophy.

"Where is it now?"

"He's bringing it in when he's finished."

"He better." Before I dug into Freddy about lending the pen, the bell chimed, and the mystery man plunged through the door. He picked at the scabs on his face, and his right eye twitched like someone had sprayed him with a sandblaster.

His eyes fixated on a neon sign behind Barry. "Hey, man. Can I buy this pen off you?"

"No. It's a gift. Why don't you fuck off down the street to Rite Aid and buy one?"

"Because I need to copy down this information now. You got any paper?" Once again, Freddy fumbled through his pockets. The only thing he had was his acceptance letter to State. Funny how no one has a piece of paper when they needed one.

"Nope," Freddy answered, a little perturbed. "Just write it down on your hand. That pen writes on anything. Maybe if you wash your hands first, you'll be able to read it." He was heating up; his red-and-black face paint ran together and he ripped down the fuzzy hood on his coat.

Frenzied, the neurotic kid yelled and spun around. "Goddammit!" He streamed his long, yellow fingernails through his bolt, and headed back to the phone. The sick bell chimed.

Freddy cooled down. "Maybe we should invite psycho to Dodger's house. Looks like he could use a beer."

"Fuck that," I shot. "Let's take him there and give him a blanket party," A blanket party was our way of letting an asshole know he had stepped out of line. Usually performed as a joke or homage to the infamous "Code Reds" of the military, we pulled a blanket over some sucker's head and beat the shit out of him until he begged for mercy. Nice, huh?

"Oh, relax, D. What's happenin', Barry?"

"Not much, Freddy. Here's them donuts."

Once again, the scumbag plowed into the shop. The bell didn't work.

"Don't be a dick, dude. I need this pen. I'll give you twenty bucks for it." One of his face pickings had started to bleed.

Freddy showed early signs of the hyperactive youth who had once lit himself on fire and jumped into the lake as a joke. "Look, fuck, just write down your info and give it back." The pleather-clad hesher kicked the door open and returned to the phone.

In an attempt to alleviate some of the stress, I stepped up to the counter in front of Freddy. "I got it, Fred. I owe you something for being a cock earlier." I reached across the counter and gave Barry my money.

FWAP!
FWAP!
FWAP!

Three gunshots rang out behind me. They shook my teeth and burnt my gums. Terror thrusted up my veins. My balls shriveled into my chest and my dick got wet. I jumped behind the counter with Barry, who had already taken cover. I didn't hear Freddy cry out, so I figured he had taken cover with us as well. Barry's employee of the month picture fell and the glass smashed on my head.

Two seconds later, the reluctant bell rang, and the gunman squealed out of the parking lot.

With my eyes closed, I propped myself up slowly. Barry hunkered down, shivering in shock. I shook so hard that the cheap imitation glass doughnut case rattled and the cakes inside fell off their shelves. With one eye, I looked up through the display case, peering beyond the mixed pile of doughnuts.

I saw the twitching remains of college student Freddy Brubaker.

It was difficult to tell where his blood stopped and his smeared makeup began. It was even harder to tell who he was. I lost control of my breathing. I looked down at my mangled life long friend, the first of my allies to escape from the town, and saw his Mont Blanc pen gripped in his hand. Engraved on the base were the words, "You did it. Love, Dad."

He shivered. His arms fluttered and his last living squirt of blood spat all over the front of the counter. I jumped over Barry as he fired up a joint.

"Breathe, Freddy. Breathe, Goddammit. Breathe," is all I

managed to get out. My heart pounded and my palms where soaked with sweat.

I tried with napkins to make the bleeding stop and I tried to plug up the three holes with my finger like Freddy's chest was a bowling ball.

"Fucker. Goddamn it, fucker," I screamed at myself. With that last look, I blacked out.

+ + +

A week later, I crossed the street to the Brubakers' house. Buck, Freddy's father, gave me the pen, saying I should have it. At first, I felt reluctant to take it, but he insisted it belonged to me. He couldn't bear the sight of this last trophy, all that remained of his youngest son.

In an attempt to console him, I told Buck the killer didn't have any idea of the pen's value.

"The bastard didn't even have the balls to face his crime." Buck sniffed. His lips quivered and his voice cracked during accented syllables.

After the killer bailed from Al's, he headed down the highway, where the local cops pursued him. While driving toward the Bay Bridge, his only escape route, *the* only escape route, he crammed the gun into his own face, fired it, and swerved off the road. Flames engulfed his car.

Coward.

The entire hell night didn't faze the cops of Kudzutown. Freddy was just another kid in the wrong place at the wrong time. Since the rest of the apathetic assholes of the town were too busy fucking off, not many people seemed to care that Freddy had been killed. Lori cared, though, and she called me.

"D, I'm sorry I haven't been in touch," she said weakly.

"It's okay, Lori. Where have you been?"

"I've been busy. Do you miss him?"

I tugged on my ear and bunched up my face so that I wouldn't break down. "I haven't had time to think about it."

"You can't just ignore it, D. You loved him."

"I love you, too."

"D—" she began. I hung up the phone.

That night, I went to visit Nazareth and bury Freddy's trophy at the foundation. I didn't think I'd ever be able to write with it.

Much to my chagrin, some neighborhood kids had constructed a rope swing by hammering two railroad spikes into the tree's hands, securing a long nylon rope connected to an old tire. Furious, I ripped down the apparatus, tearing the nails through the limbs of the tree. Then, I hoisted the plaything into the sewer.

The fiery rage pumping through my arms froze when I realized what I'd done. I weakened the appendages. Sap gushed out. The limbs dangled like the ornaments on a pathetic Christmas tree.

After my initial shock though, it didn't upset me. Without looking again, I dug a hole at the base and buried Freddy's trophy. Then, I sat down with my back to Nazareth and wrote.

CHAPTER THREE

Winter added another ring to Nazareth's long life. In that season, I spent the day home from school "sick" so I could crank out a couple poems that were due for my creative writing class. I knew they wouldn't take me that long to complete, and I wanted to leave high school with a bang, making my presence as a writer remembered. How heroic of me. I felt that nothing made people listen like the written word.

My love for reading and writing began when my mother forced me to read a bunch of books each summer. When the post-school season began, she would take me to the bookstore, where I picked out half, usually something from C.S. Lewis or Robert Newton Peck, and she picked out the other half, usually classics. As I got older, each summer would be stacked with more and more classics until the kid's books were ignored altogether. Reading became an easy outlet for me to disassociate myself from my fear of dying. I let the authors guide my life, like they did their characters'.

As far as competing with other students, I had no worries. What did I have to compete with? I wasn't afraid of the theater kids and their obsession with the bored rebellion of Holden Caulfield. I scoffed at the stoners and their Gonzo-esque carbon copies of Hunter S. Thompson. I turned up my nose at the countless caustic attempts at metaphorically mutating "roses are red" by paying tribute to Jimi Hendrix or John Lennon.

I wanted to tell something bold, something true. Oddly enough, when I was young, I always dreamed of writing horror stories. The new poem, however, couldn't be horror or fantasy. It had to be real.

After pacing in an unconstructive way around Nazareth, I concluded that every other kid in my class was going to sum up the closing of the paper mill and how it had taken its toll on our town. I hadn't taken the time to deal with Freddy's death, so I decided to leave that topic to one of the many girls in class who fancied themselves his widow. I diverted my attention elsewhere. Lori Conroy's misery and my short confrontation with her stepfather at AutoRx were the first things that came to mind.

Lori had always been a close friend, but kept secrets from me. I knew she suffered from anorexia, and it consumed her. One time when I went out to get some frozen yogurt with her, she threw a fit at the employee who refused to measure the non-fat yogurt into exactly ten ounces. She was obsessed. All the warning signs were there.

A couple of my friends and I used to make fun of her mustache and call her "Hitler." Whenever she walked by, we stood at attention and saluted her, our arms into the air, exclaiming, "Heil!"

One day she took me aside in tears, explaining that because of the affliction, her body produced a soft, thin layer of hair everywhere on her body—except for the hair on her head, which had already begun to thin. All of her friends ignored her cry for help, relying on a societal debate concerning high school females and their infatuation with supermodels. Another time, she admitted to me that she had to be re-hydrated and medicated regularly by an IV. No one knew. Myself included, we were a typical bunch of self-absorbed high school assholes.

I owed her something. I didn't want to expose her shit to my teachers or make her uncomfortable around her friends, but I *did* want to let her know I cared. I worked all that day under the weakened arms of Nazareth. The trunk supported my back and kept me attentive to the task I had outlined; however, the stench of the bog, combined with stale beer made me gag every couple of minutes. I wrote poem after poem and just balled up the shitty ones and chucked them into the water. Sure, a plea for forgiveness drove my poetry, but the result painted a picture of how I saw Lori.

At dusk, I finally produced a finished product that satisfied me. I read the poem to myself over and over. It was poetic, everything I'd hoped it would be. Lori's maze always led back to the beginning. I searched what I knew about her for an answer to her perpetual self-destruction and found nothing. Deep down I thought it a little selfish for someone to refuse food.

IV

It would seem as if Lori
Is locked in the cold,
Ignoring demise
Struggling for her
Life.

"Help me get out,"
Her gentle eyes cry.
A pile of bones,
Burying regret
Under lies.

Coaxing reflections beyond,
are her creatures within?
Eating is forgotten,
Beauty under her
Knife.

She will never know
Where and when
Death will strike.
Every calorie skipped
His sickle delights.

Those who are forced to mature
When their parents divide.
Can weep all they want,
Their tears best left
Unsaid.

She reaches for support

With her skeletal wrist,
Love for all others.
To herself
Love went missed.

If Lori is my teacher,
Why am I alone?
Am I also confined
To her spidery
Web?

As I watch Lori bowing
To her personal harm,
I notice
A bracelet,
An IV in her arm.

Excited about my poem, I went home, checked the mail, and disappointed again, called Lori to ask her to meet me at the McDonald's parking lot. She agreed.

"You can't bring this to class!" she screamed after she read the words. Her lips were bleeding. "You'll totally single me out!"

"But—"

"I don't have a problem, and I don't want to be your secret little joke. I'm not your freak."

"Lori, I just wanted to—"

"Fuck you!" She pulled a cigarette, probably the first of her second or third pack of the day, from behind her ear. In one swift, circular motion, she pulled her trademark Zippo out of her pocket, lit the cigarette, and returned the lighter to its home. She must have practiced that move so many times to get it right. I watched in admiration as she filled my car with a huge puff of smoke.

"What? You wanted to tell everyone how fucked up I am? You don't understand, D." She continued to look at my poem as tears poured passed the dark circles around her eyes and down her cheeks. For a long time, neither of us said anything, not a word. After a long time, she took a deep breath. "He fucks me, D."

I searched through my mind and came upon a frightening

realization.

"He fucks me all the time." Once she found the courage to start, she didn't want to stop. "When my mom goes out, even when she just goes to the store to pick up a couple of things, he rapes me. He beats me like his bitch and calls me by his dead wife's name. 'Angie! Angie, you whore! Angie!' All over the house! He won't stop!" Smoke clouded the car. It was too cold outside to roll down the windows.

I touched her shoulder. Unable to comfort her, I retracted my hand immediately. Lori's lip curled up as she snarled at my touch. "Rick?" Rick Conroy, stringing up his Christmas lights, whistling, "Jesus Loves Me." It all made sense. I finally understood how such a beautiful girl with everything going for her would want to reinvent herself as something unappealing, and skeletal. She looked horrible. Her thick beautiful hair had become thinned and patched, like the rodent carcasses that I sent swimming weekly down at the bog. "How come you never told anybody?"

"Would you tell anybody? My mom? She's always so piss drunk, she ignores what she may or may not know. She doesn't care." She took a huge breath, fighting down the tears. "She's so fucking stupid that she doesn't notice the ant traps that I have surrounding my bed. Rick uses greasy towels from his shop as nut rags and throws them under my bed when he's finished fucking me. I'm not touching that shit; they're covered in ants."

"Lori, as your friend I have to tell somebody. Jesus Christ, you should have told someone other than me!"

I didn't want to be the sole protector of her secret but her black eyes pleaded with me.

"No way. I don't want to be the freak. I know what people say. I hear those tweaked cunts that pretend to be my friends say they want to help, when they secretly wish they were as thin as me. I see how all of you make jokes about me. She pulled up the arm of her sweater and revealed her lifeless bone of a limb.

"You aren't a freak, Lori. You just need help."

"It's not that easy. You don't know, D. Please, please keep it to yourself. If I find out you told anyone, I'll kill you. You hear me?"

Reluctantly, I nodded.

"I'm getting out of here. I'm going to stay with my sister until summer, and I'll find out next week whether or not I got into State. My mom has the money tucked away from when my grandfather died. My grades are pretty solid, er, at least until this year." She flicked her cigarette out the window and lit up another. Same motions, same precision. I was surprised that she could lift the lighter.

"You have to quit. Now!" All I could do was offer simple solutions to her terror. Back then I didn't realize that all she saw was her stepfather's cock staring back at her from the mirror. I couldn't feel her pain.

She opened her eyes wide. "Keep your mouth shut, D. You aren't God." She pulled deep on her cigarette. "Shit, asshole, I think one of my contacts fell out."

"Okay, I promise."

"Thanks." She continued to look at the poem and cry. "Can I keep this? I'll give you my lighter." From her pocket she pulled out her precious Zippo, this time, slowly. Her fingernails were yellow and frail. It was an offering for secrecy. I shooed it away, but she insisted. "Take it. I have to quit smoking. It's killing me." We both laughed as we made the exchange. I heard her bones creak as she left the car carefully. She poked her head in and blew me a smoke-scented kiss. She followed her token of love by performing a crazy skeleton dance. She bounced around aimlessly, flapping her grossly thin body around like an uncontrollable marionette, her way of letting me know everything was okay.

The next day, I ended up turning in an obvious poem about the closing of the paper mill and how it would have affected Mark Twain. Apparently, my teacher didn't agree with my views on obscure literary references focusing on Twain and his hatred for James Fenimore Cooper's fraudulent, romantic writing style. I thought it was funny, but my teacher fancies herself quite a *Deerslayer* when it comes to grading. I got a C. At least Lori's secret was safe.

A few weeks later, Lori's friend Kelli told me that Lori had been taken to the hospital after collapsing in her physics class. According to the teacher, she'd been giving a speech, and in mid-sentence, toppled over and nailed her head. The teacher blamed exhaustion, but I knew better. Lori was in trouble.

After school, I went down to the local hospital to see if everything was okay.

The hospital sickened me. I'm sure that dirty floors and donation cans next to the ashtrays were common practice in most non-third world hospitals. Our town and everything it was third world. Just a shithole. If you were born there, you were born into shit. Most likely, judging from the upkeep of the hospital, you'd die in shit, too.

"You okay?" I asked as I yanked open the curtain that sheltered her from the molester.

"Yeah, I'll be all right. I just got dizzy and hit the ground."

At the risk of sounding like a typical eating disorder bully, I nudged at her. "Then why do you have an IV in your arm, Lori? You need to fucking eat."

"Fuck you, D. This has nothing to do with that. I think I drank too much this weekend at Dodge's house. I'm still a little dehydrated."

I grabbed a three-and-a-half-legged stool over to her bedside. "Listen, we both know that's bullshit. Don't worry; your secret is safe with me." After her reaction to the poem, I didn't want anyone to know about her condition. Seeing her pale beyond belief, shriveled up with an intravenous bag filling her with water, I thought my safest bet would be to keep quiet rather than lose a friend. I didn't want her to keep suffering though.

"I love you, D. I have your poem hidden in the glove compartment of my car. If I ever feel unloved, I read it. How's the lighter?"

"Great, except for the fact that I don't smoke."

"You will." She lit up a cigarette with a match off her bedpost.

"Miss, you can't smoke in here," a nurse walking by stated.

"Fuck you, bitch," Lori grunted.

+ + +

The phone rang at around 2:00 in the morning. My mom answered it and rushed into my room. "Honey, Lonchar is on the phone. He says it's important."

Great, I thought, Dodge must have been having another one of his epic all-nighters.

"Where were you tonight?" She'd heard me sneezing. I'm allergic to alcohol.

"Out." I ventured through the desert of writing and paper all over my floor and picked up the phone. "What do you want, Launch? I'm sleeping," I grumbled as I wiped the snot away from my eyes.

"Dude, Lori jumped off the Bay Bridge. They found her car parked out there with a note. They haven't found her yet."

I acted surprised. "What? Shit!"

"She may still be alive. I'm going up there and search around."

"What did the note say, Lonchar?"

"It was a letter from State, refusing her admission and something else." Shit. The poem. The phone dropped from my hand and I walked away. Faintly, I heard Lonchar yelling, "D! D! Are you there? D!"

Refused. No way out. Lori knew she was trapped. I walked into my room and put on my clothes. Mom peeked in through my door. "Honey, what did he want? Did something happen? Did you do something?" I couldn't help but think about my own fate if I was refused.

"Don't worry about it, Mom. I'll be back in a little while." I should have told her something, but I had another agenda.

I picked up Lori's Zippo from my bed stand and headed out. Voices in my head reminded me of recent tragedy. I didn't wait for them to search for Lori. I didn't have to. I already knew.

When I went to Nazareth to bury Lori's lighter, I saw him in a completely different light. The darkness may have been deceiving, but at night he didn't look as strong. He seemed weathered, beaten down, tired. He didn't reflect any tangible form other than a big pile of kudzu. I fell to my knees and dug directly next to the burial location of Freddy's pen. The smell of death and the town made me gag but I sucked the vomit back down and swallowed—something I'd become accustomed to over the long years in Kudzu captivity. Never looking down, I dropped Lori's flame into the hole and covered it up.

The authorities eventually found her decayed body a couple of days later. It washed up on the banks of the bay. I'm sure that even in her decomposed state she was still as beautiful as she had always been. As much as I wished it never happened, I knew deep down that she hadn't any other way out. I kept her secret. At that time, I wanted her beauty to live on forever, untarnished. Her problem wouldn't have been solved by an extra two ounces of yogurt.

CHAPTER FOUR

I was stretching out my knotted back from my hard mattress when I peered into the mailbox one unexpected spring day. Unlike the previous few months, during which I opened the box only to be showered with the avalanche of delinquent bills my parents tried to ignore, that day I found a sole letter. I knew what it was. I bit my lip, pulled it out, and my stomach howled. I felt my eyes welling up and premonitions of working the toll both on the bay bridge stabbed me in the head. As Lori and Freddy's murders proved, the bridge was the only way out.

The envelope felt thin, not a good sign. I smelled it. It still smelled like the bog. Negative thoughts shot through my mind. "Why would I, a kid from a shitty little town, beat out every other aspiring writer to get a scholarship to Palmbrook University?" The letter was for me. It was either a ticket to paradise or a sentence to death.

Luckily, my parents were gone. They wouldn't have to see my disappointment as I unfolded the letter. More thoughts raced through my mind. "Well, I could always go to the community college and raise my grades." I would then hear my personal devil's advocate answer. "This isn't about grades; it's your only chance." Fuck that. If I had to walk across the fucking evil bridge, I was going to get out of town. I hated it that much.

I closed the mailbox and headed up my walkway.

"So, D?" The mailman I had pestered that entire year asked.

"What's the word?"

I said nothing and slammed the door behind me.

"Don't shoot the messenger," he yelled after me.

I walked to my room and I sat down on my messy bed, playing with the letter, holding it up to the light, bending it for contents. I expected nothing but the worst. Was it any better than the dying town where I lived? Where exactly was I going? What did I expect to do with my life? I thought about Freddy Brubaker and Lori Conroy for the first time since they had passed.

"Is our world so fucked up and deranged? What did they have to look forward to?" I yelled at myself. "What could they change? Murderers get off because of their social status. Good people are killed for saying what they want."

What was so good about the world? Everything that I looked forward to, everything that I had ever wanted, was on that one piece of paper. Like so many other times, like the night Freddy was killed, I needed a piece of paper. It would surely fix things.

I tore open the envelope. There was a single piece of cheap paper stock inside, nicely folded—something I wouldn't have noticed, except I always envisioned my college acceptance letter printed on a thick paper, laced with gold and ripe for framing. I unfolded the first flap. What if I didn't fit in? What if paradise was a scam? What if I couldn't cut it as a writer? I unfolded the second flap revealing the contents of my life. It was only about three paragraphs in length. It was fairly unimpressive for the foretelling of my future. I read.

Assholes! They spelled my name wrong! Well, that wasn't important. I read the first line.

"Congratulations, you have been accepted on scholarship to attend Palmbrook University."

Paradise found.

Fuck. I did it.

I actually fucking did something.

When my parents arrived home that evening—my father had taken on a part-time job as an engineering consultant a few towns over and my mother worked at the local bookstore—I proudly showed them the letter. They both went to college. As a matter of fact, they both went to better colleges than the one I had gotten into; however, the military brainwash of my father's academy school and the Lutheran teachings of my mother's mid-western school didn't appeal to me. I wanted to write, and I wanted out.

"Good job, son. You did it," my father, who I called the general, said, extending his hand for a firm shake. He was a big man. He brushed his dark Pollack hair over his protruding forehead caused by years of boxing and football. He smiled.

"I don't know, Honey. Are you sure you want to leave," my mother pleaded. My mom tried to hug me in like I was a cub. She was no bear. Always a small woman, her dyed blonde hair showed roots—the result of unpaid bills. Her green eyes watered as she wiped her calloused hand across my face. Her rich parents would have been ashamed by what Kudzutown had done to her.

I handed my father the letter. "Assholes! They spelled our name wrong," he muttered.

After a good dinner, I took my letter off the fridge.

My mom, still a little shaken up that I was leaving home, took her eyes from the stove. "Are you going to go and show it to your friends?"

"Something like that." I had one last sacrifice to offer Nazareth. One last duty.

CHAPTER FIVE

Sitting on the stump of the drained Nazareth, I counted the days before my triumphant escape. The tree, which once stood proud, an enigma in our town, had been reduced to just a pew surrounded by a lump of torn kudzu and leftover bark. Unbeknownst to me, someone had leveled the entire area sometime over the previous couple of months. Even the smaller disciples across the bog had been mowed down.

It was also really nice of the workmen to knock down a power line and add to the smell of the area by electrocuting the few living creatures that managed to stick it out and survive in the swamp.

When you're forced to grow up, security blankets, crutches, idols, and even religions fade away and you lose interest. Why did I give faith to something based solely on its test of time and its importance to my past? My dependency on God disappeared, becoming nothing more than a lesson. I don't think that spending any more time there would have made any difference. It wouldn't bring Freddy and Lori back. I picked up a blackened raccoon by the tail and tossed it into the big green dumpster in the middle of the stream.

I was a realist, not a dreamer. I was sure they would build a strip mall or something equally worthless. The type of place no one in Kudzutown could afford to frequent. It didn't matter. The entire town was fucking scatter, and no matter how they dressed it up, scatter was all that it would be. All we were was a bunch of dead animals.

Bending over, I lunged my index finger down my throat, and vomited. It didn't seem strange at the time. I was sickened by everything that had happened during the school year. My agony and hatred, coupled with the smell of my world, made it easy. I didn't retract and swallow the barf back down. I enjoyed letting it go. I wiped some mucus onto my pants. I felt relieved. I felt cleansed.

Clearing away the piles of Nazareth, I dug up Freddy's trophy pen and Lori's precious lighter. I wanted to cry. Senseless. What could I have done to prevent their deaths? Nothing. First, I pulled out the lighter. I lit the Zippo flint as I envisioned Lori's one-motion trick. All I saw was her pain. It was about more than escaping for her. She wanted to be loved, but not by that fucking lazy-eyed asshole Conroy.

I held my acceptance letter up and, in one circular motion, torched it. They'd spelled my name wrong. I knew the general would make sure they sent another. The paper burned slowly away. The breeze broke the ends off and shat them into the disgusting waste of the bog below. The thin paper burned brightly, but eventually the flames burned uncontrollably. The letter doubled over and collapsed, singeing the skin on my thumb, but the stomach bile that remained on my index finger controlled it.

I held up Freddy's trophy. Sure enough, just like he'd said, it proved indeed indestructible. I read the inscription aloud to the fallen Nazareth. "You did it. Love, Dad." It was roughly the same thing that my father had said to me. Sure, the general wanted me to go to some military school, but he was proud of me, just as much as old Buck Brubaker was of Freddy. I'd tried to shut out that fateful night for the rest of my life, but certain elements always flashed by: Freddy masked behind his ridiculous face makeup, Lonchar the hero, Barry the dreamer, the speed freak coward, and me, the jealous asshole.

I'd tried as hard as I could to plug up Freddy's bullet wounds. I'd tried so hard but the blood kept pouring out. The sight of Freddy's shaking body haunted me, but I shut it out. He just lay there, begging for a minute, a second, a moment, and twitched. As his leg quivered, the blood from his wounds pumped out, as if his leg were a death machine, pushing him to the end as quickly as possible.

Fumbling around in my pockets, I searched for a piece of paper to write on. Just like Freddy at Al's Do-Nuts though, I didn't have a piece.

"If he only had a piece of paper!" Anything for that freak to write down whatever information had been so fucking important. Why is it that every time someone needs a piece of paper, they can't find one? But of course, I knew the answer to that one. The paper mill closed down.

I stomped around like a lunatic, crushing the worthless remains of Nazareth. Frantic, I threw Lori's lighter into the bog. I shredded pieces of the vine. I kicked at the stump and smashed scraps of bark.

"I fucking hate you!" I yelled at the stump. "I hate you so much!" I blacked out for a second. Time took its toll on the town and I had been just another animal. I might have felt release, but I would always be a prisoner. My arms and legs were ripped apart by limbs and bark. I was bleeding all over myself and I sucked snot into my mouth to get it off my face.

I vomited again. I jumped to my feet, unleashed, uncaged. I still wasn't free. My head banged against the cage that held me from escape. I would never be free. Just as I lifted my arm to throw the Mont Blanc, that terrible fucking pen, a memory surged through my head. *Dude, this pen can write on anything.* I stopped and slowly picked up a piece of bark from one of Nazareth's two reaching limbs. I wrote the truth. My truth. I paid my last respects to the tree. For once, it proved useful. The bog, the paper mill, the tree, they weren't my hiding places anymore, nor were they the burial ground of my friends.

Darkness surrounded the swamp, so I fished Lori's lighter out of the smelly pissing hole, put the piece of bark under my arm, proudly placed Freddy's pen in my front pocket and headed home.

For the second time that year, I observed. The dilapidated homes, the beaten up cars abandoned in the streets, the rummage growing in the yards—it was all so wrong. After an hour of disgust, I reached my school, most likely the cleanest high school in the country. Our good-natured principal hired an over abundant amount of out-of-work custodians when the mill closed. I walked by the football field and saw Lonchar kicking field goals. Since Freddy's death, Lonchar stayed late after soccer practice to warm up for next year's football season.

"Good job, D," he yelled across the field when he saw me. "I heard the news from your mom when I called you to tell you about a shindig tonight at Dodger's pad. A real kick-ass party. Honeys everywhere. Pick your own poison. You up?" I wasn't close to him, but all the same I could tell he'd been crying. His voice cracked as he screamed. I'm sure he cried every night.

"Yeah, I'll be there; I just got some shit to take care of first."

Lonchar booted a forty-yard field goal. It was all in vain; he never scored another show-time point again, at least not in high school. After he lifted his arms to signal three points, he dropped to his knees. I wanted to comfort him, but I was a bloody mess and I was out of words.

He got up from his knees, placed another ball on the tee and wiped sweat and tears off of his forehead. "Kind of a fucked up year, huh?"

"Yeah, kind of a very fucked up year." I turned around.

"Oh, your mom told me to tell you to call if I ran into you. Use the phone over there by the locker room. It's free."

"Thanks." I headed toward the locker room, listening to his grunts and groans. Provided he got that soccer player nonsense out of his head, Lonchar was going to make it out of here. I picked up the phone and started to dial my house. I hesitated, and just as easily as I had picked up the receiver, hung it up. I fell into the wall in front of me. The bricks crumbled as the dust blinded me. That time, at last, I cried. Some things are best left unsaid. Some things aren't. I dialed a different number.

It was strange how everything came together. After I walked by the high school, I caught a glimpse of something out of the corner of my eye. To be sure I wasn't dreaming, I looked down at my watch. Sure enough, April 16, nowhere near Christmas. Shocked, I dropped everything I was holding. There he was, Rick Conroy, whistling away, tearing down the lights that still covered the house like an overgrowth of kudzu.

After collecting my memories, I walked up to his ladder and shook the base. "Nice night, huh, Mr. Conroy?"

"Wha? Oh, ya scared me." He looked up at the sky. "It's all right. I can feel something's coming in from the west, though." He readjusted his hat, snorted and spat onto the ground. All I did was stare at him. I stared directly into his aimless lazy eye. I wanted to gouge it out with Freddy's pen.

"You gotta problem, son? What're lookin' at?"

I woke myself from the death stare and got myself together. "I just think it's brilliant how you leave your Christmas lights up practically all year round. It's almost like you want to constantly bring joy to the town."

"Ah, yeah," he scratched his nose, checking to see if he had a booger on his face that would warrant my stare. "Somethin' like that." He shook his head, confused.

I placed the piece of bark at the bottom of the ladder and walked away. "Well, here. I've decided to bring joy to this town as well. I hope you get what you deserve, motherfucker."

"Boy, what in the hell?" I heard him step down from the ladder, but I didn't turn around. I just kept walking. Walking away.

"Is this some kind of joke, kid?" He screamed after me. "Why are you all bloody? Are you on PCP?" I didn't answer. "Hey, I'm talking to you, ya little shit!" I continued to walk, and he continued to scream. "What does this mean? I know you Deese, ya little fucker."

He didn't run after me; he didn't understand the message I'd scrawled on the Nazareth's bark. As his rants became more distant, nearly out of my reach, I heard the police sirens. For once, a phone conversation had indeed paid off.

"Merry Christmas, rapist!" I whispered, thinking of the message I carved on the bark with Freddy's pen.

BOOK TWO

ECCLESIASTIC

"There have been daring people in the world who claimed that Cooper could write English, but they are all dead now…"
Samuel Langhorn Clemens

CHAPTER ONE

Dr. Sandler opened his pad to a new page and licked his Cross Pen. "Let's begin," he said. I looked around his office. Papers were nicely stacked and the file cabinets shined as if they were dusted and waxed hourly. There was no couch. I tapped my shoe on the floor, the same checkered linoleum pattern that covered the whole eating disorder wing of the Sisters of Prophecy Care Unit.

"Like I said before, Dr. Sandler, eating disorders are a choice, not a disease."

He breezed through my profile, and tapped my folder with his index finger. Every few seconds, he'd use both his hands to open his salt and pepper hair part down the middle at his cowlick. "So, D, you being here, in a hospital for eating disorders, is your choice. It says in your file from last summer that addiction, mainly alcoholism and drug abuse, runs in your family. How can't you attribute that to a hereditary disease?"

"First of all, being here wasn't my choice. It was the combined effort of my college dean and my parents, Doc. Secondly, as far as I'm concerned, eating disorders, drug addiction and alcoholism aren't diseases. What does it matter? It's all bullshit." I bit at my bottom lip, but inadvertently cut a sore on the side of my tongue with my chipped teeth. How the *hell* did I end up in a care unit for eating disorders?

"The three addictions you just mentioned are all diseases."

Sander's flared nostrils steamed up his glasses as he sighed. "In most cases they are traced genetically."

"Oh, fuck you. If that were true than how come kids in Africa don't shoot heroin or make themselves puke? What a load of shit. You're basing this on what we know about where we live. What med company is paying you to tell me this?" I dropped to my hands and knees in front of Sandler's desk. "God, please help me. My grandmother is an alcoholic and my brother is a cokehead. God, please help me. But wait, why do I throw up after I eat? Could it be that I learned it somewhere and I chose to do it?" I popped up off my knees and swatted my profile folder out of Sandler's hands. "Fuck you, God. Fuck you, Sandler."

"'Eff God, huh?'" He pointed at the papers with his pen, now scattered all over his sterile desk. Sandler's eye twitched a little bit. God forbid any disarray in the house of perfection. "Would you mind picking that up for me, D? And please, refrain from outbursts. This meeting is simply to get a feeling for why you have been committed to inpatient care and why you have relapsed after doing so well last summer as an outpatient. This isn't a diagnosis. I'm not here to prescribe medication for you."

I bunched up the papers and politely handed them to him. I nudged my head slightly to get his forgiveness. As he reached toward my peace offering I blurted out, "I didn't say 'eff God,' I said 'fuck God,'" and threw the papers at him. "Is this what you want, Doc? The past five years of my life condensed into a folder? Let me make it simple for you. I'm fucked up, but that's my choice. Fuck you." I licked my lips again. They were puffy and dry. "I will never tell you why I act like this. I will never tell you where this came from. I don't know and I don't want to know."

Sandler rolled his eyes back to his notes. "Then you'll never be well, D."

I tried to swallow, but the sting carried from my throat, up to my jaw line, and into my ears. The pain made me grin and jam my eyes shut. Swallowing made my ears ring.

"Do you feel that, D?" I opened my eyes to look at him and avoid pain. "That feeling isn't normal. I know how your throat feels. That's from alcohol and stomach acid ripping away and destroying your esophagus." It's called a Mallory-Weiss tear.

Eventually, you'll bleed to death."

I noticed a picture of Nazareth that I had drawn as a kid poking out of the folder. Avoiding the pain in my face and my throat, I asked, "Where did you get that?"

"Get what? This?" He looked down and pulled out the picture as if it were a planted card in an illusionist's deck. "Your mother gave it to me." He handed it to me politely. "When did you draw this?"

"I can't remember. Maybe I drew it when I was five or six."

Sandler reached for his notepad and pen. "Why did you draw this? It's a daunting picture, D."

"It was a daunting tree." I hadn't seen the picture of Nazareth in years, nor had I remembered drawing it. "It's not shit anymore."

"What happened there?"

"Some people tore it down. They leveled the entire area. They should have leveled the entire fucking town." I looked up from the picture. I held back the tears that sometimes came when I remembered my final year of high school in Kudzutown. I grinded what was left of my acid-decayed teeth. Nazareth, Kudzutown, Freddy, and Lori weren't Sandler's business. I wished they weren't my business, either.

He looked at me, noting my reaction to the drawing. I stared at him blankly, but sometimes my lip quivered.

"What else can you tell me about the picture, D?"

I swallowed lightly and bit some dry skin off of my bottom lip. "I don't like to be pissed on."

I took the last drag of my cigarette and looked out the iced window to the courtyard in front of the hospital. The other patients were in group therapy. Since it was my first day, my therapy involved getting used to the care unit. The main area consisted of one big room. It contained a common area with a crack addict television and a few couches, and connected to our dining area with its three tables. An office looked in through a dubious glass window. It was Doctor Sandler's observation room.

I felt like shit. Apparently, the human body couldn't sustain the amount of abuse I had forced on myself constantly. Who knew? I smashed my cancer stick out, and lit another. I wasn't chain smoking, but I had to counter the loss of drugs, alcohol and bulimia with something. Smoking would have to do.

I never encouraged smoking but it filled the compulsory void of past poisons that continued to pound in my head. I didn't even want to think about what it would eventually do to my heart or my lungs; I just wanted a friend, a crutch. At the moment, I wasn't looking for God. When my brother gave up his addiction to boxes of wine, acid, and coke, his counselor refused to encourage him to give up smoking. He reasoned that a guy couldn't just give up everything, every crutch, every means of self-support. I bet that self-righteous asshole relapsed.

Outside, directly in the center of the Sisters of Prophecy Hospital courtyard stood a statue of a priest. That day before dinner I smoked a cigarette and looked at the mound of shit. It seemed the hospital had fallen on bad times, or at least into a bad neighborhood, because the gray weathered statue had been trashed. Half his face was gone, either smashed or eroded off. The hands, which I assumed at one time held a granite Bible, had fallen off.

The worst thing about the statue was that some taggers had come along and written things like "fuck off" and their personalized tag symbols all over it. These were the John Hancocks of urban America. The graffiti artists didn't intend to be blasphemous. I think that the world is just running out of places for kids to write. It didn't seem like paper was an appropriate way to tell someone you despised him any longer. No one has the time to stop and read a cry for help.

I sucked the life out of my cig and noticed a vagrant trying his hardest to keep warm in the sub-zero weather outside. His long beard was icicle laced, and his skin, permanently browned by the sun of the summer, now burned from the freeze. The flesh was wrinkled and leathery, and he squinted to avoid the sun reflecting off snow. Indifferent shreds of clothing that helped to fight off hypothermia covered the rest of his body. He looked around, looked again. He desperately needed something. He came to the wrong place looking for redemption.

Then he pulled his dick out of the front of his attempt-at-a-winter-outfit and pissed on the statue. After he shook himself off, he noticed something on the ground. He bent over and picked up a butt of a cigarette, hopped over the wrought iron courtyard fence, and staggered back to the downtown streets.

I watched the effigy for the better part of the afternoon. Obviously, people didn't care about it. Patients from the large hospital, preachers, nuns, and doctors—nobody cared that it was crumbling away.

A pack of snickering nuns sipping on their Starbucks coffee walked by—not even a glance. A priest race-walked by in his Nikes, eyeing his watch. Forget it, that dipshit had places to be. A gaggle of young doctors demonstrating their squash backhands in the air strolled past. One of them accidentally swiped his fingers across the statue, but didn't stop. To top things off, a hospital assistant pushing around this old bitch in a wheel chair rolled by. She was more interested in feeding the birds.

At the very least they could have gotten the dilapidated pile of eroding rocks out of the middle of the courtyard, maybe replace it with some modern sculpture or something. Then there would be some eye candy for the old woman shitting in her colostomy bag as she threw pieces of moldy bread to a bunch of pigeons shitting all over the statue. The spray painted slogans were probably the most attention the old statue had received in quite a long time.

"D, it's time for dinner," Sandler yelled from across the room. "Put your cigarette out." I took one last look at the priest and shook my head at the poor bastard. "D, now." I put my cigarette out and got up from my smoking corner to join the three tables of girls in the observation room. They were whispering about me. I hadn't gotten into the routine yet. Sandler knew my rap because I'd spent time as an outpatient at Prophecy the previous summer.

I'd fooled them that time and I knew I could do it again. I walked over to my assigned seat; an exciting step back for someone who'd just graduated college. I hadn't stuck around to accept a diploma, but my adviser had called with the good news the day before I was tossed into the hospital. I noticed a girl with a baggy shirt that said Mariah across the front. Her face had sunken in far beyond any recognition of a human form. She stood about six feet tall with a back hunched over and twisted like a little girl with scoliosis beaten with a tire iron. As the "doctors" helped her into her seat, I noticed they placed a doughnut-shaped pillow onto her chair. I think she had liver spots, but she couldn't have been any older than eighteen.

Before she sat down, some little shit girl grabbed the doughnut out from under her and ran around the room. I figured that the ceremony happened every night, because Mariah didn't even bat an eye.

I took my spot and Sandler opened up the dinner cart. The meal didn't smell four-star.

"Hey Doc, what's with that statue outside in the courtyard?" I asked.

Sandler looked out the window and shrugged. "Don't know. It's been here longer than me."

I found that hard to believe, but instead of beginning my first supervised meal by being an asshole, I picked up my balanced meal from the food cart and headed for my assigned seat. I sniffed the food. Lingering memories of high school cafeteria lunch smelled more appetizing.

Sandler closed the steel dinning cart. "All right. If anyone needs anything, I'll be in the observation room." Making sure I was paying attention, he pointed at the window. I waved to him breaking an enormous grin that showed my wisdom teeth. Personally, I thought I was a little old to have an assigned seat and have people watch me eating, but I was nowhere near the oldest or the youngest person at dinner.

I was, however, the only guy.

"Are you gay?" the little pillow-grabbing imp asked as soon as I hit the table.

I covered my mouth to talk because I was chewing. "No, are you eight or nine? What do you know about being gay, anyway, little girl?"

"I just wondered." She ran her finger through her hair to give off the air of being an adult, but her fingers got stuck in a butterfly hairclip. "I mean you're the only boy here. I'm Brittany."

"Well, I can assure you I'm not gay," I said, swallowing a

tater tot. The jagged sides of the potato scratched my throat going down. My ears hurt. I felt especially bad for Brittany. Not only was she confused and naïve, but she was also young, much too young to be wasting her life at Sisters of Prophecy.

"What's the freaking deal then?" another girl asked. "The only other guy I've seen in here in the three times that I've been here was a schizophrenic high school kid. He had, like, four or five different personalities and was constantly spazzing out. That kid was a fuckin' idiot." She put out her hand. "My name's Kristina."

"I really don't know the answer to that, Tina. That's why I'm here." I chopped my food up into small pieces and piled them together on the dish, ignoring her hand.

"I think D's performance when he got here was enough of a reason to admit him into the program," Sandler piped in on a microphone from the observation room. I knew what he was talking about, but I don't think that my fellow inmates had any idea.

I glared at the window. Whatever happened to the Hippocratic oath? When I arrived the day before, I'd just gotten off a plane. I was still piss drunk when I collapsed at the airport. I was a tad undernourished, too. I don't believe that it's normal to reflexively throw up a bland bowl of broth after every sip.

"I bet you want a cookie? Huh, Sandler?" I said, whizzing my dessert, a rock-hard oatmeal and raisin cookie, at the observations room's window. The girls laughed. They needed a leader. I'm not saying they needed a leader to aid them against the Establishment. Rather, they needed someone to make them laugh, someone to make them feel safe about all their inhibitions toward the "man" kind—the Rick Conroy kind.

Being in the hospital wasn't an opportunity for me to get laid, but it was a way for me to repent for letting the women I really did love get away because I was too involved in self ruin.

"Great, D, you just lost your TV privileges," Sandler yelled into the microphone, regaining control of the meal situation.

I looked over to the connected common room at the Jurassic television. "Wow, I guess that would be a crime if I didn't know how to read, huh?" Under the table, Kristina nudged my leg.

"You're cool," Brittany said in pre-adolescent admiration.

I snapped back, "Yeah, so cool that I've been sentenced to months in this prison with a bunch of confused cunts." Not a word. Not a laugh. I kept my head lowered, feeling their death stares targeting my dry scalp. I waited and waited and waited until the exact last minute, and then I raised my head with a smile. "I'm just kidding."

One thing that these girls had to learn was that I took sarcasm to a new level and it never seemed to faze anyone. People accepted it, laughed it off, or ignored it. This was their first taste. We all returned to our meals. The nurses and Sandler starred me down when the doughnut girl, Mariah, picked at her asparagus and cried. The royal guard barreled out of the observation room to comfort her.

Were they going to help her? Not very likely. They snapped open a nutritional supplement and jammed it down her bent straw-like throat. She couldn't fight any more, and because she wasn't a barfer, she couldn't yack into the crawl spaces of her room. Fucking anorexic, even if she did throw up, she didn't have anywhere near enough energy to create a bouillon cube for the rats. I figured that her bare stomach would tug and pull at the little bit of nutrition in her body. I almost gagged as the poison curdled down her throat.

Her six-foot-tall, seventy-seven pound frame doubled over in disgust and Sandler pulled her up gently by her stringy hair. Her tears followed a path around her mouth, blocked by the vitamin-infested concoction that didn't make it into her body. At least that's what I thought. Later I came to find out that her bones couldn't support her body. Like Lori Conroy, Mariah was a tangled string marionette. I couldn't watch her torture any longer. I finished my meal and went back to my nest by the window and lit up another smoke. Other than Lori, I had no patience for anorexia.

I continued my fixation on the statue of the priest. I wasn't going worship him, as I may have done in the past with a tree. I just wanted to know if anybody in this world cared about him.

"Can I join you?" a voice asked behind me.

"I guess. Do you smoke?" My eyes didn't turn away from the centerpiece outside, but I knew it was Kristina. I caught a glimpse of her reflection in the window. She was the only person there close to my age, and she didn't seem nearly as tattered as, say, Mariah.

"You seem like a normal enough kid, D. I guess you're intelligent enough."

Her unmistakably Ivy League attitude slapped my ass instantly.

"Let me guess, Tina—" I began.

"It's Kristina. Thank you."

I was still looking out the window, but I envisioned her with her little hands on her hips, shaking her head. I released a nice long drag from my cigarette. "Like I said," I slammed my hands down on the table and propped myself up, "Tina." I sat back down, waited a beat, and then, "I'm just kidding. Don't you think it's funny when people try to act like badasses when they're obviously not?"

"Yeah, imagine some longhair in a clinic for eating disorders trying to be a badass. Now all you need is an Italian horn and a muscle tee."

I looked away from the window and up to Tina. She stood over six feet tall with kinky hair, a huge smile and deep brown eyes.

"Let me guess, you need to bum a cigarette." I flicked a Camel Light to the top of my pack.

She grabbed it. "Only after I eat or while I'm getting drunk, D. You have a light?" The only lighter that I had on me was Lori's. I was only person who used it since she jumped off the Bay Bridge.

"No," was the only response I came up with.

"Whatever." She grabbed my cigarette and then jump-started hers off of my ash. "How about you, D? Are you a smoke-a-holic?" She laughed and took the seat right next to me in what eventually became the smoker's corner.

"Same. Only after I eat, after the barfarama, and when I get drunk. Most of the time."

"Barfarama. Hmmm. Is that kind of like an Oral B?" She dragged at her cigarette like it was the first one she had smoked in a decade.

I rolled my eyes. "What the hell is an Oral B?" I knew the brand of toothbrush, but I'd never heard anyone use the name any other way.

"That's when you make yourself yack by shoving a toothbrush down your throat. You know, the water is running, and you can clean that acid off of your teeth in one sharp motion. Dr. Sandler calls it multitasking, perfectionism."

I knew what she was talking about. As a matter of fact, I often "washed my feet" or "took showers" after meals; however, after a few years practice, my body evolved. I puked by thinking about it and clinching my body.

"What do you use as lubrication?" I asked.

"Lubrication?"

"You know, what you eat as a side dish to relieve the powerful blow of your stomach acids. Personally, I use either a creamy salad dressing or a yogurt-type substance." Ha. All my years of careful preparation paid off.

"I never thought about anything like that. I always just used whatever liquid, Diet Coke, as a lube."

"Are you crazy, Tina? Diet Coke's no good; it's carbonated. Not only can it totally rot your teeth and your throat, it hurts when it comes up."

"Have you ever chugged Ipecac?"

"Ipecac. What the hell's that?"

"It's syrup that doctors recommend if you drink anything poisonous. Makes you hurl immediately."

"When I was about ten, Tina, I had this really gnarly cough. One night I got out of bed, because it wouldn't stop and I decided to go the shitter and pound some cough syrup. Anyway, it was really dark, and I was sleepwalking. I grabbed the wrong bottle and chugged it."

"What was it?"

"It was the crap you put inside a vaporizer. When I found out what it was, I immediately jammed my finger down my throat. It hurt like shit and tasted even more horrendous than it smelled. It felt like someone shoved a hose up my ass and shot yellow jackets through my insides."

"You're lucky it didn't tear your esophagus to shit."

I rubbed my Adam's apple. I hadn't forgotten what Sandler told me earlier that day. "I know. My mom and dad called the poison control center immediately and then commended me on my bold behavior. I think, 'Way to go champy' was what they said."

"They'll probably never do that again. Every disorder begins somewhere. You see that girl Becky over there on the couch? She used to drink like a gallon of milk and then chase it with Ipecac."

I looked over at Becky. She was a cute, early-twenties ecstasy freak with the sides of her head shaved who made butterfly movements with her legs as she curled her knees up to her chin.

Slowly, she bobbed back and forth like an autistic child. I came to find out later that this was a popular technique for most of the girls in Prophecy. It was their way to compensate for the usual routine of compulsive exercise.

"What about laxatives?" Tina asked, excited about our morbid conversation.

"Come on. Of course," I bragged, brushing her off. "The only problem was that I take too many smashes a day, anyway. One time I was trying to be the life of the party, and I lifted my leg to unleash a huge fart and shit my pants."

"That's really gross." She used her eyes to lead me across the room. "That older chick sitting over by Becky, Sylvia, she's got such a big tolerance that she maxed out on like thirty-two laxatives a day. She's really dehydrated, and her potassium and calcium levels are abnormally low. You'll see Dr. Sandler make her and Mariah eat a couple bananas a day."

"I was wondering about that Mariah girl. She's totally fucked up, isn't she?" I caught a glimpse of Sandler and one of his nameless drones walking the feeble Mariah over to her specified seat. She had her own seat. Even with the pillow, any of Prophecy's cheap-as-shit standard-issue furniture would break her in half. I didn't ask Tina if Mariah had jaundice, but I shivered at her yellow skin, teeth, and hair. She looked like an alien who just got a golden shower.

"She's nice, but nobody really knows anything about her. She always keeps to herself. I don't even think I want to know what kind of shit lurks inside her head."

"And Brittany?"

"Don't worry about that fag comment; she's only nine. Since the first time I was in here, they've gotten younger and younger. She's probably one of these kids doing it to grab some attention from their yuppie parents. You'll find that people like Brittany are a dime a dozen around here. But that's cool; they all have issues. One thing I'm going to warn you about is this anorexia superiority complex that some of these bitches have."

"What do you mean, like *Lord of the Flies* shit?" I met several anorexics in my lifetime, mainly Lori, and never experienced any class systems before.

"Kind of; they believe they're superior because they commit

themselves to full control." Tina lunged back into my pack of cigarettes. "Where do you fit into all of this?"

I decided things were getting a little too personal, so I switched gears. "You fucking Ivy League mooch."

"How did you know I go to an Ivy League school?"

"You speak to people like they should beg to give you a rim job."

"Kiss my ass, D, and let's smoke lots of fuckin' cigarettes."

"What's your major in school, Tina, women's literature or some other garbage-made-up-hippie-bullshit?"

"It sure is, and this is one of my *Awakenings*." She took another cigarette out of my pack. Impressed with her capacity to play my game, I joined in with my guard down.

"Chopin, huh. So, you're literate."

"No, it's just my education taught me a lot more than your so-called well-rounded private liberal arts school." Ivy league. They believe the educational system revolves around their curriculum and poser free-thinking liberal bullshit. School without walls? More like school without consequences.

"Fuck you, Tina."

"My name is Kristina." My short exchange with Tina taught me that I would learn more than how to keep my food down in that penal complex. I took a fresh pack of cigarettes out of my pocket, packed them and surrendered by placing Lori's lighter on the table.

"What's the story with that statue down there?" I asked.

She looked outside. "I've been here three times, and I have no idea. Probably some priest that either donated money to the hospital or did some outstanding deed for the community." She started to pack the fresh pack of Camels, opened them up, and flicked one in her mouth. "You want one?" she offered kindly.

I snatched the pack out of her hand. "What, do you smoke a pack after every meal? You're going to smoke my carton before my parents get here."

She grinned with the stogie firing out of her mouth. She reminded me of a bluffing poker player, not an ailing psychosomatic. In one motion, she scooped up the lighter, crept the end of the flame past her cigarette, and shot smoke out of the corners of her mouth. "Screw you, you pussy. I saw you come in here with two cartons. While you were busy struggling to digest that broth at lunch, I walked out of my room and clearly saw two cartons in the front pockets of your duffle bag."

"That doesn't mean I'm going to share them with you, bitch." I still had the chills from that little display she put on with the lighter. It was all too familiar, and like a lot of things about Prophecy, the healing process already hurt.

"Although this may seem like jail, Tina, I can't imagine you sneaking up on me in the night with a shank made out of a nail from the sofa wrapped in tape to steal my cigarettes."

"No, you're right, D, it's not a prison. But you'd better get used to being watched every time you eat—even an hour after you eat—by a bunch of bush-league doctors. You, unless you're full of shit, which I can already tell you're not, are already a prisoner to yourself. You're going to love when the doctors watch you take a shit."

Knowing then that having any privacy in the restroom was impossible, I decided that it was time to get creative.

"Oh, and by the way," she taunted me, "if you don't gain two ounces a day, you get your supplement intake beefed up."

"Very creative," I mumbled. The sun buried itself behind a couple of big buildings next door. A man, a custodian maybe, ventured outside, attempting to polish the statue. Possibly he was the mop-carrying mortician that could ease my strange curiosity.

I strayed from my conversation with Tina and gazed back into the yard. The statue's engineer was in his fifties, balding with a limp and a cane. I could tell by the way that he examined the statue before he cleaned it that he didn't have enough money to reload the prescription on his bifocals. However, his uniform was carefully pressed. It seemed strange for it to be so tidy after a full day of cleaning up hospital mishaps.

"What's your problem, Mr. Sensitive Godboy?"

"Just for the record, I am neither sensitive, nor do I have any kind of religious beliefs; however, I do find it frightening that Prophecy let the centerpiece of its courtyard chip away to shit. How does that make you feel? I mean, come on, if they can't even maintain their art at this place, how are they going to keep someone as fucked up as Mariah alive?"

Tina stared at me. The custodian shuffled around examining the day's beating. As he squinted and peered at it with his glasses off and on, he continued to drag the top edge of his hand under his nose, wiping away the mucus that would quickly accumulate on a bitterly cold day. Amazingly, his nose never, ever touched the sleeve of his uniform. He was one proud janitor.

"Your teeth look pretty gnarly, D. Check out these pearly whites." She smiled.

I blew a puff of smoke in her mouth. "Tell me about it. Whenever a dentist looks at them, he shoves about a thousand pamphlets in my face and then thickens them with some plaster stuff."

Tina sighed and began ripping a piece of paper into hundreds of smaller pieces.

"Check out that custodian, Tina." We watched as the custodian started from the base of the statue, scrubbing with a large brush. Carefully, he stripped away the birdshit, urine, and salt without doing any more damage to the mangled cadaver. "Why the fuck does he care?" He was like an artist making precise strokes and then stopping momentarily to wipe the build-up of ice on his brow. Although I couldn't make out the graffiti that covered the corpse, it was easy to see that it had been repainted many times in a cemetery-white color. It almost looked like stained glass. The layers and layers of paint, covered and covered again, didn't prevent the anthems and slogans from subtly shining through. "Why does anyone care about that piece of shit?"

She laughed and threw confetti in my face. "The janitors spray it white once a month." After a quick examination from top to bottom, the janitor knelt down before his masterpiece and made the sign of the cross. "Who cares, D. They're fucking Catholics."

"This is a Catholic hospital; what do you expect? What are you, Tina?"

She put her yellowed index finger to her mouth and whispered. "Well, my father's Jewish and my mother's Catholic."

"Sounds like a great combo, Tina."

"Maybe they started out as a great combo. They're divorced now. Religion had nothing to do with it."

The janitor left. A minute later, the vagrant who pissed on the statue before returned and unzipped his pants. "Look at this fucker. He didn't even wait for the smell of Ajax to go away before he pissed on it."

Tina looked. "What a dirtball."

Sandler snuck up behind us. "It's time for group, gang. And, D, if you could stay after group, I'd like to have a talk with you."

CHAPTER TWO

"I called it pulling the trigger." I shaped my hand into a pistol, fired it and rolled my head back for dramatic purposes. "Or the barfarama. It was my way of making something fratboys found acceptable."

Sandler furiously scratched away on his pad. "Pulling the trigger? Hmmm, don't you think that's filled with suicidal connotations, D?" He opened his hair at the cowlick.

"I never thought of it that way, Sandler. It seemed liked a cool way of explaining it to anyone who caught you throwing up. It's funny; no one ever caught me."

"You're proud of that? It still didn't keep you from avoiding your return visit here." Whenever the good doctor felt I was avoiding the subject or passing on half-truths, he slammed me with one of his long-arm-of-the-eating-disorder-law speeches. "The way I see it, you were only lying to yourself."

"In many respects I was, Doc. Like you said, I got caught." He had no idea what I had gotten away with. If he did, I would have been shipped down to the psycho ward.

"It started out that whenever I wanted to do it, I could blame getting wasted, Doc. As a matter of fact, it became almost 'cool' to throw up."

"I think you're stretching it. What do you mean?" Sandler bounced his Cross pen on his lip. Accidentally, he hit the gold pen on his whitened teeth.

I changed the subject. "Sandler, let me ask you a question. You make pretty good money, why do you use a Cross pen? Did it come free with your Jostens class ring?"

"This pen means a lot to me." He held it up and almost smiled. "It was given to me by my wife when we bought our first house."

"Sorry, I guess I figured that someone in your position would have a Monte Blanc or something."

He looked at his worn pen, "It has an emotional attachment for me. It means almost as much as my wedding ring."

"How long have you been married?"

"Returning to you, D, tell me what was so cool about being bulimic?"

"Well, when I pledged a fraternity, the brothers made us drink Mad Dog."

"Mad Dog?"

"Yeah, MD 20/20. It's like this dick cheap rummy wine. Really gross shit. Anyway, Doc, at the pledge meetings every night, they would make us drink so much of it that every pledge threw up. There was actually a bucket set up in the middle of the room every meeting."

He stopped scribbling and looked at me square. "What was cool about that?"

"Before we went to meetings, all of the pledges drank all sorts of different colors of Gatorade. Then, when we got to the meeting, we cracked up, as one by one we puked all sorts of neon colors. The inside of the can eventually ended up looking like one of those crappy candles that a kids make by melting crayons at camp. There wasn't any real shape, but colorful, nonetheless."

"That's sick! Did you know that hazing is illegal?"

"We didn't care; we were having a blast."

"Answer me a question, D. Why would you want to go through something like that, the initiation? You don't seem like the fraternity type."

"Palmbrook, as expensive as it was, didn't fund any activities. We had to create our own fun. Besides, Sandler, how could I have survived college without the high-fives and the date rapes?"

"Fun? Alcoholism? Bulimia? Rape? Fun? Have you ever thought that this fraternity fueled your problem?"

"First of all, the date rape thing was a joke. I was set in alcoholism and the barfarama long before I joined any organization." That was the truth. The first time that I'd consciously self-induced was back at the tree, the night I'd escaped from Kudzutown.

"So, would you say that you have issues with your weight?"

Typical question. I had the answer, because this was the only thing that I thought I could be completely sure of with my condition. Weight and food meant very little. I was an addict and it was my choice. "No, not really. I mean, I don't want to be some obese freak, but I always got off on the high. Sometimes, I do it to blow out anger. I don't get angry or show emotion very regularly." I never binged on anything. "I eat like a normal person and I flee into the bathroom like a junkie going for a fix when I'm done. The barfarama is better than booze. It's way better than drugs. It's solid, natural, and legal. Some people brag about the ultimate rush of a hit of crack or a six-hour roll while dancing on x. They don't have anything like I do. Something that makes your heart pound in your chest makes your eyes sting as the stomach acid rips onto your eyelids and nose. The barfarama is like standing up quickly and seeing the world roll around in your banged up head. It's the shit. I'm in total control of it. Control is something I never had with any drug, including booze."

"Strange, unless you're lying to me, you exhibit none of the stereotypical traits of this disorder. These aren't the problems you told your parents you were afflicted with. You don't binge, but you purge. You say weight control isn't the main issue, rather euphoric control. It sounds to me like you're an alcoholic, D."

"I *am* an alcoholic, a good one, and I know that I'm also allergic to alcohol; however, this is a totally separate issue. If I had to make a choice between the two, I would choose barfing instead of boozing. I've read a lot about this problem, bulimia, and I know what it can do. That's why I took the initiative to create tricks, you know, cheat death."

"I don't think I'm following. Do you know what something like regurgitated vodka can do to your esophagus? Remember our conversation earlier?" Sandler burned frantically through page after page of material.

"Absolutely. Rule number one: I don't mix alcohol and

throwing up. I learned that after my pledging experience and I knew what it did to my insides. From what I was told, it was like being skinned inside out. Number two: I also always mix my food with a nice, smooth lubricant."

"Lubricant?"

"Yeah, yogurt is great. After every bite of your food, I take a small bite from some yogurt. It makes the delivery a lot smoother."

"That can't be proven medically, D."

"I know, but it makes me feel better when I'm practically sticking my head into the toilet." I pierced my nose. "Do you know what the toilets smell like in a fraternity house? The lube does smooth the procedure. On that same note, I always eat my food in a calculated order and take note of that order."

"Once again, you're not making sense." Sandler found it easier to mark on his tablet, dismissing rather than listening to my twisted manifesto. I was getting to him. "You're making me sick."

"I start out with your first dish, then second, then third and so on. This way I know when I'm finished by the color and taste of the pile I'm building. It's a good way to gauge when my well is dry."

He tapped on his tablet and squinted. "Pile?"

"It keeps the puke from floating all over the place in the can, Doc. This way, as I pile up a nice stack of flavors, I can tell where I am in resurrecting the meal. It's like making a sandwich, backwards. I'm thinking about starting my own restaurant franchise."

"This is one of your little rules that isn't feasible. The regurgitation procedure itself does not limit itself like a production line. It's all based on the consistency of the food you're eating. For instance, if you ate a bowl of soup first, it would most likely manage to work its way out before everything else because the liquid makeup."

"Like I said before, lubrication. I always eat soup or liquid-based foods last. That way, I can flush that shit out and get on with my pile. Rule number three: I never try to shoot pizza. That's a death sentence. There is no way to chew a slice of pizza to compact it down to not get stuck in my pipes. I think it's the combination of melted cheese and bread that makes it difficult. If I decide to brave pizza, I chew the fuck out of it and wait until right before my forty-five minutes are up, and then do it. My stomach has a chance to break some of the consistency."

"Forty-five minutes, D?"

"C'mon Sandler, we all know how long it takes before the food is out of reach, before it's digested. You know. It's like being on a bomb squad. Should you choose the red or the blue wire? It really doesn't matter; every bomb squad knows the right cut to make simply by looking at the connections and makeup of the bomb. If I don't cut one of the wires before the timer runs out though, I'm screwed. It's totally pointless; the food has already been sucked dry of all of the good stuff I want to barf. You know, the flavor."

"Then it would be a food and/or caloric issue."

"Not true," I stated as I boasted another loophole. "If I don't get it out before then, the acid is too strong for me to retain composure. It detracts from the experience. The best bet is to deliver the package ASAP. I admire Don Ho. You know, the "Tiny Bubbles" guy. He went to restaurants and ordered big fat steaks. Right next to his feet was a big old bucket. I don't know if it was a gift from the maitre d' or if he brought the thing from home. Anyway, I heard that Don Ho would chew on his twenty-ounce porterhouse and spit the chewed-up meat into his bucket. Now that's ballsy. Imagine some star-struck eighty-year-old bitch going over to his table and asking old Don Ho for his autograph. 'One second, madam, let me throw my undigested steak into this bucket.' He had a lot of nerve. At least I have the decency to covertly hit the basket whenever I run a fast break."

"That sounds like something you read in a tabloid."

"Maybe I did. Maybe I wrote it down and then read it. Lyrically, it's far better than "Tiny Bubbles." Don't you think?" Sandler gave me the gas face by curling his upper lip. He refused to buy anything that I said. "Rule number four: Before I get down to business, I always fill the toilet with a major wad of toilet paper. I take credit for this rule, after leaving the can with splashed chunks of vomit on my face and shirt."

Sandler scribbled. "Another means of secrecy, huh, D?"

"Yeah, and when I get chunks on me, the smell is hard to get rid of; cotton, stomach acid, and food don't mix. The last rule, and I think this is the most important and strictest rule to stick to: I never use my index finger."

"Another way to hide the smell?"

"Not at all, it's a way to avoid the skin peeling and discoloration that I get on your finger from the acid. It also hurts." I showed Sandler my hand and bit off a rough hangnail. "I chew my cuticles. Open wounds don't mesh with vomit. Blech!"

"So how do you do it? With a toothbrush?"

"Ha!" I grunted. Sandler had sucked Tina's lame secret out of her. "Even better, there is a way to internally move my stomach and clinch my ribs and ass, forcing the shit out. In the beginning, after I haven't been doing it for a while, I usually have to use my finger, but once the process is set in motion, it just flies. It's similar to what Houdini used to do when he had audience members participate in his show and punch him in his stomach. He had this brilliant way of adjusting his stomach to taking hard blows from all of the meatheads who thought they could play ball with the master of illusions."

"Don't you think your body is getting used to the process and automatically regurgitates the source, thereby making it a, for lack of a better phrase, natural reaction?"

"I've heard that before. There's nothing really natural about the barfarama. What's natural about an impulse to reject food? Besides sex, I think it's the most natural instinct of the human body. You need food to live, period. I can feel the food in my stomach when I can't pull the trigger, like when I'm on a trip with my parents. It's like a tug of war. The body wants food worse than anything. After I became its servant, however, I always felt sick or stuffed." Several times I ended up in a situation that prevented me from doing the deed. I got overly anxious, and I heard my stomach digesting the food. Usually my heart sped up, and I began to sweat. Strange, I rarely sweat, even when I do physical activities. I always focused on my watch, trying to think of ways to get away with it.

"If eating is the most natural instinct, then why are you doing this to yourself, D?"

"I think that's why I'm here, Doc."

"Okay, in the last ten minutes you have compared your disorder to a bomb threat." He skimmed his notes. "Also a basketball play, Harry Houdini, and killing yourself."

"I'm impressed with the way that Houdini escaped from shit he didn't have any control over. I admire him so much that I look at him as one of the main influences."

"So, do you want to escape from here?" Sandler tried to inch further. I dug into his face, his lines. His intentions weren't to heal me; they were to get me to admit to my criminal ways.

"*Should* I want to? I don't think I want to change. My brain has a choice. I chose my path."

"What do you think you are escaping from?"

"I don't know. What was Houdini escaping from?"

"He was a magician. He fooled people into thinking that he could control any environment or situation."

"Do you know what happened to old Harry, Doc?"

"Hmmm. Yeah didn't he get caught in a tank and drown during a show?"

"We all saw the Tony Curtis film, jackass. What a load of shit. Harry's death was nothing that impressive. He was at a theater in Detroit performing on October 21, 1926, and one of the overzealous dickheads in the audience caught him off guard by punching him in the stomach. He died on Halloween from a ruptured appendix."

"You seem to know that story pretty well. I think you're obsessed with Houdini and escape."

"Actually no, I couldn't give a shit about that pickle-sniffing Kraut."

Sandler's hands left his tablet, and he threw them over his head. "Come on, now. Do you need to be racist? Why do you know all of the dates and locations?"

"Because, Doc, I was born on October 21 near that theater."

He took off his I'm-a-yuppie-pussy wire frame glasses and rubbed his temples. "D, you realize that when you speak to me everything is in strict confidence, don't you?"

"Of course I do. You have my chart in front of you. Look at the dates and places; they match up."

Sandler put down his tablet and looked at my medical chart. He wasn't amused. "You're trying to convince me of this, aren't you? How do I know that the dates match up?" He didn't believe my story. What the hell did I care?

"Well, since this is in confidence and I trust you enough not to tell anyone, he was punched on October 22, but I celebrate my birthday on that day, and I was born pretty close to midnight on the twenty-first."

Sandler rolled his eyes, and licked his pen. "While you were in school, did you take any psychology classes, D?"

"No not really. I spent most of my time in English classes and anthropology classes."

"That was when you decided to grace the other students with your presence, of course."

"Huh?"

Once again, he picked up the chart, flipped through a couple of pages and read. "When I interviewed your parents the first day you came in last summer, they said you nearly failed out of school because you never showed up for class. When you did, you reeked of alcohol."

"To some degree, that's probably true. It didn't start out that way. When I first got there, I was a good student. I prided myself on affecting teachers with stories and shit. You know, thrilling myself with the fact that I could make them cry. I also got off on fighting with teachers about stupid shit like what pussies the Romantics were, as opposed to the Realists. That was fun. I got bored with it, though. When you go to a school that small, you usually end up having repeat teachers. I had this one fucker a couple times. I hated Professor Angello."

"What happened to him, D?"

"I think it's a story I'll save for later." I never wanted Sandler to know. More important, I never wanted my parents to know.

"You never answered my question. You seem to enjoy toying with people's emotions and dismantling people psychologically. You also seem to have a pretty firm understanding of what exactly you're doing to yourself. Why no psychology, D?"

"What am I doing right now, Sandler?"

"I didn't say acting classes." He chortled. "Have you ever thought that you might have a little bit of a schizophrenic disorder? The first sign of schizophrenia is an omnipotence complex."

"I don't know, Doc. Can you tell me that there is a Christ? I've seen a lot of shit, stuff that would make you grab your dick and rip it off while you were pissing. If I wanted to be Christ, I'd have a self esteem problem."

"Once again, I'm not following, D."

"I know you don't. If there is a Christ, a God, an anything out there, I think he is doing a shitty job. Would you like me asking if I thought you had a superiority complex because you complimented the janitor who cleans the statue outside? You know the guy. He did a dandy job of cleaning up the shit dripping off the stretcher of the bum with AIDS who got shot. I know you don't admire a guy who risks his life cleaning up shit. Fuck off! You sit back studying a bunch of dumb kids while he tosses and turns every night wondering if his one-room shack is a fair trade for his life. I never want to be someone's god. It takes too much responsibility. The thing about the way I act is that it's completely irresponsible. Yes, doctor, I do have dreams. I like to consider myself a cut above the rest. You don't see me harming anyone else, waving my hand with gang slangs. Everyone has to have dreams, even if they've become nightmares by that custodian's reality."

Sandler pointed his pen at me. "You have no right to tell me how I feel about others, D."

"Trust me, my self-destruction is not as conceited as your 'polite' gestures to the shit shoveler. He knows you're looking down on him. He just doesn't have the balls or the time to even acknowledge you. He works for a living. His dreams, my dreams, they aren't any better than real life. We know what we see in the world. I tried to find paradise, Doc. It wasn't any better than a one-room shack."

Dr. Sandler didn't look up from his pad, he just closed the page, cleared his throat. "Go to bed, D."

Group seemed like a reason for the medical staff to give the patients the feeling they were in summer camp doing arts and crafts. It was time for me to make a mockery of their system. Picasso I was not, but I knew I could knock out a picture so preposterous and blasphemous they had to let me out of their cave. Besides, it was a Catholic hospital, and painting an inverted crucifix with watercolors wouldn't go over real big. Maybe a priest getting his cock smoked by a little kid would have been better.

"Hi, I'm Sheryl Desmond. I'm your artistic therapy advisor." She seemed nice enough, but I was confused by what kind of degree she had and how it pertained to any legitimate medical profession. Judging Desmond by her tightly stretched and brightly colored pantsuit, her festive "look what I just got on my trip to the Islands" hair braids, and her wacky fish-covered shoes, she would prove easy prey.

We all sat around her on the floor in a circle, as if preparing for a nursery school story time. Being a chronic nail and cuticle biter, I noticed the hangnail on my index finger that I bit off in Sandler's office the previous night starting to bleed. Perfect. What better to provide a palette for my canvas?

Desmond looked at me. "I see some new faces here since last week." Then she looked at Tina. "And some old ones who have returned. Today we're going to do some drawings that reflect the nature of our family relationships." I couldn't believe it, from Major English Writings III to crayon pictures of Ma and Pa. She rambled on about the importance of this project (blah, blah, blah), and I pumped my finger for blood, piercing it so it gushed. It was a hackneyed scare tactic, but Tina, who sat next to me, was entertained. "Excuse me," Desmond began. "What is your name?" I looked up from my transfusion.

I reacted as Tina giggled. "Wha?"

"What's your name? I'm not talking to myself here." She must have thought that the medical degree she got at Pottery Barn entitled her to treat me like a bitch.

"My name's D. I'm your newest student."

"This isn't a class; it's a therapy. What's wrong with your finger?" She looked around the group, shrugging her shoulders and acting like she had paralysis of the mouth. She loved hamming it up to the crowd. All she needed to finish her MD was a big bicycle horn, a flashing bow tie, and a set of rainbow suspenders. The advertisement for Operation: The Wacky Doctor's Game plagued my memories. The blood gushed from my hangnail, smeared all over my finger and trickled down my hand.

I didn't answer. I carried on with my drilling.

"Listen, D. You are disrupting the other group members and embarrassing yourself. Let me get you a tissue for that." She pulled a small travel tissue packet out of her purse and passed it to me through the group. I believed that it must have been in her purse since the last time she decided not to wipe her nose on her sleeve, probably a couple of years before I became its owner.

"I don't need no stinking tissues. I'm just dipping my pen. We are doing art, aren't we?" I looked at her seriously, but decided to back down. "Oh, I'm just fucking with you. I'm listening."

Desmond's face flushed white as Tina giggled again and then nudged me to stop. Desmond turned to look at little Brittany and then raised her index finger in my direction. "Umm, D, we are in mixed company here, and I do not find foul language acceptable." She crossed her arms declaring she was the law. I looked around the circle. All of the girls were bobbing back and forth in their Indian-style seating positions to stay active. I was sitting in a dilapidated house of toothpicks.

"Mixed company? What the fuck? Are you a drag queen?" I stared her down as I heard a few chuckles from the peanut galley. I refused to look around and suck up for approval. I wasn't going to resort to the comic buffoonery of Chuckles the Eating Disorder Unit Clown.

"How dare you! You know what I mean. Brittany. She's too young to hear language like that. And if we are in mixed company, then I guess you're the," she raised her fingers for air quotes, 'odd man out.'" She looked through the corners of her eyes, pouting her lips and nodding her head.

"Wow. You got me there. Where did you learn to throw such zingers, Doctor? Wait a minute, didn't you play a wacky orangutan in a movie?"

"First of all, I am not a doctor," she began.

I acted surprised. "No shit. Then what are you?"

"I am a social worker who is on her way to becoming a doctor." Social worker, huh? Hippie. If she'd said that to begin with, I may not have been such sadistic prick.

"I'm sorry, you don't need me to misbehave. Please ignore my interruptions. Tell us about our project, Ms. Desmond."

She nodded her head in victory, brushed her way-too-long and greasy Crystal Gayle hair over her fat lunch lady arms, and continued with her project.

Our first project, at least since I had been there, was to draw a portrait of our families. Simple enough. I shut my mouth, grabbed my crayons and construction paper, and headed over to the window. I figured cigarettes and the statue of the preacher outside would inspire me to come up with a picture completely lacking insight and depth.

"You're a total prick," Tina said as she came over next to the window, stole a cigarette, and sat down beside me.

"Oh give me a break. You know how silly this is, Tina."

"My name is Kristina, jackass. Some of us don't see it that way. Trust me, D, it's better than sitting around and being forced to tell the entire group your problems or being grilled by Sandler in his office." She grabbed for Lori's lighter.

"I really wish that you would quit using this lighter. It means a lot to me."

"Whatever." She lit her cigarette and threw Lori's lighter down on the table. "Fag."

"I bet you wish that stealing cigarettes and my lighter are enough to piss me off, Tina. I let things that get in my way slide right down my sack."

"Typical. You're a mental freak. I can tell. Let me guess; you compensate for pathetic social skills by controlling yourself in the bathroom."

"Wrong. Let me guess, you compensate for not looking out the window on the second floor because you're afraid of what horrors may attack you in the real world."

"Wrong."

Agoraphobia. I knew about the affliction because my Godparents' thirty-eight-year-old son never left the house. When he did, when it was absolutely necessary, he shook and cried. I remember visiting him once while I was in junior high, and he explained to me why records were so much better than CDs. At the time I didn't know that he had the disorder, but one thing stuck out in my mind. Whenever he played an album, he put the cover on the wall above the stereo. Below the brackets was a brass sign that said, "Now Playing." I was young, and I thought it was pretty cool. I envied him because he had his own little radio station that he controlled. I looked up to him as a kid, and thought he was super swass. You know, always at home, kicking it, and sticking it to The Man.

Anyway, after buying his story about CD quality opposed to vinyl, I asked him to go out and help me pick out a few records. I knew he wouldn't dig my taste in music, but I thought what the hell, we'll have a blast. We didn't end up going, though, and my taste in music was irrelevant.

She snapped her fingers in my face. "Hey, D, I said, 'wrong.' Agoraphobia? Your skills in psychoanalysis are even worse than Sandler's. Brother, I party my ass off. I can't get enough of the outside world."

"Wow, you're such a riddle. At least you could've acted like there was something traumatic out there, in the sky, across the street, whatever."

"Listen, we have all day to screw around with these drawings. I already drew mine." She spun around her construction paper revealing a woman holding a crucifix, opening a door with a cartoon bubble that said, "Divorce, asshole!" On a bed there was a man in a yarmulke getting head. It was fucked up, yet funny. "You can find out about me later. Everyone here knows my deal. I have this feeling that I won't find out yours unless you tell me soon. They aren't going to let you stay much longer unless you relax."

"Relax, huh? Why are you so curious? Are you taking psych at your Ivy League school?"

"Of course; my parents, who are both therapists, by the way, would have it no other way."

"They don't expect too much from you, huh?" From what little I knew about Tina, I imagined that a bitter divorce left the kids and their problems buried. Either that or her parents buried her in the hospital to keep her out of their hair.

"Tell the deal, D."

"I can't say that it's a short story or one that I'm very proud of." I had no idea how she had managed to even get me this far into the conversation. I guess I really liked her.

"Kiss my ass. We're not going anywhere."

"I suppose you're right, gash."

CHAPTER THREE

I visited Palmbrook College when I was a junior in high school—before anything happened to Freddy and Lori. It looked like a country club. There were hot girls everywhere, a huge swimming pool, and a sun deck overlooking an enormous freshwater lake where water ski and windsurfing classes were required once a year.

Nicely groomed palm trees covered the campus and made the carefully constructed stucco buildings seem more like cabanas than classrooms. In the center of campus stood a huge park surrounded by a cobblestone path. Every two or three bricks on the path had the name and the graduation date of an alumnus. The only names that I recognized were Jed Clampett, Norman Bates, and Mr. Rogers. The campus was picture perfect. During my visit, my parents kidded with me about how Palmbrook looked like a travel brochure for the Bahamas. The general checked out every piece of ass that walked by. I couldn't figure out how the institution could afford to keep everything that well-attended, until I saw the outrageous tuition, room, and board prices. The only reason I'd applied was because my mom had wanted to go there as a kid. Her father wouldn't let her. I'm glad she didn't.

The small, ritzy town surrounding the campus featured the likes of Laura Ashley, Neiman Marcus, and Ralph Lauren, as well as French bistros and a throwback bar directly across the street called The Library. The first time I saw the gold sign I laughed and thought about leaving a message on my answering machine that said, "Hey, if you're looking for me, I'm at The Library." I'm sure I wasn't the first person to come up with that brilliant idea. I never felt guilty about lying when my parents called while I was getting wasted, rather than studying. As odd as this may sound, with Palmbrook being a college and all, I thought that all of its beauty was a front for its lacking academic standards. My bad. The academics there were great, and it wasn't an easy school to get into. That is, if parents had the kind of money to keep their kids' dirty little habits buried while they got an "education."

My perceptions didn't change much when years later, I came back as a student.

My experience at Palmbrook was more like confinement. It had been too easy to escape from a shithole like Kudzutown to a place that presented itself as Shangri-la. I should have known. The only true difference was that in Palmbrook, the evil was hidden in the shade of palm trees, rather than engulfed in the Kudzutown's virus vines.

A calm graveyard outlined the campus and the town. I thought all graveyards were cool, and this one had its own specific charm. It wasn't made up of rows upon rows of pauper graves. Every grave had its own uniqueness. One, for instance, the grave of Audrey Littlebury Rowe, was this immense stone covered grave with really cool cement doves and vines. Even the real vines, completely different from the kudzu I'd fought in the past, were brightly colored and swirled and swished around the grave. Under her name and years, the epitaph read, "Fiat Lux," the Palmbrook motto. "Let there be life."

Fiat Lux was an ideal motto for those who spent their days drinking by the campus pool in the scorching sun, whether they were shamed from their families or not. The student body was like no other I've ever seen. Typical of boarding school brats from the Northeast, there were pretty much two solidly definable groups of people: the moderately rich and the extremely rich. Most of the students went to class in pressed Ralph Lauren oxfords with the buttons never done up, and starched khaki shorts. Surprisingly enough, most of the kids listened to the Dead and the Allman Brothers. Hippie music went hand-in-hand with the underlying drug culture that dominated the school.

I didn't fit the Palmbrook standard. Even when a fish is dropped onto land, he squirms. Either he wants to be thrown back in the water or he evolves. I'd already escaped from the water. The most difficult part of my evolution was developing lungs without announcing my naiveté.

+ + +

On my first day of orientation, one of the school's representatives welcomed me at the train station.

He was a scrawny, five-foot, six-inch Irish kid with a healthy tan and burn. No sun, however, could ever cover up his rosy red cheeks and his awkward gin blossom. He was touring the campus that day, shirts-optional with no sign of shoes. He had two different colored eyes: one brown and one green—that is, as I later discovered, when they weren't red and drooping from a full night of hitting the sauce. His right eye had a small birthmark on the bottom lid. I found out later he had gotten there a week early for a school-sponsored hiking trip. With a beer in his hand, he looked at my high school sophomore picture, a required element to be added to the "freshman meat book," then at me.

"Are you D?"

"Yeah. Who are you?"

He hesitated and put out his hand to shake. "Thank God. I was looking at your picture and I thought you were a flamer. My name's Casey Kelly. I'm your roommate." I grabbed the picture out of his hand. Shit. My mother neglected to inform me that she sent the administration a picture of me as a sophomore in high school with bleached blond hair all curly and in my face. I looked like eighties fag Howard Jones.

"This is an old picture. As you can tell, I don't look like that anymore."

"We'll see what a fag you are, kid. Here." He yanked two beers from his backpack. He turned them both on the side, and with his room key, he broke open the cans at the base, shredding the aluminum. After handing me my tipped beer, he cracked opened the top of his, lifted it, and shot-gunned the entire thing. Reluctantly, I did the same. I was quicker, and smashed the can like a tough ass, and threw the empty on his foot. Talk about an introductory showdown. Before I could act tough, Casey picked up my empty can, turned it upside down, and poured out the backwash. "It's a Cooper." He threw my can into the nicely trimmed bushes behind him and emptied his onto the sidewalk—not a fucking drop.

I wiped the beer foam residue off of my mouth. "Cooper? What the hell does that mean?"

"Well, it means a lot of things. For one, it can be used as a noun. Your cooper in this case is the backwash you left at the bottom of your beer. You're going to find out that a lot of the rich-ass kids around here party this way. Fucking idiots." He sat down on a park bench and cracked another beer. "Take one little sip." He took the tiniest of sips, barely touching any liquid to his tongue. He looked around and said, "I'm finished." After wiping his mouth, he staggered around. "It really pisses me off. I actually learned about it from my old man. He's hacked. Sits in the garage all night in his reclining chair with a half rack of PBR and pounds them until he's positive my mother and little brother are asleep."

"The second kind is called A Cooper." He stood up from the bench swaggering again like he was the town crier. He spewed out indecipherable words like a retard and then toppled, dropping all his weight onto the road.

I looked around. Maybe someone walking by knew what this kid was talking about. "In this case is a cooper the sounds you made or the fall?"

"It's the fall. Funny, sometimes idiots do it for attention. You know, like the first time they ever drank booze, and it looks like this." Cooper stood back up, faked a dry heave, and plotted out his fall. His hands picked the shot like a movie director. When he had the perfect shot, he collapsed. It took him an entire minute to reach his final destination, the soft grass below.

I was enthralled. "What else? What else?"

"Well, there is The Old Cooper. That's just some old man

who can barely walk, crossing the street and fucking up traffic." Cooper looked around and pointed off in the distance at an old man walking with his granddaughter. "Like that guy over there." The little girl was hyper, jumping up and down, screaming to get on the swing set, and the old man shuffled through the sand behind her, step by step. Cooper yelled across the street. "Punch the kid, old man! Punch the kid!"

"Is that it, Casey?"

"No, I don't think so. Anyway, everyone calls me Cooper." He lunged into his backpack and grabbed us two more beers.

"PBR, huh? We drink The Beast where I come from."

"It's all the same piss. We're young, and it'll get us drunk. I'm bullish on PBR though. It was always easy to snake out of my old man's fridge in the garage." He lifted his can. "Cheers." We both sucked down most of our beers. "What does your old man drink, D?"

"He's a Scotch man."

"Cheers to your old man. That shit's tough. I try and stick to beer and shots of hard liquor."

"Yeah, me, too."

Cooper reached into his pocket and pulled out a shitty pack of GPCs and lit one with a match. "You need a butt?"

"Nah, I don't smoke. It's always kind of grossed me out. My dad chain smoked while I was growing up."

He flipped one to the top of the pack. "Get over it, pussy. You're already dead. Do you honestly think during finals you're going to be able to deal without something in your mouth?"

"Whatever. I figured by the sweet way you were talking to me that you planned to have my cock in your mouth by the end of the week."

"Cheers, D, you fucking ball buster. Let me show you our penalty box."

"Penalty box?"

"Yeah, our room, fag."

A BMW screeched to a halt as we headed toward campus with my luggage.

"Hey you dickheads, move it," the driver screamed.

Cooper shook his half full beer and threw it at the car, just missing the windshield. "Fuck you, rich boy." He looked toward me and raised his finger as if he were giving me a lesson. "That beer was not a Cooper, D."

+ + +

A word to the wise: don't pick a fight with a literature teacher on the first day of class.

"I am Natty Bumpo," he announced, introducing himself to our American Literature class. He pointed to his foot. "And this is my leather stocking." He was dressed as James Fenimore Cooper's famous romantic character from books like *Last of the Mohicans*. I could tell that he got it from a costume shop. The outfit looked more like something a Washington Redskins fan would wear than something an American Indian would wear. "Can anyone here tell me the importance of Natty Bumpo's, and Fenimore Cooper's view of industrialism?" No one raised their hands. "Feeling a little hung over, are we class?"

I looked around and saw blank stares. I had a hangover, but I raised my hand.

"Yes. You, please stand up and introduce yourself to the class."

"My name is D."

"Hello, D, I'm Natty Bumpo."

"That's strange, my schedule says that your name is Professor Angello."

Angello, Natty Bum-fuck's real name, was a sixty-something, dark-skinned gent. On top of his head was a gray anarchy of hair prepared to attack and overthrow the world at all costs.

I looked around the class for some applause. No one was paying attention. Shit, that joke would have killed in high school.

"I'm trying to make a point, wiseass. Continue."

Against my better judgment, I blurted, "Cooper, like most Romantic writers, was opposed to the industrial revolution."

"And, why is that, D?"

"I don't know. Because Cooper was kind of a Romantic ninny."

"Romantic ninny, huh? I guess that someone in this class reads Mark Twain." He got close to me. He had the nastiest set of snaggle teeth, accompanied by breath so pungent that it shot my hangover into overdrive. I tried not to inhale.

"As a matter of fact, he's my favorite author. I think that Twain made some great points in his essay about Cooper's literary offenses."

"Do you think that essay just might have been written out of jealousy?"

"Not really. It was satire. Why would Twain be jealous of Fenimore Cooper, anyway? Twain made real points about the real world. Fenimore Cooper essentially wrote romance novels. Real life isn't like that. From what I understand Natty Bumpo was the eighteenth century equivalent of Fabio."

Angello got closer, almost right in my face. "Were you alive during the French and Indian Wars?" He stood right next to me. I gave up holding my breath and inhaled. I cringed.

"No, were you? For that matter, was Fenimore Cooper?"

Angello backed off. "So, class, it looks like we have a regular Samuel Langhorn Clemens," he pointed at me, "over here."

"I'm sorry. I don't know enough about the author or his books to really make any critique on his views of the Industrial Revolution. When I think about the Industrial Revolution, I think of Upton Sinclair."

"Exactly. You don't know enough about his writing. Sit down, D, and maybe you'll learn something." My problem, other than being a smartass, was I spent too much time reading and not enough time listening.

"Sorry, professor. I'm here to learn."

"You see class, James Fenimore Cooper despised the aristocracy and wealth that was bought through the Industrial Revolution. He therefore used Natty Bumpo as a device to convey his message of a tranquil, natural world. In "A Letter to His Countrymen," Cooper criticized the wealthy and made a social statement about taking the Native Americans' land."

I raised my hand. "Too bad the guy didn't even know any Native Americans. That dick was a phony."

Angello spun around from the rest of the class and stomped toward me. "Wrong. Wrong. Wrong. I am making a point here. We'll let you make your point when you have to write your senior thesis. That is, if you make it that far before mommy and daddy have to buy a new field house for the campus."

"What's that supposed to mean? I thought that we were in college to learn."

"You can't have an opinion when you haven't read the

literature. My point is exactly what I just said. Just because you are all a bunch of silver spoon-fed brats doesn't mean that I'm going to be easy on you. This is not a remedial freshman class. Participation is encouraged and you can only miss class four times. If you miss five, you fail. So, D, since I can smell the booze all over you, I suggest that you don't drink the nights before my class." He turned around and dove into a chalkboard discussion of the French and Indian War and the Industrial Revolution. No one else decided to participate for the rest of that first class.

I understood that he was old and a little jaded from the centuries of getting shitfaced after teaching a bunch of thankless wealthy kids five days a week, one of the few things I respected about him, but I think lashing out about my opinion was a little heavy that early in the school year.

I was one of ten kids in the class. The problem with a school so small: the teacher knew if you missed a day, a minute, or even a second. At first, I believed that our incompatibility was my fault. It could have been, possibly, I was jealous of him and admired his knowledge. That didn't mean I couldn't fight.

+ + +

Over the next couple of months, Cooper and I became closer. Between classes, after class, and all night long, we spent our time at our jolly-colly, getting inebriated, sunning at the pool, and hanging out with another friend of ours, Bunky. His real name, although most people's real names were irrelevant at Palmbrook, was Charles Mitchem. He was a pretty boy from the West, and we spent much of our time making fun of him. After several months of opening up random pages of a phonebook, and testing out possible identities for him, we picked him a name: Bunky. We were all in the same hall in our dorm and got along well despite our different nurturing. Bunky often said, "Fuck you Cooper."

I didn't even have to be in the room to see Cooper acting condescending, calling Charles "Flunky" or "Stinky" or whatever variation he had on the nickname that day. Even after he had branded you with the nickname he thought appropriate, he found ways to mangle and twist it ever so slightly every day.

After only a month at school, Cooper began calling me Dirtybird. He decided that this name befitted someone who got as grossly drunk as I did and stuck his dick in whatever bitch was willing. We had a bet early in the year that I couldn't hook up with twenty girls in a month. Well, I lost and only snagged eighteen. All the same, my conquest was an incredible feat for someone who escaped entering college a virgin by only a margin of one.

Our promiscuous bet was worth a case of PBR. As we drank them together, Cooper decided that since I had the balls to attempt something so gross, my nickname should fit my behavior. Later, Dirtybird would mutate into Shitbird, Stinkybird, Fuckybird, and so forth.

Bunky came from money. Cooper always joked that we were on The Bunky Scholarship. Whenever we went out and spent time at a bar or anything, Bunky would pick up the tab and throw it on his mom's platinum card. Cooper's abuse of Bunky's wealth made him look like a hypocrite. It wasn't like he was sticking it to the Man; it was more like he was using the Man and returning the favor occasionally with sincerity in his bi-colored, dueling eyes. Bunky even got us our first fake IDs.

There isn't much you can do with a Polaroid Camera, poster-board, and a laminating machine, so all our names on the IDs were Kevin Vaughn and we all came from Kentucky. Going to the bar as a team was difficult, but spacing ourselves out down the street always seemed to do the trick.

Bunky had been shuffled through several boarding schools through his life, something quite common at Palmbrook. He and his brother were the type of kids that mother wanted to keep tucked away as she devoured her fortune and fucked her latest twenty-year-old flavor of the month. I didn't find out until much later that she was a serious lush as well as a crack addict. From my little hole in the world, I thought crack was a ghetto drug, a cheap high for people who couldn't afford coke.

Bunky reminded me a little of my brother. He was a preppy, good-looking, standup type of guy. Although he came off as a rich kid, he was cool, and he got older pussy, while Cooper and I were dicking around with the girls our own age.

It was a boring Saturday and there wasn't much to do. During the weekends, most of the older students who were allowed to have cars took off for the beach. As for the rest of us, well, the school never sponsored any activities, so we had to create our own fun.

For Cooper and me, fun was to get as drunk as possible and be as obnoxious as possible.

Cooper pounded on Bunky's door. "Hey, Bunky, can Bird and I borrow some money to go down to the store?"

"Fuck off, Cooper, I'm sleeping."

Cooper looked at me with a shit-eating grin and pulled his validine out of his pocket. The validine, or "dinyo," was our meal ticket. At the beginning of the year, our parents had picked a meal plan that suited us and all the food in the cafeteria was accessible when we were hungry. The food card became the perfect way for me to put no value on food. The dinyo also gave us free reign to buy anything we wanted in the bookstore. Copper banged away at the door, and then, he took his card, pried it between the door and the wall, and pulled back quickly on the doorknob. Bingo. "Watch this."

The door creaked open.

"Hey, assholes! What do you want?" In the center of the room, Bunky was on his knees sucking down lines of blow off the glass dorm table that he had purchased from the local European furniture shop. Bunky tilted his head back, shut off one of his nostrils with his left hand, and sucked it down. Cooper didn't seem fazed.

"Junky, get off your ass; we're going to the store to buy—"

Before Cooper could finish his sentence, we heard a voice yodeling down from Bunky's loft. "Charles, can you bring me a line up here?" I didn't recognize the voice, but I was pretty sure that it was one of the older sluts he hung out with.

"Shit." Bunky paused, looked up to the loft, and then at us. Out of frustration, he reached into his pocket and threw about a hundred bucks in scrunched up cash at us. "Get out, you fuckers. I'll talk to you later."

On the way out, Cooper pretended to fall over the fridge in the corner. There was a big old sack of blow on top. Bunky flew through the air, and Cooper bent over and plunged into the fridge to pull out two Heinekens. Before Cooper could even acknowledge the absurdity of the cocaine, the coke whore in the bed, or the lameness of someone who stocks his fridge with

Heinekens, he threw them back into the fridge and looked at Bunky.

"Bunky, you've got to find yourself some new bitches. Come on, Bird; we have things to accomplish. Later." Cooper opened the exit and slammed the door behind us.

"Did you know that Bunky did coke?" I asked Cooper like the dumbass kid that I was at the time.

"Do fish fuck in the lake? Almost all the cunts at this school are coke whores. I knew he wasn't getting tail because of his good posture or his queer sweater vests. Didn't you know about his old man, D?"

"No; just about his mom and his brother. You'd think that would be enough to make him stay away from that poison."

"Fuck, Bird, that's nothing. When Bunky was a kid his old man used to own a surfboard company. To make a really long story short, he ran into a bunch of competitors who were trying to drive him out of business in the seventies. Anyway, his dad started importing coke inside the foam. It seemed like a good idea at the time. Until the FBI wised up to him. They busted him with two tons of blow."

"Two Tons?"

"Yeah, Bunky told me the whole story one night. To make things worse, while his dad was in jail, he and his mother and his little brother had to live in a fucked-up cabin in the woods.

"Apparently, the FBI agents constantly went out there to taunt his family. You know: take their clothes, trash their pad. Well, anyway, while his dad was in jail, he started a new surf company. When he was released, he was instantly rich again. Too bad he had no interest in his family anymore. Bunky Sr. paid them off, and I guess they never spoke to him again."

"That's pretty fucked up," I said.

"You think? I might not have the perfect family, but I know nothing will ever break mine apart. We're happy with what we have, and although it ain't shit, we have each other. As much time as my dad spends tinkering in the garage, sitting in his recliner, and drinking, he'll never lose my mom or me and my brother because he loves us and provides for us. We're all he has. He's pretty happy, you know, to have a kid in college. He never went to college and my mom didn't either."

"Whatever, crybaby. Look where you're going to college. Attending class when you want isn't considered a good deed."

Cooper scratched his chin and looked back at our dorm. "No shit. They've never seen the school and most likely they never will. Come on, dick, we have to go to The Library to study a couple cocktails." Before we got too far away from the dorm, Cooper flicked a quarter out of his pocket—I think it was the only money that I had ever seen him create on his own—and dialed Bunky's extension on a payphone in front of our dorm.

"Flunky. Campus security is towing your fucking Benz, dude." We waited out front as Bunky ran out of the dorm in his boxers. His head shot around like a groundhog seeing the sun for the first time. When he realized he had been totally dicked and humiliated, he gave us both the finger, the gas face, and re-entered his little pimp pad. "What a jerkoff," Cooper muttered as we headed to the bar.

Three months into our college careers, we could enter the bar together without the aid of Kevin Vaughn. We were regulars at every bar in town. Before making our first pit stop, we walked to the graveyard, dug a small hole, and put our IDs to rest. Our alias, Kevin Vaughn, was a name of the past.

"Bird, check it out." Cooper pointed across the street at a costume shop. "Let's go over there." We walked to the shop after burying our first reliable friend and went into Phillie's Costume shop. It took the kid seconds to find what he was looking for. His eyes lit up and his gin blossom shone like Rudolph the Red-nosed Reindeer.

In the corner of the shop was the Holy Grail of silly things for Cooper to wear, a leprechaun outfit that looked like a green-tailed tuxedo with a ridiculous pipe and an even sillier green top hat. "I have to get that."

"What are you talking about? Don't be stupid. We've only got like a hundred bucks, and we need that to drink."

"Fuck you; I got a credit card in case of emergencies."

"And this is an emergency? What's wrong with you?" There was no talking him out of it.

I saw this costume on Cooper many times. He probably thought that because he was Irish, he might as well play it up a bit. When we got to the curb outside the shop, Cooper raised his hand at a passing cab.

"Hey, Bird, let's do something different today."

"What do you mean?"

"You'll see. Hey, cabby, do you know where we can find a

Chuck E. Cheese around here?"

"Chuck E fucking Cheese, Cooper? Are you kidding me?" I hadn't been to a Chuck E. Cheese since I was ten.

"Excuse me, Charles Emerson Cheese has cheap-ass pitchers. Henceforth and hitherto, we are off." His logic seemed acceptable—even though his attempt at old English was preposterous. At least he was wearing that ridiculous leprechaun outfit. Maybe if we were lucky someone would mistake Cooper for a guest performer and hook us up with a free pitcher. Realistically, he had a better chance of being arrested for attempted pedophilia.

As the year passed on at Palmbrook, the seasons never changed. The leaves never dropped, snow never fell, and the coldest it got was around fifty. A tree like Nazareth could never have lived in that thick, muggy climate. College was a dream world encased in plastic-looking, yet perfectly natural, vegetation. With all of the evils of Palmbrook, I was surprised anything could thrive.

The combination of conditions called "humiture" was year-round. It was either boiling and humid or blazing and damp. If I woke up dehydrated and hung over, I almost passed out the second I stepped outside. It felt like getting hit in the face by a hot washcloth, even early in the morning. Going to class became more like a chore than a learning experience. I'm surprised that more students didn't keel over every day considering the alcoholism in the student body and the overpowering heat of the climate.

Cooper, Bunky, and I continued to knit together, and soon became almost as close as old friends. For a while we even got Bunky to lay off the cocaine.

"Bunky," I began as I used a couch arm as a crutch. "Cooper and I think that you should stop using coke."

Cooper, tripping over his shoelaces, placed his hand on Bunky's shoulder and joined in. "We think that you're a fucking idiot."

After an hour and a half of the two of us pathetically

attempting an intervention, Bunky finally had enough. "Are you two shitfaced dicks finished? You can't even speak."

"But drinking is legal," I pointed out.

"Yeah," Cooper added. "It's also fun." Eventually, Bunky agreed to relax a little, and we spent a lot of our weekend time going to the beach, passing out in the ball tank at Chuck E. Cheese, and hooking up with bitches at The Library.

Everything in our college lives centered on getting wasted. As for me, throwing up my food had taken on a life of its own, and I kept it well concealed from everyone. Anything that was edible had to be expelled. I didn't even have to eat any longer. I always felt sick and hair-of-the-dog was my only medicine.

One time, the three of us headed out to the cheesiest of lowbrow beaches, and Cooper and I decided to get completely demolished on the sand. As usual, Cooper wore his leprechaun costume—although the pants were rolled up and the hat left back at the hotel. For some aberrant reason we decided to ignore the open container law. Either that or we were too blind drunk to read the huge signs that stated, among other things, No Drinking on the Beach.

Well, the local law enforcement decided to take Cooper and me to the local drunk-tank. Bunky, being a little more sober stayed back at the hotel and got hammered poolside.

We met some interesting characters in jail. One guy, a ragamuffin with a shaggy beard and covered in sand was thrown in with us. According to the pig that tossed him in the can, he resisted arrest after selling some rock to an undercover cop. His name was Frog, and he made the jail experience entertaining. The entire time we sat on the floor of the cell, Frog yelled at the cops.

After three hours of having a blast with Frog in the county tank, Cooper and I finally made a collect call back to someone on campus, who managed to page Bunky back at the hotel and told him to bail us out. Not that we weren't having fun entertaining each other. He and I acted like we were hammered and pretended to collapse in every corner of the tank.

After he was through "teaching us a lesson," Bunky let us know that he was real happy that we interrupted the fresh move he was putting on some trashy local "prosti-tot," whose pants he was trying to get into before we got our one phone call.

I understand that he was unsure about almost every obstacle

that he was confronted with through life, but damn, did he get angry when he had a sure thing and we fucked it up.

When spring rolled around, we all pledged the same fraternity. When I first got to Palmbrook, I'd no intention of joining any organization; however, beach trips and Chuck E. Cheese were no match for an endless supply of free booze, something the college never supplied to its students. To Cooper, Bunky, and me, hazing was a present.

Alcoholism became a series of events rather than a social activity. One of my favorites was a tradition called the "wine and cheese party." Now, this wasn't your typical picnic in the park with Burgundy and Brie. Rather, we had ten minutes to drink a bottle of Mad Dog and eat an entire dispenser of Cheese Whiz. Every one of us barfed, in a very communal, fraternal collegial environment.

Another one of the pledge events was called "Lock and Load." In this exciting ritual, twenty of us had an hour to finish a keg. To make the event a little more entertaining, we weren't allowed to exit the room. In the center of the room was a garbage can. By the end of the affair, everyone had barfed, pissed on themselves, and fought each other.

The most Herculean event of all was one called the "Fifteen Hundred." In this race, we had one minute to shotgun a beer and another minute to ride bikes around the center of campus, fifteen times. Not only did everyone barf, but everyone also ended up with some serious battle wounds from toppling over on the bikes.

"Cooper, I didn't even notice this restaurant was here."

Cooper nodded his head across the restaurant to an opening, which connected Nusstorte to the Library. "How long have we been drinking over there? What's wrong with you?"

I looked around. The dark, musty restaurant was dressed-up like an Octoberfest at Epcot Center. Although a decent attempt at mimicking Switzerland or Germany, it was obvious that everything was bought half-assedly at a souvenir shop. From the beer steins to the lederhosen that drooped off of the waitresses, I hoped that the food was better than McSchnitzel.

"My parents own both of them. I'm Monica. I'll be your waitress."

"Hey, I know you," Cooper began. "You serve drinks."

She pulled her ordering pad out of the front of her pants. Her manners weren't classy, but they were hot. "Yeah, and you two drink drinks. I see you fools in here all the time." A strand of her long curly blond hair swirled over her big brown right eye. She blew the strand back in line with the rest of her hair. She pursed her thick lips on the end of the pen to extract a little ink. Too bad my pen was about to shoot off a little more than a little ink.

She was hot. She was also young; I'd say no older than sixteen. Trying to attract her attention, I played the ethnocentricity card. "Well, Monica, I can't read the menu. Can you recommend anything?" I looked at her ass. Unusual for her size, she had a shelf ass that looked like a bitch in a rap video.

"Probably nothing you drunks will like. None of the kids from Palmbrook appreciate my father's food. It's Swiss." She licked her pen, waiting for us to give up and order liquor.

"I'd like to try something. I've never had Swiss food before."

Monica leaned over me to point at the menu. I felt like a dirtbag looking at her tits. "Try this, Zürcher Eintopf."

"What is it, Monica?" I tried to keep my eyes on her face. I didn't want to get busted looking at her chest.

"It's potatoes and veggies and shit, thrown into a bowl with some pork."

"Sounds good. I'm D."

Cooper threw his menu down on the table. "God, Bird, you're such a scumbag."

"It's okay, Casey. I know both of your names. Like I said, I see you in here all the time."

"My name's Cooper."

"That's not what your credit card says," she returned.

"Monica, we'll both have the thingy that you said."

"Bring extra pork."

"Fuck you," she said. "Neither of you two lushes could get it up anyway."

I settled the conversation that was headed downhill quickly. "What does Nusstorte mean, anyway?"

She looked me square in the eyes, "It means nut cake."

+ + +

Being vulnerable one night in the dark trenches of The Library, I did the unspeakable. Unbeknownst to my friends and family, I had been making myself throw up since that horrible night back at Nazareth. It was an easy way for me to forget about all of the evils of Kudzutown. It became my escape. For some reason, I felt that I should tell Cooper.

"What do you mean you make yourself puke? You mean so you can drink more, D?" Cooper asked me.

"I make myself throw up. Usually not when I drink, though; that fucks up my throat."

"Are you fucking kidding me? What are you, gay?" Cooper laughed. "What is that anorexia, or something?"

"No, I think it's actually bulimia."

I knew the scientific term for making myself puke, but I played stupid.

"Yeah, I knew this girl in my high school who did the barfarama," I continued. "She was all freaked out. She would go to a party and get all emotional and then clean out the cupboards. It was goofy."

"Whatever, Bird, just don't let me catch you doing it around me. I understand twenty guys in a small room all hurling in a bucket, but making yourself barf secretly is just lame."

Cooper changed gears. "You know Bird, one day you and I will own this place. My vision is to somehow get our hands on the deed by blackmailing someone. We'll get rid of these jacked-up prices and faggoty beers and have only PBR in cans and Jack Daniel's on tap. Imagine, you and me, owning a bar. We'd never make a cent. Before it went banko, we'd have a fucking blast. I have an idea," he pointed at Monica. "Why don't you start banging the cocktail waitress and try and swindle her out of the deed."

"Her name is Monica."

"Anyway, you've got to stop this puking thing. Dirty, you're my best friend. Let it go. It's girls' shit."

"Don't tell anybody, dickhead, about what I do," I scolded in my most serious tone.

Later that week, Cooper went to the school nurse and got some pamphlets on bulimia. After reading the propaganda the surgeon general aimed at diverting teens away from the barfarama, he decided to become my savior. First, he told those in charge of our fraternity. Then, they decided to take the problem into their own hands by handing that information over to the dean of students.

"D, your friends are concerned about your health." Not being a fan of fraternities to begin with, Dean Adams looked at this as a way to punish ours. "Although none of your teachers have complained about your behavior, except for Professor Angello, who seems to think you purposely pick fights in class, I think that I have to take steps to see this problem gets resolved before it progresses any further." Dean Olivia Adams was one of the hottest women at Palmbrook. The fact that she still passed for a coed, ten years out of school, was miraculous.

Like most of the female student body, she had bobbed, natural blond hair, a perfect tan, and she wasn't afraid to break all dean stereotypes by wearing somewhat revealing clothing.

"Don't worry about it, Ms. Adams; most of the things you've heard are either blown out of proportion or they can be resolved easily."

She looked down at my file. I tried to look down the front of her blouse. "I have a campus security report here that says your student I.D. number has been written down on several occasions; urinating in public, stealing the security golf carts, riding a bike around campus intoxicated. Your brothers are concerned that you act in a self-destructive manner. Bulimia is a serious problem." She slammed the file down.

"Excuse me, Dean. Bulimia is binging and purging. I only do the purging part."

"Let me remind you that you are here on scholarship. If these incidents are not resolved, the school is going to contact your parents and tell them what's going on." I didn't want that to happen. The general wouldn't take the news of his son having a "girl's disease" too well.

It was time to beg.

"Listen, I don't think that's such a fancy idea. I'll do whatever it takes. My parents can't find out about this. It isn't something they'd understand."

"Okay, I've gotten the board to sponsor an outpatient therapist for you to see every week."

"Therapist?" I rolled my eyes. "Fuck that."

"Don't you dare scoff at me, D. I'm giving you a chance to sort this out. This is a problem that develops in a lot of new students and it isn't one to be taken lightly." As I was leaving she added, "Don't even think about missing one of those sessions D; I *will* call your parents." I crumpled the paper in my hand. It was all bullshit, anyway.

Just what my parents needed to find out. A year ago my brother shocked them with drug dealing, re-hab, and a grandson. Fucking Cooper! What? Tell everyone how screwed-up I am. What I did or didn't learn from Lori Conroy and her drop from the bridge made me sick. I understood why she didn't want me to turn in the poem I wrote. Exiting the administration building, I stopped by the private bathroom and unleashed my anger, my fury. I hadn't had anything to eat that day, so I puked stomach bile and foam.

Something was different, though. I saw blood and what appeared to be flesh in the toilet. Most likely, it was scrapings from of the sides of my esophagus. I knew that it was flesh because I fished around in the growler bowl until I plucked it out and held it in front of my eyes.

Before I intelligently assessed what happened, I was whisked away by the snowstorm of flurries that lightly danced in my eyes. I never noticed the flurries before. My head tingled like the guy with shampoo in his hair in the dandruff ad as my body buzzed. My insides were numb and warm, but my skin was freezing. My face tightened to my skull and my eyes rolled around. After silently dry heaving for about three minutes, I threw my backpack, which was filled with the beer I picked up before my conference with the dean, and headed back to my dorm. For the time being, I was cleansed.

Angello scratched at his nose. "D, my attendance record tells me that you have missed my class three times already," Angello warned me one day after class. "You know my rule."

"Professor Angello, I'm totally sorry. I guess I have to get my shit together."

"You're damn right you have to. You're not a dumb kid. You're not like some of the other retards that attend my classes. You need to listen. You may think that you're wiser than me with your high school education, but I assure you, you're not. I didn't like your assessment of Gillman's 'The Yellow Wallpaper.' It seems obvious that you haven't read the story." He twitched, agitated with me.

"That's interesting; I guess it would seem logical for me to find the *Cliffs Notes* version of a ten-page story."

"I'm not saying that you took any shortcuts to write your paper, D."

"Then what are you saying? How could I know the characters and the premise of the story if I hadn't read it?" I was definitely going to stand my ground on this minor war; I'd read the story several times.

"Well, here's your paper." He handed it to me and I noticed the big fat "F" above the title immediately. It also had a little bloody nose mucus in the corner. "I've made my notes. Don't be late for class again and be more attentive when you're here." He scratched at his nose more. The bulbous end was purple.

"Do you feel okay, professor?" *Fuck you, Prof,* I thought.

"I'm fine, just a sinus infection. I have to go to my next class." He rushed out of his office.

I looked over his notes, and other than a couple of, or actually quite a few, grammatical errors, I had every right to convey my opinion of the story. I got up from my seat in his office and headed into the bathroom down the hall. I needed to get high. I needed to give myself a kick in the ass. I needed to feel at ease with my situation.

I got wasted and barfed all weekend.

I convinced Cooper, since my therapy was his fault, to come with me every Tuesday to my new doctor. It didn't take much convincing. To begin with, whenever we went, we made up these absurd stories about what was wrong with me. Cooper was a great liar and our imaginations together were tough to beat. Of course, for him to take an hour out of his afternoon, I had to pay for us both to drink at night. The administration and Dean Adams were pleased that I was seeking the much needed help and my fraternity brothers were safe from any possible situation that might come up during some back-and-forth heckling at an intramural sporting event.

I woke up the day after our fraternity hell week dripping in my own sweat and urine with the smell of booze pissing from my pores. Like every other day that year, my successful freshman year of college, I just wanted to go finish my classes, grab Cooper, go to therapy, and then finish things off with our final trip to Chuck E. Cheese. I did just that. Angello handed out our final grades, and I managed to get a B- in his class. I thanked him. I knew that he would have loved to flunk a little shit like me, but he knew teachers rarely flagged students during their freshman year. Besides, I did all the work. I shook his hand, and to his dismay, I promised that because I'd chosen English as my major the day I got to school, we would see each other again. It was a safe bet in a school that small with a total of about ten English teachers.

"Maybe then you'll start coming to class a little more often with some actual facts rather than just opposing opinions," Angello suggested.

"Yeah, I guess I'll just have to do some more research."

After I wiped his bullshit off of my pant leg, I headed back to our destroyed dorm.

"Hey, Bunky, have you seen Cooper?"

"Bird, Cooper had to leave." He was struggling to clear his head and tell me what was going on.

"What do you mean? Did he already bail and go to The Library to check out Monica? Figures, the lush. He knows I want to fuck her."

"No, Bird, he had to leave school."

"What are you talking about? Cooper told me that his grades were fine." The shaky snips of Bunky's voice were confusing me more than helping me understand what was going on.

"There was a problem at home. His dad fell asleep in the garage last night. He woke up because he smelled gas. He woke himself up and went into the basement, and—"

"What the hell are you talking about, Bunky? Spit the shit out."

"Well, he went to the basement, and there was a gas leak. He opened the door, and the house exploded."

I cleared my throat, trying to take the story in. "Is everyone okay?"

"No. His father was thrown from the house, but his mother and his brother were killed. The house was completely demolished." Bunky wiped away the tears from his swollen face. Neither of us had ever met Cooper's family, but we both knew how close they were. Bunky grabbed me with a strong hug. His teeth rattled together as he struggled to make sense of the tragedy.

"He left an explanation or a note or something for you. It's inside."

I opened the door to my room. The stench of our debauched drinkathon filled the hall. The door crept ajar, and I noticed that Cooper's desk light was on. Sitting on the chair by the desk was the green outfit with the top hat, folded nicely, and arranged like a snowman from the bottom up. It was Cooper's pride and joy, the leprechaun suit. I picked it up and out of the pockets rained what seemed like millions of Chuck E. Cheese coupons that we'd collected over the year. The room was plastered, wall-to-wall, with notes and pictures from our freshman year.

On the band that sectioned off the brim of the hat was a piece of paper. I opened it as I sucked in. Explosions filled my mind.

The note read, "Bird, this stuff is yours, now. Your friend, Cooper." Then, below it read, "Quit fucking puking and stay away from the things that will fuck you over." I knew exactly what he meant by bad things. He meant Bunky. It wasn't my place to cry, but I'd lost my best friend.

I picked up the green outfit and sat in the chair. I put on the ridiculous hat. Like Cooper's dad, whom I could imagine only through the stories that Cooper had told me, I grabbed a PBR out of the mini fridge and sat back in the chair. I didn't know how to react or who to react to. Should I have cried? It seemed like those days were so far behind me.

I realized that my imagination, which was where Cooper's family lived, within "me-scape," always leads me back to where I began. I never wanted to use the name Cooper in a bad way again.

I called my dad that night and told him that I wouldn't be coming home for the summer. Instead, I wanted to stay at school and take some classes so that I might graduate earlier.

CHAPTER FOUR

Tina stared at me and put her Prophecy meds in her mouth. "D, that's fucking terrible. Do you still talk to Cooper?"

"No. Not any more." Remembering him so candidly made me feel as if a hammer followed me through life, creating a wave of catastrophes in my shadow.

"Do you know if anything has gotten better for him?"

"No."

"Nice, dickhead."

"Hey, fuck you."

"There is one thing that you didn't explain, D." She paused and frowned for a second as she chose her words. "If you were worried about everyone finding out about your bulimia, why did you tell him that you threw up, anyway? That seems like something you would have kept secret." Tina had a point. She'd spent a good portion of her life shuffling around secrets.

"Have you ever wanted to tell people your secrets, like the fact that you make yourself yam with a toothbrush?"

"I guess I have." She hesitated and gnawed on the side of her tongue. "But whenever I did it, it was for attention." Brittany, the hospital's answer to *Home Alone* ran by us with Mariah's doughnut pillow. "It was something I did a lot when I was Brittany's age."

I shrugged. "I felt that Cooper was a trusted and trusting ally. I understood that deep down he just wanted things to be better for me. He always had this father-like quality. He took me under his wing. But I never looked at his actions as anything other than throwing my secrets around." I shrugged again. "I guess it wasn't that big a secret after all. I got drunk and I opened my mouth. It was my fault and it's possible that I was looking for attention. Looking for attention is one thing. Telling a meat and potatoes kid you suffer what people think is a girl's disease is another. I don't know. Maybe I just wanted to tell somebody."

Tina looked me in the eye. "When I'm hiding from the world, I want someone to understand my pain. As careful as I am, someone could easily have come quietly in the bathroom and seen my balls and ass hanging out underneath the stall."

"Why do you puke naked? Is that some sort of turn on?"

"No, dumbass. I keep my pants around my ankles so if anyone comes into the bathroom I can sit on the toilet quickly and make it seem like I'm taking a smash. Who would believe someone is shitting with his pants on?"

"That's why you should only use private bathrooms, amateur."

"That's why I invented the barf bag in a locked room. I was panicky Cooper would unlock the door one day and find me chucking in a grocery bag at my desk. If he didn't know, he may have caught me. Telling him was a way to avoid being called a 'lightweight alcoholic.' The people he told, he did so out of concern."

I sighed and leaned back before continuing.

"When you see one of your best friends fucking himself up, you try and take action. Of course, the intervention was a little out of control. I didn't have to hear a bunch of people who were concerned about what Cooper described to them. I'm sure he told them a great story."

"I doubt he made fun of you, D, but telling your fraternity brothers was a sure way the bulimia got back to your parents." Tina pulled hard on her cigarette, and then told me that her first year in the league she suffered similar, if not worse, results. "And what happened to Bunky?"

"Tina, that's where the story begins."

"So this is what you aren't very proud of?" The voodoo doll pins of shame instantly overcame any short-lived sense of pride.

"Try totally, abso-fucking-lutely ashamed of."

A voice from across the room interrupted our conversation. "Kristina, D, come join the group. You guys have chatted long enough." Sheryl Desmond, the wacky social worker, called over to us. And to think I'd actually been enjoying the therapy that I was getting from talking with Tina. It didn't even bother me that she'd been abusing my cigarettes and using Lori Conroy's lighter.

Desmond crossed her legs and shot me a thumbs up. "So, D, since you've been so vocal today, why don't you share your picture with the group." I reached into the drawing tablet that I'd brought with me to Prophecy and pulled out a picture that had nothing to do with the family assignment.

It was a picture of a nasty winged gargoyle nestled on top of a pack of cigarettes. Rather than having a huge body structure with comic hero muscles, its shoulders were drawn in either from dehydration or malnutrition. The creature's legs couldn't support it; they barely hung onto the pack of cigarettes. The wings were frail and lame, clipped and filled with holes. Instead of having an exaggerated mouth filled with piercing fangs, it wore a sullen look on its face. Like most of the monsters I related to, the circumstances involving their terror were purely invoked by misunderstanding. Most monsters would have been more fulfilled locked away and hidden. Those who weren't, were the ones who suffered at the hands of others. That was always the great thing about classic monsters; they weren't evil, they just wanted to flee, and get away.

"This is a nice piece of art, D," Desmond began, "but I don't understand its relevance to your family." Neither did I, but I figured I could shift my eyes and make something up. When I drew the picture originally I'd been thinking about Lori; the monster she saw in the mirror and the devices that broke her down. The same creature came in the middle of the night with a silencing hand and a dim bathroom light. Lori crept back into my head again. Whenever frail Mariah spoke, I saw Lori plunging to her death off the Bay Bridge.

"Well, it's not a family portrait." I laid the bullshit on extra thick. "It's more of a portrait of the relationship between my father and me. My old man was really tough on me growing up, and I remember him and the odor of his cigarettes. The gargoyle is me—a bird incapable of flying, that many would rather see as an atrocity rather than a human." Desmond took the picture, tilted it around and tried lethargically to make sense out of it. Every so often she would utter, "Hmmm," or "Huh." She handed it back to me.

"That is an excellent assessment of your life. So you're telling me your father and his overpowering nature prevented you from ever realizing your potential and your flight."

"Kind of. I don't blame my dad for holding me back at all. He loves the shit out of me and provided me with plenty of opportunities all through my life. He attempted to make me see further than I did because my brain was fucked-up. What was preventing me from flight was a cloud of my own smoke and bullshit."

"I think that this is a very therapeutic step in your recovery, D. Good job." Desmond turned away to look at the next drawing, and I looked at Kristina and winked. She shook her head in disbelief. She'd just seen something that couldn't be taught at an Ivy League school. Bullshit came naturally.

"Mariah, can we see your picture?" Mariah opened the piece of construction paper that she had folded in half, scanned it, and then refolded it. "Come on Mariah, everyone has to show their picture." It was painful watching this girl even do the simplest tasks. She couldn't sit on the floor with the rest of the patients (she had to sit on her doughnut), and every time she moved, I heard her bones squeal and shake. The sound of her body was horrible. Her neck wouldn't even support her head. Her body, no stronger, folded over on itself and her crumbed twig-like digits clenched inward.

"It stinks." She faded out when she breathed. Other than the screams and grunts she made when the staff attempted to give her a caloric supplement, Mariah never spoke. She had innocence in her voice, but her broken English betrayed her lack of education. She wasn't proud of her picture, or of any accomplishment in her life for that matter.

"We are not here to evaluate you on your art, Mariah. We just want you to share a part of your life with us."

Mariah picked at the corner of her drawing. "No!" Tears formed in her sunken eyes. I saw Kristina shaking her head out of the corner of my eye. Something horrible must be scrawled on the paper. I hated confrontation, even when it didn't involve me. Trouble filled the room and I didn't want to watch the fog come in. Suddenly, little Brittany grabbed the picture out of Mariah's hands. In her condition, the carcass was no match for the Machiavellian eight-year old. "Give it back," Mariah pleaded with the little shit.

I chimed in. "Hey, Brittany! She doesn't want to show it. Give it fucking back to her!" The giggling little urchin opened the picture and laughed. Then, she held it up for all eyes to see. I don't think she understood the picture. She couldn't have.

"D, don't swear in front of Brittany!" Ms. Desmond screeched at me. The social worker had no idea what was going on. "Brittany, give Mariah her drawing back."

"Look at this! It's like all scribbles and stupid stick figures. It looks like the pictures my little brother draws." Brittany coaxed Mariah with the picture skipping around her and holding it out of her reach. Impish. All poor Mariah could do was raise her arms halfway up and swat at it. With the energy she used to reclaim her picture, she dozed off in between swats like a smack addict after a two-month spell of going cold turkey. King Kong had a better chance at swatting down a team of stealth bombers than she did of retrieving her picture.

Tears flooded her face and wet her bones. The rest of the group bounced back and forth like a tribe of autistic children, the climate rising and the fear level intensifying. Sweating dripped all over the place. I felt claustrophobic, and my stomach warped and bent. I was boxed in. I felt my aorta smacking my right earlobe against my face. Pain prickled my right arm, up to my armpit and tore into my chest.

"Give it back," Mariah tried to scream as her crying caused her weakened lip to collapse. Her voice cracked and whimpered. In a last attempt to nab the drawing, she lost her breath. Her torso filled with air like a blowfish. She coughed and convulsed. She was defenseless.

My heart raced and my skin heated up. I gathered enough energy and grabbed the drawing from Brittany. Sandler, finally coming up from his afternoon latte, jumped up to escort the little shit to her room.

"D, you don't have the authority to scare Brittany like that," Desmond scolded me as she brushed off her pants suit.

"Am I on crack here?" I was hyperventilating and shaking like a methadone freak. "Are you retarded, you bitch? Why didn't you stop that? You pathetic pseudo-social-worker cunt.

Why didn't you stop it?"

"Brittany is at that age when she has to learn from her own mistakes."

"What a load of shit!" I yelled back at her. "Maybe if the little brat had some structure in her life she wouldn't be in here to begin with!" I folded the picture back in half and took a good look at it.

Brittany was right, the drawing was the equivalent of a picture a four-year old drew and placed on the fridge. Crude and unconnected lines and doodles tore at each other and created a maze of disarray. I stared at a picture seeing complete and total psychosis. It was a picture of a big stick figure on top of a diminutive other one. The big figure had an arrow pointing to it that said "Daddy" and the little one had an arrow pointing to it that said "Mariah." I hoped nobody else got a good look at it. I placed the picture back on Mariah's lap, and I walked back into my room down the hall. Red-faced and delirious, I hurled a plastic chair at the observation window.

I rolled my finger in my ringing ear. "I hear things, Doc. Every time something gets me amped up, angry, sad, I hear and see things from the past. Very vividly. I can see shit so well in my head I can hear it. Maybe I'm trying to tell myself something. Maybe I'm trying to justify acting like an idiot." I didn't want to share the details of the picture Mariah drew with Sandler, and I had no interest in providing him with details of Lori Conroy and Freddy Brubaker in Kudzutown. They were the voices in my head. Mariah's picture, something about it, made me start to hear things.

"It sounds like textbook delusional behavior. Let me ask you a question. When you threw the chair, did you feel a sense of omnipotence? Did someone tell you to throw the chair?"

"Don't speak to me like I'm a child. I know exactly why I threw the chair. I think this place is a crock of shit. Mariah, Kristina, and I all have the choice to stop acting this way. The only answer you have for me is fucking Prozac. I just graduated from college. Sure, I didn't graduate with honors, but I want to get on with my life. Let me choose how to live it."

He leaned back in his chair and steepled his fingers. "Maybe you're afraid of the world."

"You're damn right. Look at it. My fear is of the world. My only hope is escape. This barfing shit didn't start last week. My behavior was learned and only in a shitty society like ours would it matter. It's a bad joke."

"Let me ask you this. Do you ever have thoughts of suicide?"

"No. At least I don't think so. I remember being spiteful and pissed off when I was a kid. I always thought about how my parents would feel if I were dead. If my memory serves me correctly, I picked up that attitude after reading *Alexander and the Terrible, Horrible, No Good, Very Bad Day*."

"I am not familiar with that."

"*Alexander and the Terrible, Horrible, No Good, Very Bad Day* is a children's book about a little kid who woke up one day and everything was complete shit."

"When you say 'shit', do you mean there was a death in his family or something tragic?" I couldn't believe that anyone hadn't read that book. When I was a kid, I read it cover to cover a couple times a day.

"No, nothing like that. It was stupid stuff, like his older brothers got cooler tennis shoes than he had at the store. The ultimate goal of the story was to teach kids that not every day in their lives was going to be perfect. Judging from a lot of shit I've gone through in my life, I'd say that I've learned to deal with getting the white tennis shoes like Alexander. I purposely got white shoes when I was a kid and wore them around when I wanted people to feel sorry for me."

"Hmmm. Then why do you consider yourself the embodiment of self-destruction?"

"Now who's thinking on an omnipotent level, Doc?"

"Well, let's look at the facts. The books you favor are depressing and realistic. The music you listen to—" He picked up my chart, paged through it, and said, "Skinny Puppies."

"It's Skinny Puppy."

"Whatever; I've heard it coming from your room. It's morbid."

"It has a positive message. I just like its aggressiveness and truth. Have you ever listened to something, music, and felt it captured what you were thinking at the time, even if you weren't catching the lyrics or the message?"

"Well, D, when I was in school, I listened to a lot of Pink Floyd."

"Syd Barret, huh, Doc?"

"Who is that?"

"Barret was Floyd's first guitarist; he lost his shit. I think he left the band and now lives under the care and guidance of his mother. A real fucking waste."

"I guess I listened to them because my roommate played them and I grew to like their sound."

"Hey, Doc, can I see your degree? I want to know what mind is studying mine."

He turned back to his tablet, making no attempt to acknowledge my wit. "I want to know more about what happened when you were six with Tommy Horton in your back yard, D."

"Why?"

"Because I can't help but think that some of your problems can be traced back to that."

"Sure, Doc. You tell me how you'd feel if I pissed on you right now."

"I can't say I'd like it, D. Did you like it?"

"What, are you kidding? Tell me how much you would like being on your knees with some kid shoving his cock in your face, peeing all over you? I can't even be downwind from a hot dog now. His family ate cold hot dogs for dinner and whenever they had me over, that's what they served. All I remember about Tommy is his grinning and mashing a cold frank around in his mouth. Fuck, was he gross. Can we change the subject, Doc?"

"You have to let go of it, D."

"I know."

"D."

I stopped in front of Mariah's door. I tried to never look into her room. Her business was private.

"D, can you come in here?"

I didn't look. "I might get in trouble," I said.

"Thank you."

"For what, Mariah?"

"Thank you for sticking up for me."

I turned into the room and faced her. "You're welcome."

"I have something to tell you." She struggled and sat up on her bed. "I'm not that different from you."

Hesitantly, I took two steps into her room. I didn't want to look into her eyes. The way she looked scared me. "I'm not following."

"Come closer. I can't talk very loud."

I took two more steps. "Dr. Sandler will get mad at me for being in here. I don't think this is a good idea."

She used her right arm to control her jaw. "It's okay. I'll take the blame." She sat hunched over with her shoulders aligned vertically. Her left arm rested on the bed with her hand curled up. I walked closer to her. As sick as she was, she had beautiful blue eyes. Her eyeballs took up half of her face because other than her facial hair, the face itself didn't exist. I could see my breath in her room. "It's okay. Thank you."

I tried not to look her in the eyes. "You don't need to thank me. Brittany was being a little shit. Are you cold in here?"

"It's not anorexia, you know."

"What's not, Mariah?"

"Me." She picked at a fuzzball on her blanket with her free hand. "I'm not anorexic. They can't figure out what's wrong with me. I've fooled them."

"Mariah, you're confusing me. If you're not anorexic, then why don't you eat?"

"It might be about not eating, but that's not why I look like this. They can't figure it, D. They can give me all of the tests in the world and they'll never figure it out."

I looked at her square. "What is it? I saw the picture. Is that it?"

"I'm kind of like you."

"In what way? Do you know some way to throw up in here that I don't?"

"It's not like that. I've never made myself throw up." She picked up the doughnut pillow and tried to throw it. She was unsuccessful. "I've never used laxatives."

"What is it, Mariah? What's wrong with you?"

"It's worms."

I walked closer, thinking she slipped into insanity? "Do you see worms?"

"No, D. I eat worms."

"I don't understand. Is that some kind of diuretic?"

"No. I pick worms out of cat poop and I eat them."

I froze. My teeth clicked and my cheekbones dug into my eyes. It couldn't be true. "Parasites? Mariah—"

"My sister brings them in to me. I promised her I'd let her do it when the time was right."

"Mariah, that can't be true."

"It is. That's why the doctors can't find out what's wrong with me. They think that I starve myself and that's it. I don't want to be touched anymore, D."

"I know you don't but—"

"Now you know. It's our secret. Thank you."

Like an asshole, I didn't acknowledge her. I didn't believe her story. It was too horrible to be true. She was delusional. She had to be crazy. There is no way something like that could work. Could it?

"Tell them to turn up the heat in your room." I turned around and left her alone. She was always alone. Everyone at Prophecy besides Brittany was scared of her. I was no different. I couldn't even bare to look at her.

"It's our secret," she said as she collapsed down on her bed.

Days pressed on at Prophecy, and something became clear to the doctors and the staff. No matter how many balanced meals they fed me, I didn't return the favor with any signs of weight gain. Like Tina told me on my first day, if I didn't gain two ounces every morning when they weighed me, I'd be punished. The staff thought that if I wasn't gaining any weight while participating in the program, I was up to no good. When I came into the hospital, I was about fifteen to twenty pounds under my so-called ideal weight. The problem of my gaining weight wasn't because of the food, however; it was the lack of binge drinking.

The nurses searched my room for bags, loose floorboards,

or a jimmied entrance into the locked bathroom next door. No luck. They monitored me extra closely when I was in the bathroom. The entire time I was in the hospital, I took the absolute minimum number of smashes that I could. I wasn't interested in having a sixty-year-old nurse looking at my cock while I grunted and made disgusting facial gestures. They also tried searching my shit for ephedrine or water pills I may have had someone sneak in for me. No luck again.

Finally, the staff started administering supplements, which were tastelessly disgusting. Desperate and without many resources at my disposal, I devised a clever little plan to momentarily throw them off the scent.

Being the elusive genius I claimed to be, I decided to conceal heavy objects on my body. My problem was concealing the objects in a way so the nursing staff couldn't see under the near-translucent robe they weighed me in when I woke up.

I started out by shoving D batteries in my ass. Bear with me a second. I know that sounds totally fucking gross, but I didn't shove them all the way in. More accurately, I would clench them between my cheeks and my underwear. After a while, I taped them to the fronts of my legs and under my sack. Don't even ask how painful those were to strip off. I felt like a human Christmas tree. I knew that the nursing staff was hesitant, seeing as how I was male, about feeling me up so early in the morning. Sure, they searched my mouth and my arms, but going near my genitals was a gray area not discussed in their job descriptions. Not only that, the nurses seemed to find me charming. My cunning behavior was reminiscent of Alex in *A Clockwork Orange* when he attempted to convince the jail priest that he had changed his ways.

"You're kidding me." Tina laughed and shot the foam from a Coke out of her nose, putting out her cigarette that was sitting on the side of the ashtray in the smoking corner. "That is the most inane thing I've heard. You get away with that?"

"Of course. I know what these nurses will do and what they won't do. Look at it this way; these nurses are here to help define a psychological problem. Hell, I don't think they would touch my ass or my balls even if they thought I had colon cancer."

"How long do you think you can keep this up?"

"They'll let me out of here before I get to that point, Tina."

"Shit, Mariah has a better chance of getting out of here than you, battery boy."

"Leave her alone, Tina. I think she's troubled."

"What do you mean?"

"Nothing."

"What?" Her eyes narrowed as she studied me. "What do you know?"

"Let's just say, I'm not even in the same league as her."

"Yeah, but you also aren't admitting you have a problem. You think these bloodsuckers are gonna let you leave before they squeeze every last cent out of your insurance? Boy, are you fucking stupid, D! You'd be better off just playing the game." She had a point. Since I had been there, I hadn't made any progress at all. Why was I listening to her? She'd been at Prophecy several times, and hospitalization didn't seem to be doing her any good. "Why don't you tell your parents when they come today that this place is just a big waste of their insurance premium?"

"Maybe I want to find out what's wrong with me, Tina."

"Give me a fucking break. D, you're never going to want to know what's wrong with you. It's fun for you. It's a joke to you." Tina sucked on one of my cigarettes and raised her voice. "Just remember I might laugh when you show and tell a bunch of pictures of demons during therapy time, but I'm actually pissed off. Not everyone agrees with your shitty view of the world."

I rolled my eyes. "Shut up. Why don't you tell your parents why you've wasted so much time here, bitch? Oh, I forgot, they don't visit you, because your old man is off plowing some twenty-year-old in Greece, and your mom, well, I guess no one knows where she is. Do you think I can take anything seriously coming from a girl who would rather suffer behind a windowsill than deal with the real world?"

"Fuck off!" she screamed. "You don't know anything about me. How dare you? Do you think this is shits and giggles for everyone here? Get over yourself."

"You're right, Tina. I'm sorry. I'm a total asshole. I won't tell my parents to get me out of here yet, but I'll tell them to wait on the car battery."

"Car battery?"

"Yeah, I still haven't figured how the hell I'm gonna fit that son of a bitch in my ass."

"You are so screwed up, D." She laughed.

+ + +

It was uncomfortable the first time my parents came to visit me at Prophecy. I expected my dad to be all freaked out about my being in the hospital with a bunch of scary-looking girls and my mother to be nurturing, but I got the opposite reaction.

"So how are things coming along, D?" my father asked, giving me a big bear hug. My dad looked around the Prophecy common area, trying to get a look at the living train wreck that was our little wing of the hospital.

"I guess they're okay. I'm learning, and the people seem to be pretty cool."

"That's not what Doctor Sandler tells us," my mom interjected. She caught me off guard and I didn't know how to react.

"What are you talking about, Mom?"

"The doctor says not only have you made no progress, but you have been extremely difficult, and on one occasion violent." I knew my little incident with the chair would come back to haunt me. How dare Sandler take the story out of context and distort it in a way that made me look like I was purposely being deviant.

"It was no big deal, Mom."

"No big deal. No big deal, Andrew! Like we aren't paying enough to have you in here. You're just like your brother. That's all we need, a bill for a huge window."

The kinder, gentler general chimed in. "Honey, we don't know what happened. To tell you the truth, I don't want to know. At least, as far as I can see nothing critical went on and everyone seems to be okay."

For some reason I knew anything Sandler told the general would be taken with a grain of salt. My favorite shrink was the kind of guy my father would have beaten the shit out of for jumping the border during the Vietnam draft. He was, as the general would say, a "pinko faggot." My mom, on the other hand, believed anything that someone with a medical degree told her. She was still waiting for me to walk across the stage and get my diploma before I could defend myself intellectually.

A few years earlier, my mom was diagnosed with ovarian cancer. I was away at school, but I knew my father didn't cotton to our family doctor. During her time of need, my father was gone a lot, trying to stay with a fulltime job during a shitty economic situation and get back on his feet. He tried to be by my mom's side whenever he could, but to pay the medical bills, he had to work. Her doctor on the other hand was always helping her through her sickness. I'm surprised the general didn't kick the shit out of the wacky doctor after my mother recovered. I never liked that doctor anyway; he made jokes one time when he was giving me a rectal exam.

"Hey, baby, can you go wait with Doctor Sandler?" My father kissed my mother on the cheek.

She gave me a hug and a kiss and brushed my hair out of my eyes. "When are you going to get this cut?" She gave me one last look and headed for Sandler's office.

"You do understand why your mother is so angry, don't you, D?"

"I guess so, dad."

Brittany, who wanted to show off her parents, interrupted us. "D, these are my parents, Doug and Linda." The general looked at me. It was obvious that he disapproved of a little girl addressing her parents by their first names.

Brittany's father looked at me like I was not only strange, but as if I posed some threat to his daughter. Brittany's mother, on the other hand, stood behind her protector and simply nodded her head. "Nice to meet you, D. Linda and I have heard a lot about you."

"Ah, yeah, and this is my father, Dave."

My dad put out his hand to shake. "Hi, I'm D's father. Nice to meet you." I bet if the circumstances were any different, the general would have crushed the guy's hand. Spasmodic as always, Brittany dragged her trophies to the next victims.

"Well, Dave, D," said Brittany's father, as he was dragged away, "it looks like our little Brittany has more introductions in order. You know kids. Take care."

Being a kid at one point in my life, I wanted to inform old Dougie that what he had was a couple of species removed from a human child. Doug and his wife gave me a once over and then continued on their tour. I looked around the room; Tina was nowhere to be seen.

"You have to understand, son, your mother isn't mad; she's concerned. When you faxed us the letter with your grades last year, it was almost like you had copied your brother's cry for help word for word. Then, when I picked you up from the airport, I almost had to carry your ass off the plane. We love you two very much, and we don't like seeing you in pain." The general embraced me with another hug, gave me a care package filled with cartons of cigarettes and some cover-less paperback books and went to join my mother in Sandler's office. He may have been crying, but I doubt it.

It was nice to see my parents, and when they left I wasn't angry with my mother. She had every reason to think I fucked up and I'm sure Sandler's perverted stories didn't help pave the way for a brighter future for her youngest son.

Almost everyone in the unit had gone to bed, but I stayed awake and puzzled over the statue in the courtyard. At night, the statue was semi-lit with one yellow fog light that attracted winter moths. During the day, the icicles and snow camouflaged the statue, making it more or less a snowman built out of slush and pissed-on snow. During the night, it seemed more human. I couldn't see the bird shit and the graffiti that covered his body. Even the ugliest creatures look their finest at night. Like everything, the night is deceiving. Trust can become your worst enemy when you can't see a foot in front of your face.

The statue reminded me of when I had to go to church as a kid. Even at that age, I thought of the carriers of God's word as nothing more than panhandlers in uniform. Think about it. What do they do? They spout out some long-winded performance so they can pass around a collection plate, which, by the way, is shaped like a pan, and take your money. Fuck, at least when it came to drunks and bums, I knew the payoff would be a good filthy joke.

My friend Phil used to abuse the power the typical workingman had over vagrants. Whenever they asked him for spare change, he'd offer them five bucks to show their cocks or their tits; then he would take a picture. His ultimate goal was to make a coffee table book filled with naked bums. Phil was obviously a little "touched," but I think it would have been great to do similar things to God's soldiers.

I never understood church. It seemed like a cool place if you wanted to make a horror movie—bad music, scary rituals, and haunting effigies of a guy who got hammered to a cross, but it scared me more than it entertained my optimism. One thing I never did, however, was patronize someone based on his or her belief system. If a person truly had found something to believe in, something that would make him happy at the end of the day, then I tipped my hat to them. The believer was far better off than I was. In my world, the end of the day meant reliving infectious memories. I would be a lot happier if I could prove the existence of a god. I guess that's the most difficult test to overcome. My personal assload of issues aside, shitting on someone for their beliefs is how wars get started.

"So what did you do during your summer vacation? Did you go home?" I quickly pulled the blind down, covering the window. Tina had managed to sneak up behind me. "Thank you," she said. "I guess all it took to close you off from that window was a good bitching."

"I'm really sorry about what I said before."

She shrugged and looked away. "It's over; we all have our hang ups in here. Yours are just too obvious. You need to not let your emotions take over, D."

"Why do you want to hear any more of this story? I don't want to tell any more. I'll tell you that the only summer I came home was last summer. That's when I dropped my issues, as well as my shitty report card, on my parents."

"I guess I'm intrigued. I'm a closet shrink. If you grew up with two psychiatrists for parents, it would've fucked you up, too."

"No, instead I grew up with a Vietnam vet who served two duties and the rich daughter of an abusive father and a drunk mother."

"Well, at least you were curious about one of them." She meant alcoholism. What a cheap shot. It figures; it was a typical Ivy League comeback.

"Nice. Really nice. Anyway, no, I never went home for the summer. I didn't like home. It had nothing to do with my parents. There was a lot of history and bad memories in my hometown."

"Fuck that boring shit. I want to hear about all of the things you regret. The stuff you told me you weren't proud of."

CHAPTER FIVE

Going to Palmbrook College, and escaping from the Kudzu were the two proudest achievements of my life. However, that same achievement threw me into a world I didn't understand—one of money, snobbery, and debauchery— forcing me to be more resourceful. Resourcefulness wasn't foreign to me; I always liked to think of myself as a chameleon in different environments. When the rule makers least expected it, I jumped in front of the camera, took center stage, and overthrew the standard practices. Being an escapist, a man of many faces, led me down a path of bullshit glory that managed to crumble my pride.

Palmbrook was no place to flaunt intelligence. I was a little turd in what quickly transformed into the world's largest cesspool. It wasn't different from my hometown; it just looked and smelled better. While I checked my naiveté at the door, I spaced the things that I knew were right. After all the lessons that I'd learned, it seemed appropriate that I would fall prey to those things that I used to brush off with a snide, "that'll never be me." I speak of course about drugs, my brother's near-death involvement, and his near-jail experience.

My brother was a pretty typical kid. He threw mud clods at passing cars, wrecked housing developments, piled shit on doorsteps, and spent most of his time fucking around. He wasn't a bad kid, though. He was a model citizen, in fact, except for his tendency to act like a boy. As he grew up, he became an exceptional musician, playing the trombone in the school band. I think his discipline at the time drove him to lash-out when he reached college. Like most, or at least like those who don't want to remember their pasts, he escaped to college with one thing in mind: to change his identity and how people perceived him. He left his talents at home in a box with his old comics and his trombone and became someone else. I don't know if he thought he was a geek in high school, but he wasn't that person ever again.

It's funny; I can remember my brother as an awkward teen, participating in Bible retreats with the family preacher and the rest of the young lacking-in-religion Lutherans of Kudzutown. Fortunately, my parents had become consumed with their professional careers by the time I got to that age. The only time my father had for God was when he was at the Vietnam memorial or when the threat of losing his job shook its ugly-assed face. I can't imagine going on a camping trip with a gaggle of God people, even though leeches and mosquitoes have a perfect affinity for priests and Bible thumpers.

Max wanted to enjoy all the other fruits of life that he might or might not have shit away during all those years studying and making music. In that sense, the truest form of escape, my brother and I were identical twins. Sure, a lust for paradise drove my escape, that and a need to escape from the kudzu-covered carcass of the paper mill. These things represented shitty, broken down houses, rapists, and speed-addict murderers. On the other hand, my brother really just wanted to get away from himself. What he found in his attempt to reinvent his persona was his own fear and it drove him into the ground.

I understand he didn't want to go back to what he was. He ran away, cutting himself off completely from his loved ones, and then returned to his boring former existence. Don't get me wrong; my brother wasn't a misanthrope or a dork. I think he got laid for the first time at a much younger age than I did. Max wanted to encompass decadence, and that was something he achieved.

Finally, it seemed he had refocused his life. He begged my parents to put him in rehab. Then, his girlfriend from his façade life moved in with my parents. She neglected to tell Max while he was being rehabilitated that she managed to become nine months pregnant.

When your daily routine involves two boxes of wine, a case of beer, ten hits of acid, and uncountable numbers of bong hits and rails of coke, you *become* addiction. You become a pure chemical compound. I think to this day, after leaving his delusions and skeletons behind, he still hears the trombones playing in his head with every second he spends with his son.

Sophomore year started and Bunky introduced me to Chuck Drost, whom we called Roast, since his name sounded so much like Chuck Roast. Although the word roast carried connotations of stoner society, it couldn't have been more unfitting. He was proper; he had the obnoxious habit of announcing when he was going to speak by prefacing every sentence with, "Ahem." Apparently, he and Bunky had been sent to some oddball reform school together out West. Bunky was in for running drugs in high school, while Roast blew up a big, wooden mailbox structure outside a ten-story condominium building with pipe bombs. He would have gotten away with the prank if the shrapnel hadn't shattered the glass of the building. Federal convictions, such as blowing up federal property like a mailbox, don't apply to those with coin. Such was the case with Chuck. Those convictions got buried and forgotten.

On one of those post-Cooper nights, Bunky decided to stash away his razorblades and mirrors for the more socially accepted alcoholism. Don't misunderstand me: alcohol is no better for you than coke, but it is legal. He took me to an orgy off campus with some of his other friends. A few familiar faces gathered there, most of them late-night callers to Bunky's pit of cocaine insanity that I would run into nightly while visiting the shitter to drop off my dinner.

As with most off-campus parties at Palmbrook, this ditty lacked nothing in the realm of hedonism. A huge glass table, most likely a '70s gem picked up at the Salvation Army, dominated the center of the ring. Several mounds of blow covered. On the outskirts waited several kegs of free-flying coopers, crushed and mangled. It was a new arena for me, but not one where I figured I couldn't be a contender. Over by the bar, in front of the host's kitchen, several red-in-the-face tweakers lined up to arm wrestle. At the center of this hormonally packed event we found Reno Lee, the baddest motherfucker, second only to the general, I ever met.

"Hey, Bird, this is Reno," Bunky said. Hillbilly by choice, Reno dropped an overzealous preppy kid's arm onto the bar, nearly breaking the kid's knuckles. "Reno, this is the Dirtybird." Before I could extend my hand out to shake, the 200-plus, six-foot monster grabbed the preppy kid's head and smashed it against one of the banisters that supported the bar. I noticed out of the corner of my eye that Roast had already partaken in the glass table's offerings.

Reno licked his index finger and dragged it across a gnarly scar that parted his hair slightly off-center. "You see this coke, you dumb son-a-bitch? You owe me this times two." The kid shook off Reno's attack. The thickly southern-accented and gravel-voiced Lee gave his victim a farewell speech. "Hey, boy, when y'all are done getting my shmodes, you can clean out that stinky old pussy of yours."

Most of the cokeheads at Palmbrook called cocaine shmodes. I never knew what it meant, but when I heard it, my stomach growled and my nose itched. My allergies were always in season for blow. Reno extended his hand after he was through fucking up the prep. "Dirtybird, huh? I heard of you. Ain't you some kind of drunken faggot?" I put out my hand to embrace the devil, and Lee crushed my bony hand in a vise, lubricating the shake with the sweat and blood of his last contender.

"No. Aren't you some kind of fucking red rider?" I asked. Reno pulled away his sweaty wrestling clutch. He looked at me, then at Bunky. Quickly, he grabbed me by my nasty unwashed hair and pulled me underneath his shoulder. My heart started pounding. Smart, D, fuck with the biggest, most coked-up, shit-housed drunk guy at the party. He tightened his sleeper hold on me with his solid pipes, and the perspiration from his arm-wrestling matches dripped all over my face. He reeked like a cow—or someone who spent the night tipping cows.

He licked his finger and dragged it across the scar. "What you say, faggot?"

"I was just fucking around." I tried to act tough, a joke in itself, but my voice cracked with fear.

He started laughing. "I'm just playin', Dirty-shitty-little-man." He let me loose from the vise and signaled to one of his boys. "Hey, Snif, go to the store and get me a handle of Old Grandad." They called Wade Smith Snif because of the rash that had built up around his nostrils from cocaine abuse.

"You got any money left, bitch?" Snif replied in what his birdseed-ass thought was hard. It was big talk for a kid who was an emaciated abnormality with a booze-swollen face. He looked like a stop sign.

"Ahem," Roast chimed in. "More coke, please."

Reno turned red and licked his finger again, this time covering it with dip spit. "Fuck you, pussboy, get me some whiskey for me and my new bitch, the Dirtybird." I didn't know whether to be honored or scared that Reno knew of me. If I had a brain at the time, I would have chosen the latter.

Pissed off for being treated as a subordinate by Reno, Snif let me in on his most hideous character trait.

SNAP!

The kid bit into and chewed on a stick of chalk—a way to cope. Like another trait he'd developed at school; sucking on an entire box of throat lozenges during a one-hour class. These methods helped him get his fix of artificial coke drips—a way to fool his body into thinking he was doing blow. Being someone who can't even stand the feeling of chalk in my hands, much less the feeling of writing with it, the sound produced a shivering freeze down my arms and left my hands chapped and dusty.

Reno and I sat in the corner as the party emptied out over the next two hours. We got sloppy, sucking down the last of the bottle of Old Grandad. "So, what's your story, Dirty-shitty-little faggot?" Reno asked me. Over by the table, Bunky, Roast, and Snif power slugged Kiwi Lime Mad Dog and blew through a gram and a half of coke. Every once and a while, some of Palmbrook's most notorious coke whores would pass in and out of the house to jump into a few fat rails or beg Bunky to roll a fatty. Sometimes Snif would play along with the girls, teasing them for an impromptu lap dance.

"Nothing special; I came here from a small town last year on scholarship to write."

"Write what, boy? About grabbin' mens' sacks while you're

getting' it from behind?" Reno didn't think I was gay; he just had petty way of belittling people and reminding them that he was a badass. I searched for an answer as Reno began packing a container of Kodiak. His big fingers slapped against the tin's cover and bounced loudly off the walls.

"Well, I know that when I was younger I always wanted to write horror stories, but since I've kind of gotten a little older, I think that's all hack bullshit. I'm kind of a fucking literary snob. Where the fuck did you pick up that chafed neck and that broken language you call English?"

"I grew up in the Bible belt, boy." He opened the tin and stuffed roughly half of its contents in front of his gums. "Accordin' to my daddy, I'm one of the few male descendants of General Robert E. Lee."

"Wow, impressive. He won the war, didn't he, Reno?"

"Fuck you, son. He didn't win shit except for takin' to the hides of a couple hundred niggers." As racist as Kudzutown was, I'd never heard anybody ever use the word nigger as freely as Reno.

"Niggers, huh? Do you really think in this day and age that nigger is an acceptable term?"

"Fuck off. I don't mean nothin' by it. Look at your buddy Drost. He's a fucking kike. We get along like champs. Besides, racism bleeds a patriotic color."

"What color is that Reno? Bullshit color?"

"Red, white, and motherfuckin' blue, you Yankee shit."

"Whatever, Reno. I mean I know we're both fucked up, but I can't say I like talking about things like that. What's the deal with your name—your first name?"

"My momma got knocked up while my parents were in Reno gamblin' one summer. They never went back, and I'm an only child." If I'd had a kid like Reno Lee, I wouldn't roll the dice again either. Someone told me in passing that in high school Reno belonged to a group of skinheads. Despite their affluence and Baptist school upbringing, the small group would cruise around nights in Reno's pickup and beat the shit out of people for no reason. Stories of his capers ranged from gouging eyes out to biting ears off. It was all hearsay though, and I never paid it any mind. These were the types of kids I knew better than to associate with. Even the chameleon can only change color when in a foreign environment. My color that night was white.

"What's the deal with Snif? He seems a little drawn to the entire coke thing, huh?" We looked across the room, and Snif unleashed his bones from his T-shirt, staggered around, and pushed Bunky.

"He's all right, just a little green. Cokeheads from barn towns usually play the fool. You gotta stick around here Bird; More-ganja is showing up later. You'll like him. He's a fagboy like you."

"Who's More-ganja?" I asked.

"Miles Morgan."

At first, I picked More-ganja as a cliché in Palmbrook. He listened to the Dead and the Allman Brothers, kept a collection of bootleg DAT tapes from shows, covered everything with tapestries, and smoked a shitload of pot. Oddly enough, for someone who constantly had his lips wrapped around his treasured three-foot bong, he was sharp and attentive. The nickname suited him on many levels.

When I actually got an opportunity to hang out with him for the first time, one of his hang-on girlfriends was showing him pictures from a party. After looking through all of the faces and poses of the coed and her friends, one thing caught More-ganja's eye and made him interested in the free-for-all. It wasn't the picture of Jenni sucking down a yard of beer or the herd of sluts showing off their tits. Rather, faded out in the background of an overexposed picture was a faint shadow of a bong.

"Check it out, Bird; there's a three-foot, glass Graffix with butterfly slide." He pointed at the paraphernalia proudly as if I were Sam and he were Quincy the forensics expert.

"How do you see that?" I studied the blurred picture. I couldn't see anything other than a dildo between some girl's rack.

"What do you mean? It's just like mine. Fucking sweetest binger ever. As soon as you pull out that slide, a nice, clean bowl gently clouds your lungs. Ah, heaven." I was still naïve at this point. I didn't grow up close to the drug culture, except, of course, for the stuff I learned secondhand from my brother and a couple of high school friends. This was knowledge that grew straight from a boarding school. I, one of the few non-boarding-school students at Palmbrook, had never learned the ins and outs, the hardware and software of pulling tubes.

More-ganja was the laid-back stoner of school who spent his boarding school days playing lacrosse, being a punk, and waiting by the shore for washed up bales of pot. Unlike Bunky, Snif, Roast, and Reno, however, he thought he knew when to say when. Rather than waste our time kissing up to the party culture of the school, something I'd felt I needed to do, to fit in the previous year, we had more fun sitting around and getting wasted and doing stupid shit. Our favorite idiotic thing to do was distorting the lyrics to songs that we hated. If my memory serves me correctly, the song "Wild, Wild West" by Kool Moe Dee ranked the highest on our list of absurd, retarded songs. In that respect, being with More-ganja filled an empty place after Cooper left.

One thing that especially intrigued me about More-ganja was his tendency to break into a feverish sweat every time he headed towards the airport. So much so, on the way to the airport, he sucked on a plastic imitation cigarette dugout full of pot shake and ranted aimlessly about how great the Dead were. To make things uneasy, I would often play the hardest music I could find from my collection. Slayer or Ministry usually did the trick. He tried to calm down and find a happy place, but that couldn't stop the buckets of sweat that soon became permanent fixtures on my vehicle's interior.

More-ganja didn't fill Cooper's shoes. He was different; different from me and in some respects the same. Some people even began to refer to More-ganja as "Dirty Miles."

"Bird, why are you here?" More-ganja asked me as he tugged at his bong, and sucked down smoke.

"Do you mean in like a metaphysical sense?"

"No, dickhead. I mean, why did you to come to school here. You don't seem like the type. You know, Daddy's little pissant." I thought for a second. There were several reasons why I was there, I just hadn't really figured out how I was using these reasons to benefit my post-college career. As far as everyone else knew, I was only good at one thing—being drunk. "I mean," More-ganja hesitated for a second, "do you think that those guys in your fraternity are really your friends? All they do is laugh at you when you get hammered, and can't walk." Funny, my fraternity brothers often said something similar about More-ganja, except the word "stoned" replaced "hammered" and "think" replaced "walk."

"I'm a narc," I joked. "No, I really don't know. It seemed like the ideal place to escape to. A place to learn and a place where nobody cares about anything except debauchery, fucking, drinking, drugging. I don't have a whole lot, and I don't ask for much, either."

"Then why do you puke when you eat?"

I hesitated and went flush. Exposed. I hadn't decided whether I was embarrassed or angry. "How did you know about that?"

"Come on, dude; everybody knows about it. Your fratboys have big mouths when they're drunk and smoking pot." He lit another huge bowl and sucked down the entire chamber without batting an eye.

"Let me guess. Bunky and Roast."

"Yeah, but don't tell them I told you that. It was kind of a mistake. Roast was going off about 'finger sandwiches' and 'eating Dirtybird's seconds' and shit. I was like, 'Hey, why are you talking about Bird like that?'" As he spoke, with the mouthpiece resting under his chin, he held the bong hit and let it fester in his lungs.

"How noble of you."

He paused for a second and blew the hit out. "I didn't know your deal. You have to admit that it's kind of weird, though. Why do you do it? You're not, like, fat or anything. It does explain why you get so fucking stinking drunk."

"Actually it just intensifies the fact that I'm allergic to alcohol and makes me a lot drunker, because there is nothing in my system to mop up the booze."

"Well, just don't let me catch you doing that shit." He meant it. Not even in his presence, whether we were out to eat or just getting drunk at The Library. I did it once. As I recall, I excused myself from the table and went into the shitter. I knew that time was ticking, and throwing up all of my food in the time of a standard piss was difficult. I had to be quick, precise, and efficient. Sometimes, unfortunately, you'd end up with a slew of complications.

When you unload a big pile of barf, it usually slides into the toilet as one big blob. This happened especially if you jump the gun on a barfarama and threw up something dense like a sandwich before the digestive acid had a chance to break anything down. The result was that I backed up the toilet. It was a combination of a few poorly plotted moves. First of all, I flushed the toilet before beginning to throw up to lower the water level. I flushed depending on the type of toilet I decided to face. In this case, it didn't have much of a lip. It was more bowl shaped. Secondly, I yacked fast, which is occasionally noisy. You have to take the good with the bad when you're not careful. Thirdly, there was an anxious drunk outside pounding on the door.

"Hey, fuckhead, hurry up!" The guy outside kept yelling as he pounded on the less than secure plywood. Fearing capture, I rushed and flushed. With my heart smacking my ribs, my head circling, and eyes filled with snow, I desperately struggled to find a plunger. No luck. I rolled up my sleeve and reached into the plumbing that was filled with bar piss and tugged on the dinner plugging the pipes. Still no luck.

"Hey, asswipe," the drunk squealed. "You'd better not be taking a fucking shit in there. I'll throw up." With time ticking away on what should have been the time allocated to take a leak, I stood up, still shaking, and took the upper deck off of the toilet. Using my drunken plumber's first instinct; I tugged on the chain mechanism connected to the plunger.

"Goddamit! Hurry the fuck up, or I'll bust a cap in your ass. Are you jerking it in there?" Finally, after minutes of tooling around, I achieved success. With the aid of my right hand, I pushed the mound of bile into the pipes as my left controlled hit the mechanism above. I got up and brushed any chunks off of me, washed my hands, and glared in the mirror. I didn't get a really good look at myself, so I didn't recognize the fact that I was soaking wet and had a busted blood vessel in my eye.

"D, are you okay?" Monica met me outside of the bathroom door that night. She was counting her tips. Sadly, I was attempting to count when she was going to be legal.

"Yeah, I'm fine. How are you doing, Monica? How's the Nusstorte?"

"You remember. I can't believe it. What ever happened to Cooper? I haven't seen him around all year."

"He had to leave school."

"That sucks. Did he fail out?"

"No. It was something else." I got my composure together. "Monica, do you maybe want to go out sometime?"

"Yeah. You, Wade and I can go drinking later this week."

"Snif?"

"Yeah, we're dating. That will be awesome." She noticed the broken blood vessel and put her hand on my face. "What's wrong with your eye?"

"Nothing. I'll talk to Wade."

"Cool, D. Take care of yourself."

More-ganja didn't catch me in the act, but by the time I got back to the dinner table, he was wise to me. Being the enemy to the sad game, he disqualified me by breaking a beer bottle on my face. I've still got a scar on the bridge between my eyes. The wound was my fault. That's the reason if I had to puke after a meal at a restaurant, I had to play the "my stomach hurt and I had to take a smash," card. This play not only allowed me plenty of time to let my eyes dry up, it also gave me an opportunity to chew on toilet paper to distill my breath. The postmortem procedures often varied depending on whether or not I managed to get a chunk of food lodged in my nasal passage. On that occasion, however, I was busted. There was no excuse for busting a blood vessel in my eye. I didn't tell Snif that I'd unsuccessfully asked Monica out. I didn't feel like getting my ass kicked.

After dinner, More-ganja brought up the barfarama again at his off campus house. "Do you do it because you feel alone?"

"No. I think that we're all alone, especially here. Even when I'm in a room full of people, I feel unworthy."

"Yeah, I know how that is, Bird. When I get lonely, I know where I can turn. We all have vices that never go away. They only get worse. I've been alone for most of my life. At least I have this." He toked away on his friend, the bong.

My sophomore year progressed and the year started to wind down. More-ganja and I became more and more blended. I taught him what I knew about alcoholism, and he taught me what I now know about drug abuse. Great, another monkey on my back to add to my shopping list of issues. I think More-ganja was more depressed than he made out to be. He fell into the bracket of students whose parents wanted to hide their dirty little secret. He sometimes got acceptable grades, and he said he attended class, which was something that I couldn't say for myself. Drugs became his solace, his Nazareth. He felt like a burden on his parents.

"Do you ever feel like People don't want you around, Bird?"

I shrugged my shoulders and scratched my temple. "Not really. I feel that everyone enjoys my company. That's my main flaw. I tend to think of myself as a performer rather than an acquaintance."

"Whatever, dick; if anything you're a jester. You amuse everyone with your drunken buffoonery."

"No shit. It's a way for people to notice me. I don't care what they think as long as they're talking about me. Why do you ask? Everyone seems to like you. I don't see you lurking in the dark at parties. You sure fuck a lot."

"That's not what I mean. Maybe I'm just baked, all paranoid and shit."

"Well then why are you asking me, More-ganja?"

"It's just that, I know that you and your dad don't have the greatest relationship, but you do have an understanding."

"Yeah," I said, "I understand that he can kick my ass if he knew I was hanging out with a lowlife tycoon like you smoking pot."

"Fuck off. I'm serious!" His voice contracted and his usual carefree tone grew somber. "I don't have any friends like you, Bird. I mean I like Reno and Bunky and Snif and those guys, but all they aspire to be is fucked up. They want to live like this forever, worthless and rich. I want to do something. When I was a kid I used to have to go out and be my parent's little trophy. It was terrible. I had to go out to dinner with them and my father's business associates, and I wasn't allowed to even open my mouth. I had to sit there like a bitch and only answer when spoken to. That's how I'm beginning to feel about this school." Ganja leaned back, thinking that a pillow was behind him to support his back. There wasn't a pillow there and his guitar broke his fall, making him a little heated. "These stuck-up assholes and their money. The teachers; they're no better. They know this place is a country club. They don't take anything, even the sincere shit, seriously. They're total dicks. If I get bad grades because I fucked up, my dad will beat the shit out of me. Like the time I decided it would be clever to fart at one of my father's little dinner dates. My brain collapsing at school would be a lot worse. I wouldn't have a family anymore. I wouldn't have anything. They don't understand.

"I have dyslexia, Dirty, and it sucks for me to concentrate in all these classes. It doesn't help that I burn through about an eighth of smoke every day, but my parents were more likely to excuse anything I told them as me being difficult."

His eye twitched slightly, holding it all in. After a couple seconds of fighting his emotions, a tear trickled out. Then, a few seconds later, he let loose. Unlike Freddy Brubaker, More-ganja's disorder centered on his inability to see words correctly. It's a wonder he ever got into college. I got uncomfortable. I never knew whether to calm a crying person down, shut them up, or leave the room and ignore the entire situation. I felt unable to cry, even when I knew it was appropriate. To protect More-ganja's relaxed façade, I left this conversation unsaid and dismissed it. He sucked down another bong load. It was a lot bigger than the two previous ones. He blew it out a lot quicker though, because it was too big for his lungs. He coughed and gagged out a huge ball of phlegm. As many wars as he had fought with himself and who he was, he loved the ones that centered around his body versus his bong. The more I thought about it, the more I believed he wasn't crying, he just sucked down too much smoke and his coughing made him well-up. What did he have to cry about anyway?

"Well, I've always felt that the best way to feel relaxed in a situation is to outwit everyone you're in the company of and play by your own rules. That way, you control the situation. What are you worried about? I'm more of an outcast here than you."

"Well, what scares you then, Bird?"

I picked up a straw on the table and started playing around with it. "Lately, I'm afraid of my reflection. I'm unable to come to terms with what I see in the mirror."

"Yeah, I read something about that and people who don't eat."

I defended myself. "No, it's not like that. I mean, I'm not real happy with the way I look, but I'm less happy with the way I feel. I feel strung out, wasted. When I shave, I only wipe clean the surface of the mirror that shows the area on my face that needs work. When I pass my reflection, I ignore it. There was something I saw in my eyes I didn't like the last time I was really fucked up and brushed my teeth. I don't like what I am. I see only the bad, and I have a fear that something is going to creep up behind me." It made sense that I felt unease and paranoia. I was more than an addict as my heart flickering on and off reminded me.

"Just because you're fucked up, Bird, doesn't mean someone can't tell you shut up and beat your ass."

I rubbed at the scar that he left between my eyebrows and accepted his rejection rather than have him analyze me. I appreciated friends like More-ganja and Cooper and their caring about me, but how could they understand something I didn't understand myself?

"Yeah, you're right. Maybe there is something that we can do. I mean, I can't get you in class and make sure you're doing your homework, but I can help you out with other stuff."

"What do you propose?" More-ganja asked.

"Cocaine. Lots of it."

Bunky walked into the room. "Where?" he screamed.

CHAPTER SIX

"Oh big fucking deal," Tina scoffed while packing a cigarette on the three-and-a-half-legged Prophecy table. "So you and your buddies did a bunch of coke. Wow, D, what a dirty little secret. Who hasn't done coke?" She shook her head and rolled her eyes. "What a pussy story. I can't believe you roped me into this lame load of shit."

"Okay, to begin with, you were the curious one. The story doesn't end there. I'm tired of you running your mouth. If you don't think there is going to be any payoff to this story, then fuck you. I'm not telling you because I believe you'll think of me as a hero or a bad boy. You wanted to know my deal. You have been hounding me about it since the second you decided I was going to be your cigarette pusher. By the way, I don't condone smoking and I have yet to see you produce an ID. As far as I know, you're Brittany's age."

"Fuck you, asshole. Would a nine year-old have a set of these?" Tina tried to stick out her chest by arching her back and cupping her miniature breasts with her hands.

"Do you really want me to answer that, you scrawny bitch?"

"No." She looked down shamefully. "I just thought that maybe you liked having someone to talk to. It's the things that I fear most about this place that sucks me back. It's easy for you to escape your faults, especially if you don't tell anyone what you're afraid of. I like hearing about someone else's misfortune, hoping that someday I'll find someone screwier than me. I remember when my brother used to take me skydiving. He used to say, 'Tina, it's the fear that makes the experience fun.' After that first dive, I was totally addicted."

"That's cool, Tina. I *do* like talking to you. I tell you a lot more than I tell Sandler. The thing is this; if I want to get out of here, I need to censor what goes out and what doesn't. Have you told anyone anything yet?"

She focused on the ashtray and fiddled with her cigarette's granny ash. "Kind of."

"What did you say?"

"I'm sorry. I told Brittany about the batteries because I thought she would get a kick out of it. She got scared when she first came here when her parents left. You know how kids are. Fart jokes and footballs in the nuts still reign supreme in that age group."

"That's cool. Just don't say anything else. Sandler has my parents' number, and he isn't afraid to twist and mangle stories to suit him." I covered my mouth and let out a huge yawn. "Let's get some sleep. We best be well rested for the bullshit I have to ham up tomorrow during group." Sticking batteries up my ass to make my daily weight was the least of my worries.

The next morning, I woke up feeling good. Not great, but good. After serving a few weeks at Prophecy, the structured meals actually made my body feel a little better. Usually, when I woke up at Palmbrook, I felt so gross, sick and hot, that I slept until dusk. I didn't want to face the world. In my condition it wasn't pleasant for the world to face me either. It didn't hurt that the hospital had no drugs or booze for me to get into. I was finally flushing out all of the years of garbage built up in my body. Despite the fact that my voice and throat were shredded from the pack of cigarettes Tina and I smoked the previous night, my body didn't ache. One thing about the barfarama is the toll it takes on your body after a while.

To begin with, my lower back hurts constantly. So much so, if anyone ever tried to give me a back massage while I was throwing up actively, I screamed in pain when they touched the area directly underneath my ribcage. I can't prove it scientifically, but I think my kidneys were banged up beyond repair. This, combined with the dehydration of drinking myself into another plane of existence, didn't heal my body. I was a dehydrated shell incapable of retaining nutrients. I felt like the stump of a rotted old tree.

Another problem was my bones. I needed some essential vitamins such as potassium, iron, and calcium. It wasn't a coincidence; it was the reality I'd created for myself. My health was my choice. People often asked me, "Don't you think eventually all of this abuse will catch up with you?" I knew I wasn't indestructible, but I didn't think it ever would. I felt maybe one day I would heal. I told myself I was one in a million. Good luck. Malnutrition doesn't repair itself without a price. I felt sure the same feelings would come back and beat me later in life.

When I began the progression and decided this would be my "Road Less Traveled," I neglected to consider the good things about the "Road Already Paved." If I was indeed looking for some type of sympathy initially, the addiction devoured the novelty. If a person is willing and able to self-induce vomiting, even in my case dating as far back as to when I regurgitated the vaporizer juice, then he'd better be willing to do it again. I would disagree though, that the vaporizer liquid instance was the starting point. That was too painful to lead to the gradual enjoyment I got from the barfarama. It was just the first time that I knew I could do it. After being presented with the idea, which I really didn't know anything about until the day I visited Lori Conroy in the hospital, I created my own actuality, not original or visionary by any means, just my choice.

I got out of bed, stretching and looked out my alley-facing window. I was cold, so I paged a nurse to unlock my bathroom and let me into the shower. I know what you're thinking. "How come you didn't puke in the shower?" It wasn't possible. All of the water filtered out of a little hole in the side of the tile. If I did throw up, which wouldn't have made any difference any way because I was only allowed to shower in the morning before breakfast, the drain would have clogged. They had everything figured out. Shower barfs were never a good idea. The pleasantness of a toilet bowl, the big welcoming mouth, wasn't there. Smashing food down a pinhole drain constructed even more of a problem when it came to getting the stench off of the body. Vomit is a very pungent concoction: It's the smell that keeps on giving.

The winter sun felt great and I took my time drying off. It was nice outside, but in the hospital I was still in jail, a white-walled hell constructed by a bunch of Catholics. It was a quiet morning at Prophecy. Most weekends were. Usually, I heard Brittany terrorizing someone, bouncing around on the couches in the common area or raving about the latest guy on one of her budget Saturday morning neon soap operas. No such luck. I figured that Sandler either muzzled her or upped her dosage of antidepressants. Either one suited me fine. The muzzle appealed to me the most.

I hated antidepressants. I thought Prozac and the like were bullshit drugs. From what I saw, they only made things worse. I stretched one last time and headed to the common area to create mischief. On my way down the hall, I realized that Kristina had something to do with my sudden burst of optimism. Maybe she wasn't qualified to be my therapist, but she seemed interested in what I had to say.

"You have to go back to your room, D," Sandler belted out as I started walking down the hall.

"Listen, Doc, I'm sorry that I slept in so late, but I feel great today. Tell your staff that I left a few nut rags on the floor next to the bed." The halls, with the exception of Sandler and me, were empty. "Did you slip one of your little crybaby cocktails to me while I was sleeping?"

"Just get back to your room, D. I'm serious."

"I'm serious, too. I want to go play Scrabble and shit. Want to put that medical degree on the line, champ?" I slapped him on the shoulders.

Sandler pointed in the direction of my room. "Listen, D. If you don't comply, I will have to get security down here to take care of you for me. Go, now!"

"I want to go down to the common area and do something. That's why I slept so late, so I'd be all smiles today." I formed a huge grimace with my fingers and Sandler immediately realized that I wasn't going to budge. He pulled a walkie-talkie off his belt strap. Had that been there before? "Sandler, come on. Don't you think that it's getting a little too police state in here?"

He shit into the walkie-talkie not taking his eyes off me. "Security, I have a disturbance on the second floor." Then, he blocked me from getting farther down the hall. I licked my lips and clenched my fists, preparing to dart. His eyes set into mine. Bad choice. My eyes weren't going to give away my running direction.

"Let's see, Sandler. I'm nowhere near as weak as I was when I first got in here. Do you think that I can outfox you and get down to the common area? You feeling lucky, old man?"

He stayed focused on his communication with security and his eyes never left me. Like a Little League basketball player, he steadily stood square in front of me, his feet directly aligned with my body. The absurdity of the situation made me rely on a head fake to the left and a cunning dash to the right. I guess he didn't know that I was right-handed, because anyone could have seen that follow-up move coming.

"D! Get back here!" He returned to the walkie-talkie. "That's right, the Center for Eating Disorders. This is a serious situation." I ran down the long white hall, which appeared even more sedate than ever with the girls' closed doors. I laughed my ass off as my head flung around to salute and say Godspeed to Sandler. Crazy like a fox, indeed. I didn't have a feeling of freedom; that was difficult to create even with my random imagination in the hospital. I did feel carefree. It was an emotion that I hadn't experienced since the days and nights that I sat around with Cooper or More-ganja. Just when I heard the elevator bell chime out that security had arrived, I realized why everyone had been banished to their rooms that day.

It hit me like a wrecking ball. I will never forget the feeling of shame that struck every pore of my body. The realization of what I had done didn't hit me, at least not right away. It was the contact between my body and the stretcher. I knocked into a shrouded, wheeled bed, I slammed into one of the orderlies, knocking him on his ass, causing him to lose control and drop the bed's contents all over the floor.

"What the fuck are you doing, you stupid fuck?" the orderly screamed at me.

"No!" Sandler yelped down as he ran towards me, losing his breath. "Oh God, no." He stopped and evaluated the atrocious accident. With my head bursting and dazed, I looked at the orderly. My heart thundered, but I couldn't figure out what was going on.

"What?" That was all I could bring myself to say. That instant, that second, I realized what had occurred. The contents of the stretcher were what were left of Mariah, the artist. Her twisted torso tucked itself into a fetal position on the floor. Her arms braided themselves together. Her glazed eyes, wide open, glared at me, but they didn't see anything. I wanted to reach out, be her crutch, her doughnut pillow, but the sight of her scared me. I wanted to stitch her back together, but I knew I couldn't hold a needle and thread with my shakes. I retracted and cringed. Was I the one dead? No voices from my past chimed in. The horrible memory of her batting at the drawing after Brittany grabbed it crunched my head and pounded me in the face. The trust she showed me when told me about the parasites drowned out the yelling of Sandler and his staff. I'd desecrated her. She lay dead, and I felt soulless.

In the middle of the night, Mariah had given up her fight. There was nothing left of her, nothing that resembled a human being. I kept thinking that maybe it was the arts and crafts incident that set her off, but she had been strolling carelessly on her twine-like deathrope for much too long. Her body imploded. Her ribcage collapsed, folding her like an accordion. I guess her will to live wore tired of wringing out every inch and every corner of her body, searching for a morsel, a scrap, anything that resembled nutriment. The parasites made sure her last meal was theirs. The clock had timed her out. Father Time had bargained with his last second, tired of waiting for a sign of restitution. I thought of Lori Conroy.

I peered down from the white-walled jail cell. I clinched my fists and pumped at my arm that hadn't been thrashed by the clumsy physician's assistants who decided to shove a blood-drainer into every crevice of my arm looking for veins. I wanted to kick holes in the walls, to thunder around like a mad torpedo, and spit on my reflection, but I was out of fight. Even the things that I had once felt so strongly about didn't matter any more.

They, like my wish to succeed as a writer, were buried back at that fucking tree, Nazareth. Everything was encased in a couple of theatrical performances I'd lifted from lame books I'd read as a kid.

If I looked at the world through the eyes of Mariah, someone so unfortunate that she disintegrated like an object, a possession, maybe I could see that any guiding force—such as a finger—had to be better than a stalking predator. Unfortunately, the predator always catches up and slaps you down. If slapping weren't enough, the predator's hands are likely to scrape at your face, rip off your pants, and beat you black and blue. I didn't know Mariah's dad, or stepfather, whoever he was, but I hated him. I hated him just as much as I hated that worthless pederast Rick Conroy.

I tried to force myself to believe that Lori and Mariah were somewhere else, dancing around. Nobody need dance in this world anymore. Hate mongers and hate-fuckers overshadowed the time for festivals and thanksgivings. I mean, not only did Mariah and Lori have nothing to be thankful for; they wouldn't have eaten at the great feast anyway. Stuffing themselves with their families meant something else in their lives. It meant fear. It was a light peering into a dark room. It was a sweaty hand over their mouths and a cock shoved into their asses. Why didn't they say anything? I understand why no one wants to be an outsider. But if only they had said something!

With my missiles waiting to launch, I wanted to pound on something, to empty out the build up inside. I couldn't. I couldn't release. I was buckled in, shouting. Caged. No one wanted to hear. I focused on the priest statue, a broken man without religion or God. Maybe I needed a mentor, an ally. However foolish it sounds, I believed in nothing the bastard once preached, but I believed he, like so many others, suffered the test of time. His God, and his gospel had crumbled.

If everything was so lost, then how can some people place themselves in a constructed fantasy, an unproven paradigm, and find guidance? If God was indeed leading us somewhere, then how come even they, these perfect souls, aren't immune to the poison in God's toilet? That's all it is, was, and will ever be. I could scream and cuss all I wanted to. I could have burned down Rick Conroy's house with his fucking Christmas lights. I could have hunted down Mariah's intruder. It wouldn't have done any good. The statue proved it, shit on like the world, revenged on like those self-absorbed assholes outside who couldn't give a damn about their own heroes and heroines. They were outside. I was in. Their god remained too far out of my reach. From my window view, he didn't look too promising. I wondered what it would feel like to pound cement. So I did.

Later on Tina studied my wrapped hand. "What happened exactly?" Her hand shook her granny ash and it fell on her shoe.

"I don't know. I wasn't thinking at all. I just thought Sandler was being a dick. I swear. It wasn't like I had any idea, or even wanted to have any idea, what happened last night. I thought that she was all right, that the doctors had it under control. I didn't know." I tried to bite at a cuticle. It was a way for me to veil my face and the tears from Tina.

I felt like a total piece of shit. The picture of the stick figures that she had drawn and then her, a stick figure, lying on the floor, motionless was all too much to think about. Seeing a dead body never gets easier on the eyes, it just makes you remember the time you saw one previously. I thought for a split second that I'd killed her.

Kristina put her hand on my shoulder. "I bet Sandler is pissed as shit, but I believe you, D. I know enough about you to also know that you would have never done anything so careless on purpose."

"You got that right, but it still doesn't ease the pain. What's worse, Tina, the pain of death or the pain of life? Sometimes I think the world, our society, is so painful. It's filled with nothing but setbacks, evil, and a complete lack of happiness. We're all so fucked. How did we get here? How did we get to this point?" I felt tears on my cheeks. They were unavoidable. "Why am I in this hospital, expecting some kind of sympathy, when there are people starving in places? There are messed up people all around the world, and for some reason I feel like someone should give two squirts of piss about my issues and the bullshit that I have willingly created with my imagination. It's all so fucking wrong." I was right. I was full of shit. I was selfish, and everything seemed wrong. The world was wrong. God was wrong.

"D, it wasn't your fault. You couldn't have done anything for her."

"Save it." I kicked out my chair and adjourned to my bedroom for the rest of that afternoon. I was no better than the Brittanys of the world, and I had my past to prove it.

+ + +

Later that day, Sandler had words with me. He more or less accepted my apology about the unpleasant episode with Mariah. I was the one who couldn't deal with it. I told him that I wished he had said something to me; that he'd let me know what had happened. It was a communication error provoked by my lack of good judgment. I found out that he had another agenda all together.

"Some of the parents of the girls believe that you might be a threat, D."

I scratched at my bandaged hand. "I don't understand. How am I a threat to anyone?"

"D, you are a male, and you are over twenty. Some feel that you may be filling their heads with evil thoughts. Like, for example, if they were to catch you masturbating in your bedroom."

"Doc, as you know from your past year's dealings with me, my sexual deviance, if you want to go as far as to say that, takes on quite a different form. I was kidding about the nut rags next to my bed."

"I understand that because I'm your doctor. Some of the other patients are underage and shouldn't be exposed to sex talk."

It was payback. After spending years of treating females like shit for my own entertainment, I eventually got tired of it. I had many sexual experiences after having such a catharsis, but I rarely had sex to orgasm. They checked me out when I first got to Prophecy and couldn't find anything physically wrong with my equipment. I could get hard. I just wanted to control another piece of my life. The whole orgasm thing was all part of the façade. I was a fake, and my actions proved that I was only out to please myself at the expense of others. I only loved a few people. I thought not cumming would make for a more satisfying experience for the girls I banged, but it turned out that girls despised my sexual behavior. The whole silly premise, possibly, could be traced back to the fact that I don't ever remember going through puberty or having anyone talk with me about it.

"Anyway, Sandler, that chick, Susan, the one who hangs out sometimes with Brittany—"

"Yes."

"She's fourteen years old and she's got Norplant. So if my language is the issue, I hate to be the one to inform their parents that these kids aren't the angels they appear to be. What about Mariah? Do you know what she was doing, Doc?"

"I know from our private conversations that she was in a lot of pain."

"She was eating parasites out of cat shit. That is completely nuts."

"Don't lie—"

"I'm not lying, Sandler. She invited me in her room and told me about it. She actually thought that she was bulimic. Mariah thought the worms that her sister was bringing her in from her cat's litter box were making her skinny."

He didn't believe me. Although he didn't take his eyes off of mine, and scratched something on a pad on his desk. "Okay, D. I just wanted to give you a heads up. I'm sorry about earlier. I should have been more like a doctor and less like an enforcer. How do you feel about what happened?"

"It's terrible. I saw it coming, though."

He plucked out bits and pieces of my chart and dove into the one I wanted to avoid the most. "Did your voices warn you?"

"Not really, and I told you that I didn't want to talk about that stuff. I'm not ready."

"I think I'm going to agree with you. You need to spend time on your own. Maybe you should write things down."

"This isn't the Psychic Friends Network, Sandler. What do you think these figments of my imagination mean? I remember all the situations vividly, and as far as I can remember, I didn't do anything wrong. They seem like warnings clouding my brain."

"Hmm. Have you thought about asking your parents what they may be?" He reached into my folder. "Do you think that this picture is important?" He held up the crayon drawing of the tree that my mother had given him.

"Nah," I scoffed. "That's just a picture I drew when I was a kid."

"Well, maybe you should think about that. It is possible that your parents have answers for you that you and I couldn't begin to explore."

"That's cool, Doc. Thanks."

"You can go back to the common room, D."

Desperately trying not to look at Mariah's room, I left his office and headed back to the window. Tina was waiting. "So do you want to hear the rest?" I asked her. Something about Sandler's gentle tone left me uneasy.

She smiled. "Wow, for someone who prides himself on secrets, you sure seem to want to open up."

I nodded and took my usual seat on the sill. "You're right, I do want to, Tina. It scares the shit out of me. Have you ever regretted anything so much that you tried to bury it? I mean really bury it?"

"Did you kill somebody and bury him at the beach or something?" she asked.

"I don't mean it that literally, you dumbass. I could have prevented a lot of things from happening. I mean, I can't say that I could have prevented all of the tragedy in the world. I don't have ESP or anything lame like that. I regret many of the behaviors that I took on."

"Everyone does drugs at one point in their lives—"

I cut her off. "My parents haven't."

"Mine have. I used to get high with my mom whenever she came to town."

"That's lame, Tina."

"Well, my mother and I are more like best friends than mother and daughter." I had heard that story one too many times in my life. I will forever hate those hippie-assed parents who think getting high with their kids and letting them do what they want, whenever they want, is the correct way to raise a child. Sure, I got to certain points in the relationship with the general where I got pissed and said shit like, "I'm running away." It was always bullshit. If I ran, he always ran faster.

"Anyway, it was complete decadence," I began. "Friends turned against friends and everybody wanted to be the most macked-out gangster. I know what you're thinking; a bunch of white, East Coast faggots going to school at a country club thinking that they could hold a gun in the ghetto. It's completely stupid. When you're that whacked, you think you're someone other than yourself. It's typical for someone to have money for the first time to think that they are bad shit. Look around. This place is a fucking mess. Everybody wants to be a gangster. These shit-eating little pricks in places like Little Rock with their colored bandanas and full arsenals of hardcore warfare parading around like they grew up in the hood. What a load of shit. Unlike the real hoods of the world, these pampered idiots got their bandanas free when they bought their guns at Wal-Mart."

"I think that I've decided to come clean. At least to myself." I sucked on a butt and glanced at the preacher outside. His one floodlight had conked out, leaving him in darkness. He must have worked extra hard that day. It really didn't matter that he was invisible to the world. When you're too weak to fix what's wrong, you let things spin and pervert. Rather than spend the time to fix things, like a lighter or a pen, you take the easy route and throw away the evidence. Besides, not every toy becomes a collector's item.

CHAPTER SEVEN

The summer after my sophomore year, I took more classes and a job at the college cleaning boats for the influx of professional water-skiers who stayed the summer to sharpen their skills. My newfound friend in drugs had disappeared for the time being. Waking up at six a.m. and working until sundown was rough. Only on the weekends would I practice any raucous activities, and during that three-month rest, alcohol and tobacco were all I could manage. I never liked smoking pot. I did it whenever I was around More-ganja, but it made me bored and tired. Coke, on the other hand, became my thing. Addiction. The summer passed, and before I knew it I found myself picking up More-ganja at the airport. He was stressed from the flight, so he sat in the backseat alone and smoked. After five hours locked up in a Ziploc bag, he needed to fill his lungs with something natural.

"What did you do over the summer, D?" I shrugged without taking my hands off the wheel. "I hung out here and worked around town. I met some of the locals. They didn't seem to mind me like they hate other college kids." Zipping around the rental car tourists who had no idea where they were, we pulled out of the airport onto the highway.

More-ganja puffed away on a fatty and found sarcasm. "Sounds killer. That must have been a blast. I don't see a gun rack in your car yet, you fucking bumpkin. Why didn't you just go home for once? Isn't there some bitch at home who still wants to fuck you?"

"I hate where I come from, Ganja."

"Why? Are you embarrassed or something?"

"Not really, a bunch of bad shit happened there and I won't go back unless I have to. How about you? What did you do? Sit by the pool and get stoned all day?"

"Fuck off, Bird." More-ganja coughed and blew out a mushroom cloud of skunk. His dealer from home didn't hook him up. "After my old man saw my report card and found out that I was on probation, I had to work at one of his development sites. You know, doing construction for sixteen hours a day and shit like that. It sucked cock."

"Ganja, you didn't tell me your grades were all fucked up. What happened?"

He got quiet and fumbled through his pockets for some papers. "That cocksucker Angello happened." Angello. I guess I wasn't the only one he tormented.

"Did he fail you?" I asked.

"Yeah, and so did my Astronomy teacher." He licked the edges of the poorest joint he had ever rolled, looked at it, and then dumped the shake inside back onto his jeans.

"Maybe we should take it easy."

"Shut up, D. Let's hear your little idea." More-ganja had a good memory. I must have mentioned my plan over the phone when he called to get a ride home from the airport.

"Remember last year when I said I had a plan?"

More-ganja, pissed about his inability to roll a good blunt, started sucking away on his homemade tin foil bowl. "Was that the thing about lots of coke? Bunky, you and I must have sucked down about an eight-ball that night."

"It didn't help that we also munched about a handful of ludes as well," I added with a nod. "Yeah. I'm amazed you remember that."

"Hey, bro, I wasn't the one who fell off of my barstool twenty thousand times. Snif's chick, Monica, had to drive you home from the Library. Man, was he pissed, not that he could have gotten a hard-on anyway."

I was too drunk to touch Monica that night, but if Snif ever heard that I tried to kiss her, I wouldn't have been there picking up More-ganja from the airport. I would have been dead. "Eat me; I'm allergic to alcohol."

"God, Bird, that excuse is really old. Why don't you admit

you're a total waste? I can tell that you gained a lot of weight over the summer."

"People in glass houses, Ganja. Not everyone has their little daddy's development business to work for. I bet you were a foreman the entire time."

"Whatever, Bird. That makes a lot of sense. You can rag on my life all you fucking want. I'm not the one who's afraid to ask his dad for help. Let's hear it, Blue Collar Man. Let's hear your little idea."

I calmed down our pissy battle before I got hurt.

My plan was brilliant, at least in my mind. As I'd told More-ganja at the end of the previous year, it involved a lot of coke. That was just the beginning. At Palmbrook, a college filled with the richest of the rich goldbrickers, it made sense to me that to make money and become gods was to create the biggest cocaine ring anyone had ever seen. We all knew that most of the drug dealers in the United States ran their action from our central location, up the coast, then out and ultimately inland. Point A was always a better place to start than point B. Although the big time dealers' tricks and practices weren't our concern, they made us feel connected to something illegally legit. I knew nothing about actually being a dealer, but at our school, it didn't matter.

My plan was flawless; it involved More-ganja and our wealthy, flaky friends: Bunky, Reno, Roast, and Snif, whose parents had recently sold their budget fertilizer company to a big name chemical conglomerate in the coastal farmland area. My plan: everyone would dump in an initial grand into a pot to buy the first shipment of blow. Then, we sell the product and broaden our user base from there. Six-G worth of shmodes was a lot of sniffing, especially since we knew we could empty out the pot in a week. We also knew, judging by the weekend party consumption of the student body, we would have no problem establishing ourselves on campus. Most of the coke residue found around campus was usually left somewhere around Reno, Bunky, or Snif. For the most part, we already had the eyes and ears of the students. They safely came to us or they went into Cracktown and risked their asses with some real gun-packing dealers.

Cracktown, a purgatory, lay outside the town center, the graveyard, and the golf course that surrounded them both. More rotting corpses, lost souls, and gravestones haunted it than did the pristine graveyard, despite all the rich motherfuckers buried there. Fiat Lux it was not. Unlike the structurally sound stucco buildings and palm trees of the campus, the plastic-flowered parks and the high-rent, gold-covered storefronts of the town center, Cracktown was a broken-down pissing hole that reminded me of dilapidated Kudzutown. It was permanently under construction. One of my anthropology teachers told our class that what we called Cracktown was actually the first completely black-run city in America. In fact, it was the first to have an all black government and population. I guessed we could have colonialism to blame for its demise. More likely than anything else, the college sucked the life out of it, and only the money from rich drug addict's mommies and daddies made up for what wasn't selling at the corner liquor store. As if being a trashed crack town wasn't bad enough, it was on the other side of the train tracks that I'd ridden into town my first day of college.

I thought that we could make a kinder, gentler answer to the common drug dealer; we were the faces that the students saw in class. What wasn't to trust?

That night, More-ganja and I briefed the rest of the assholes on the idea. They were hesitant at first about coming up with six grand. That was until More-ganja, crafty bastard, told them the second part of the idea. The school Validine, or identification, was more than just a meal ticket, more than a means of jimmying into someone's locked room; it was also the way for students to purchase their books and other expensive things (such as sunglasses) in the school bookstore.

My preliminary plan was simple. We were going to break into the school's identification office, naturally by jimmying in with our cards, and create a bunch of fake school IDs that would, of course, display our pictures. We would wander daily into the school bookstore and buy a lot of thick, expensive books. Science and math always showed the greatest profit margin. Eventually, over the next week, we would return the books for a cash refund. The most brilliant part of my scheme was that we knew the bookstore gave cash-only refunds, because it was too difficult to un-bill a parent that wasn't there, or in this case, that didn't exist.

Most important, when the bookstore employee swiped the

magnetic strip through the system, it would be charged to some bogus account. For instance, Kevin Vaughn. We had no intention of stealing from any of the other students, so fake accounts were perfect. It existed in their computer, so it wouldn't be detected until the end of the year when the school sent out statements to the parents.

After a week of hard drinking at The Library, we ironed out the details, and we decided to proceed with the plan.

To think that I was wasting my time with English. I should have been a business major. It was ambitious but my overly enthusiastic cockiness was going to get me nowhere. If I had half a brain—not filled with drugs, booze, and lacking food—when I devised my strategy, I would have recognized that my plan was utterly fucking retarded. Nothing ever ran that smoothly.

We were all college students, or at least that's what we told ourselves between flaking classes, shitting on girls, and having pipe dreams about being the Mafia. Since we were fairly well educated, though, we decided to take our little venture from a business angle.

The enormous redneck, Reno Lee, plunged a syringe filled with Jack Daniels and blow into his veins one night and suggested we create a system. Despite his lack of reliability, we decided to put him in charge of the money and money-related activities after he nominated himself. He didn't need money or acceptance; he just wanted all that coke and the glorified illusion that was synonymous with it. Reno grew up treading water behind a father who owned the largest bank in the South, and since no one had the balls to step on his feet when he made a decision, we all hastily thumbed him up. My thumb shook at our stupidity, but who better to watch our coin? No one stole from Reno.

Roast, who was not known for his strength in confrontation, patted Reno on the back and injected, The perfect man for the job. Hear, fucking hear! Roast probably would have rather had the money detail himself because it fit perfectly with his nickname, social image, and flawlessly annoying English. But why argue? We were all pals, right? I'm sure if anyone else's name was thrown into the hat the heir to the hardware throne would most likely have gotten bitchy. Roast fought his wars with unnecessary cut downs and spitting: hence why he described my problems behind my back as "finger sandwiches." To me, it didn't matter if his intentions were harmless, which I'm sure they weren't; he didn't have any tact or remorse when it came to stepping on others. It was a stupid idea to put Reno in charge of our well-being, but if Snif or I handled the money, we would have been accused of theft. From humble backgrounds come thieves.

Roast ended up getting the cake job. He was the clearance guy. He made the call on to whom we sold to and whom we wouldn't. His overcautious nature, which I first witnessed when he sniffed me out before he decided to lump me into the "friend" category, was a great instinct. We weren't afraid of narcs at the school; we all realized any institution that wouldn't pay for any function for students didn't give a fuck about what their students did in their spare time. It was almost as if they enjoyed the stigma of being a party school. That explained why, despite an awesome academic staff and extremely difficult classes, they never made a name for themselves as a top-notch school—and also why they didn't care if their student turnover rate was close to fifty percent.

Roast's second job, and most important to us, was providing us with the necessary packaging for our deliveries. We weren't big on plastic Zip-loc bags. Cracktown methods didn't correspond with the aura that we wanted to create. With our expensive, agreed-upon prices, we needed to make drug dealing flashy and make it seem like we were really providing these spoiled addicts with four-star services. Luckily for him, and I guess us, his father owned that chain of hardware mega-stores and had recently opened a franchise about twenty miles away from school. All Roast had to do was flash his corporate card and pick and choose anything he wanted. He should have picked up a shovel, because he shoveled so much shit into our heads that Helen Keller could have robbed us blind.

We put Bunky and Snif in charge of getting us the product. Bunky had pals all over the country that provided his family with their needs growing up, and Snif, on one of his late night, monthly missions to go dig through cow shit for shrooms, had met a bunch of farmer dealers over on the Pan Handle. The sources seemed reliable; Bunky's more so than Snif's stand-up gang, but we needed a backup resource. We ended up using Snif's guys more regularly, because they didn't cut the coke with as much speed. Besides, it was our job to water down the coke.

Bunky honed his art skills once again to provide us with the mock Validines. Unlike a real driver's license or state identification, the Validine didn't have any holograms or tricky state seals, so they were very easy to replicate. Bunky created a huge piece of poster board, carefully constructing the exact background of the look and feel of the ID with huge rub-on letters and numbers. The technology seems pretty archaic by today's standards, but it worked well before the age of mass computers and Photoshop.

We had all of our pictures and backboards knocked off with an instant camera; they worked great, because we easily peeled the backsides off, giving us a less bulky ID. As it turned out, our little thief friends Snif and Roast broke into the school's I.D. office one night. Their mission was to steal about fifty I.D. backs, program the magnetic swipe strips and log information into the school's dated computer network that corresponded with our fake account. According to them, the job was less risky than we originally thought it to be; Roast spent his summers working in the credit department at his father's store. I'm sure the only problem was Snif using the newly acquired IDs to cut rails while Roast did the account work. Laminating the magnetic backs to the instant photos wasn't a problem either. Roast had stolen a laminator from one of his father's stores when he was in junior high.

More-ganja got the choice job. He was indentured into the "Trustafarian" culture, and had seen Dead shows since the day he was able to shout "Jerry." His job was to be the middleman. He took orders, and made himself visible at parties. If anyone needed anything, like a rush order at a rave or something, he was in charge of the extra kilo or so he had hidden in his room. He was our PR guy and our man on the street.

Regrettably, I got the shit job. My scholarship entailed my working off some of my extraneous loans by assisting in the school post office. Therefore, I was the delivery boy. Given that I had worked there since my freshman year, I had a pretty good rapport with the office manager.

He would rub his belt loop with his gloved hands, sniff around for the smell of booze, and ask, "Why are you late, D? Yesterday, you delivered all the wrong shit to all the wrong boxes. That's your seventh infraction. I'm afraid that you'll be working the nightshift from now on."

And so I'd earned the opportunity to come to work when they were closed, right after the mail was delivered in the evening, and fly solo. "I'm sorry sir." I hung my head in what I hoped. "I deserve the punishment. I won't let you down." It was actually more effective in getting everyone's mail into their boxes before they got up for classes the next morning, and it became standard practice and schedule for the post office for years to come.

The nice, small packaging boxes, which Roast got us in all sorts of different sizes and shapes helped. If I ever got caught, it might have looked like I was delivering gifts to friends. I tried to glorify the situation, but it was still the most risky of the tasks since it involved putting my loyalty to the college, my scholarship, and, well, my escape from Kudzutown on the line, not to mention the possibility of federal charge. My loss of focus and need for acceptance clouded what I would have seen as a daft idea, and one that went against everyone I loved.

Our scheme in the bookstore nearly went sour one day when Reno decided to get coked-up and drunk.

The clerk rushed over to him after he knocked over a kiosk of sunglasses. "Excuse me, sir."

"What the fuck do you want?" Reno looked over to Snif for a wink. Snif headed to the door and left.

"Umm, I believe you're drunk. Could you please come back tomorrow and purchase your books?" Reno said nothing. He passed out in the middle of the store and pissed his pants.

When you find yourself abruptly provided with an artificial security in life, especially after never having it before, you get into a certain groove. Unlike Snif and Roast, who decided it would be a great idea to become as flashy as possible with big-screen TVs and tricked-out car stereos, I decided that a good portion of my share would remain in Reno's hidden pot of money. Sure, I took what I needed—I am, after all, human. But I used that money to buy things like nice dinners for friends and drinks for everyone at The Library. I didn't really need anything else. I just wanted to really live life. I wanted people to know who I was. I wanted to be accepted in a world that under other circumstances rejected me. I finally felt unconnected to Kudzutown.

Since we were in college, it made sense that if we were to continue on this cycle, we would have to keep our grades and schoolwork at an acceptable level—especially since More-ganja had found himself swinging in the hell that is academic probation. First, I apologized to my fraternity brothers and asked for their forgiveness. I really missed a lot of my friends there and, even though Roast advised against it, they provided more bodies for us to feed. I trusted them. My motives weren't all completely earnest, though. They had something we all needed. In the dark basement where Bunky and Cooper and I had spent hell week were two vast filing cabinets that contained previous tests, A-plus papers, and the notes and documents to get us through the year effectively. Of course, these measures didn't ensure good grades, but they did provide most of us, who were always flaky about attending class, with the backbone of what we were supposed to be learning. After I paid the balance of my dues, we were in business.

During my down time, I also helped More-ganja deal with his dyslexia. He was a great writer and also an English major. I sometimes found myself jealous of his incredible ability to create situations and creative spins on characters. It was reading that was his major ordeal. First, we tried *Cliffs Notes*. That didn't work as well as I had expected. Even though Miles could translate plots and dig deep into an author's intentions, his main problem was deciphering what would have been the easiest code of all to everyone else: words on a page.

We decided upon several different means of overcoming this problem with the time we had. One, we watched movies every week on Roast's enormous TV. Two, we bought books on tape. Both of these methods gave us half of what we needed. The books on tape were usually so condensed that any insight was deleted. Similarly, the directors of many novel-to-film translations took liberties with stories to make them plausible to an audience in the era of the big-budget action film. Since my mother had made me read a certain number of classics every summer, such as *Of Mice and Men* and *Huck Finn*, I had the classics covered, maybe too well for More-ganja's own good.

We were lucky. By this point, we had managed to conquer most of the British drivel and the Romantic shit. Don't get me wrong. I'm not justifying my deviance by channeling my good deeds to others. This was a friendship thing and a way for us to continue what we already started.

+ + +

As soon as we had successfully built our drug domain, Snif began coming up with get-rich-quick plans. Somehow, he convinced Bunky to drive More-ganja and me with him out to the Panhandle to pick mushrooms. I hadn't felt well all week. I had a permanent build up of snot and shit stuck in my throat from puking. The closer we got to our destination, the more it smelled like farmland. The reek of the farmland that Snif called home smelled far worse than the smell of Kudzutown.

SNAP!

Snif bit into some chalk. "Why the fuck couldn't Reno and Roast come with us?"

"Reno doesn't like picking through shit," More-ganja answered as he sucked away on some shake from a bat. "And Roast said that it wasn't in his job detail."

Snif sucked some coke off of one of Bunky's CD cases. "Fuck those queers."

Bunky blew through a red light. I most likely would have stopped, seeing as how we were all carrying a couple grams of blow and were really fucked up, but he didn't care. What was one more DUI to him? I felt faint to my surroundings, but my stomach ached like I had eaten a handful of thumbtacks. I was about to embark on a new adventure: the involuntarily barf. I held it in the best I could, but finally mustered, "pullover, Bunky."

He did as he was told, and I crawled to the curb.

"You okay, Bird?" More-ganja yelled from the car. "What the fuck is wrong with him?" he whispered to Snif.

My throat brought up a dry thud as I unleashed an unearthly amount of stomach acid and booze. It foamed, flowed out, and it hurt like a motherfucker. I felt the scratching of the cocaine dragging itself through my esophagus. The barf tried to latch onto skin. The skin felt like a spaghetti noodle caught in the passage.

Bunky jumped out of the driver's seat to help me out at the curb. "Hey, Bird, what's up?"

"Fuck him, Bunky, he's having his faggy problems again," Snif chimed in. I didn't have a comeback for the little farmboy-turned-addict. I couldn't talk. As the acid burned through my lips and my head rotated from the intoxication, I looked at my hand. Blood. A lot of blood.

"Bird, we gotta get you to a doctor, man." The concern in Bunky's voice reminded me of the passion that he showed after Cooper's family's house exploded.

"I said, fuck him. We gotta get to the pasture, pick our shit and get out of there before we get caught. Farmers don't fuck around. Trust me." Snif was far from a friend. His only friend, ally, accomplice was himself.

I swallowed down chunks of shit and throat lining. All that did was make them hang the opposite way down my pipes. "Don't worry about it, Bunky." My problems were bad, really bad. "I think I drank too much."

Snif hopped into the driver's seat and slammed Bunky's door. "Yeah, right, Bird. Why don't you take a trip over to one of the sorority houses and join them bitches as they line up at night to try and knock off that 'freshman fifteen.' C'mon Bunky, let's leave that girly faggot. I gotta meet Monica at the graveyard."

According to Snif's lore, every once and a while he and Monica went out to the graveyard to fuck. I figured the risk of being classified as a necrophile was his way of building up his badass image. What a joke. Anything that involved Snif fucking Monica pissed me off. I spent too much time worrying about her age. I figured that it was better for that shithead to go to jail for statutory than me.

"Just give him a second, Snif, you dick. The kid is sick. We don't have to do this tonight."

"Bullshit we don't. I need money."

I gasped for a little air and tried to loosen up my throat flesh with my tongue to try and break it off. "Fuck you, asshole."

Snif took off his shirt and swung the car door open. "Everybody knows about you, you lush. You're a fucking loser." His wiry frame slithered around as his right index finger massaged the tingling in his nose. "You gotta problem, bitch?" I couldn't beat up Snif. He wasn't intimidating, but I was a total pussy.

My neck collapsed and I banged my front teeth on the cement. "No problem, Snif." I hacked up one last load of whatever it was and got back in the car. My throat spaghetti continued to dangle, but I had no choice but to accept it. I had no idea where I was.

"That's what I thought, faggot."

SNAP!

Snif snapped into a piece of chalk, proclaiming victory by thumping his chest with one fist. I remained quiet for the rest of the ride.

+ + +

There is nothing better to accentuate the feeling of nausea than standing in a cow pasture. I was knee deep in cow shit with a garbage bag half-full of 'shrooms. More-ganja walked over to me.

"You okay, Bird?" he asked again.

"Yeah, I just had to get that shit out. I'm sorry that I threw up in front of you. I'd appreciate it if you didn't beat me up."

"Don't worry. It wasn't your fault. *I'm* about to puke right now." A cow walked by. "Bird, why are we doing this?"

Snif yelled across the pasture. "Hey, faggots, get back to work."

"Why? Are you late for a Def Leppard concert?" More-ganja yelled back.

"What the fuck is that supposed to mean?" Snif held up his arm, which was covered in cow dung up to his elbow, to show off a machete.

More-ganja pointed at the pants. "You know what it means, farmboy. Look at those jeans." I laughed to myself. Snif's jeans were torn into hundreds of slits from top to bottom. Sadly, the rips weren't from wear, he bought them that way. "Yee haw."

Humbled, Snif went back to the pile of shit he was working

on. "Just work, dick."

"Nice." I whispered to More-ganja. "That'll shut his ass up for a while."

"We should leave him out here. You know, with his people, D."

"What's his problem with me, anyway?"

"He thinks you want to fuck Monica."

"Well, I do. I'm never going to admit it to him, though."

"I think she told him you asked her out on a date or something."

"Fuck him. I hate that kid. I hate the way he looks at me without saying anything."

From about fifty yards away, Bunky started humming and making guitar noises. I didn't think he heard More-ganja making fun of Snif, but apparently he had. I looked at him and bit my lower lip.

When he got to a part of the song that I knew, I nudged More-ganja and started singing, *"take a bottle."*

Bunky shot me a thumbs up, and, almost unable to control his laughter, he shook his hips. *"Shake it up."* The camouflage waders he was wearing started to slip down his body.

I smiled at More-ganja. He had no idea what was going on. I avoided looking at Snif, but I felt his machete aimed at my back. *"Break the bubble,"* I sang.

More-ganja scratched shit onto his cheek. "What are you guys doing?"

"It's 'Pour Some Sugar on Me' by Def Leppard," I said.

He looked at Bunky, then back to Snif's jeans. "Oh shit, wait a minute." He stretched and bent backwards and used a huge spore as a microphone. *"Break it uuuuuuuuuuuuuuuup."*

The three of us, now laughing hysterically, all sang together. *"Pour some sugar on me. Ooh, in the name of love."* More-ganja grabbed my arm and we started square dancing around the cow. We made crazy hillbilly faces at each other. *"Pour some sugar on me. C'mon fire me up."* Bunky fell over into a huge pile of crap. He was laughing so hard that he didn't even notice that his waders were around his ankles and he had shit all over his face. *"Pour your sugar on me, oh, I can't get enough."* We were screaming at the tops of our lungs, not realizing how loud we were being.

"Shut the fuck up!" Snif threw the machete into the ground

and started walking toward us.

I looked him directly in the eyes and grabbed the large spore from More-ganja. *"I'm hot, sticky sweet. From my head to my feet. Yeah."*

Bunky got to his feet and began pulling up his waders.

Snif yelled again. "Shut the fuck up, pussy."

"Hey! What are you doing?" The ceremony ended abruptly. Everyone went quiet. I saw a flashlight shine on Bunky.

"Run!" More-ganja grabbed my bag of shrooms and chucked it at the cow.

I grabbed his shirt and threw him to the ground. "Maybe no one saw us. Look." Bunky frantically tried to run, but his hip waders tripped him and he twisted his ankle. I looked around; Snif had already taken off. "Just stay down." By the time Bunky got to his knees, a farmer was standing over him with a shotgun aimed at his head. More-ganja vomited into the mountain of shit in front of us. I did the same.

"What are you doing out here, son?" The farmer aimed his gun steadily at Bunky's head. Then, seeing Snif running in the distance, the farmer fired at him. Snif just ran. The bullet missed him. "I asked you a question, son. What are you doing here on my land?"

More-ganja was shivered. "Dude, we're so fucked. What if we die out here?"

"We aren't gonna die. Relax. Keep your head down." I vomited again and buried my head in the shit.

"Umm, I'm looking for my dog," Bunky's voice quivered. "He's lost." I looked up. Bunky was on his knees with the farmer's gun in his mouth. All of a sudden, the cow shit in my mouth didn't taste so bad. More-ganja inched down further. He grabbed onto the back of my pants as if he were going to grab me to flee.

The farmer pulled back his gun. "What's the dog's name, son?"

Bunky looked in our direction. My heart sped up and More-ganja was almost crying. "My dog's name is Bunky."

The farmer looked down at the two bags of 'shrooms next to Bunky. "Come with me, son."

+ + +

Bunky was arrested for trespassing and attempting to distribute illegal drugs. Luckily, the farmer only saw Snif flee the scene, so he figured they were the only two out there. Moreganja and I cleaned off in a lake and Roast picked us up the next day.

In Bunky's absence, Snif held a dangerous new level of control over the group. He had brought in all of the coke through his connections, and that made him the top dog. It sucked. Reckless by nature and often forgetful, Snif ended up doing us more harm than good. When he forgot to go on a run, a pissed off Reno would jump in his jacked-up pick up and drive through Cracktown. *Better him than me,* I always thought. Of course, thinking like this was a negative sign that we were starting to fall apart as a unit. Snif was always involved with his own personal dilemmas. His time was consumed by either mentally or physically abusing Monica, or locking himself in a room with a glass table for fourteen-hour coke binges. He was more lost and belligerent than ever. Constant kicks to me like, "Fuck you, pussy, why don't you do something?" and "Whatever, girl," didn't help me in making any decision other than to detest him.

The hardware heir, Roast, had also fallen out of the loop. He and Bunky were always in the drug dealing together, because they went to reform school together. With Bunky gone, Roast started to get lazy about coming through with the packages he stole from his father's store.

"Ahem. Why don't you go get it?" he asked when we were struggling to make a deal go through. "It's not your butt on the line. What if my dad decides to check my account?"

"What are you talking about?" I returned. "All the boxes are free; they're shipping boxes." The boxes that we used were what his father's company had sitting in some garbage room waiting to be recycled. Third-party companies sent screws and nails in them. Roast's Hardware was the home of the scoop-a-bulk full of nails, screws, and fasteners. If his father hadn't created buying product in bulk, we might never have been able to buy three hundred pounds of granola and gummi bears at the grocery store.

Roast lashed out because he knew reform school wasn't the place for him. "Ahem. Whatever, Dirtybird. Your ass isn't on the line."

"What are you talking about, Roast? Mine's on the line the most. I'm totally fucked if I get caught. I'm the one actually dealing the drugs, asshole. Unlike you, I choose not to show it off to everyone."

"Would you queers mellow out?" More-Ganja unleashed a huge fog of smoke. "It isn't Bird's fault. Everybody's fucking up. Reno, why don't you just tell us where the money is and we'll stop doing this shit."

Reno was reluctant to let go. He licked his finger and dragged it across his scar. "Fuck off, Pussy. We ain't quittin' nuthin'!" He liked the fact that he decided the fate of our corporation. He knew where the money was, and we didn't. None of us had the balls to ask him where he hid it. I had a suspicion that his plan was to take all of the money when we were finished and bolt anyway.

"Roast, just do your part of it man," I recommended nicely. Snif sat in the background, veiled by More-ganja's smoke and ticked out little giggles as we argued.

"Ahem. Whatever! You can just get your damn boxes yourself and take your wannabe drug dealing nonsense and shove it up your faggot asses. I'm not failing out with you jerks. I need to go back to school. Isn't that why we're here?" He looked at me, maybe because I was the least threatening of the group. "Huh, Bird? You're the one who brags so much about being such a great writer. Oh, the author, the poet. What are you gonna write about if we get busted? Huh? Getting a covered wagon in jail?" Roast felt free to pass back an expression that I had given him. A "covered wagon" was having your teeth punched out in jail and then being forced to orally pleasure the inmates in your cell. It happened after the inmates fixed the mattresses upright to cover the sides of the bottom bunk. "What about you More-ganja? Findley told me your grades aren't improving. What the hell? You've got Bird to read you to sleep at night. Read any good alphabets lately?"

"Whatever, asshole." More-ganja never showed it, but Roast's words were a body blow. Whether or not the story about Findley, our shared advisor, was true, Roast had crossed the line like he had so many times with me.

Roast continued to rant. "Ahem. You're all a bunch of losers. Snif, do you think that when you get your face out of the snow you can come pick up all of your crap over at my house?" Snif looked up for a second and acknowledged him with a salute. Roast didn't make eye contact with Reno; that would have ended in certain tragedy. "Hey, I have an idea. Why don't you call me when you guys decide to quit playing gangster?" He grabbed his backpack and shoved his way past me.

"Hey," Reno grunted.

"Yeah," Roast replied, not looking at Reno.

"I fucked your girlfriend." And that was that. Roast was gone. Even though we laughed at the pussy way he left, it unnerved me. I was becoming uneasy about us losing cohesion at a dreadfully brisk rate. Roast, despite his abrasive arrows aimed toward me at all times, was the smartest of the group. I never saw him again.

It turned out that all we had to do was go and ask the manager at the hardware store if we could have the boxes.

+ + +

I was in the mailroom later than usual one night when I came across a name on a package that I didn't recognize. "Who the fuck is this package for?" Apparently, More-ganja had taken in a new client and had either forgotten to share it with us or he was hiding something. I guessed the latter.

After I finished up, I met More-ganja in his room and asked him about it. "Hey, Ganja, there was this weird package delivery into a nameless box. Did you bring on someone new?"

"Ah," he hesitated. "No." He sucked on his bong, and his eyes slowly peered up and looked to see if I was buying his lie.

"Well, great asshole, then I have to go back and get it. It looked like two eight balls. If we don't get that back we're busted."

"Why don't you just let it be, D?" he snapped.

"Dude, what in the hell is wrong with you? I know you know whose package that was. I guess I better go ask Reno and Snif." Pushing More-ganja with threats of feeding him to the lions would get a quick answer. He jumped up and grabbed me by the shirt.

"Don't, asshole. I paid for it. Relax!"

"I don't care who paid for it; I delivered it. Who was it for?"

"It was for Angello, D."

"Are you fucking insane, asshole? Are you trying to get us all thrown in jail? That motherfucker hates my ass."

He tried calming me down. "Shhh. Relax. It's gonna be cool. That prick said he was gonna flunk me unless I gave him some blow."

"How regularly, Ganja? You have to cut this deal off. That guy will take us down in a second. Jesus, if Reno and Snif find out about this, we're as good as dead."

"He's cool about it. I've done shmodes with him a bunch of times in his office. He's got this Conan Doyle thing going on. It's kind of freaky. Look at his fucking teeth man. Are you telling me that you never suspected that he was a coke freak?" Morgan justified his actions to himself. My flesh crawled.

"Good job. I can't believe this."

"Bird, how many times have I told you that I *have* to graduate? I'm on probation, man, and this is my last chance. I'm doing well enough in all of my other classes. He was the only loose end."

"It looks like you just opened up a bunch of new loose ends. Dude, I can't believe you just had me deliver, in the school's post office, where I work, for my scholarship, drugs to a teacher. Are you that disabled? Maybe you should lay off the pipe and get your fucking head straight. That way you might be able to read a sentence that doesn't look like hieroglyphics."

More-ganja smashed his bong against the wall and bum-rushed me with the intention of ripping my voice box out. "Take that back, asshole." He pinned me to the ground with his strong right forearm as he bitch slapped me with his wrist. Over and over he pounded on my face. "Take it back!"

"What the fuck?" Reno Lee kicked the door open. I couldn't see anything because the impact of my head hitting his glass coffee table caused blood to roll down into my eyes, but I knew his voice. More-ganja didn't want to let go. At the risk of Lee discovering his deal with Angello, he hyperventilated as he beat away.

"Reno! Get this dipshit off of me!" I whimpered. I was no match for More-ganja's power punches. They were as lethal as *Of Mice and Men*'s Lennie Small petting a puppy.

"Forget it, boy. It's about time you learned to fight your own battles. I ain't your momma." With that, More-ganja stopped his barrage and left the room. I don't think he intended to hurt me. I pieced myself back together. My head was split open and gushing.

Unsympathetically, Reno picked me up by my torn shirt. "What was that all about?" he asked. More-ganja deserved to be ratted out for making such a poor decision, but I didn't want Reno to kill him.

"I just said a bunch of stupid shit about his dad. I'm pretty drunk, Reno. Can you drive me to the emergency room?"

"No problem, faggot."

"Why are you here? I thought you and Snif were going to the shore for a shipment."

"The deal didn't go through. Snif's little farm boys fucked us over again. I came by to drop this off for Ganja." Reno dropped a vial of rock on the broken table.

"All of you dumbasses are smoking crack, aren't you, Reno?"

Reno smirked and threw me over his shoulder. "Wasn't obvious enough for you, was it?"

The ride to the emergency room was silent except for the blaring Hank Jr. that I believe must have come standard when Reno purchased his pickup.

Reno spoke as he knocked back some whiskey from the flask that perpetually filled his center console. "You want to know something funny, fagboy?"

"If it's about all of you dipshits losing your minds and totally putting my neck on the line, no."

"Whatever, Sissybird. You'll think this is funny."

"All right then," I agreed.

"You want to know where I hide the money?"

"I don't think that it's a real good idea that you tell me. No." I never wanted the money to begin with.

"I bury it out at that graveyard next to that nice old grave. You know, that old lady."

"Audrey Littlebury Rowe?" I scoffed.

"Yeah, that's her. How do you know that?"

"Have you ever heard of the Rowe Student Center on campus, Reno? She donated it."

"No shit. Goddamn is that funny. I think it's also the grave where Snif fucks Monica."

"What? You're kidding me. Now that's funny. He's been going nuts for almost a year trying to find out where that money is, and the entire time it's buried right beneath him." I tried not to laugh. My face hurt too badly.

"D, your head looks okay, but I have another question for you," the doctor said as he re-entered the room that I had been waiting in for two hours after Reno carried me in.

"What would that be, sir?"

"Judging from your blood sample, there's something wrong with your hormones. You have the lowest blood pressure I think I have ever seen for someone your age, you're underweight, your heart is exhibiting palpitation, you're dehydrated, and you have a vitamin deficiency. It doesn't add up. When was the last time you saw a doctor?"

"Good question. I don't know. Maybe about five years ago. I'm not real big on doctors unless someone beats me up, sir; hence why I'm here tonight." I tried to play it cool. The last thing I needed was to get busted for the barfarama.

"Would you like to tell me what's going on, D?"

"Not really; I feel great." My stomach burned. I felt blood, not from my brawl with More-ganja, trickle out of the side of my lip. I looked up slowly at the doctor. He wasn't looking at me. I wiped up the evidence.

"Ah ha," he said, "Your file says that you were seeing a therapist around town for," he turned toward me. "Bulimia?" The jig was up. "Is your current state a result of this? Are you experiencing a relapse?" Relapse? I didn't want to ruin the doctor's day, but I never quit.

"No, sir. That's out of my life. It was a mistake."

"Well, I think it's a good idea that we keep you here overnight and give you some nutrients intravenously."

"You mean like an IV?"

"Yes, D. I'll tell your friend, Mr. Lee, that you'll be staying here tonight." I hated IVs. They scared the shit out of me. They reminded me of Lori Conroy and the Bay Bridge.

The next day, I apologized to More-ganja, and he did the same to me. When I asked him about the crack, he assured me that it was only something he had dabbled in a few times and didn't really like. I decided to keep the secret of the delivery to Angello from Reno and Snif. It seemed like More-ganja had the situation under control. Maybe it would have been smarter for me to do the same thing instead of pissing around corners to keep my head above water in his class. I assumed that as long as More-ganja got off probation and his head back into a school, we would be all set for our climactic senior year.

On the final day of our junior year, I went to say my goodbyes to everyone. Reno's house happened to be my first stop. "Hey, Reno, what are you doing tonight?" He pounded away on a punching bag. Reno was huge. It was cool watching him beat shit up, even though I knew most of the fables about him were untrue. His body was thick. I don't mean that he was fat; he wasn't at all. He was just a six-foot tall mass of a human. As he pummeled the insides out of the bag, his dog, Rebel tore at his shoe.

"Don't know, boy. I figured that maybe you me and More G could go out somewhere. Get shitty frunk and try and fuck some hogs."

"What the hell is frunk, Reno?"

"Fucked up drunk, boy. Besides More-ganja needs some cheerin' up."

"Why is that?" I asked.

Reno stopped, shot me a confused look and scraped his sweaty hair out of his eyes with his forearm. "You pussy. He had trouble with one of them teachers of his. You know, that same cocksucker who flagged him last year."

I asked, even though I knew the answer. "Angello?"

"I think he went to the Dean's office to try and get an incomplete in the class so he wouldn't fail out."

"Fail out!"

"Yeah, boy, that's what they do to you when you're on probation."

"Why didn't he tell me any of this?"

Reno shrugged. "Don't know. Maybe he felt bad because you spent so much time licking his wounds and trying to help him out. That's your problem, pussy. More-ganja's a crackhead."

"Reno, please tell me you're fucking around."

He didn't look at me. "No way, boy."

It was time for me to come clean about More-ganja and Angello's arrangement. "Reno, he was hooking Angello up with a few eightballs every week. There is no way he was going to flunk him."

Reno bit into his finger, licked it and dragged it across his scar. "How do you know that?" His eyes reddened in anger. He gripped onto what was left of the fifty-pound bag, getting ready to unchain his madness. His fingernails dug through the tough vinyl cover, and the contents spilled out and mixed with oil on the floor of his garage. Rebel ran away.

"Who delivers the drugs, Reno? Dammit, why aren't you with him? Why didn't you tell me right when I got here? What the fuck is wrong with you?"

"This isn't my fault, asshole. Get out of here. Go run to your little girlfriend. Tell him I'm going to beat the living piss out of him to for being a fucking dipshit."

We were all fucked. Why did he do it? Why did he have to jeopardize everything? Shit. As I made my way down the block, I heard Reno rip his bag out of the ceiling and attack it. He screamed ferociously. If Angello hadn't gotten to More-ganja yet, then Reno sure as hell would soon.

It took me about ten minutes to get to More-ganja's house. Everything looked normal. He wasn't known for his cleanliness, so the fact that his room was totally trashed didn't bother me. I looked to the broken table with one sharp edge of glass in the corner with a few cut-up rails on it. Normal. The bong tipped over with water drenching and stinking up the carpet. Careless, but normal. A couple of tapestries with about twenty darts thrown at a picture of Angello from the yearbook. Not good. Suddenly, More-ganja's neighbor blasted through the door.

"Who are you?" he asked.

"I'm D. I'm a friend of More-ganja's."

"Good God, son, open the frigging garage."

"Huh?"

"There's a fire or something in the garage." Both of us ran into the garage. It was filled with a smoke so dense I couldn't breathe. We looked but couldn't see any fire. I cuffed my face under the collar of my shirt and looked around for the garage door button.

"Cover your face, D. The car is running." As certain aspects of what we were witnessing abruptly became clear, I found the button. Slowly, the door opened and smoke sashayed out into the dusk. Light blew little holes in the smoke, and I made out a body near the rear of the car.

"Over there," I pointed to the neighbor as I coughed and vomited on my chest. The neighbor knelt down.

"Call a paramedic, D. Call now!" He began coughing. I froze. As more and more of the smoke filtered out, I saw More-ganja. He was lying on a pillow with his face planted directly in front of his car's exhaust. His bottom lip was stretched and melted onto the bottom of the tailpipe. The weight of his skull tugged at the lip, but that didn't rip the skin from the metal of the pipe.

Another friend was dead.

I learned later, as I'd figured at Reno's house, the dean had dismissed More-ganja's plea for one last-chance probation or an incomplete in Angello's class.

Unlike many of the disturbances that I had somehow survived over the past couple of years, such as Cooper's family's loss and Bunky getting busted, this one was preventable. The neighbor turned off the ignition and picked the body up, carrying it out to the yard.

CHAPTER EIGHT

I peered through the window of Prophecy Hospital as nightfall frocked the priest's statue. At his feet lay the faithless and faceless vagrant. He wasn't praying. Some scaffolding on the statue's head prevented snow from falling onto the bum below. Prophecy's crack painting team may have been touching up the enormous iron cross on the Prophecy sign. Crosses were easy to paint out of the picture and left to dry. Like the vagrant, they didn't have faces anymore, either.

"Hey guys, I could use a little paint down here," I giggled to myself, emulating the priest statue. Kristina, my personal shrink, interrupted my short attempt at cheering myself up.

"So did you guys get busted finally or what? God, that Angello was an asshole."

"No, we didn't get busted, Tina. I guess Angello decided to blackmail More-ganja rather than live up to his side of the deal. He didn't know anyone else was involved. He probably thought Ganja got the coke from Cracktown, snorted down all of the leftover rails, and forgot about the whole thing. But, just like I figured, More-ganja, Reno, and Snif were smoking a shitload of crack. When they did the autopsy on Ganja they said he had even more rock in him than an overdosed cop killer'd had the night before. It wasn't looking too good."

"Well?"

"Well, what, Tina?"

"What happened next? Did your buddy Gambler—"

"His name was Reno."

"Yeah, yeah. Did he kill Angello or something?"

"No. Even though I told Reno and Snif what went down between More-ganja and Angello, they probably didn't care. No money was missing, no one was wise to our dealings, and More-ganja was gone. That's all they understood."

"And so, in spite of the fact that you understood what you were doing was wrong, you decided to lay low, cleaning boats or whatever, around town. What the hell is wrong with you?" Her motherly tone cracked at my shell. I wasn't a hero and I longer held my head above others because I was just as bad, maybe worse, than those I had condemned in Kudzutown.

"It wasn't quite that simple, Tina."

"Why? Because you had to bury another friend? I'm sure you got over that just as soon as you had another shipment of coke. Aren't you fucking great?"

"No, I didn't bury More-ganja. I didn't go to his funeral because his parents buried him near their estate and didn't even know I existed. I was invisible to them, just like we were both invisible to everyone else at school."

"You are such a selfish prick, D. Do you think that you deserve any sympathy? No matter how fucked up you are, you were driving the car that plunged one of your best friends to his death." I grasped at my temples, trying not to remember the sight in the garage.

"I told you that I hated myself for what happened. I'm not here because I want sympathy. I'm not here because I fell apart after I witnessed More-ganja's death. This shit, these situations, they didn't start at college."

She raised her voice. "What a load of shit. The drug dealing was your idea. You were the instigator, not the victim."

"I know what I was. I know who I am. I just wanted us both to find what we wanted. Even if it meant aligning ourselves with dangerous fucking people."

"What was that? Drugs? Popularity? Oh my God. That's the most pitifully romantic set of ideals and dreams I've ever heard. But in a way," she pretended to fiddle with a contact lens in her right eye, "I understand."

"I don't want you to understand. I'm only telling you all of this because I want to understand it myself, and because I want to get it off of my chest. When I say the story didn't begin here, I mean it. I don't know what my reality is, because I side step through life following voices and memories that don't exist anymore. I can't follow what I hear and see because I know the afflictions of the world firsthand. I think that I'm a toilet that sucks up everyone's misfortune." I grabbed on to my index finger and crushed it. Blood popped out of the cuticle. "I don't have enough sense anymore to tell them to fuck off. I can't see beyond that gate outside anymore. I'm dead." I inhaled, and it became increasingly difficult for me to communicate without falling in and out of sadness. I was lost, and when you're lost in paradise, a poor man's version of fame looks a lot better than a busted up old paper mill and a dead tree.

For the first time since we met each other, Tina bent over to grab something other than a cigarette. She grabbed me. "It's okay, D. You're not dead."

+ + +

When I entered Dean Adam's tidy office, she pointed me to a seat. "I'm sorry about the death of your friend, D." The Dean never had the time to tend to any one student, so it seemed appropriate for her to cut right to the business at hand.

"Why? You didn't kill him," I said, still smelling More-ganja's carbon monoxide tomb.

"That's not why you are here, D."

"I got the feeling that this wasn't a sympathy visit. How did you know that More—Miles—and I were friends?"

"You share the same advisor. Professor Findley told me that Miles always had nice things to say about you. Findley is also very worried about your health."

I leaned back and rolled my eyes. "Here we go again."

"Your grades are unacceptable. I'm afraid I have to put you on academic probation going into your senior year."

"I figured as much." I picked and pulled at my cuticles to try to create motion that would divert her from my condition. "Listen, Dean Adams, I know I've let my grades slip."

She interrupted. "I think there is more than that, and I have decided that since you have not stayed true to your promise to me, I have to make your parents aware of the problems involved here."

"Wait a minute, Dean, we had a bargain. You weren't going to say anything if I stayed on top of it. Besides, I've stayed here every summer to take classes. I'm going to graduate next winter."

"True, your credits add up, but if you fail one more class, you're out. You haven't made any progress with your problem, anyway. Have you seen yourself lately? You look twice as bad as you did then. I mean, listen to this." She tapped a file on her crossed legs as she read back the analysis of my former therapist. "D and his friend Casey showed up to sessions late, both smelling of alcohol. They made jokes at my expense and pretend to fall asleep in the laps of other patients in the waiting room. On one occasion, the two called me 'Mr. Munch,' danced around my office, and then instigated fights with each other, knocking things over." She pushed the file over to me on her clean desk. "Take a look?"

"No, that's okay," I said. If the tone of the conversation wasn't so serious, I might have laughed, remembering Cooper's and my antics. You see, Mr. Munch was the drummer and leader of Chuck E. Cheese's backup band, "The Make-Believe Band." Munch was this big, hairy blue guy. My therapist resembled him.

"I don't really think that this is funny at all. The only reason I overlooked these negative notes then was because you managed to pull off decent grades your freshman year. Since then, it's been nothing but downhill. You're failing out, D, and I have no choice but to alert your parents to your health issues. Listen to this. 'D seemed to be proud of his addiction referring to it as a triple-threat or an inning.'" She looked up at me. "What do these things mean?"

"A triple threat is like three strikes, a complete fucking cleansing." I rambled and she shot me a blank stare. "It's when you piss, shit, and barf all at the same time. What do you know about it, anyway?"

"I don't know anything about it, D, and I would prefer if you didn't use profane language in my office."

"Then how do you know that there are health issues? Even if Miles did express his concerns to someone, my advisor, for example, I know that Findley never passed that information on to you. He thinks you want to fire him. He's what you call the 'old guard.'"

"Well, someone did, D."

"So, now you're going to take it upon yourself to be my lifesaver and completely smash me in front of my parents. Didn't I tell you before that my parents are going through a hard time right now?" She closed the file and rolled her eyes.

"I just got off the phone with your father; he doesn't seem to be going through any type of personal struggle. He is a very reasonable man." I couldn't rely on the fact that my father was laid off from the paper mill any longer. His consulting job had turned into a fulltime gig and my parents were doing fine.

"Dean, you already told him?"

"No, that's your job." All I had to do was lay low and clean up my act over the summer. The general never had to know the intricacies of my private life, my eating disorder, my drugs, my drinking.

"No problem, Dean Adams," I said, trying to act like I had learned my lesson. "I'll go back to my room and call him. Wow, this is going to be a tough summer."

"I don't think that's the way it's going to work this time." She turned the monitor to her computer around and tapped it flat-handedly. "Your father informed me that your phone has been turned off. He blames himself for not providing you with the money to keep in close contact with them. You're going to write him a letter now. He is waiting by his fax machine at work for your transcript, which I promised him I would send after our conversation." I was trapped. Dean Adams had played me from the second I walked in to her office and let me fall right in. She knew that I was going to try and take advantage of her, and she was prepared. I mumbled under my breath as I scratched uncomfortably at my chest with my thumb. Suddenly, I felt an alien bulge in my front pocket.

"Let me ask you a question, D. Why do you do it? I mean, why do you harm your body like that?"

"Have you ever felt like you've had your body overhauled with a long, steel pipe and a couple flasks of acid?"

"No, I can't say that I have." The youthfulness of the dean came out in her disgusted face. She couldn't have been more than ten years older than me. "But I can tell you that I wouldn't like it."

"You'd be surprised," I said. "It's actually quite a refreshing experience." She handed me her keyboard. "No thanks. I'll write it freehand." The protrusion in my pocket was the pen of my best friend from Kudzutown, college-bound Freddy Brubaker. I didn't remember placing it there, but I was glad to have him with me at that moment. I wrote then what was to be the letter that I'd dreaded writing since I started on my crusade, my confession that I wasn't as strong or as bold as the general. Sweat built up under my flaming skin. At times like that I needed to purge—the times when I knew I couldn't. This was the letter that I figured he had been waiting for my entire life.

A few days later, the general picked me up at the airport. I didn't want to talk. Instead, I covered my body with my backpack and silently sat riding shotgun in the general's tank. He'd never been big on words, especially when disappointed. I'd seen it when my brother returned from his war, defeated, and I saw it then. The ride from the airport began completely silent. If the circumstances were different, I suppose we would have had a lot to talk about since I had seen him three years earlier.

"It doesn't look like you cut your hair in a long time, son," he finally mumbled. "You look like a girl." After that, I knew that my fall from grace wasn't going to be easy. My father had hated men with long hair ever since his experiences in Vietnam.

"Yeah, I know." I didn't come out fighting. The odds weren't in my favor and any sign of lip would be instantly fattened.

"Your mother hasn't been doing too well, so I told her that you were coming to visit her today."

"She knows?"

"Yes, I told her. She said that it has something to do with all of those strange broads you were with in high school."

I tried to occupy myself with what had changed in the world I had escaped from years earlier by diverting my attention out of the passenger side window. The general didn't know exactly what had happened to Lori Conroy and I wanted to be sure that all of the blame lay on my shoulders. Like when my brother and his wife had their kid, I didn't want anyone to point the finger at someone who was innocent. I wasn't interested in the hurtful memories outside, but they seemed a hell of a lot more inviting than any eye contact with the general, who I could tell, after receiving an abridged file of my life over the past three years, was pissed off.

Kudzutown was the same shit I'd left, but the town was banking on the quick-forming Resurrection Ministry and its flamboyant leader, Reverend Jackson Christopher. Although we didn't pass through the immediate area of the crimes against my youth, the influence had overflowed onto the outskirts like an airborne black plague preying on anything that lived. Houses were boarded up. People were coughing on their dogs as they walked them through their own shit on shoestring collars. More and more businesses were closed, and shopkeepers loitered outside their once semi-prosperous enterprises, begging alongside the same lawless vagabonds they once swept away from their storefront sidewalks with the night's cigarette butts. A combination of new odors replaced the smell of the pelt, finally cleansed from the air. It was, as I had feared, an expired land, one of your god's toilets. I came from a place just like Cracktown.

"Is it because you like to eat and you don't like to gain weight?" the general quizzed. He tried to understand. Behind the mound of his body and what he had been trained to know, he also had a side that resembled normal human compassion. I feared his stare like Roast feared Reno's. His voice overpowered the oldies radio station that he kept programmed on his radio dial. It reminded me to hold it together and not let my guard down. Sure, it wasn't playing taps, but at that moment "Little Deuce Coup" sounded no better. I didn't want to beg for forgiveness by showing weakness.

"Yeah, it's something like that," I said very softly. The general acted remarkably composed for someone who just saw his son's dreams nearly flushed down the shitter. His first reaction to my brother's debacle was anger. I continued to look around outside the glass. I wanted to explode, release, but it didn't seem justified, because I didn't know if I was feeling sorry for myself or absorbing the pain of my home.

"It's going to be all right, D," he said reassuringly. "We can get through this together. Men don't have this problem."

"I know, Dad. I don't know what I've been thinking." I felt bad. I hadn't told the complete truth about why I was returning home a broken and dishonorably discharged grunt. Telling him that I dealt drugs to a bunch of egocentric rich kids was probably a more suitable indictment than the one Dean Adams forced me to expose, but I stayed true to my silent comrades at Palmbrook. Maybe, at least for an instant, I wanted to reconcile the bad I had created for myself. That night the three of us sat in my parents' place and attempted to come to terms with my problem.

We decided conclusively that I would seek help at the Prophecy Center for Eating Disorders as an outpatient over the summer and go to summer school at the local community college to make up for some lost schooling before returning to Palmbrook for my last semester. My mother had heard about Prophecy's success rate from the personal physician that had been helping her deal with cancer that year. I was surprised at the one-day turnaround at which they came to this solution. It didn't involve me in any group therapy, which I feared. Mostly, my punishment was seeing a nutritionist every week. It was the least that I could do. I hated what I had become. I was a liar and a failure. With so many issues still unresolved back at Palmbrook, however, I knew that Prophecy was my only choice.

Prophecy hospital was a stale dump downtown, across the bridge from Kudzutown. White walls and the smell of Ajax overpowered the old charm of a hospital that served a purpose. Or at least, one that had before the respected University down the street stole Prophecy's thunder. The old hospital became a jail for addicts. Ironically, I was listening to Howard Stern on my way in one first day. He was talking about Karen Carpenter. According to him, Carpenter died after she quit using laxatives. She couldn't survive the tolerance she built up and her body turned off.

My nutritionist's name was DeeDee. She worked as an intern at Prophecy hospital. In a strange way, I found her optimistic funk amusing. On the other hand, an hour a week of her high-pitched voice was enough to drain the power out of a nuclear plant.

"Let's get on the scale, D-ster," she sang in a spunky tune.

"Your progress is awesome, dude." I got flushed. DeeDee was only a few years older than me and her attempts to be hip and fresh offended my intelligence. At least she meant well. While I was on the scale she picked at my hair. "What is up with this dude? You need to comb out these dreadlocks. Are you Jamaican, Mon?"

"No. I just don't wash my hair," I said to get her hands off of me.

"Ewwwwwwwwwwww! Okay, step on down, D. Well, whatever makes you happy. Ha. That's funny, just like that reggae song. You know the one, "Don't worry. Be happy," she sang as she opened her hospital-issue garb to reveal a heinous shirt with a big smiling face on it covered with big badge-like pins displaying flimsy messages such as, "word up," and "wild thang."

Laughing subtly, I shook my head in disgust. "I'm not too sure that's really considered a reggae song, DeeDee."

"Well, 'excuuuuuuuuuse me,'" she screamed, bobbing her head and sticking her tongue out at me. It was incredible; she was like a walking one-liner, a catch-phrase doll that had its cord ripped out and was left speaking in horribly dated clichés. We sat down in Sandler's office, and she checked away at my chart.

"Everything looks good, and you, my friend, are getting right back on course."

"DeeDee, I think that still remains to be seen. I have two and a half long months ahead of me."

"If it were up to me, D-ster, you'd be going back to school tomorrow."

"Ahem. It's not up to you, DeeDee. You can go now." As the childish intern left Sandler's office, she turned around, crossed her eyes, and made a monster face. "That will be all, DeeDee." The door slammed shut by a button Dr. Sandler controlled under his desk.

"Yes, sir," DeeDee humbly whispered back from behind the door. I glared into Dr. Sandler's icy eyes; my reflection was all I could see. It was the first time we had met.

"She was just trying to cheer me up, doctor," I began. "From the looks of this place, I could use it."

"Why? How does the hospital make you feel?" He opened a new pack of pens and began writing.

"I don't know. It's kind of scary. You know how it is. Earlier, a gang of nuns with axes tried to lift my wallet in the parking lot and this weird guy in a black outfit tried to sell me some book of lies called the Bible. I told him I didn't read science fiction. I had plenty of hangnails to deal with, Doc."

"Let me begin by saying that the only reason you're here is because your mother's doctor is a good friend of mine, D. We usually don't accept walk-on disorders. As a matter of fact, we have a long waiting list."

"Gosh, Doc, I thought it was hard to get into college. Maybe I should grease you up like I did the admissions board at school."

"Maybe if you'd done something while you were at school, you wouldn't be here at all." He cleared his throat again. "Would you mind if I got some water?"

"No."

"Would you like some, D?"

"No, thank you, I have to drive home." This wasn't going to be as easy it was with Mr. Munch, the shrink Dean Adams had appointed me. The fact that DeeDee had lightened my spirits with her casualness led me to believe that Sandler wasn't such a stiff cocksucker.

He sat back down. "Let's get something straight here. You are at Prophecy because your parents believe you have an eating problem. Our aim is to heal you of this problem. We take this seriously here, and we don't have time to joke around. That is, if indeed your problem is as severe as you've told your parents."

"Listen, Doc, I don't want to be here. I think this whole thing is a joke."

"Then we agree on something." He cracked a slight smile. "Anyhow, our intention at Prophecy is to get you back on course. However, you need to help us as much as we're helping you."

"I'm not a lost soul, Sandler. I just strayed away from the norm a little bit. You see, I'm a writer, and sometimes I find it easier to laugh off or hide behind bad situations."

"Continue."

"I find it really easy to relate to fictional characters' actions. Sometimes I even find myself disassociating myself from reality and placing myself in fictional situations that I know worked out."

"So, D, you rely on fantasy to guide you through the difficult times. Interesting."

"Not necessarily," I started again. "I find it easier to be guided by someone I respect rather than by someone who knows that they are my authority. I know it sounds kind of stupid."

"No, it's actually very common. Let me ask you a question. Do you believe in God?"

"No."

He scribbled away on his tablet. "Why not?"

"I guess that I haven't found a god good enough to believe in."

"But you do believe that some hand guides your fate when you leave reality and enter the lives of fictional characters."

"No," I answered. "People think that you're a bad person because you don't believe in God. That's the way it's always been for me. I imagine it's the same in here. People alienate me because my fantasies are based on a real world that can't be glossed over by a belief that if you're good, you'll be saved. I don't want to be saved. All the same bad things are going to be waiting for me with knives and Christmas and shit. It gives me an upper hand to fight people with stories that already have conclusions."

"Your theories don't make a whole lot of sense." He took off his glasses and placed one of the ear-pieces in his mouth. "They seem to conflict with what your parents told me about you in our initial screening."

"They don't make sense, Sandler, because they're all bullshit. Can I go now?" Sandler tore out the first page of my file and threw it in the garbage can.

CHAPTER NINE

It was easy to convince my parents to send me back to college for my senior year. Think about it. To begin with, they wanted to ensure that I received a college diploma. They knew that without it, I could never be as happy as my brother because I hadn't run into the fortunate experience that led to his son and wife—a true blessing in disguise. Secondly, since they didn't understand the magnitude of the disorder, or for that matter, anything about the disorder at all, I did a great job making it out to be a secluded and short lived incident—the fact that it was a girl's disease really helped me plead my case. Lastly, they knew I had one last chance in school. I was a good enough kid growing up that I usually learned my lesson after one fuck up. The only things that stood in my way—because I really did want to get my education and forget about what I had done, were Snif, Reno, and my trusted professor, Angello. I only had to make it half a school year. My grades sucked, but I had the credits in order.

As far as Sandler went, he was a piece of cake. Although he related my case to several different standard studies, as if he knew more about me than he actually did, I found out ways to weasel my way around his medical book armor. As always, I could fall back on the fact that my eating remained healthy around my parents—and that I'd performed very well in school over the summer. I think Sandler may have tried to throw a monkey wrench in my situation by asking my parents either to keep me at home with them for another semester or have me finish at a local state college (which probably would have been smart). Luckily, my scholarship prevented anything like that. Besides, my parents realized that the state school closest to us, I think it may have been called Kudzu U, amounted to capital punishment for me.

As for my eating, well, it got a lot worse when I returned to school. For the first time, I actually began to hone in on the weight and distorted self-image aspects of the barfarama. One thing came from seeing Deedee, the nutritionist, over the summer and that was I learned more about the problem than I needed to know. In other words, before she or anyone at Prophecy evaluated the condition, they injected a bunch of insane images and stories into my head. I never knew that some things were good for you and others weren't. I didn't know that some foods were worse to throw up than others, and I had never even thought about the digestive process. I guess I could thank Deedee for teaching me the cherished forty-five minute rule and a couple other theories of food breakdown and digestion. Even though she was foolishly tangled in a web of promises, charities, and other hippie garbage, she taught me more realistic ways to go about my shortcomings than a teacher like Angello could. A very informative bluff, if I may say so myself.

All my new wisdom did, however, was completely sack my brain. The worst of my new collage of fears and expectations for myself sprouted from the awareness of evil foods. Over the summer, I had nearly reached my "desired weight" as insurance to go back to Palmbrook. No matter what I did to control the dismissal of my food, I knew now that some portions of a meal were impossible to flush. In other words, the barfarama wasn't the foolproof method I'd thought. So, I took different measures—very extreme measures.

I came up with a few of these one night as I hurried to flush my food without being caught—while making the mistake of having to take a shit at the same time. I'm sure you can imagine how that worked out. As I sat on the can to take a shit, I attempted to throw up between my legs. Well, that ended in travesty. I barfed all over my cock. While wiping myself down with toilet paper like a baby, I realized that there had to be an easier way to puke. It was completely twisted, so I decided that it would be in my best interest to attempt some drastic preventative methods. Mind you, I still didn't know a whole lot about what I was doing.

My first new technique was actually quite basic. I stole a clean syringe one night out of Reno's stash and filled it regularly with windshield wiper fluid, WD40 or free-based rat poison—whatever—and injected it into the food Deedee told me made for an unhealthy and unproductive diet. It was kind of like cutting old or lacking members of your team because I remembered never to touch those items when I ate. I thought of it as training a dog not to shit in the house. If you rub his face in his own mess, he'll always remember the smell. Whenever I ate at a restaurant with buddies, I either sprinkled poison on my food, cut a notch in my knee with a razor blade, or convinced myself that I hated the food by filling my skull with memories of the smell of defecating. The latter rarely worked when you needed to find control; it reminded me of when I yacked on my dick.

My second inventive technique was less complicated, less dramatic, and less dangerous. Whenever I ate, I stuck a small dip of Kodiak under my tongue. That always made me vomit when I ate. The only problem was controlling the backlash long enough to escape from sight. Even though my taste buds were useless at this point, I could still taste some things. I built a strong fixation with hot sauces on food. One time the year before, when I was totally down on funding, Roast bet me I couldn't drink a whole bottle of Tabasco. The exchange was a carton of cigarettes that I really needed. I fulfilled my end of the wager, no problem. If I did eat, which I knew I needed to do some time, I enjoyed it. However, the nose tingling aroma of a bottle of Tabasco mixed into a salad grossed a lot of people out.

My final addition to the regiment was the one I disliked the most. I decided to compliment my already horrid physical well-being with ephedrine and laxatives. The ephedrine, which we called "cross tabs," served as a way to speed the fuck out of my heart—like the coke wasn't doing that already—and the laxatives were another way to be sure I unplugged myself if I ever got caught in one of those uncomfortable time-ticking situations.

Laxatives hurt. As quickly as you build up a tolerance, you lose control of your bowels altogether. I believe that's why they were a short-lived routine to my regiment. The more I took, the more trips I had to make to the bathroom (sometimes as many as five or six visits an hour) with no real results other than kidney pain, stinging dehydration, and constant dry-heaving. I also found it disgusting that whenever I took a shit that it would pour out so fast that it ran all over the backs of my legs.

None of these were desirable behaviors. I never would have thought of them though if it hadn't been for Deedee. Soon after I returned to Palmbrook all evidence of the hard work that I had put in during the summer to prove my worth to my parents, was gone. My fear of my reflection got worse as well. By that time, I didn't even like to see my shadow. In some lights, my disfigured body reminded me of a cloaked figure, like death in an old Doré engraving.

Back to school and miles away from my family, I was back where I started in my college. I was back in class with Angello.

"Well, well, well, it looks as if my old friend D has returned to my class in his attempt to graduate. Ironic, isn't it? Your senior seminar, graduation, and fate are in my hands. Let me guess. You want to write about Mark Twain. Do you think you can make it to class this time, Huck?" His words hurt because I knew what had gone down between him and More-ganja.

I kept my cool, stood up and addressed the entire class. "I've turned over a new leaf, Professor Angello."

He flicked at his nose with his thumb. "That's good to hear." Asshole. Killer. Fucker. "Maybe in the two years you have managed to avoid me on campus, you learned a little bit about literature." His sniveling voice and cheap shots brought the smelly memory of carbon monoxide into his classroom.

"I sure did, sir." I stared into his shaking eyes. There was nothing there. No regret. He looked around the room, as if he was afraid that I was on to him in some way.

"Well, good," he replied. He searched the room for his next victim as his eye twitched. "The world doesn't really need another prose writer who emulates Mr. Mark Twain, anyway."

"You don't think so, huh? Personally, I believe that if people actually opened their eyes to reality that maybe they wouldn't be so careless."

Caught slightly off-guard, he turned back to me. "I think that it was careless of you to recommend I conduct the foreman's duties in making your thesis a reality. Do you enjoy punishment?" Angello was colder than I remembered him, and it wasn't because of what he did to More-ganja.

"I'm the one who elected to accept the challenge, Professor."

"It won't be a challenge. I make the rules here, and I am the warden of the grade book." He clinched his cherished grade book, the one that he marked missed days with a bleeding red marker. I prayed he didn't know that More-ganja and I were friends. Rarely had the two of us been seen together around the English department.

+ + +

A strung-out voice grunted into the other end of the phone. "We need to talk, boy." It was Reno. His unnatural desperation signaled that for one second, one instance, his guard was down. No longer did the intimidating mass pump out the energy of fury. No longer did he seem like an uncaged fuck up destroying everything in his path. Reno Lee was falling apart.

I played out the late night call with caution, remembering how easily he gutted his punching bag.

"About what, Reno? Are you okay, man?"

He drooled and coughed out his words. "Yeah, just a second." He dropped the receiver and I heard about two minutes of fumbling and shuffling around. He could have been doing one of many things—smoking a glass dick or hammering a needle filled with whiskey into his arm. He picked up the receiver again, coughed, grunted, and spat some more. I could hear his lips resting on the phone and his overbite scraping up and down the holes of the mouthpiece.

"I'm coming over to pick you up. We got business to take care of."

"Should I be scared, Reno?"

"Not of me."

Even someone as evil and racist as Reno Lee stirred a little of my sympathy. After all, there was a much filthier adversary shaking around in my head: Snif.

Hearing Reno in such a bad way reminded me of a scene from Steven Crane's *Red Badge of Courage.* Not because it was about the Civil War, but because the way the soldier in the passage died was horrible.

"After four years of arduous service marked by unsurpassed courage and fortitude the Army of Northern Virginia has been compelled to yield to overwhelming numbers and resources."

+ + +

"You didn't tell any one about the money, did you, boy?" He clawed at me as if I was the one to fear. I noticed that since his performance at the punching bag, he had lost nearly thirty pounds. His eyes were glued shut as he felt around the road for curbs. "Hold the wheel," he shouted as loud as he could without spewing out the shale in his throat. I did as he commanded. As quickly as I had my hands on the wheel, Reno was tying off his arm and thumping around for a vein.

"Reno, why don't you just drink the shit, dude?" I never understood his obsession with the spike. He couldn't be bothered with an answer. Three shots later, he regained control of his car.

"My daddy made me do steroids as a kid to get bigger. I like it this way." Blood bubbled out of his nose. He licked his finger, dragged it up his face and smeared blood up his nose. He didn't make it far enough to catch the scar. "Where's the fucking money, boy?"

"You know where it is, asshole. You hid it out by that old lady's grave."

"Yeah. Fuck." He dribbled.

Did we all look like this? What was left of us? I didn't know. My paranoia of my own reflection and the fact that I had avoided any contact with Reno and Snif made me think we had all nearly vanished from existence. We were no longer just invisible to authority. We were also invisible to the human race.

"Bird, we gotta get the money out of there before farmboy finds it. That money is all we got." I had no idea how much money we had accumulated or how much Reno had hastily thrown out on crack, but it seemed like the only thing keeping him alive.

"Dude, I don't want the money. I don't want anything to do with this anymore."

He looked at me with his razor slit eyes that barely revealed the absence and delirium inside. He was cashed in, and no matter how much money was left at the graveyard, it wasn't enough to restore so much time already lost to addiction.

He screeched to a halt inches in front of a stop sign.

"What are you talkin' about, motherfucker? We need to go get the money." The scar on his head dripped blood.

"I realized the other day how fucked we all are. I mean, we never get into trouble with the law or anything, but we're screwed. Have you looked at yourself?" He continued to stare at me with blind anger. "Look at yourself, Reno. You're a fucking mess."

He exhaled. His teeth were almost black. "What are you talkin' about?"

I pushed up his sleeve. "Look at this. Look at you. You're not even a functioning person anymore." The track marks consumed his arm and the veins were crushed and collapsed. At the top of his arm, where his monstrous biceps formally pounced and broke the bones of anything that stood in his way, I saw a permanent chafing caused by whatever he used to tie off his life flow.

"You got a lot of nerve, boy. For someone who's just a fucked—" A gastric pain in his abdomen caused him to double over. "You got a lot of—" He couldn't concentrate on his words long enough to produce a full sentence. A dribble of blood formed on his earlobe. He shook his head, trying to remember where he was. "My name is Ransom."

"Ransom? Reno, how in the fuck have you been going to class like this?" Probably a question I should have been asking myself. I knew the answer though; either I wasn't going at all or I was hiding in the back, staying awake by coughing.

"I haven't, boy." He exhaled and sucked in and out a few more words. "I failed out last year."

"What?"

"I haven't been in school for a long time, son." His temples were noticeably pounding away, and I could sympathize with the pain and struggle to focus. Squirts of blood pissed out of his ear. "I failed out. I'm too fucking stupid for college. The only reason I got into school with my GED was my old man. I've been living off of the drug money, my tuition and my allowance. My parents don't even know."

"Then why did you stay here? Why are you here now with me?"

"I need to get the money before Snif tries to get it from you, pussy." His fumbled speech grew more disjointed. "I need to pay my old man back for the school I wasted."

"Why? What the fuck? He has plenty of money."

"No, he don't. He needs me to graduate from college so I can get my inheritance and get him back on his feet." The story wasn't making sense, but I got the gist. The selfish redneck asshole couldn't get his money unless he had a college degree. Well, since that wasn't going to happen, he was going to pay off his father and try to convince him to send him to another school. This wasn't about an education or pride. It was completely about trust funds and old money. This was about Reno Lee and his world. Although I came up with the drug plan, I was the pawn the entire time, the pawn in their game of wealth. I grabbed for the door handle as the mighty Reno tugged my shirt with everything he had left.

"What about Snif?" I asked, already knowing the answer.

"Same. He failed out before me."

"You assholes used me." I clinched onto my heart and rubbed above it, to sooth it. I didn't need to get excited in my state, but the twisting and pulling and clogging and farting continued. I needed aspirin. I lost breath and began snorting. I went for the door handle.

He licked his finger and his truck swerved. "Where you goin'?" His mouth distorted in slow motion, and he barfed on my pant leg. "We ain't through yet, son." His face was covered in his stench and he resembled a rabies-infected hound panting through the final stages before psychosis.

"I'm out of here. It's over." I knocked the door open and fell out of the car. As I tried to lift myself up, the flurries of snow buzzing around in my vision clouded and grouped together. It wasn't a pleasant euphoria like it used to be. It was horror. I got one last look at Reno and saw my reflection, my state. I didn't need mirrors to know what I had become; it devoured everything around me. My anger blew everywhere and fumed like alcohol shooting out of my cock. I was dead. Reno's car peeled out. He hit a curb and headed toward the outskirts of Palmbrook. He needed more crack before he went to claim his prize. I threw up all over myself and buckled into a nearby ditch.

The only reason Reno needed me at all was because he'd forgotten where he hidden the money.

Some time had passed until I felt a hand shake at my body. I wanted to respond, but I couldn't. I was buried alive in pity, hatred, and deceit. It shook again. I couldn't respond. I didn't want anyone to see me like I was, but I couldn't do anything to prevent it.

Vines of plastic flowers encased my body, intending to suck the life out of me and shove me back into the world as a bogus apparition, another drone robbed of identity. The only thing I could feel was my urine-drenched pants scratching a rash onto my legs and pelvis. The only thing I could smell was my own waste. The only thing I could think was a replay of Reno's mouth opening and nearly releasing his lower jaw. Over and over the sight haunted me. I wasn't being chased, but I was running. I wasn't tired, but I was out of breath. I was so out of breath that my skin stuck to my chest like a straight jacket. I wasn't dying, but I wasn't alive. Dried vomit accumulated around my mouth, and as I challenged my respiratory system to one last bout, chunks of esophagus vibrated and hummed as my body struggled to blow them out of the way.

"D." The voice comforted me, dancing around in my dreams as the kaleidoscope of blizzards and emaciated euphoric states broke up.

My hands dug into the mud. It was raining, and I attempted to lift myself and see who was resurrecting me from my coma. I got to my knees, and then the dead weight of my ill body plunged me back into the ditch.

I blacked out again, for who knows how long.

"D," the voice insisted. I opened an eye. My heart flip-flopped in every direction and felt wrung out and dense, like a blood-drenched towel used to sop up the mess of a slaughterhouse before an inspection. I dry-heaved. Blood. Flesh. Acid. It burned as it crept down the inside of my shirt until it stung at my delicate fingers exposed by too much cuticle biting. I was nothing, contorting my body into a fetal position as the mud battered my body at every point. A tree limb drove itself into my hand and pierced it ever so slightly. I couldn't see the speaker. I felt hands pick me up, and I complied by leaning against the host. The body was warm against mine. In an attempt to regain composure, I tried to dream up a situation in literature, my last fading passion. I tried to separate myself with this conquest of my fears. I dove into my catalogue of happy endings. I hoped for a light, a memory. Rather than Twain, I was cursed with one page, one scene from one book. One vision remained in The Library after the others fled. Everything else was checked out, and the doors and windows were boarded up. It was the same passage from Steven Crane's *Red Badge of Courage* that reminded me of Reno—a vision of a soldier running across a battlefield as his grotesquely mangled arm fluttered.

I recognized the voice on the phone in the next room. It was Monica. I shivered under three goose-feather-filled blankets on her couch. The tingling of my body was under-shadowed by the pain of dehydration.

"You're kidding me," she shouted into the phone. "Get the fuck out of here. Tell Wade to fuck off." She slammed down the phone and turned to me. Her eye was swollen from a deep cut underneath it. I knew where it had come from. She twisted her curly dirty-blond locks and bit at her lower lip. Strangely, I felt myself getting aroused by her. It wasn't her youth that stimulated me (she was just eighteen at the time). Rather, it was the adaptability and street sensibility that made her the most popular cocktail waitress at the Library.

"Wow, you look gross," was all I could muster. My voice was hoarse and the drying abrasions on my throat tickled as they burst. I took every precaution not to purge as I spoke. I found it difficult, though, to produce moisture and swallow. I felt around my body; she had cleaned me up, and I was naked. I hoped she burned my clothes.

"You're one to talk. You're lucky I found you, D."

"Why?"

"Because you'd be in jail right now with Snif if it wasn't for me. The cops were out in full-force last night after what happened. It must have been a full moon."

"Full moon? What are you, a hippie? And jail? What happened?" At least someone had the sense to lock up Snif.

"Oh, not much, he just beat the shit out of me in front of my father at The Library."

"Wow, your dad's pretty big. Did he beat the shit out of that birdseed?"

"Nah. I'm a sucker. I love that idiot, so I called the cops before my dad could get to him. My mother helped out."

"Why are you with that guy?"

I still found Monica attractive. I always had, ever since the first time Cooper and I ate at Nusstorte. Maybe it was the way she cared for Snif, knowing he was a total scumbag that drew me to her tomboy attitude. This was the closest I had ever been to her.

"I guess I love him." She caressed her eye with an ice cube and then threw it across the room. "Fucking asshole. Anyway, we have to stop making this a pattern, D."

"Making what a pattern?" I asked. "Did I have sex with you or something?"

"Right. Don't flatter yourself. I couldn't even get you to stand up. What? You don't remember the time like a while ago when I drove you home from The Library and you got out of my car before it stopped moving?"

I shot her a blind stare. "Uh, no."

"You're kidding me. It was that night you and all of your good pals came to the bar all fucking wasted on Quaaludes and Mad Dog. I thought you remembered. It was pretty funny."

"Funny in what way?"

"Well, when I pulled my car over to see if you were okay, you tried to kiss me. After I said, 'No, you don't,' you made me take you to your place and wait until you checked your answering machine to see if any girls had called you. After you stumbled around looking for your answering machine for a while, you collapsed. I sat there with you for about an hour to make sure you were okay, and then I left."

That's one of the things about my blackouts; I never remembered the part of the night that involved getting home. On most nights, I figured I just got there.

"Weird. Well, why didn't you kiss me?" I asked.

"Because you're gross, you crack addict."

"Crack addict? Not me, Monica."

She giggled. "Well, you sure look like one. What are those, dentures?" I noticed that it was getting dark outside. I had slept for quite a long time.

"How long have I been here?" I asked looking to my smashed watch.

"Since about four in the morning. Good thing you weren't with Reno, huh?"

"Why? Did he drive his car off a cliff, that bastard?"

"What do you mean, D? Reno got the shit kicked out of him in Cracktown last night. He got shot like five or six times by some black drug dealer. The cops said he said the wrong thing to the wrong person."

"What? Holy shit. Is he dead?" In the moment before Monica answered me, I found that the thought didn't bother me. I didn't feel his loss, and even though I hated him for what he had done to me and told me the night before, I knew he shouldn't have gone to buy crack in his disarray. There had been something wrong with him when he talked about the steroids and called himself Ransom.

"No, he's not dead. But I heard that his father came and had him flown out of the hospital to avoid any trouble with the Johnny Law." Typical. His daddy and his trust fund were there for him once again.

"Good riddance," I said. "Let him go home and explain this one." After a minute, I added, "Thanks for helping me, Monica."

"*Sie sind ein ruck,*" she spouted.

I thought I was hearing things. I shook my head and tried to knock some more of the deliriousness out of my ear. "Huh?"

"It's German for 'You're an asshole.'"

"German?" I queried. "I thought you were from Switzerland."

"Dumbass. My parents came over here when I was two to get their piece of the American dream.

"Do they still have their Camaro?" I joked.

"What does that mean? Both my parents drive BMWs."

"It's a joke. You know. It's a generalization about immigrants. It's a stereotype that when an immigrant becomes successful he buys a Camaro, the American dream."

She stared at me with a pissy look on her face. "Well, it's not very funny. I've got to go to work. My dad is about to kill me for last night an—"

"No problem, I'll get out of here."

"Don't worry about it. Stick around. There's food in the cabinets. I think you should stay away from the booze, though." The thought of drinking made me gag. "And, D." She glared at me. "Don't steal anything. I can kick your little ass."

Snif was jailed for the first-degree assault of Monica, and the timing couldn't have been more perfect. With Snif and Reno out of the way, I needed to cut back on my plagues and focus on school. As with Kudzutown, escape was the only thing on my mind. As far as the student druggies were concerned, the reign of terror was over. I heard about a sophomore kid who decided to pick up where we left off, but he didn't do his homework. He stole a key from the mailroom and got busted. I no longer worked there; I worked out a deal with Dean Adams to focus on my studies and pay off the school in the form of a loan. Anyway, no one ever knew about my connection to the gang.

In an attempt to redeem myself in Cooper's eyes, I stayed away from the bad element and ended up spending a lot of time with Monica. We didn't get sexually involved, but she had the balls to keep me in check. She was a fiery little bitch with so much spunk and "fuck you," I sometimes felt speechless when I was around her. Unlike most people, it didn't bother me that she spoke like a retard. For example one time she said, "Cherish the thought," when she intended to say, "perish the thought." Other people laughed at her. I thought it was kind of cute.

Monica was a real person who didn't take shit from anyone. She was the perfect combination of her parents. When she wanted, she could be delicate and classy like her Swiss-French mother, who was the hostess and public relations side of the restaurant. On the other hand, she could also be tough as nails like her father, a former European heavyweight boxer. He was the cook and business side of the restaurant.

"So why did your father let Snif treat you like that?" I asked, finding myself curious in the "hows" and the "whys" of their atrocious relationship. It seemed to me to be more based on cutdowns, fighting, and cemetery fucking than love.

"It's weird. I managed to keep Wade's punches and drugs out of the bar. My father thought he was a pretty good guy. To him, Wade was like this pauper in a world where princes are a dime a dozen; that's actually what he told me. They shared common interests. As you know, Wade grew up on a farm up north. Well, my father grew up moving from relative to relative on several farms around Switzerland. He never had anything for himself, until he met my mother, the ultimate prize."

"If your mother was such a prize, Monica, why did you tell me he spends all his time at strip clubs?"

She shrugged and looked away. "I guess after you get the prize you forget why you wanted it to begin with." For someone without much formal education, years in a bar developed Monica's extremely intuitive sense of character judgment. "I know he loves my mom, just like I thought Wade loved me."

"Well, what else? I mean I see people I sympathize with because they are similar to me, you know, not from very extravagant backgrounds. The thing is that they're the people I fear the most. They're hungry, and they're not afraid to kill to get food."

"Well, Wade and my father share a taste for a drink called absinthe. My dad's brother smuggles it into the country. Every once and a while the two get really wasted on it."

"Absinthe? I've never heard of it. Is it like Jagermeister or something?"

"No. It's illegal in most places. They banned it because it's poison. It's like this bitter, shit-green stuff that they mix with sugar on a spoon, or something."

It sounded familiar. "You mean kind of like freebasing?" I asked.

"Yeah, D," she returned, "like freebasing, you retard."

"Weird. How did a farmboy like Snif find out about this shit?"

"I told him about it before I introduced him to my dad. You see my dad doesn't like the kids from the college, even though they shovel thousands of dollars into his business. I knew he'd hate anyone I brought home from there. At the time, it seemed like a better idea than having Wade show up at my house with his shirt off and a bottle of Mad Dog."

"No shit. Why does he always do that?"

"I think he considers himself this badass gangsta." She laughed, and her excitement tickled the underside of my ears. "I've kicked his ass before."

"Really?"

"One time I went to this lame college frat party. After about an hour of looking around for that dumbass, I accidentally went into the garage. There he was, snorting lines and banging some bitch."

"Ouch," I said, thinking that both cocaine and sex sounded tempting.

"Yeah, that's what he said when I clocked him in the face and kicked her in the tits."

"You are a badass, aren't you, Monica? Such a defiant redneck."

"Yeah, I kick ass."

"What's the deal with him chewing on chalk?"

"I don't know, but it creeps me out. He said it stimulates him, makes him aggro without doing coke."

"It makes my skin crawl. Shit, I can't even hold chalk. The taste of eating it must be like digging your teeth into a chalkboard." Many things made me uneasy when Snif was around. He was a terrorist cell's dream; he slithered around undetected, and no matter where you directed his ferocity, he was bound to detonate.

"We all make mistakes, D," she said solemnly.

"Why do you call me that?"

"What?" Monica asked.

"D? Everybody around here calls me Dirtybird."

"It's better than that stupid nickname all your fucked up friends call you. What is your real name, anyway?"

This time, I was the one who looked away. "I don't know," I said.

+ + +

With Monica's help, I struggled to get back to reality. The

problem was, even if I wanted to, I was past the point of going cold turkey on everything. I brought my grade point average up slightly, just above the required limit. I had to keep my head above water to get a diploma. Because Angello based his seminar and thesis mega-class solely on one paper, I wouldn't be able to judge the exact average I needed until I won a buy-in from him. Shit, it sucked knowing that no matter what I did to reconcile a student/teacher relationship, I'd dug my own hole with him my freshman year. Even worse, I had become increasingly bitter—every time I saw him in class, I thought of More-ganja in that garage. I had no intention of letting him off with a slap on the wrist. Ganja had been a great friend.

"So, Mr. Langhorn Clemens, have you finished your thesis on Mark Twain yet?" Angello asked me as the year finally wound toward a conclusion. Every student in the class, with the exception of me, sat poised, ready to deliver his or her neatly bonded masterpieces and stared.

"Yes, I'm almost done—"

"Almost," he announced to the class. "What? You can't find enough relevant material to support your theories?" From the corner of the room, a sharply dressed ass-kisser giggled a comment into the ear of a girl sitting across the table. The girl pinched her lips and pretended to sneeze. I smirked back at her and brushed the side of my nose with my thumb. She bought coke from us regularly.

"It's not the material, sir. I wanted to ask you if I could get an extension. Everyone else had your personal attention in the writing of their theses, because their subjects were almost covered in the seminar." I didn't want to point out his favoritism, but I did want to make it known that I took an enormous risk wanting to write a thesis on an argument that in no way coincided with the studies of the rest of the class.

"You wanted to ask what?" he joked. "Doesn't that seem a little unrealistic to you? I mean, according to you and your arguments against the Romantic works, we live in a world that doesn't give second chances. You said it yourself many times."

"I don't think it's fair of you to mock me in class," I said.

"Oh, good heavens above. Mock you? Are you kidding me? I'm going to enjoy every minute of seeing you squirm out of this one, Mr. Langhorn Clemens." He spaced out Twain's name as if it were some pitiful song composed to animate his apathetic children that smirked and gasped at his holy insight.

"It's just that—"

"It's just that what? Just that you didn't do it? You haven't been paying attention in class?" He stared me down as he pouted his lips. "Is it just that you don't like what the teacher teaches?"

"Listen, asshole. I know the paper is late. I've read your fucking syllabus. I also read that you knock down the final grade one mark every day. The way I see it, the worst I could do is a B if you were a real teacher." I was tired of playing into his hands again and again. With my sobriety came cockiness. This time I had him trapped. I knew my thesis was worthy of an A by any other teacher's standards.

"That's funny, Mr. Langhorn Clemens, because the syllabus I remember writing clearly states 'Any student who wishes to postpone his thesis delivery date should consult with the teacher.' Funny, I don't remember you and I having a conversation about you turning in your paper late." I didn't have the outline any longer; I'd used it as a sifter to cut some coke with aspirin. He was right.

"You can't fail me, Angello. It was a mistake. I'll get it to you tonight. I swear all I have to do is edit the thing."

He glanced at his Victorian pocket watch. "Unless you get it here by the end of class, which is in about five minutes, you're SOL, pal."

"There's no way I can do that, Angello."

"Welcome to the real world. Good bye class; I enjoyed teaching you literature." I sat in my chair, delirious. Without even sharing another look, Angello packed up a box filled with all the other papers and slammed the door behind him. I couldn't move.

I told myself that everyone has a heart. After thoroughly fine tuning my thesis, I even put it in a nice binder that I bought with my fake Validine in the bookstore. I looked up Angello's home address in the school directory and headed over to make my last plea. I knew it wouldn't work, but I wanted to see in his eyes that he felt no regrets about what he had done. I was desperate. I looked at the extravagant door that attempted to mask the teacher's modest home and lightly tapped with the gold-plated knocker. I heard some shuffling inside. The door crept open, releasing a spray of uninviting feelings.

"What do you want, D?" Angello growled as he used his palm to crack his lower jaw. My heart raced.

"I decided to drop this by." Cautiously, I raised my thesis up to his chest. My hand shook, not because I was afraid of his response, but because I felt myself stumbling out of the conversation. I was losing coherence, only minutes before my funeral.

"What is this?" he asked blindly.

"It's my paper. It's my life. You have to take it. All I need is a C to graduate. Please, Professor Angello, you have to take it." His shadow cast over the light from the inside of the house that was blinding me. "I don't like to beg, but I need this. This is all I have left."

He snapped the binder out of my hand and read the title aloud as if his cats were now his class. "Miles Morgan," he said. "I thought that this paper was about Clemens. Jesus, I thought about actually accepting this. Not only did you turn it in late, but you also obviously changed your topic. I can't accept this. You're just like all the other little shits I've taught; you think that no matter what you turn in, it will be acceptable because you have the money to go to school here. If I had a nickel." He looked at the binder again. "Miles Morgan."

"That's right, asshole. I know you were buying coke from him. I know how you blackmailed him. I know." My skin bubbled. My insides froze.

"What are you talking about?" Angello made his arms go limp, his eyes crossed, and he stuck his tongue out. "The retarded kid?"

"Retarded? What the fuck is wrong with you?" My eyes steadied and my upper lip crept into a sneer. "He was my friend. He killed himself because you blackmailed him. I know that he was giving you coke so he could pass your class."

Angello flipped the binder at my feet. "Even if you could prove anything that absurd, who would believe you? The way I see it, *you're* trying to blackmail *me*."

"I know," I started to well up. My attempt to tell the truth like

I had with the bark of Nazareth had backfired. It was the truth. It was the fucking truth. "I know," was all I kept repeating.

"Sorry. You have failed my class. The real world that you have spoken of so highly is ultimately your tragedy. I don't hate the realists, and I don't hate you, D. You just didn't do an acceptable amount of work." Angello looked at the binder one last time.

Take it, Goddamn it. Take it. Take the fucking paper, I kept shouting over all of the voices in my head. He turned around and closed the door to his world.

As shabby and fake as it was, I wanted to belong so much. I didn't want to hear the voices of my dead friends and gods any longer. I stood defeated at the door for an hour, wishing he would reconsider my offer. In the end, in a place with no rules like Palmbrook, his tenure eclipsed my truths. Just like I had outwitted Palmbrook with my master plan to be accepted, Angello lived outside the law, tucked away in his gold-plated shack. I neglected to retrieve the paper. I finally saw that the beauty of the plastic flowers of Angello's Paradise could never host the melancholy of my Kudzutown and Cracktown. Like I had before in the face of my own fears, I retreated to my closet and eroded away.

I was over, trashed, no longer human. What was I going to say? There would be no redemption. I'd betrayed my parents' trust, betrayed myself and forgotten my mission, my escape. I'd shat my life away and I had no way of beating Angello. He was the teacher. The thing that really pissed me off was that I'd actually tried so hard, fighting by his rules to win his game. I failed, because I didn't believe in anything, anymore. His controlling hand swept my life away in one definite "Fuck you." He washed his hands and crucified me.

I retreated, hid, cried, and fled into my trench. I looked at my reality, my shit. My room was upside down and tortured. My inflatable mattresses were dismembered and torn inside out. Urine covered my walls; the electricity was gone, turned off and the heat swelled and encased the room as thunder sounded and hurricane winds pushed against my door. The sight reconfirmed the fact that I was back were I began. My life had fallen apart. I was Kudzutown, once again, to face baptism. There was no one pounding on my door; they had given up long before.

All I could do was whisper, "Someone please help me." I fantasized I was to be cured from my transgressions. But no one wanted to hear me anymore. It was all bullshit.

I slumped down farther and farther, deeper under the hills of filth, passed-out-in and pissed-on clothing and tried to shake the pain out of my chest. I felt like I had to burp, release, but nothing came out except agony. The skin on my torso again tightened to my rib cage. I paced myself and breathed as slowly as possible. I held my breaths in my mouth and released them in intervals. I focused on my broken watch, the second hand stuck between 10:16 and 10:17. The single, eternal second went nowhere but back and forth. Nothing in the world could save me. I would end up another failed nobody. I'd quit before I started, because my influence was driven by my jealousy for others' affluence.

I dragged myself to the bathroom, knocking my head as I found my way. It was all I had to guide me in the dark, because my hands collapsed on themselves, attempting to fight the pains in my chest. I felt disappointment burning icons into my flesh. One of my clenched hands scraped across a broken vanity mirror on the floor. I bent down and licked the sharp edges, trying to find a leftover morsel of coke to ease the pain. I closed my eyes to avoid my reflection. I licked at the mirror like a dog, and a sharp edge cut my mouth, making it bleed.

I trekked beyond Nirvana to my bathroom. I inched across the floor on my side, shaking to advance. I left a trail of blood that would lead me back to the trenches, and then, success. I felt the fear and hatred in my stomach knocking from the inside out. I sucked in, holding back. My throat whistled as a clump of something unusually large, part of my organs, pushed to get out of the trap I had laid. I reached my goal, the mechanical god of my being. I lifted the lid and began eating away at my insides, forcing out what was left of my fight. Acidic tears cursed me and mixed with the blood that smeared all over my face. I shrieked.

"Dispel!"

"Purge!"

"Forget!"

Nobody could hear. Voices in my head sang in time with the deafening power of my heart as it radioed to my eardrums and rang. The pain was so rabid that I plunged my head into the cold water. My teeth knocked against the undertow of the toilet. As a last ditch effort, I grabbed onto the back of my hair with my crippled hand. A toilet full of blood and puke showered onto the cracked linoleum, mixing with my piss.

I looked into the porcelain god and saw what remained of my reflection. No longer was I the fresh-faced, naïve kid who wanted to belong. I had withered away into nihility. My mind was mud, my energy searched past its reserves, and my body was about to suck itself in and disintegrate. Every second that I looked at myself, I forgot more of who I was. The blood and tears began a rapid barrage on my reflection until I couldn't see myself anymore.

+ + +

Two days later, I emerged from the bathroom and embraced the red light of dusk. My eyes, encased with muck, were no match for the power of a new day. I sat up. My mind was clearer, but my body had diminished. I tried to roll my shoulders like a pitcher warming up during the seventh-inning stretch, only to feel the insignificance of my frame. I could have broken those bones in my sleep. The blades that once carved Rick Conroy's fate on the bark of Nazareth were the balsa frame of a cheap, one-day kite.

Carefully, I picked myself up from the nest of rubbish embedded in the disgusting tile. My cupped hands supported my skeletal frame. I flicked at my beer belly and made sure I still had some nutrition left. Luckily, my gut churned constantly with the caloric sustenance of alcohol. Even if I evaporated, it would survive. Booze had become my meal. But where was my god? The world had forgotten his conquests a long time ago. I flicked a damp, stale cigarette off the floor and into my mouth. I grabbed my plane ticket home. It was stuck to the coffee table that stood against the door, barring it. It was time to check out.

I struggled to walk four blocks to The Library. Students passed by, returning from their dinners at the hippest new restaurant. They brushed against me and laughed at my horrible march. "Look at that drunk," some dipshit announced to his pals. "Hey, buddy, have another." I ignored him and fixed my eyes on The Library sign.

"You okay, Bird?" the doorman asked, extending his hand. I put my hand up to his and welcomed it. He pulled me in close. "Hey, can you hook me up with a couple of grams, bro?"

I gazed into his eyes. "Fuck off." I shoved him aside and made my move up to the bar. The bartender, Shelly, had known me for years. She began pouring me a beer, but stopped halfway when she noticed my condition.

"Dirtybird, are you wasted again?"

I shook my head yes because my voice, all I'd ever had, was gone. I managed to spit out a sentence. "Where's Monica?"

"Shit, Dirty, she doesn't get here for another hour." That was good enough. I had enough sense to ask a question. So, she continued to pour. Everything was spinning and struggling around me. I shifted my gaze around the room and noticed that no one was looking at me. I became paranoid as I sipped on my dinner. The bitter taste of the alcohol singed the wound on my mouth. Beer mirrors surrounded me. I drank more and my pity looking back at me with a big Budweiser or Heineken advertisement plastered across my forehead. I came to a mirror that painted Pabst Blue Ribbon across my head. Cooper. Why didn't I listen to Cooper? I held onto something in my front pocket. The Monte Blanc pen.

I cursed my shaking hand as I tried to write a note for Monica, telling her that everything would be okay. I owed her that for all she had done for me. Feeling defeated, I evaluated my note to see if it was in any way coherent. "Merry Christmas, rapist!" was scribbled over and over again. The words overlapped each other, but I could read it. I ripped into the bar napkin and tore away in a frenzy. I was unable to communicate. The only thing I loved, my passion, my fuel was empty. The door thrust open behind me.

SNAP!

Teeth dug into chalk.

Snif. As usual, the coke rash around his nose was in full effect. A sea of purple infection surrounded zit upon zit, piled on top of each other. Likewise, his eyes were stretched open and burned with the fire of broken blood vessels. Snif looked more like Grendel than the fresh-faced farmboy with cowshit on his vinyl loafers.

He waved at a drone across the bar and whispered, "Hey Dirtybird, we need to talk." He flicked a disguised coke sniffer, a bullet, out of his pocket and grabbed a quick slice of his toxic heaven. A few snowflakes descended onto the shoulder of my black shirt. As he breathed heavily into my ear, the musty smell of Mad Dog and chalk puffed from his mouth. My heart was already flying out of control, and I felt bile backing up in my esophagus.

"What the fuck do we need to talk about, Snif?" The bile forced its way up the passage into my mouth. I chewed at it with my back teeth and swallowed it. Snif grabbed me and shoved me into the Pabst mirror on the back wall, knocking it off. He pushed his pussy mug in my face. It wasn't the time for me to be a wiseass. I couldn't, even if I'd wanted to.

"You know what we need to talk about."

I bluffed. "What, that I'm fucking your ex-girlfriend? You know her. Her parents own the bar. You beat the shit out of her."

"No, I want my fucking money."

He inched closer to me, and I felt a bulge on the right side of his jeans. It wasn't a boner. That birdseed motherfucker meant business. Why did Reno have to tell me where the cash was?

"So, as soon as you're done puking up whatever you ate today, meet me in the graveyard and don't bring any of your faggot friends, asshole." I pulled a shard of glass out of my shoulder, and I found my voice. Not the buried Bird. My voice.

"The graveyard, huh? What, are you going to fuck me? Should I bring some lubricant? Can you even get a hard on?"

Snif's eyes, bugging out and then twitching closed, made him resemble the speed freak that axed Freddy Brubaker in the doughnut shop back in Kudzutown. That time, I hadn't seen it coming. The guy who killed Freddy had been fucked up, really fucked up. Snif was a spoiled brat farmboy. He never had to answer to anybody but that selfish, drug-eating brain of his. I looked in the broken Pabst mirror and saw Freddy Brubaker lying in doughnuts and face paint and blood.

Snif headed for the exit. In an attempt to strut, which is difficult to do after about two bottles of Mad Dog and about a gram of coke, he tumbled over on the corner booth next to the door. Quickly, he spun around to make sure no one was watching. Luckily, nobody cared. Everyone in the happiest hour on earth was absorbed in their own miseries and defeats.

SNAP!

I cringed. He kicked the door open as he bit into a warn-down piece of chalk, most likely one he stole from the specials board by the entrance.

I looked at Freddy's pen and read the transcription. "You did it. Love, Dad." I remembered the site of Freddy Brubaker, the college kid, with face paint smeared and covered in blood. I was painted in remorse and it suffocated me. I'd lived through the incident in the doughnut shop, and I'd let everyone down. I sighed as I scribbled out a semi-legible note for Monica on another bar napkin and an extra pump from my heart nearly dropped me off my barstool creating a fluttering of Cooper's whisper in my ear. "Stay away from the things that will fuck you," he'd said.

They were all talking to me. It was time for me to face my demons. I paid my tab, gave Shelly a hug, kissed her on the cheek, and walked away. As I left my home of three and a half years, the pony-tailed drone at the door added to my fear by reminding me that Snif was looking for me.

The graveyard where I began my college journey didn't look as inviting as it had before. Everything looked placed, fake. The beautiful gravestones weren't as massive as I remembered, and seemed easy to kick over, as if they were props in a cheap stage play. The beautiful flowers hadn't changed at all; they were exactly the same. Everything was lifeless and unsettling like the world they boxed in. Beyond the perimeter, a wind blew in, bringing the forgotten smell of Cracktown. No matter how much its inhabitants knocked on the gates and pleaded, they would never be able to enjoy the luxuries of Palmbrook. I looked at Snif across the graveyard. He paced himself and walked cautiously over to me. He lifted the gun and took aim at my head.

"Where is it, asshole?" I started to dissolve again. My heartbeat was so faint that I couldn't feel it behind my ribs.

"Why do you need it, Snif? Why would you risk coming back here to get it?" It was just some money accumulated by a bunch of wannabe drug dealers. Pennies for pussies. That's all we were. Big game, big plan. Peanuts.

SNAP!

He bit into his chalk. "Where is it, Pussy?" he demanded. His hand shook and the revolver of his pawnshop gun rattled. He aimed the barrel on my head. I wanted to cry but I was too dehydrated. I wanted to pray, but I didn't know who to pray to. I wanted to give him a reason to spare my life, but I couldn't think of one. Without considering he was going to bump me off no matter what I did or said, I pointed to the grave of Audrey Littlebury Rowe, the gravestone that stood for every bad thing about Palmbrook and "Fiat Lux."

He looked at it and chuckled. He reached into the pockets of his low-hanging jeans with his free hand and pulled out a mound of cocaine in his palm. With his eyes still fixated on me, he buried his nose in it, snorting away like a farm pig in the mud.

"That thing better be loaded, boy." Snif looked at me with a coke mustache under his nose. I hadn't said anything. Neither had he. Before I had time to collapse, before Snif had the chance to turn and face the voice, Reno Lee swallowed him. I never really wanted to see Lee in action, but I learned in a split second that the legends of his brutality were tame, compared to the living wrath: Reno Lee's retribution. After planting his knee in Snif's spine, Lee snapped both of Snif's arms backwards and let them dangle around. The scrawny crackhead cried for mercy, but Reno wouldn't hear of it.

"You think I'm fucking around, farmboy? I get shot buying you rock and you don't think I'm gonna come after you?"

Without even breathing, he moved onto the legs. He kicked

Snif to the ground and hammered on his kneecaps with the sole of his boot. The sound of bone run over by a train bounced off the trees as Lee hammered relentlessly on both knees until they gave. A flock of crows fluttered and retreated. Even they knew better than to stay and watch. The shirtless farmboy on the ground convulsed and shifted into a state of shock.

It was far from over, and I couldn't take my eyes away from the scene.

Reno plucked Snif up into the air by his nostrils and threw his head against the gravestone. His skull cracked open on the granite base as Reno limped over, breaking off a tree limb that got in his way. He still wanted more. I decided to get out of there. As I turned to run, I heard the dense pine branch pouncing off Snif's chest. Rib after rib lit like firecrackers, one after the other. Again and again, Reno mashed Snif into an empty plot next to Littlebury Rowe.

"You gonna try and frame me, asshole?"

I scurried to the perimeter as the relentless bombing continued. Escape. Please. Somebody let me escape.

Reno licked his finger and dragged it across his scar. "Where you going, fagboy?" The topside of my body twisted around to see Reno looking directly at me. Snif lay at his feet, and blood and mayhem drizzled out. I didn't have anything to say. I didn't want to know what had gone down between the two of them. My drug-selling plan had propelled them into a little side game.

"I—"

"Shut up, boy. I'm just fuckin' with you. You want your money?"

"No. I just want to leave. I never belonged here."

"Can I drive you to the airport?" he asked gently. I must have looked worse than what he had just done to Snif. At least in my case, he seemed to care.

"That's all right, Reno, I'll manage to get there somehow."

Snif reached up for help. Reno flipped open a massive Buck knife and drove it into Snif's leg, pulled it out and put it back in his pocket. He walked toward me.

"You ain't gonna tell nobody about this, are you, boy?"

"Why would I? I'm just as guilty as you are."

"That's right, boy; this was your mess. It's a good thing your pal Reno was here to clean it up for you." I looked back toward the grave.

"What was it, Reno? What the fuck was in the grave?"

"Nothin', really," was Reno's response. That was just it, nothing at all. He had spent the money a long time ago and he purposely told me where it was located. They were all assholes looking out for themselves and their money.

"Who's Ransom?"

Reno didn't say anything. We both walked away. I accepted the hallucinatory events that transpired that night in the graveyard and held on to them as if they really were the conclusion to my tale.

But real life doesn't end that way.

CHAPTER TEN

"D, could you come in my office?" Sandler's attempt at being the vice principal of the ward warned me that I was in some kind of trouble.

"Yeah, give me a second." I took a drag from my cigarette.

"No, not just a second. Now!" I didn't think psychotherapists were supposed to take such angered tones with their patients. I put my cigarette out and followed him through the swinging door.

"You better make sure that's locked, Doc, I heard these patients are the Berserkers. Shit, we might as well put down the impenetrable titanium door."

"Explain."

"It's a random reference. It seems that like in any cheesy movie about the booby hatch there's always a hidden ward of horrible creatures. They're always secluded from the other patients and are just that much crazier than the rest. The only problem is you can't control them. They haven't any rhyme or reason. They're berserk! Mad! Insane!" I laughed. Sandler didn't find my allegory amusing, but he knew what I was talking about. I also knew that he would try and analyze it to death, especially the "you can't control them" part. It was total bullshit. If anything, I was trying to make him feel like a buffoon for making sure the swinging door was locked. I'm sure it's really hard to control a bunch of girls who weigh under a hundred bucks.

"D," Sandler began, "it has come to our attention that you are making this experience unproductive for some of the patients."

"What are you saying? That I killed Mariah? Sandler, I barely even talked to that girl."

"That's not what I'm talking about."

"Well, fill me in."

He lifted his favorite little tablet. "Let's see. Apparently, after you didn't gain weight once we put you on the hospital's structured diet, we began to doubt your story."

"Wow, that couldn't be because I'm not allowed to get piss drunk every day."

"In any respect, we found out that you were hiding large batteries and other items on different parts of your body to ensure the daily two-ounce gain."

"You have been misinformed, Doc. I only shoved such items into my asshole. Who told you that, anyway?"

"To answer that would violate my oath, D."

"Bullshit. I know who it was. It was Brittany. Like I care. What other hard crimes do you have on me?"

He put down the tablet, took off his glasses, and started acting like it was heart-to-heart time.

"D, I think that the problem is that Prophecy should never have mixed sexes in this program. People know you like to instigate fights, and that some of the girls find that amusing and join in." Hoping I would give in, Sandler yawned and stared at me with tired eyes. "That is not a productive part of the healing process."

"What are you talking about? I should be condemned because some of the girls find me to be a good male role model? Christ, for once in these people's lives they don't have to fear a guy. You know how messed up they are, Doc."

"And you're not? You haven't been hired as the guardian angel at this hospital. You came here to get help. What have you done since you've been here? Let's see. You've lied, acted belligerent, crossed authority. That isn't healing, that's summer camp. Look around you! This isn't summer camp, D."

"I couldn't tell from the arts and crafts portions of the group."

"For some that is very therapeutic."

"Like for Mariah. You made her draw a picture with crayons

of her family, her father who raped her. What the fuck do you think pushed her over the edge, Doc? What kind of therapy is that? The crayons, the picture. You forced her to relive getting fucking molested." I kicked at his desk. "Let's be honest. You've had worse patients than me in here. How about that chick that tried to OD on Prozac and then bolted through that shaky little swinging door? I never tried to pull anything like that."

"Probably because you wouldn't let us put you on Prozac."

"Or Zoloft, or Lithium, or whatever miracle-drug-of-the-month your pretentious quarterly dish rag recommends. It's all bullshit. This is more than about an eating disorder or manic depression. I refuse to believe that I'm a depressed person. I like what I do. I like throwing up. I've never hurt anyone and it's not illegal. I made my bed. Let me fucking lie in it. It's a choice. An eating disorder is a choice."

"Denial. You'll die."

"Fuck you; that's not denial. Listen to me, Sandler; the only thing that I regret about my life so far is that I ended up in the wrong place at the wrong time. I've had great friends, great experiences; my life isn't a total fucking tragedy. Just because your system didn't work on me, or as far as I can see anyone in here, you automatically think that I'm in denial or depressed or schizo. Now, you're booting me out of the hospital because you can't find out what's wrong with me. It looks like you forgot how to do your job, Sandler."

"It's a little more than that, D. Brittany's parents are worried that you might do something." I knew where he was headed and I didn't like the implications.

"Please don't even tell me what I think you are alluding to. Do you honestly think after all the shit that I have seen, all of the shit I have witnessed toward women, that I would touch a little girl?"

"What are these things you've seen? You haven't told me anything. Do you even *remember* anything? Why would you expect me to trust you?" He looked deep into me for a confession, a memory. I didn't have any. He paused and announced, "You're the final male that we will ever have at Prophecy as an inpatient. We made a mistake thinking that this would work out."

"I know for a fact that I'm not the first guy in here. Why is it a mistake now?"

"Because you don't want to use this as a therapeutic opportunity." Hoping it was time to see the last of me, he looked at his watch. "You are using this as an escape from whatever it is out there you're afraid to face. I don't know if you have ever even had a problem. You don't give us anything to work with but a bunch of stories. I can tell you right now that I don't know the first thing about your problem, or for that matter about you. I know bits and pieces of your life. You tell me that you're an alcoholic and a bulimic. The typical bulimic patient that comes to us for help binges and purges. From what you have told me, you just purge."

"That's where you're wrong, Sandler. Drinking is my binge and food is my purge. I *do* have a problem, and I don't want to make light of it or trivialize it. However, it's a difficult problem to cope with. It's not easy being a regular kid who has no earthly idea why he loves to barf. I didn't come here to tell you about how I have a poor self-image. I came here to find out what's wrong with me. I hate being alone, doctor; it terrifies me. But you just proved to me something I already knew. I don't belong anywhere. Not at home. Not at college. Not here."

Sandler chewed on the end of his Cross pen for a second before continuing. "Were you ever abandoned, or have you ever felt that way?"

"You want to know why I hate being alone, Doc? Because I know what I do to myself when I'm alone." I stood up from the metal chair, and saluted Doctor Sandler. "Call my parents. Tell them I'm ready to go."

"Your parents have already signed your release papers and they're waiting for you in the main lobby."

I didn't want to cry, I just wanted out. With my back turned, I unzipped my pants and pulled out my scrotum. I turned around for one last look at Sandler. "Look, Doc, I sat in some gum. Are you going to say I sexually harassed you now?"

He rolled his eyes. "D, before you leave I have to get some long-term goals from you. What do you want to do? Are you moving?" His eyes stayed focused on mine, avoiding contact with my balls.

"I am going to move west. After that? Fuck. Who knows? It's all bullshit. Sandler, I know I gave you a hard time. But there is going to be a lot more tragedy walking in and out of this office. I guess in that respect, you got lucky with me. It's the ones you make relive their agony that are going to haunt you."

He sighed and shook his head. "When are you going to relive your agony? It builds up inside, doesn't it? It makes you angry, and you can't relive it because you refuse to face it. Come to terms with it." He reached into my folder.

"I don't fucking know what it is. Do you?"

He looked down at his notes and handed me the picture of the tree I'd drawn as a kid. I grabbed it, and with one sweeping motion lit it on fire with Lori Conroy's lighter. "Fuck off, Sandler. This picture doesn't mean shit. Am I a pyro now? *Please* give me drugs." I threw the picture in his garbage can. Sandler scrambled to fill the can with the pitcher of water on his desk. He succeeded.

On that, I shoved my sack back in my pants and left his office. It had been a long time since the day I'd ratted on Lori's father. I wasn't a hero anymore. I didn't want anyone to know that I suffered. Sandler might have known something, whether he got it from my parents or his notes, but he didn't want to tell me. He wanted me to figure it out on my own.

I didn't kick open the swinging door. I just unlocked it and headed back into the observation room. I found Tina waiting for me.

"What was that all about?" She asked. "What's up with all that smoke?"

"It's nice to see that my cigarettes are going to your cause rather than mine." I popped a quick stogie up from the pack I left on the table and lit it. "Sandler told me that I was getting booted."

She didn't seem too surprised. "When?"

"Today. I'm going to pack up my shit right now and meet my parents downstairs."

"And his reasons?"

I shrugged. "They can't figure out what's wrong with me and they think that I am not taking my therapy seriously." I didn't want to include the part about Brittany's parents. The poor little girl was dealt a shitty hand, and if the officials at Prophecy thought that I was even the tip of her psychological nightmare, then they should take a look at Mariah's empty bedroom. If her father wanted someone as harmless as me out of the hospital, then so be it. I'd like to see what he was hiding. Besides, I had officially escaped another one of life's mazes. Sure, it wasn't as heroic as my grand escape from home, but my balls had literally gotten me out of jail.

I was a scumbag. I didn't deserve to interfere with this mess. I didn't have the right to trivialize these girls and their problems. Whether it was these kids or the fact that their parents wanted closure to their issues, it wasn't my place to pass judgment. I'd fucked up, and I regretted it. No longer did I have the delusions of grandeur that got me by for so long. No longer did I possess the arrogance that made me believe I could outwit anyone.

"That's bullshit. Anyway, come here, I have a gift for you."

"You don't have to give me anything. You already did." "Tina, really quick, I just wanted to tell you that your ear listens well. You're the one who helped me figure this out, and unless you're a narc, I guess I owe you for your time."

Tina put her arms around me and gave me a hug. "Is that the best you can do?"

"I love you. You were there for me and you will always be there for me."

"That's all I wanted to hear. Is that why my parents are so into their work, because they feel love?"

"No, Tina, they don't know what your love feels like. Why were you here so many times, anyway?" She owed me an explanation. I wanted a piece of her to take with me.

"Whoever the fuck you are, D, my story's not as much a convoluted mess as yours. The first time I came here, I was really young. Brittany's age. Anyway, my parents had just gotten a divorce, and my dad was off fucking younger women."

"The rabbi?"

She laughed. "Fuck you, he isn't a rabbi. Why all the stereotypes?"

"Well, it just seems preposterous. Anyone who knows me realizes that I'm not racist, and it makes for fun to emulate dipshits who think that every Jew is a fiddler and every Mick is a fighting drunk. If I ever offend anyone, I'll apologize and then piss on them behind their backs."

She shook her head. "You really do have some kind of attitude. Anyway, I came here really young. First, I was diagnosed with anorexia."

"Like Brittany."

"Yup, and then next time, bulimia."

"So they do go hand and hand, huh?"

"Although Sandler and his gaggle of super doctors would like to think they are helping every pathetic girl, person, who walks through that door, the truth is that this is nothing more than a breeding ground for different sub-classes of the problem."

"No shit? Go on, Tina."

"Well, I admit now that I wanted attention. Back then, anyway. Now, I'm just absorbed with the problem. You might think in your omnipotent little mind that you have this thing under control, D. Truth be told, like any other addiction, it rules you. I got carried away. My father didn't want to hear about it. I never tell him anything. My mother is a fucking lush. I guess I like to be raped of my dignity by coming here. This is where the real problem began, and this is where I think I might find my answers. I like to be punished. You know, the Catholic thing."

"Tina, let me tell you something that I've learned here, and please don't think that it's preachy. Believing that Bible is better than the Torah or the Qur'an is no different than thinking that *The Adventures of Huck Finn* is a better book than *Last of the Mohicans* or *Lord of the Rings*. It's all fucking fiction. Besides, you're only half Catholic."

"Yeah, the dark half. If I told my parents any of the shit that went on in here over the years, they'd take away my shelter." She lowered her head and closed her eyes. "Sometimes I feel like a paper doll. I didn't cost anything to create, there are hundreds of duplicates of me everywhere, and eventually I'll either whither or be blown away."

"Take it easy. I see the pills you're taking. Lithium, Tina? Are you kidding me? I'm surprised you aren't catatonic in the corner, mumbling to yourself. Statements like that aren't going to get you out of here. Apparently, Prophecy's rag-tag bunch of doctors don't see it that way; they own your ass. Whenever I wised up or made a derogatory statement, they gave me thirty lashings. You open your mouth and tell them to bite your cunt, and they up your dosage. What kind of bullshit is that? Fucking pigs. I bet your old man kicked on an extra wing to this place, and they keep you here so that you can stay out of his way when he's fucking around the world." She shut down and walked over to the fridge. "What did you bake me, a cake?"

"That is where you are dead wrong, my friend." She opened up the freezer, revealing two cartons of Camel Lights neatly stacked in the corner. She turned around and hugged me again.

I think she may have even been crying.

"You bitch, Tina! You mean you mooched all my cigarettes over the past couple of months—"

"Yeah, my brother sends me a care package every month. I guess I could have told you. Surprise. Besides, I figured since your parents always came up here to visit you, I wouldn't have to waste my bro's moolah.

I grabbed the cigarettes and gave her one last look. I headed down the old hall to my room and packed. Some of the things Tina said to me got under my skin. Not like the shit that Mariah had said that day at group. Whatever Tina was hiding from, escaping from, why here? Life is filled with little riddles like that. Why did that guy kill Freddy? Why did Reno save my ass? What was in the grave?

Tina was disturbed. I was happy that they didn't convince me that I needed to be on Lithium. They'd messed her up. To be quite honest, she was the best therapy that I'd found in that godforsaken place. Sandler didn't even have the balls to tell me what he thought was wrong.

Before stepping out of the building, I heard someone coming behind me down the hall. "Hey shithead, you never told me how you managed to graduate. How in the fuck did you kiss Angello's ass to get another chance? Fuck, I would have loved to have seen you on your knees begging for mercy."

"I didn't have to."

"Why? Did you convince the Dean to make him change his policy? Something behind the scenes?"

"No, that night, the same night that he told me I had failed his class, he had a heart attack. He never returned, and he neglected to pass on the information that I'd failed my seminar and my thesis to the administration. They didn't even think twice when they found my paper on his doorstep dampened by his sprinklers."

"So?"

"I guess they figured all the coke in his system caused him to accidentally drop it out front. The rest of the papers were inside, and the one he had been grading before his coronary had a fat bump of blow on it. They ended up passing the paper on to Findley, my advisor, who was head of the English department. He graded it. Findley had me for a couple of writing classes and figured that I'd probably missed most of my seminar, but he sympathized with failures. To make a long story short, Findley called me the day before I got to Prophecy. I ended up getting my deserved C. I graduated with a solid 2.077 average, lowest in my graduating class."

"You have to be fucking kidding me," Tina crowed as I kept walking. I wasn't kidding and I wasn't proud. But at least that asshole got his.

I was heading down the elevator when I looked at my watch. Four o'clock: time for my buddy to wash off the statue in the courtyard. That ritual had been my true obsession over the last few months, and I wanted closure. My parents could wait.

Maybe it was none of my business, but if anyone could, that guy could tell me what was going on with our fallen Prophecy leader. I rushed outside, passed the nuns with the basketballs and the yuppie/hippie doctors. I flew past the crippled old lady who fed the fat shitting birds. I saw the priest, ecclesiastic in his ways, torn and twisted, draining life from the courtyard. At one time, he was a proud protector of the hospital, but now, he was armless, tattered, and dismissed. The statue was larger than it had appeared from my second-story view. In my time spent analyzing him, I never really got to see him in the four o'clock sun.

Just as the caretaker was finishing up his service, I caught him. He collected his cleaning utensils. I walked up behind him.

"Excuse me, Sir." I didn't know how to approach the question, if there even was one.

He turned back to me. "Yes, young man?"

"I was curious. Well, I see you out here every day at four cleaning this statue that's totally trashed, and I wondered why the hospital even has this eyesore in the courtyard? Obviously you take care of it, but is Prophecy so poor that it can't afford to fix it or put a new statue here? Maybe they could erect some modern sculpture or something. Don't get me wrong; I think that it's therapeutic."

"Son, this is a dedication to Father Jason. It has been here for many years. At one time, he was held in very high regard by the hospital. I used to clean his chamber. He was a very nice man."

"You still aren't telling me why nobody cares about this statue, Sir. What the heck is the story? Did some big corporation buy out Prophecy? Can I make a donation to you? Should I go into the chapel and put money in one of those bedpans? What? God only knows that I had to sit up there on the second floor and look at this eyesore every day and wonder why it's so trashed." I lit up a cigarette. "I'm going to be honest with you, I'm not a very religious person. However, as far as I'm concerned, this is an important piece, a memory of this place. Someone besides you needs to look within their pockets and fix this thing."

"Father Jason is no longer affiliated with the hospital, son. After the allegations, he became very sick. He didn't have the will to spread the word of God any further. He just crumbled away."

"Allegations? What did he do, give someone too many Hail Mary's?" The caretaker picked up his cleaning supplies, knelt down and did his much-rehearsed sign of the cross.

"The allegations by the little girl. The rape. None of it's true." He tilted the brim of his hat and scraped some birdshit off of his shoe. "Nice meeting you, young man." He walked away, and everything made sense.

I looked up to the eating disorder unit to see if Tina was there. I knew she was right in the middle of ruining one of Sandler's pathetic group meetings, and I also knew that she didn't pay any attention to what went on down here. Through the iced windowpane, I thought that maybe, just maybe, I could make out a shadow, a figure. I pictured her being walked away by another figure, Sandler.

I was beginning to well up, so, I did what I thought was my best tribute to my friend trapped at Prophecy. I zipped down my fly for the second time that day, and let loose what I now knew about Prophecy, Sandler, and Father Jason.

Unlike when I'd unleashed myself on the world in high school, I didn't have that fury any longer. It seemed like every path I had crossed, every human contact I had ever made, the world, had just devoured itself and shit all over the place. When was there ever going to be anything better? All I asked for was some reassurance that this wasn't it. Where the fuck was I? On the bottom of the entire mess, sucking at its ankles and barely walking away. These are dark times and gods don't exist.

I decided to ditch my parents and take a walk around and enjoy my freedom. The only thing standing in my way was the hospital's kindly vagrant.

"Can you spare any change, mister?" he asked.

"Here you go." I handed him the two cartons of Camel Lights and dug around in my pocket. It was still there. I grabbed onto it tightly one last time and let it go. The lighter that Lori Conroy had given me in the car when I read her my poem had officially exchanged hands. "Take care of yourself. This should help you stay a little warmer."

"Thank you. Are you sure you don't want this stuff," he asked, his toothless gums smacking together as they cried out for a sampling from his newfound pot of gold. Being so close to him, I noticed that he wasn't much older than me.

"Take it; I have to quit smoking. It's killing me."

"What's your name, son?"

"My name's D. What's yours?"

He tore into a pack of cigarettes. "It's whatever you want it to be," he said.

"It's not St. Peter, is it," I asked, fixated on the gate that held me back from freedom.

"Nah. Name's Tom."

"Nice to meet you, Tom." I extended my hand to shake his, but it had an opened pack of cold hotdogs in it.

Cold hot dogs made me sick, so I offered him some advice. "You should be able to warm those up with the lighter. Maybe you can build a fire in a garbage can or something."

"No need. They taste better cold. I've eaten them this way forever."

I took one last look at the prison and leaped over the wrought-iron fence and into the backyard of my life.

It was time to escape again. Funny, when I was younger I'd always wanted to write horror stories. It took me a long time to realize that all I ever had to do was look around at the horror of the world, the horror of reality.

BOOK THREE

RESURRECTION

"God pours out love upon all with a lavish hand—but He reserves vengeance for His very own."

Samuel Langhorn Clemens

CHAPTER ONE

It was like planting a seed in concrete. That's how I felt upon moving to Los Angeles. Without knowing exactly from where the seed came, there was no way to possibly predict what the final outcome would be.

Sowing myself without confidence into a world that once again, I didn't understand; I bounced around aimlessly, never quite making it to any fertile soil. They say it takes an acorn quite a few years to become a tree. The tree, when untouched, outlives the human. In my case, with such a premeditated self-loathing in my sprouting process and without any answers to the questions of why and how, the chances that I would make it in a city piled high with crooks, gangsters, hookers, bigots and junkies seemed highly unlikely. I thought of myself as somewhat street smart. All preconceptions planted by the media aside, the cruel paths of Palmbrook were actually paved with gold compared to LA.

Do you know who you are? I mean, when you look at yourself in the mirror, what do you see? Can you even begin to answer that? Me? Not so much. Since I avoided mirrors at all costs—reflections grew increasingly more twisted—I never got a chance to get inside and count my rings. Like the tree never hears when it collapses, I hid. I buried myself so deep into the world that if there were answers at all, the only place they could be found was in my head. As my brain vomited furiously, I no longer needed escape. I wanted to return. Not return to Kudzutown per se, but return to where I had been mentally before the tragedy began and consumed me.

I'd outwitted death and now I had come to the conclusion that it was time to live. Like any living creature, I wanted to surround myself with others so that I wouldn't be the only target.

Count my rings. I wasn't the progeny of Mark Twain, no matter how badly I wanted to be. My stories, the ones so unspeakable to me, seemed like naptime to the citizens of my new world. I wasn't afraid of being caught; I was scared of never coming to terms with where the story really began. It was a race to see which would ultimately succeed in overpowering the other, the progression of the rings, or the deconstruction of my bark. You see, no one can tell you what has actually happened to a tree by simply looking at the rings. Sure, they can tell you the simple things like wet seasons and dry seasons (my liver, I'm sure, recorded quite an intense wet season) but they can never pinpoint the hardships, the fears, the forgotten.

So it began, my struggle to resurrect and cleanse myself from the dirty bog where I was born.

A city like Los Angeles couldn't be veiled behind such dreamlike names as Palmbrook or Kudzutown. Gunshots and helicopters reminded me of its reality every night. I couldn't breathe and the riddles of my existence plagued me more than ever. Nobody spoke to me anymore. I was alone.

I moved west to Los Angeles, as I told Sandler I would. With an inflatable mattress, some money my parents gave me for graduating from college, a Mont Blanc pen, a computer and less than a handful of dreams, I headed west after my welcome at Prophecy expired. Moving was my one final attempt at escape. I looked at the world with street smarts. I had no intention of illegal dealings, self-pity, or aligning myself with criminals.

I had never even been to a place like LA where people prided themselves on being fucked up. Everyone who ventured to LA had a dream. No matter how far-fetched, no matter how silly, they all had something ticking in the backs of their minds that said, "That could be me." Rather than take the role of the star-fucker, I decided that the big city appeal was not for me. I couldn't care less about the best-dressed asshole at the Academy Awards. My dreams were simply to escape from my past. With all of the phonies in Los Angeles, I was sure to slip through the cracks like every other sad dreamer who longed to get away from their pitiful lives.

I left Dirtybird at the city limits. The voices of my dead friends still haunted my daydreams. My nights were filled with dreams of losing teeth, missing class and not remembering my locker combination. I ignored them. I was content with my confusion and simply wanted to move on, get over it. Self-pity in a town of fallen angels was the duty of street corner musicians and vaudevillian boardwalk performers.

I was unpacking my car and moving into my new house when I became a target for a shirtless neighbor watering his front yard. "Where you from?" he asked. He was an older man with graying hair and a twitchy eye. Although not very defined, I could tell that he lifted weights or had worked fairly hard doing some type of manual labor at some point in his life. Like the general, his scars from years of hard work never went away, they just expanded.

"Out East," I replied as I grabbed for control of a huge box of clothes that was slipping out of my hands.

"East, huh? Whereabouts? My cousin lives out there."

"You know, a couple different places. I can never seem to find a place that I like enough to stay."

"You runnin'?" he asked as he stiffened up and picked at a scab on his left nipple.

"Running? I don't think I understand."

"Runnin'. You know. People don't move into this area unless they're runnin'." He hacked and spit onto his walkway. Then, in a split second, he flashed the hose and sprayed the phlegm off of the cement. I think he may even have caught the snot before it reached the ground.

I shook my head. "No, I'm not running from anything. I just wanted to get away."

"Well, you picked the wrong place to get away, boy. Ha!" The box in my arms continued to slip gradually down my chest.

"My name is D." Giving up on my slipping grip, I casually

dropped the box and headed over to shake his hand.

"Get the fuck off my property, boy!" He sprayed me with the hose to the delight of some kids playing craps across the street. I quickly back-stepped my way onto my property.

"Sorry. Umm, My name is D."

"Your name's gonna be ghost if you don't stay off other people's shit. I just put seeds in this yard. It's gonna be spring soon."

A female voice shrieked from inside his house. "Cappy, what's goin' on out there? Who you yellin' at?"

"Some white boy with green hair is movin' in next door. He's runnin' from somethin', he just ain't sayin' nothin'." He turned back one more time as I started to pick up the box. "What's up with that hair, boy? You look like a goddamn booger." It's funny, as soon as someone cuts you down to size, pitiful attempts at being the center of attention automatically become stupid.

"I don't know."

"Don't know," he began. "If I was your daddy, I'd beat your ass. You'd better change that clever little attitude of yours livin' up in here." He braced himself on his screen door and burst into laughter. "You're a walkin' target, dumbass."

"Thanks. I can take care of myself."

"Ha! You can't even lift that box. Do you know where you are? Don't be comin' up in here showin' how weak you are with your booger hair. Those kids across the street will jack you up like a BMW, and take them shoes off like hubcaps."

I had nothing to say. I just felt like a naïve kid being scolded for ripping a hole in a new pair of pants.

"Sorry, I didn't mean to offend you."

"Ha! I'm just messing with you, booger," he said as he entered the house and bolted the door shut. I got a good handle on the box and proceeded with my move in. As soon as I got behind the wooden gate, I lifted my belongings out of the box and took them in one by one.

"He doesn't got any good shit," one dice thrower yelled to his friends down the block. The rest laughed as if their decision to waste an hour casing me was in vain. They were right; I didn't have shit, and I was scared.

I got situated in my new place as fast as possible. Day after day, I developed a routine. I crossed my tiny yard, listened behind the gate, and then carefully hurried to my car to get a paper to search through the want ads. To my chagrin, every time I exited the house, Cappy would be sitting in his backyard. A feeble chain link fence divided us. He was always doing Cappy things. Sometimes he would be reading a book. Other times he would be eating. On the worst days, the days that he felt the need to start drinking before noon, he played with one of his many guns. The fence, although a clear barrier of our different lives, didn't have the protection of the graveyard that kept Cracktown away from me at Palmbrook. Now, I was in Cracktown whether I liked it our not.

"Where you going, Booger?" Cappy yelled one day. "Ha! You gonna to get yourself a paper to find yourself a nice, high-paying job?" I rarely answered him, but it was a nice day and I felt froggish.

"That's right, the sooner I get a job, the less I have to hear from you."

"Ha! You're funny, Booger. You gonna go get one of them high-paying artist jobs?"

"What do you mean?" I asked.

"You're some kind of artist, aren't you? I see your computer screen right through that window." Beside the fact that my house was almost less than livable, my landlord refused to purchase any blinds or curtains. Due to my lack of credit and money, I existed on an "as-is" renting policy. I'm sure I could have filed a complaint with some renter's rights bureau. It wouldn't have done me any good though, because even the cops refused to come into my neighborhood. I made sure that whenever I left the house I turned off my computer and made sure the monitor wasn't facing the window.

"I'm not an artist." Actually, I was quite flattered that someone would even think of me as an artist, romantic and silly as it may sound.

"Then why are you livin' here? Go back where you belong, son."

"Fuck you," I said before thinking. "I have just as much right to live here as you, Cappy."

"How do you know my name?" He shot up from his lawn chair and crept slowly toward the fence.

I was scared, and my attempt to look for help nearby was a giveaway. "I don't know. I hear your wife screaming it out all night long."

"Then you must be hearin' ghosts. My wife is dead." He slammed his fists on the fence, and one of his guns reflected the sun in my eyes.

"I'm sorry, man."

"Man? Who you callin' man? When you address me, you call me sir."

"I'm sorry, Sir, I just—"

"You just what? You just fucked up and said the wrong thing to the wrong person." His eyes poked at me, and I felt his trigger finger itching like it was covered in poison oak.

"I just didn't understand why you asked me if I was an artist."

"You have a lot to learn, boy. This isn't a safe place for you at all. What are you runnin' from?"

I bit my lip as I thought about a bottle of cold water in the fridge. He stared into me, like he was picking and choosing which of my secrets he wanted.

"You gonna answer me, Booger? Are you afraid of me?"

I didn't want to answer him. The second I admitted how afraid I was, he and his gaggle of neighborhood errand runners would roll my house. He just looked at me as he picked at the scab on his nipple.

"Nothing to say, huh, Booger?" He turned around and went into his house, slamming the screen door so hard behind him that something from inside crashed to the floor.

"What the fuck is going on out there, Cappy?" the mysterious voice called.

"Nothing, baby. I'm just messin' around with the white kid next door. Ha!"

"What an asshole." I mumbled quietly.

When I returned home and walked past the dividing fence, I looked out of the corner of my eye to see if Cappy was up to his lounging around for the day. He wasn't. I released a sigh of relief. I needed a break from his constant barrage of "messin' with." He was out doing his artistic thing. When I thought about what I knew about Cappy, I laughed, remembering scenes from 'hood or gangsta films. I never figured that the action would take place in the humble backyard that was covered with worthless shit, like the retired radios and appliances Cappy worked on. In the movies, the Original Gangsta, the OG, always drove a nice new car and worked in a sweet office overlooking the city. I guess those were hard times for everybody.

When I reached the safety of my door, which was actually about as sturdy as the rusted old screened entrance to Cappy's house, I found a couple of photocopied pages from the local newspaper. At first, I flattered myself into thinking that the local paper had heard about a hotshot young writer who had moved into the area and went out of their way to find me. Then I remembered that I had already interviewed, unsuccessfully, for a job with them. Unless I wanted to work in the mailroom, I was SOL. Frustrated, I ripped the rag off the door. The headline on the top article read: "What Constitutes an Art District."

I knew that I'd moved into a shitty part of town. Not that I'd had much choice in the matter. I was poor, unemployed, and had nothing to show for my life other than a mutilated set of teeth and a diploma I'd managed to pull out of my ass because Angello had a heart attack. How bad was the area? Let's put it this way: The term "Art District" didn't reflect Hemmingway's Lost Generation and their trips to France. It was a pleasant way of dressing up a gang area.

According to the articles, an Art District was given that title after something so horrible happened there that it inevitably became a ghost town if measures weren't taken to cover up the bloodstains. For instance, my area was dubbed one of these districts after a local security guard, a twenty year-old who dreamed of becoming a cop like his old man, got gang raped, shot twenty-seven times at a bank machine, and finally gutted. The entire machine was ripped out of the wall of the bank.

To the north, out in the valleys, another Art District was conceived after two hooligans rushed the town hall with AK47s and shot the mayor after a hearing didn't go the way the townsfolk expected. In yet another birth of an Art District, a man tied up his entire family (twelve in all, including uncles, parents, kids), slit their throats, and then threw their corpses off a tall building. If at any point I'd thought that I came from a hard, unforgiving world, I'd been blind to what was really going on. The Art Districts were the real shit. If Cappy, who I figured had left the clippings for me on the door, decided he wanted to frighten me, he did a good job.

In creating an Art District, a few prefabricated measures were always taken. One of these was to replace one of the corner liquor stores with a snotty coffee club. These places always had hippie music, brightly painted and oddly shaped tables, and a spoken word or open mic night. The one on the corner in my neighborhood was called Dandelion Wine. If the name alone wasn't enough to make you want to kill someone, the clientele and the employees would.

The charade was unbelievable; these fucking pompous assholes would risk their lives to sit inside a shitty little coffee "pub" with their laptops so they could keep it real. One time while walking by (I still opted for one of the corner liquor stores), I overheard this "cultured young lady" dissecting Richard Wright's *Native Son* with a white slam poet named Obsidian. I wouldn't have caught his name, or given a fuck, because he was a complete jackass and it most likely wouldn't have stayed in my head, but the girl felt it necessary to pronounce his name poetically at the beginning of every sentence. The audacity of these people made me want to sew my foreskin back on and then dip my dick in turpentine. They gave me the shivers. Don't get me wrong; I was in no way down with my neighbors, but at least I knew better than to announce the fact that I didn't fit in. I hid in my shitbox and kept my mouth shut. The joke was on them, though. There were much better stimulants on every other corner of town than those at Dandelion Wine.

Another part of creating an Art District was to hold a yearly art show in the town center to showcase local artists. I don't believe that I saw any of the locals participating in the show, though. The year that I did go, I saw Obsidian and his followers selling their depth to the masses. High society directors and producers entered town in big numbers during a festival. I only stayed at the festival for about fifteen minutes. Whether a painting entitled "Homeland" or a statue shaped like a huge phallus, I didn't give a fuck because I needed the old hair on the dog. The art was shit and I couldn't drink in the streets. That was unless I was carrying a brown-bagged forty, calling it a metro. Ironically, the showcase of fine local art was located at the exact same point where the security guard was shot up. I'm sure that his father found the show a great tribute to his son's memory.

The single positive element of the Art District initiative was the antique stores that also moved into the town square. They bought everything. Since the town had been there quite a while, the unemployed locals had nothing but family heirlooms to call assets. Case in point, the radios in Cappy's backyard. I figured he played around and fixed those to sell to the snobby cocksucker at the antique shop. Still, just as fraudulent as the rest of the camouflaged town center might be, the taking of people's memories by a snotty collector was fucked. The collectors drove twenty miles and jacked up the prices.

Politely, I asked Cappy, "Why did you leave those clippings on my door?"

"What did you say, Booger?"

"Why did you leave the newspaper articles on my door?"

"I don't know what you're talkin' about," Cappy returned as he peered out briefly from behind his copy of *People* magazine. I held up the articles that I'd been taking to the trash.

"These. Cappy. What? Are you trying to scare me? Is that what you want to do?" He continued to focus on his magazine, cleared his throat, and shot a ball of phlegm across his yard.

I opened the trashcan and dumped the articles. "I want to let you know something. I didn't move into your neighborhood because I thought I was a badass, or even an artist, for that matter. I don't have any money, and I don't have a job. I have no other choice. This is where I can afford to live."

"What are you goin' on about, Booger? You still not feelin' well?"

"What do you mean? I'm not sick." Reflexively, I felt my head and shook it.

"It sure sounded like you were sick last night. I heard a whole mess of vomiting coming from your house."

"I don't know what you're talking about."

"Yeah, you do. Is it heroin, Booger? Is that what you're runnin' from? Run no further. I can show you who the dealers are around here. Ha! They're a good bunch of fellas. They'll like you."

"I don't do heroin," I said knowing that Cappy overheard my barfarama ceremony. "I don't know what you're talking about. I was working last night." I was getting careless. Before,

I always prided myself on my stealth ability to quickly get rid of the bad.

"Workin', huh? Ha! I thought that you said you were unemployed." Finally, he put the magazine down in his lap and took off his glasses. Rather than look me in the face, though, he pretended to look through the front window into my house. "I bet you're hidin' a bunch of money in there."

"What do you know about work? All you do is sit back here and fuck around with me, read your magazines and books, fiddle around with all that shit you have all over the place, and clean your guns."

"That's right, Booger, Old Cappy retired a few years ago. I didn't have the mud for the streets any more."

"Tired of busting caps in people, Cappy?"

"Ha! That's it, Booger. Old Cappy was one hard man. That's how I know you're runnin'. Don't worry. It's gonna catch you. It always does."

"Then how come it never caught you?" I asked.

"It did. And that's why I retired. One hard man." Cappy flashed me a last look and returned to his magazine. I turned and went back into my shitbox.

+ + +

A pounding alarm went off on my front door as I recovered from a night of bad résumé fixes and even worse alcohol.

"Hey, Booger! Open up this door. Your rent is past due. If I don't get it by the end of the day, you're out." Before I could get up to answer the call, my landlord was gone. On the back of my plywood door, I found an eviction notice. Wow, if I collected a few of those notices maybe I could have covered my windows.

I was desperate. I couldn't sell my computer; that was the only way I could get a job. Although I'd learned plenty from my arts and crafts sessions during therapy at Prophecy, I don't think that a résumé written in crayon would impress any potential employers. I'd managed to retain almost enough money to pay the rent, but I was still about two hundred bucks short. I tried to come up with an answer to my dilemma. Maybe I could sell drugs. No, I wasn't quite that desperate. At least, not anymore.

Maybe I could write poems for the patrons of Dandelion Wine. Yeah, right. I would have been better off dancing with my pants down in front of the liquor store. My poetry was too white bread for those wannabes. I'd managed to avoid my landlord for a week or two, but it had finally came to the ever-desperate eleventh hour, payday. After about forty-five minutes of ridiculous ideas, I felt the unthinkable bulge in my pocket. As much as I tried to ignore it, it wouldn't go away. It was Freddy's pen. It was the only thing of worth that I had left.

As much as I had tried and wanted to escape who I was, my unfortunate circumstances once again burst into my head. The voices returned. Ignoring the voices, I went down to the pawnshop, sold Freddy's pen, and paid for another month in the shitbox.

My shitbox was indeed a little piece of shit. It was a one-bedroom, one-shitter backhouse. I made things much worse by stacking up old dishes and leaving beer cans around. Another contributing factor to the offensive nature of my abode was the stench. My place reeked of vomit for lack of ventilation. Things could have been a little better if my landlord had bothered to paint it or clean the rugs before I moved in, but that probably would have driven away the family of possums that lived in my caved ceiling. They were about the closest things to companions that I had. Quite a change of events from the solitude that I'd lived for at Nazareth; now I lived to have someone to talk to. Being alone in the Art District made me paranoid.

Despite Cappy's constant attempts to drag me down and feel like a complete waste of air, I managed to get a job as an associate editor of a porno magazine after a two-week process. A literary critic I was not, but porn paid the bills and I moved closer to my goal of being a writer. None of the friends I made while working outside the Art District limits came over to visit. They must have known—judging from the disarray that I called a desk—that my house was gross, but I guessed that they had no interest in risking their lives to see someone who stood at such a low level on the smut totem pole. They were people to talk to though.

The working world was something of an anomaly to me. Through all those years I spent pissing about in high school and the four that I had spent shitting on myself in college, I feared the working world. One time, during a group meeting at Prophecy, Sandler had said that I was afraid to move because I was afraid to work. Everyone is afraid they won't meet expectations. Everyone is afraid of personal failure. It wasn't so bad, though. I wasn't exactly a best-selling author, but I was starting out, and the work made me happy.

\+ + +

"You're working where?" the general asked, laughing somewhat, but not letting on to my mother that I was a smut peddler.

"I'm working for Denny Donnelly, Dad."

"You have got to be kidding me, D."

"No, I'm not."

I heard my mother call out in the background, "Where's he working?"

"Don't worry, dear." He muffled the phone with his hand. "He's *working*." He took his hand off of the receiver and returned to our conversation. "Which magazine?" he whispered.

"Are you familiar with *Thruster*?" I whispered back playfully. He stalled.

"No. I mean, I may have seen a couple at the newsstand."

"Where's he working?" my mother yelled out again, excited. "Is he working on a movie?" My father laughed and tried to cover for me. I believe he wanted to save the big surprise for when we were off of the phone.

"You know he doesn't like screenwriting. That's for hacks." *Good job, Dad*. She did, indeed, know that. At least I hadn't compromised my morals in that sense. "I'll tell her later, D. Can you send your magazine to my office?" He giggled discreetly.

"Yeah, Dad, I can do that. Should I send it in the blank envelopes that we have to send to subscribers in Salt Lake?"

"Um. Yeah. Make sure you do that. How is your apartment?"

"Well, I got a small backhouse in an Art District. It's pretty cool."

"Art District. Wow, they must pay pretty well for a junior editor."

"Something like that. Take care of Mom." Luckily, it was

a quiet night. I didn't want my parents to hear gunshots and helicopters when I spoke with them on the phone. I promised myself that as soon as I had saved enough money, I would go repurchase Freddy's pen. The guy at the shop promised me that he would keep it for me until I returned.

I noticed that the quiet nights made Cappy act the strangest. Every once and a while, I peeked through the towel that I draped over my corner window and watched what Cappy did to pass the time. He never wanted to be inside with the mystery woman. She yelled for him to come in, calling him a "motherfucker" every half hour, but he kept himself busy. That night, he was especially drunk and his guns made for modern Shakespearean props for the tragedy that was his life.

"Get the fuck out of here!" He mumbled as he aimed one of his guns at a tree. "Get on the ground." Then, similar to the way I had performed this act (without the guns of course), he would either stumble over or stagger around until he placed his ass in his favorite lawn chair. "What are you looking at?" I ducked, but he wasn't talking to me. He was speaking to memories. Possibly, I thought, they were memories of drug deals gone wrong or a traitor in his gang. Whatever the circumstances, they were memories of whatever caught him when he was running.

FWAP!

Cappy unloaded a round. I ducked again. I hadn't heard a gunshot that close since the farmer shot at Snif the night we went out picking shrooms. It was just as loud, just as fucked up, and just as terrifying.

"What are you doin', motherfucker?" The mystery voice shouted from inside Cappy's house. I slowly pushed my head up under the towel and watched. Cappy was all right. He wasn't passed out, but his head rested on his chest as the smoke from his gun circled his hand. A heavyset black woman ran out of the house. I couldn't believe it. She wasn't afraid of this drunken man swinging guns around and firing them off in her yard.

"Cappy? Cappy? Are you all right baby?" She glided her hand over his receding hairline and wept. "Baby. It's okay." Her voice became less frantic as she soothed him. Cappy didn't answer. He stared into the darkness at his bare feet. "Let's go in now, baby. I'm not gonna let my man die out here drunk tonight." She picked him up and struggled to get him back in the house. His wife wasn't dead. He'd been fucking with me when he told me that. I decided to keep my voyeurism into his world a secret though. Some things, even when looking in from the outside, are best left unsaid.

CHAPTER TWO

The constant threats from Cappy, my initial fear of the neighborhood kids, the blasting of guns, and the circling of helicopters every night convinced me that I ought to put some security measures in place to ensure that I could make it to work every day. Besides, content for porn couldn't write itself. Foolishly, I thought that my landlord would see my need for some type of alarm system. No such luck. Halfway through the hour-long conversation, I realized that he wouldn't even spring for blinds. To even ask for something as expensive as an alarm system was a waste. Near the end of the pointless conversation, I remembered something I had seen in the classified ads when I was looking for a job, an advertisement for a Great Dane rescue organization out in the country.

When I was young, I'd had a Great Dane named Nicky that looked just like Scooby-Doo. From what I remember—I don't remember a lot from when I was that age—Nicky was playful. So playful in fact, that after we had him for about six months he decided to grip my brother by the neck and carry him around the house. Say what you will about the docile Great Dane, it is an animal that was trained as a worker, and every worker feels a little disgruntled sometime in his life. We ended up giving Nicky away to a family who had a lot of land to keep him busy. I never saw him again, and my parents elected to get a sheepdog after that. But a work dog seemed like just what I needed. He could keep busy keeping my place safe.

I named my Dane Ripken after Cal Ripken, Jr. The dog was a massive hound and similar to Nicky and me in many ways. However, he was socially inept. Standing at about six-foot-three and weighing around a buck eighty, he sat in my front window all night and day. If any neighborhood "art dealers" came by to investigate the contents of the white kid's museum, Ripken would surely let them know that it was closed. If someone had a gun and wanted whatever was in my house, he or she would be more likely to shoot a dog than a person.

Ripken had uncropped, floppy Dane ears and big brown eyes that were clown-like when he winked with his unkempt eyelashes. I never considered cutting his ears, not because I'm a hippie, but because the cropped ears made Danes look like Dobermans. Anyone can overpower a Doberman; an angel in disguise was a lot more dangerous.

Ripken was a confused dog. I adopted him from a woman named Tracy Ward—the wife of television sidekick Burt Ward, who played Robin on *Batman*. She had found him wandering around in the desert aimlessly, jumping on random people, and wrestling them to the ground against their will. It took Tracy, three guys from Animal Control, and an assload of sedatives to get Ripken down. If only her husband hadn't been so busy paying the phone bill, I'm sure he would have used something in his utility belt to ease the situation. Tracy told me that Ripken was so purely bred and that he was meant to be a show dog. He looked different than most Danes. He was more retarded, with an enormous oblong head that looked like a Viking helmet. Unlike Nicky, who was a tan and black fawn, Ripken was a white Dane with a big black spot. I thought he was all black with a white spot, but she assured me that it was the other way around. It didn't make a lot of sense. Unfortunately for the Dane who would be king, however, his left nut didn't completely grow into its sack, making him useless as a show dog. So the owners apparently decided to throw him away in the desert. They must have figured that an animal that large would die from dehydration in a matter of hours.

His one nut situation didn't bother me at all; I had to get him neutered the day I picked him up as part of the adoption agreement anyway. I knew after sitting in on the surgery that nothing could ever hurt Ripken. He growled at the vet and refused any type of anesthetic. He didn't even flinch for a second when they sliced into his nut sack. Instead, he panted and licked my hand. When the operation was done, he attempted to maul a half German Shepherd, half-wolf mutt in the lobby.

"You can't control that dog," the shepherd's owner howled.

"Good," I returned. "You don't know where I live." Take that, Jack London. Buck from *Call of the Wild* would have been an appetizer for Ripken.

As our time together progressed, I discovered a lot about my dog and his past. For instance, he didn't like tall men. Color didn't necessarily matter at all, just tall men. Whenever someone he didn't perceive as friendly approached, he would lunge for the jugular. His previous owner was probably an abusive large male.

I spent a lot of money replacing windows over the next couple of months. Whenever I was delinquent paying electricity or gas bills, the big black Goliath that protected my house jumped through anything to mangle the state employee who came to collect my past-due bill.

Another strange thing about Ripken was his inability to consider the motorcycle a satisfactory means of transportation. I can't even begin to tell you how many times, whether riding in my car or during a walk, that he nearly tore my arm off trying to get two-wheeled death machines off the road. Once again, I thought of his previous owner. He was a big abusive man who rode a motorcycle. After he was through having his way, he would jump on his hog and leave Ripken cowering and shaking in his own piss.

Like most dogs, Ripken hated fireworks, gunshots, and thunder. I found his hatred of noise peculiar considering his bark had enough vigor to shake the windows on my house. Any noise would send him to the window. If a prowler was going to break into my house, he had better have been so slimy that he didn't register any footsteps. Unfortunately for a prowler, even a snake couldn't get by Ripken.

To me, Rip was a kind dog. Whenever he knew that I was in a bad way—he could hear me vomiting in our shitbox)—his hair would fall out. I had him checked several times for fleas and mange, but the result was always the same—he was upset. If I was upset about something, so was he. If I was mistreating myself, he would bite away at his skin until it bled. He bled a lot.

One Ripken quirk that I found frightening was his inability to understand commands. Whenever I scolded him—say for eating the keyboard of my computer—he wouldn't cower. Instead, he growled at me, the master, and went about his business. When he ate something like a remote control, he didn't gnaw away at the corner; he ate the entire thing. He even ate batteries. I bought several phones, because Ripken didn't appreciate the ringing noise.

He was far more powerful than I was, but I wasn't afraid of him. He was a good dog whenever he sat next to me like a guardian on the couch. His past did make me a little uneasy about his loyalty, though. But unable to understand his own size and power, he would sit in my lap like he was a five-pound Chihuahua. In a lot of ways, especially his size, he reminded me of Reno Lee.

Like most Danes, he ate a shitload of food. So much, in fact, that it probably would have been cheaper for me to suck it up and get an alarm system installed. I had a plan though, to save the money I was making from work and get out of the Art District. Besides, I loved the dog. The more I got used to his, "oh, you were sitting there, find a new place to sit" attitude, the more I liked him. He stood by his guns, as if I were able to, I would have stood by mine.

The first day I let Ripken stroll around my yard to find a good place to drop one of his bombs (they were huge), I got the exact reaction from Cappy that I'd expected.

"Booger!" I didn't answer. "Booger!" I peeked out from behind the towel and watched. "Booger! Motherfucker! You've got a Goddamn horse in your yard." Holding in the laughter, I went outside to introduce Cappy to my security system.

"Hey, Cappy. Don't worry; this is just my new dog."

"Dog? Where did you get that thing?"

"I went out to the country. There is a ranch for misplaced Great Danes. Say 'Hi' to Cappy, Ripken." Unsure at first, Cappy got up from his lawn chair and shuffled toward the shaky fence. Ripken lunged toward my neighbor with his jaws open. Spit and drool flew from his gums.

Cappy grabbed his chest and hopped backward. "What the fuck are you doin', Booger? Are you tryin' to give me a heart attack?"

Ripken tore at the chain link fence with all his fury. All of the things that he hated about big men who beat him focused on Cappy. After a five-minute display, I let Ripken back in the house. When I returned, Cappy was no longer shaking next to the fence. He was back in his lawn chair. "Ha! That sure is a big dog, Booger."

"You mean you're not afraid of him, Cappy?"

"Should I be? Is that why you got him?"

"No."

"Ha! If someone wants your shit, they ain't gonna care about some dog. All that dog means is one more bullet to them." Ignoring me, he pulled out his reading glasses and a crossword puzzle magazine that was folded up in his pocket. As Cappy settled back into to his chair, he pulled out a pen. It was college student Freddy Brubaker's pen in Cappy's hands.

"What are you doing?"

"I'm doing a crossword, son. You had better get back and tend to that animal of yours."

"That's my pen."

"No it isn't, Booger. I traded in one of my radios for it at a shop in town."

"Cappy, you have to give it back to me. Please." I wanted to beg, plead, but I didn't know what to say.

"I don't see your name on it. All it says here is," he pushed his reading glasses up a little. "'You did it. Love, Dad.' Ha! I don't see your name on it anywhere."

I turned around and went back inside my shitbox. My big day of triumph over Cappy had turned into my biggest tragedy. Not only was he not afraid of Ripken, he had Freddy's life.

Safely across Los Angeles from the Art District stood the town of Beverly Hills. I called it Kingdom Cum. I didn't call it that to protect the identities of those who lived there; I called it that because even in a place as surreal as Los Angeles, the mask of happiness had borders. It was what the rest of the world saw of the entire population of the angel-less city; it was hidden and secluded within its fabricated movie set exterior. The beauty inside was built on the broken backs of every other poor soul who wanted in. The town's history helped me supply it with an appropriate name. It was built to house and hide the beautiful people from the rest of the horror, and it served as a safe ground from the whores and bums that never made it onto the big screen at a theater near you. Almost everyone in Los Angeles made it onto TV one way or another. Usually, though the mega-stars-to-be were eyewitnesses to shootings on the local news.

Everything about Kingdom Cum was fake. The citizens who pranced around with their show dogs, fake tits, and plastic faces added to the overall feeling of an artificial environment. Even the town and its vegetation were a lie, not just the people. Unknown to many, palm trees are not indigenous to LA. They were the result of a democratic decision by the Powers That Were in a vote to shelter the city from the rest of the undeserving world and mask it within a wall of trees. After the original concept to build a moat around the city was deemed unfairly cruel, they decided on a more friendly way to perpetuate their ideal system. It was decided after many martinis that the reality of Los Angeles would be kept light years away, either by the aid of the palm tree or the ficus tree. Although I had no idea why the ficus was shot down, I figured that its expulsion from supremacy had something to do with the bourgeois nature of the fig. Besides, figs gave people gas. Gas seemed unacceptable in a world without character.

Whenever I got the good fortune to be invited inside the confined city, I was observed by the brotherhood of faultlessness as a vagabond. Unlike these misled souls, I never felt the need to dress to the aces to shoot down to the market and pick up a pack of smokes. When I went inside, it was usually for a job interview. Sadly, what I thought acceptable attire for interviewing probably cost less than the insoles for their shoes. I would have gladly given the shirt off my back to have those Italian imports (comfort at its finest) step on me. I didn't look at these people with jealousy. Even though their world stimulated me in my dreams, the Beverly Hillians made sure that I knew where I came from. Not directly, mind you, but in the way they spoke and looked at me. Parallel to my revoked membership to Palmbrook, Kingdom Cum had as much tolerance for my simplicity as Ripken did for a toy poodle that he tried to maul when I took him for a walk one Sunday afternoon.

"You can't handle that dog," yelled a shaken middle-aged man that I recognized from a movie.

"I'm really sorry. I just got him, and I'm trying to train him."

"What if I was a little boy, or God forbid, a little girl?"

"God forbid is right. Listen, I'm really sorry, mister. He doesn't know any better. He's scared." The flimsy poodle shook behind its owner's rollerblades. "Maybe if your dog was on a leash this wouldn't have happened."

"Are you trying to imply that this is in any way my fault, young man? Is that what you are saying?" He pulled his cell phone out of its holster. "Maybe I should call Animal Control on your dog."

"Please don't, mister." I pointed to the sign behind him that stated that walking your dog off of the leash was illegal. As I tried to bargain my way into a deal with the cocksucker, who might as well have been the overlord of the Kingdom, Ripken lifted his leg, making it clear that he was a far stronger candidate for the ruler. I knew that this guy thought he was hot shit in town. After growling at the rollerblades, Ripken squatted in the sewage drain and took an enormous smash. I was pretty sure that the runoff from the drain ended up back in my front yard, but it was still funny. The cell-phone-equipped fruit booter scoffed in disgust and continued on his way, repeating, "You can't handle that dog."

Knowing that he had no real case against me, even in his magnificence, I impishly returned a comment. "At least my dog doesn't look like a fucking Q-Tip." He glanced back for one final sneer aiming his fuck-you stare in my direction. I thought about acting on a disgruntled impulse and unleashing Ripken to finish the job, but it wasn't the poodle's fault. He was welcomed into Kingdom Cum by the arms of the rollerblader's eighteen-year-old girlfriend. At least there was someone to walk the dog while she finger-fucked her way into his medicine cabinet and heart.

Cosmetically designed to convey an unblemished world, Kingdom Cum was indeed close to perfection. The buildings, for example, were so pristine that they didn't even have any smudges or fingerprints on the windows. I hypothesized that each establishment had a window washer who worked around the clock to help preserve beauty. The price of perfection is matched only by the willingness of a few to forget who they are. There was no cemetery or hospital in Kingdom Cum, so even these perfect people weren't truly native to the area. No one was born there and no one was laid to rest there. It seemed like a good system. They only let the deserving in, and only until their fifteen minutes were up. Then they were booted and replaced.

The streets were pristine as well. According to the street signs, the street cleaner came by on Tuesdays, Thursdays, and Sunday nights. This prevented the citizens from showing off their new fleets of cars. There was a similar street cleaning sign outside my house in the Art District, but I think that it was just a reason for traffic cops to give out tickets. I never saw or heard any street-cleaning machine. I figured that one of the local artists jacked the driver and took the truck for a joyride, followed by a high-speed chase. In the eyes of the locals of Kingdom Cum, two days and one night a week that they couldn't flaunt their dollars probably made for a good tax break when it came to dispelling the riffraff that lived on the other side of the moat.

The surrounding palms also acted effectively to suck up most of the pollution that scurried over from downtown. The brown cloud of years of hedonism was unmistakably lowbrow. Strangely enough, the fog didn't exist in Kingdom Cum. Although the trees weren't indigenous to the perfect climate inside the city limits, they did a good job adapting. I was no different from the many praying mantises that sat on the palms' majestic leaves, gnawing away at the pollution and wishing one day to be accepted inside. I was on the outside, and even though I respected the trees and their replanted assimilation, I knew that I would forever be stiff-armed by these seedling sentinels.

Everything in Kingdom Cum was controlled by and wrapped in its own perfection. Like me, though, I knew that not every tree imported as a guard would successfully grow and aid in the battle. It's not that easy to plant a tree in concrete; the seeds always bounce back to their origin or sink into a crack.

CHAPTER THREE

My greatest fear had become a reality in my quest for freedom and escape. I was alone. Sure, I had Ripken. The stare you get from a dog when you're trying to carry on a conversation with it is worse than the looks you would get from people watching you talk to the animal. Ripken was my guardian angel in a city with so few angels to speak of. He was also a great companion. When he felt like it, he would sleep on my feet or hog the pillow on the inflate-a-bed. This was his way of telling me that he was there if Cappy or anyone else in the Art District decided to make an unexpected visit late at night.

The only words that Ripken understood were "food," "walk," and "outside." Any guidance or helping hand that he could offer was pretty much relegated to "You keep me happy and I'll keep you alive". He wasn't the smartest hound in the world, but he did have a keen sense of protection. As far as loneliness goes, prayers for company are rarely answered; however, sometimes desperation sends out a mating call.

"What are you doing here?" I asked, excited to hear a semi-familiar voice on the other end of the phone.

"I decided that I wanted to do something different with my life," Monica said. "So, in October, I packed my shit and moved." Her voice, though distorted by the phone that Ripken had judged enemy when he was alone, was just as enticing as it had been when it called me back from the ditch one shitty night.

"Why, to become an actress or something?"

"Get the fuck out of here. It's good to see your wise ass hasn't changed at all."

"Then why are you here, Monica?"

"I came out here to go to a school for special-effects makeup. You know, work in the movies and stuff."

"Cool," I said with envy. Special-effects reminded me of a time when I'd been consumed by horror: books and films.

Monica, Snif's cemetery-fuck punching bag moved to Los Angeles attempting to find, maybe stumble across, a dream. She didn't know what she wanted from life. Her choices when she was growing up were delegated by the laws of her parents and their needs.

There was something about her that I loved. Maybe it was the way she denied being just Snif's bitch, or maybe the way that she carried herself as the ultimate badass. I looked forward to the chance to be able to ogle that snappy bartender behavior of hers. It was sexy to me. "Do you want to get a drink, or something?" Even for a day, a drink, a conversation and a mutual past was better than staring into the oblivion that was Ripken's mind.

"I'd like that, D," she began. "I have nowhere to stay. I got here a week ago and the dickhead that I was staying with, some jerk I met on spring break a few years back, turned out to be a total crackhead. He lives with this freak hooker slut." I wanted her to keep talking.

"Crack addict. Wow, I thought by now you would be a little more accepting of people and their positive attributes."

"Oh, fuck off. That was a long time ago."

"It wasn't that long ago, Monica. Promise me that you're not going to bring any of that shit back into my life again."

"You act like I was the one dealing. Wake up prick; it was you." She was right, or at least right in part. Who was I to make any laws after breaking so many? I was the one who fucked around and shit on her town. "So, do you want to meet somewhere?"

"Actually Monica, I kind of have to wash my dog."

"And?"

"It's not as simple as it might sound." I looked across the room at my protector. Ripken had not only kidnapped my pillow and started tearing the stuffing out of it—he had also popped my inflate-a-bed and pissed on it. He sat on the floor and growled. Not big on balls and Frisbees and toys, he had his right leg tightly noosed around a doll that I'd bought him at the Goodwill.

"Do you want my help," she asked. "I mean, how long can washing a dog take?" I looked back at Ripken as he jumped to his feet and rushed toward the window where a centipede had decided to take a Saturday afternoon stroll.

"Uh, Monica, can you hold on for a second?"

"Sure," she said. I covered the jagged edges of the phone mouthpiece with my hand. If she was going to come over and help, it was better she remain clueless about the magnitude of the bathing situation.

"Ripken, no." I tried to create a focused command at whispered decibels. "Ripken. Goddamit, Ripken." He blew around for a second, shot me a scattered look, and then began pawing playfully at the window. I threw a CD at him, but it had no effect.

"D, are you still there?"

I tried to tiptoe sideways across the room and spank the beast on the ass. To my misfortune, the phone cord was tangled and wrapped up around a chair.

"Monica, can you hold on for another second?"

"Hurry up; I'm calling you from my cell phone." I put my phone down and proceeded to creep up behind him. His tongue dangled, throwing slobber on the backrest of my couch. Just as I was about to reach his hind legs and pull him away from the disaster ahead, the center of the window gave and glass crashed all over Ripken and all over me. Unafraid or even fazed by the mess, he went back to my pillow and, in an exhausted state, collapsed. *Hard work, huh, asshole*? As he licked at the blood and caterpillar guts on his paw, he reclaimed his little dolly and sneezed up mucus from his nose. Suddenly, an alarm system made from beer cans and fishing wire didn't seem like such an impractical idea.

Nearly laughing myself to tears, I composed myself and picked up the phone. "Yeah, that would be cool," I said trying to sound excited.

"What would be cool?" she asked.

"I think I need your help."

"Are you okay, D?"

"Yeah, just some technical issues with my house that needs to be addressed as soon as possible." I gave her my address and jumped in the shower.

When Monica arrived in the Art District, she surveyed the mess. "He did what?"

Ripken sat proudly in the shattered remains of my window with his head peering through the hole he had created. He liked Monica; I could tell right away. At one point, while she was leaning on the house and commanding my full attention, the dipshit dog tore the cuts in his paws more by sitting up like a little gentleman, resting on the jagged edges of the glass. I didn't want to look away from Monica—she was such a welcome sight to me—but I also didn't want Ripken to bleed to death.

"Ripken, get the fuck down. Anyway, while I was on the phone with you, he saw a bug on the window. Apparently, I don't feed him enough."

"How much do you feed that beast, D?"

"More than I can afford."

"What kind of dog is he," she asked as she cautiously approached him and began rubbing behind his silly clown-like ears.

"He's a Great Dane."

"I thought they were supposed to be mellow and carry booze around to people lost in the snow."

"That's a Saint Bernard, you retard. The woman I rescued him from told me he was supposed to be mellow, though. A regular house dog."

"Yeah, if you live in a mansion."

"Exactly. As you can tell, Ripken hasn't exactly learned the house-training part of being a house dog yet."

"You mean he shits in the house?"

"No, he doesn't do that, but he does turn everything in the house into shit. Sometimes, if he's really pissed off, he'll take a leak somewhere. It doesn't really matter to me; I don't have anything of value."

"Did you wash him yet?"

"No," I told her, a little embarrassed by my lack of strength. She slung her nightbag over her shoulder and took initiative. The bag and its possible sleepover contents made me smirk.

"Let's get that done. I want to take a look at those cuts on his paws. You're lucky I showed up when I did."

I breathed a sigh of relief. My loneliness seemed to be coming to an end. She snapped her fingers and Ripken trailed her into the bathroom. I followed.

"Okay D, I'll get his front end while you lift up his back legs." Ripken looked at us. He hated the bathtub. So much so that I hadn't bathed him since I picked him up. Although it probably would have been a lot easier to hose the idiot down, it was cold outside, and I knew that I would have to pay my landlord a rental fee for the use of his leaky hose.

"I don't think that is gonna work, Monica. I can't lift too much." Just then, the frightened mule dog let out a huge whiz in my face.

"Goddamit!" I screamed as I punched him as hard as I could in the ribcage.

"Rowllll!" He choked and ran to the corner of the bathroom.

"What the hell is wrong with you?" Monica shouted.

"He fucking took a leak in my face." I blindly searched for a towel. "What the fuck do you think is wrong with me? Goddamit!" I ripped the metal towel rack off the wall. I was pissed. I wanted to hunt my unruly pet down and beat him into the piss-stained carpet.

"He was scared, asshole. Settle down." Monica grabbed the rack out of my fist and put her hand on my shoulder. I took a breath and toweled the urine off of my face. My heart was racing. Fucking dog. Ever since Tommy Horton pissed on me when I was a kid, I've hated even thinking about urine. I shut it out.

"I'm sorry, Monica. I've never tried to wash him."

"You should have thought about that before you got such a huge dog."

"It seemed like a really good idea at the time. As I'm sure you may have noticed, I don't exactly live in the safest area of LA."

"Are there any?" she scoffed.

"Any what?"

"Good areas in LA? I've been here a bunch of times. I even lived out here for a couple of months when I was sixteen. The entire city is a dump."

Confused, I asked her why she decided to move back.

"I just wanted to do something different. Wade and I weren't getting along."

"You mean Snif?" I shook my head incredulously. "You got back together with that scumbag?"

With her index finger, she picked at one of her front teeth and looked away from me. "He was in bad shape, D. He needed my help."

Rather than risk ruining my chances of sleeping next to a human being, I tried to understand and move along with our reunion. It wasn't as easy as I thought it would be, though. "After you and Reno beat the shit out of him, he wasn't right," she added.

"Me? That asshole pulled a gun on me, and then Reno beat the shit out of him. I had nothing to do with it. Something strange was going on between the two of them that I wasn't even a part of."

"Did you watch?"

"Kind of. You remember the shape I was in. I couldn't run. I barely walked away. Reno had his way with Snif so quickly; I didn't even have time to turn. As far as enjoying it, well, I'm not going to lie, I would have enjoyed seeing any wannabe gangster getting his ass kicked after shoving a gun in my face."

"You loved it. Tell the truth."

I laughed. "Okay. He got what he deserved. Let's forget about it."

"Well, I went to the hospital after you went home, I guess. Wade had some major problems. The doctors told me he was lucky to live. His parents showed up and stuff and I was left responsible for him after they officially cut his little ass off."

"And Reno?"

"Who knows what happened to that psycho? Anyway, the next thing I knew was that I was driving him out to a ski village in Colorado. That's where I've been for the past few months."

I frowned and gave Monica the gas face. "That's odd."

"Not really. Chuck and Julia had been living in one of Chuck's parents' vacation homes. It was really nice."

"Chuck who? Is that one of Snif's drug-dealing buddies from the Panhandle?"

"No," she said. "Chuck Drost. Roast. He started dating my best friend. You know, the red-haired bartender at The Library. Speaking of, Chuck and Wade started a band together and played at The Library. Wade told me that music took his mind away from the fact that he could barely walk." As far as I was concerned that asshole hadn't earned the right to walk.

"Is he in a wheelchair?" I tried really hard to act somewhat concerned. In the back of my mind, however, I wanted nothing but misery for him.

"Not anymore. He walks pretty well with a cane now. He actually got the balls to go snowboarding on the mountain with us a couple of times."

"Well then, why did you leave him? I mean, it sounds as if you all had a great life." Again, I gave Monica the gas face. This time I flared my nostrils. "Wait a minute. Chuck and Snif hated each other."

She dug further into her tooth with her cheesily manicured nails. "I guess Wade realized that Chuck had a lot to offer. He's really good about helping out people he used to know. He even started a fund for that high school he used to go to."

"You mean that jail he and Bunky went to? How nice can Chuck actually be? I know I wouldn't want Wade to represent me at my father's business. In their case, I wouldn't want Wade to suck down all of the inhalants in the store."

"First of all, Chuck doesn't work for his father. He started his own company, a competitor. Secondly, Wade never asked him for a job, just a place to live until he got back on his feet."

"At the risk of sounding like a dick," I began, "judging from what you told me about Wade's injuries, 'until he got back on his feet' might as well have been eternity." I still respected the hell out of Roast. He proved to me that he was the only one out of all of us with any brains. Even though he'd made disparaging remarks about me to my face and behind my back, he never meant any harm.

"Chuck is really proud of you, D," she began again. "As soon as he found out that you were working for that magazine, he went out and bought a bunch of copies, telling everyone that you were following your dream to be a writer. It drove Wade nuts. He *really* doesn't like you."

"It's not exactly my dream. Working for a porno mag and a dirtbag like my boss is kind of shitty. I don't like pornography."

"Why? You're a guy."

"It's more than that. For example, there is this man there, crazy fucker. He's a cartoonist who drew a comic for my magazine called "Donald Fondle." It's gross molester shit.

Anyway, I found out he used to take his work home with him. He did some time in jail, and then the magazine hired him back the day he got out." Vomit crept up my throat. "It makes me fucking sick, but I need money."

"It's got to be better than dealing drugs, D."

I shrugged to concede the point. Attempting to leave my past back at Palmbrook forever, I changed the subject once again. "Can we just wash the dog?"

Monica wasn't in the mood to let me get off that easy. "I know the drug dealing was your idea, D. You're the reason all those bad things happened."

"Believe whatever you want," I snapped. "Yes, technically it was my idea. I'm not the one who started dicking people over and carrying a gun so that people thought I was a badass gangster. Can we please stop talking about it and wash the dog?"

"Fine."

I'd been asking myself these same questions ever since I left school, and I didn't need to be on trial by anyone else. Before I got a chance to see what was in the overnight bag though, I wanted to find out what drew her to Snif. I guess I wasn't ready to completely drop the conversation after all. I just wanted to turn it away from me and the questions I still couldn't answer.

"Really quick before we stop talking about this." I took a deep breath. "Why did you leave him? It sounds like, even though I know what an asshole Snif can be, that everything was going really well between the two of you."

She looked away from Ripken and met my gaze. "He's not a bad person, D. From the little I know of you, you two are a lot alike. You want more than anything for people to like you and accept you. For the most part, I got to see what Wade was really like. He's really nice."

With that, she picked up the front end as I struggled to lift the caboose of reluctant Ripken into the tub. Within seconds, he squealed and struggled as the three of us plunged forward. With a couple inches of water breaking our fall, we all got soaked. The dog hurled himself from the tub, wrapped himself up in the shower curtain, and then sprinted from the bathroom.

Monica and I sat there, freezing, wondering how we were going to disinfect the uncontrollable dog. I opted to ask for the landlord's hose, but Monica said that she had

a better idea. We dried off and headed out to her truck. "Follow me, D. I know how we can get Ripken in the tub."
"How?"

"Chez Vron."

"Chez Vron? I've never heard of it," I admitted. "Is that some fruity pet shop in Beverly Hills or something?"

"They might have one, or even a few in Bev Hills." I watched her closely. Her toned arms struggled with the stick of her huge International Scout. Sayings like, "You can take a girl out of the South," filled my head. Monica was finally a woman. I loved her sense of youth and invincibility. She wasn't anorexic, like most of the girls that I was attracted to. Rather, she was rugged, a tomboy with perky tits. She had kinky long blond hair that hid the tactfulness of a longshoreman. I watched her closely, and the recent memory of her trying to lift Ripken into the tub brought me to the conclusion that she would have no problem kicking my ass. I also remembered back at Palmbrook, when I stayed with her for a spell, she had told me about beating up Snif for cheating on her. She also said something about kicking the girl he was with in the tits or the cunt. Monica wasn't a bulldyke. She was just real.

"Why don't we just go to the hardware store and get a hose?" I asked.

"To begin with," she decided, "the spigot on the side of your house is broken and I don't have any money. And from the looks of things, I doubt you do, either."

"Is it that obvious?" I looked at my jeans to make sure that I didn't present myself like an oil-stained mechanic. I even brushed a little dandruff off of my sleeve.

"No, it just looks like you haven't eaten anything in a month. Don't worry; Chez Vron will have everything we need. Here we go." She bent her arms frantically and pealed into a gas station, cutting off three lanes of oncoming traffic.

"Chevron?" I asked.

"Yup. We can get beer, food, and all sorts of shit. I'll use my parents' gas card. They never bitch; it gets charged back to The Library for tax reasons." Once again, it looked as if The Library was my home even when all the way across the country.

"I understand the beer and food part of this puzzle, but what does it have to do with giving Ripken a bath?"

"He eats a lot, right? I figured we'd buy some sandwiches or something and then throw them in the back of the tub. Then we can bum rush him when he's not paying attention. By that point, he probably won't even care."

Monica's absurd and pricey plan worked. Not only did we get Ripken nice and clean, we also got ourselves nice and drunk.

We stayed up most of the night and talked about stupid things. Monica would talk to me in the silly voice that she had created mocking her parents' foreign accents. I told her about my job and the intricacies of the "money shot." We fixed the window with some empty cardboard boxes and then washed and patched the inflatable mattress.

"This thing isn't going to do, D," she pointed out as we began to doze off next to each other. "Tomorrow, we're going to go get my shit out of storage. It's pretty nice furniture. I stole it out of my parents' house."

I chuckled softly. "How about dinner after that, Monica?"

"I know a great French restaurant," she slurred back.

"Chez Vron?"

We slept next to each other that night, and the possums that lived in my ceiling didn't bother us. I didn't touch her. I knew better.

"Why did you get so pissed when Ripken peed on you?" she asked, whispering, just as I was about to doze off.

"I don't like to be pissed on."

About three months after Monica moved in, we started getting her mail forwarded to my house. It came in quite a peculiar way. About every week or so, a nice box would come in the mail with the contents of her past. Sure, I wanted to open the boxes, but it wasn't my business, even though only my name was on the lease and therefore, the mailbox. Monica had never done anything to warrant any paranoia on my part. She was there for me. She was a true giving person. She was the Mother Earth to my lost humanity. She picked me up off of my ass whenever I got drunk, even lectured me if I urinated anywhere that wasn't proper, and she bought me what I needed to survive from Chez Vron. She was an excellent, almost perfect, example of what a girlfriend should be. She was also someone to talk to and curb my loneliness. Although she didn't—and sometimes didn't care to—understand some of my more pretentious comments, she had a voice, and I loved having that voice rustling in my ear as I went to sleep.

"Hey, Monica, there's another package here for you," I said, delivering it with a kiss on the cheek. It was a good way to preface my dumb mistrust. "Wow, that post office up there in your little ski village must be pretty sweet."

"What do you mean?"

"I mean, whenever I move and get a change of address, they just slap a sticker on every piece of mail. About three months later—if I'm lucky—I'll get a letter that looks like it served as the toilet paper for about fifteen different mailmen and their horses."

"That's how they do it in a small town, D," she scoffed and then snagged the package out of my hand.

"Those boxes are pretty cool. You must be in good standing with your creditors."

"What gets into you? Do you know how many people live in a small ski town in the summer?" I must not have hidden my paranoid curiosity as well as I'd hoped. Her eyes curled up in anger as she posed the question.

"No, I don't spend a lot of time on the slopes. I kind of hate the cold."

"Well, then. The answer is none! Nobody lives there except for a bunch of bums and locals. Why do you think people who live out there paint ducks and knit blankets and make fishing lures?" I got her point; I was being a jerk.

"I guess I never thought about that," I admitted. "I'm sorry. Does this mean that you're never going to paint my dog?" I kissed her on the forehead, "Or, knit me a blanket…" and then on the lips, "…or, lure me with your fish?" I got down on my knees, pretending to snap at her pussy.

"You can be such a jackass sometimes, D. I have to go to school. Ripken needs to be walked; you need to send in the insurance payment on your car, call the gas company, and please do something about those fucking dirty dishes. I love you." She pecked me on the cheek.

"That's cool, Monica."

I had almost forgotten Cappy. Lately, I was always with

Monica, in or out, and she was the focus of my time. She made the lonely feeling go away and the darkness of my past seem as distant as a half-forgotten nightmare. In the back of my mind, I knew that Cappy had kept to himself for far too long. Something about the weather outside made him feel playful. Monica had asked me about him many times: what he did over there, what his deal was, how he treated me. I told her Cappy was dangerous.

"Hey pretty lady, you shackin' up with Booger?" Cappy yelled across the gate.

"Excuse me?" she returned snottily.

"I just wondered if you came here to clean Booger's pipes."

"Are you implying that I'm a hooker, asshole?" Without even seeing the look on Cappy's face, I knew that Monica's intense ability to be a bitch had thrown him for a loop. I wanted to get up and make peace, but I figured she was a big girl. At least, that's what she always told me.

"Listen motherfucker, D is an old friend of mine and I'm staying here, looking out for him until I can find a better place for the two of us to live. I would prefer, during that time, if you would quit your bitching, calling him 'Booger,' and scaring the shit out of both of us with your guns and your homies and your bullshit. That's right motherfucker, I see you over there at night with your Goddamn guns all night acting like a big fucking man."

She was making me nervous. From what the clerk at the market in the center of town had told me, Cappy had killed people for littering in his yard. The uneasy memory of people like Freddy Brubaker getting shot for much less than Monica defending herself made guns go off in my mind.

"How do you think your wife would feel if she knew you were talking to other women like that? Huh, dickhead? If you feel the need to come over here on our property, then do it. But if you feel all you're gonna do is sit over there and play with yourself and make racist comments about me and my boyfriend, then fuck off." Finally, she huffed and puffed, probably flashed her tits, and stormed through the front gate. Ripken barked furiously like a tornado had touched down in the yard.

"So that's how it is?" Cappy mumbled under his breath. That was mistake number two.

"What did you say, asshole?" Monica kicked the gate open

like she was ready to jump into a bare-knuckled brawl. "You must think you're some kind of badass motherfucker. If I were you, I would sit there quietly and do your puzzles before I let Ripken loose in your yard. Leave us alone!" She finally screeched.

Frantically, Ripken ran around in circles and pounced on the already broken windows. Then, like a hurricane that blew in and out in a matter of minutes, she was gone.

Not until Cappy was absolutely sure that she was far enough down the road did he mumble a little more. Then he laughed.

"Ha! I think you got a live one over up in there, Booger. She's much better protection than that dumb animal of yours. Ha! You must think you're some badass motherfucker," he said, mimicking Monica's voice. "Ha! A live one is right."

I agreed with Cappy. She was alive and on fire. She made our living situation bearable. She made my life happy. It didn't even bother me that I had neglected to save any money for us to move out. She was worth it. I think it was that moment that I realized how much I'd always loved her. People, romantics, always have these stupid revisionist stories about the first time they realized that they were in love with their mates. Most of these are bullshit about gazing into each other's eyes during a full moon and a hayride, or the man surrendering his coat during a chilling sunset beach walk. Monica's tenacity and ability to say the things that I never had the balls to express made me love her more. She gave me back the voice that I'd lost.

Cappy never bothered the two of us again.

+ + +

"How long have you been doing that, D?"

"Doing what, Monica? Washing my feet? Ever since they've been dirty and smelled."

"Don't treat me like an idiot," she sneered. "I know what you're doing in the bathroom."

I tried to play it cool. I doubted if she actually knew what I was doing. She'd just made a guess. I could bluff. "Okay, you busted me. I was jerking it. I'm sorry. I guess I should ask permission next time I pleasure myself. That's what relationships are about. Mutual consent, right?" Masturbating made a more feasible explanation. After all, how many men make themselves throw up?

"Didn't I just ask you nicely not to treat me like an idiot?"

"That depends," I said, smiling.

"On what?"

"What your definition of the word nicely is."

The smile didn't work. She wasn't having any. "I know what you do in there," she accused. "Chuck and Snif used to make jokes about it all the time. I know about you in the hospital. Every night when you're done eating dinner, you go into the bathroom and turn on the faucet. Do you honestly think that I don't know what you're doing?"

"Wow, maybe I should try a new lubricant."

"Stop!" The concern in her voice turned to anger. I tried to divert my tearing eyes.

"I'm sorry, Monica. I just always thought that if I made fun of it, it was humorous."

"It's not funny. It's lame. What are you, anyway? A thirteen-year-old girl?"

Now it was my turn to get angry. "That's a little strong. Now who's treating who like an idiot? It's really none of your business." Anger. It's the easiest way to be concerned or defensive.

"It's not, huh?"

"No, it's not." I felt my eyes narrow as I looked back at her. "Yeah, you're right. You've been living in my crummy little world with me, and I know how bad it sucks. It's not a ski chalet where people have time to handcraft little boxes and send personal messages to people they don't even know. I realize where we live right now is miserable. You just have to let me deal with changing our living situation and have this one thing that makes me happy."

"Then what is your alcoholism? A chaser?"

"Fuck off! I didn't ask you to move in with me and be with me so that you could pick apart and criticize my faults. Since when do you get off pointing the finger at an alcoholic, anyway? I don't see any DUIs on my driving record."

"There's none on mine, either, asshole."

"Oh, I forgot; Daddy hired an expensive lawyer to have that

minor infraction slapped off of your wrist."

"*I* paid for the lawyer, D. I'm still paying for it. Don't even start comparing the two of us. I can't remember the last time I blacked out and fell down."

"Gee whiz, Monica; neither can I."

Her face turned red and her eyes were as teary as mine. "That is so fucking stupid that it's sad."

"Well, I can't mentally remember doing it."

"You know what I mean," she said sourly. "Do you honestly think what you do to yourself is healthy? Do you think it's normal?"

I looked away again. "Who's to say what's normal, anyway?"

"Would you stop with all of the hypothetical nonsense? I left Snif because I was sick of taking care of him. I was sick of watching him destroy his life. Don't you realize that you have something to offer the world?"

"Who told you that? Me? Have you ever even read anything I've written?" She sawed away at her front tooth with her fingernail. "I didn't think so. All you have to gauge my ability is my penchant to pound on my own chest and declare myself great. I write for a porno magazine, Monica. And as far as Snif goes, come on. You left that scumbag because he was cheating on you."

"That was part of it. The other part, the main part, was that I was tired of this self-pity shit that all of you dickheads try to push on people. I grew up serving years of you thankless assholes who went to that shitty school. Great, I babysat a bunch of dysfunctional little rich crybabies my whole life, and now I live with one. Sure, they were all willing to tell me their life's story, as long as they knew they were going to get me into bed at the end of the night. Or how about bailing them out of jail? Even better, buying them crack."

"I don't know who you're talking to, but I don't appreciate it. I put my hand out so that you could have a place to live. I'm sorry if I fall down and get drunk and that I fist fuck my throat after I eat. It's who I am."

She softened her voice. "You still haven't answered my question."

"Which one?"

"How long have you been doing it?"

"I can't remember. A pretty long time, I guess."

I wanted to talk about something else, make fun of her parents' accents, anything. I hated being put on the spot when I knew deep down that I was wrong. Even worse, I didn't know how to make it right.

"I'll try to stop doing it," I finally said. My empty promise just made things worse.

"Do you think stopping it for a month is going to make years of this shit better? Imagine what's going on with your body. Is anything inside you still living?"

I lit a match and fired up a cigarette. "What the fuck do you want me to do?" I threw the match at her. "Should I roll over and play dead, Monica? It's not an issue that I can just turn on and off. Barfing is my choice. I don't know why, but it's all I ever think about. When we're eating, I always wish that you'd be called away for a while so I can take care of my business. That's how I think. Sometimes, I just want to be alone with my business."

She looked at the match burning a hole in the carpet at her feet. She stepped on the match. "With that attitude, D, all you're ever going to be is alone. Don't you have any desire to live, be true to yourself, and then die and go to heaven satisfied with your life?"

"If dying and going to heaven means being nonexistent and void, then no. I choose misery. As shitty and as fucked up as the world is, we only have one chance, and after that, nothing."

"There. You just said it yourself. Why don't you seize that one chance? Who gave you that chance?"

I puffed away on my cigarette. I wanted the conversation to end. I didn't want to get into a religious debate with my girlfriend. She told me one time that while she was living in that ski village that she had spent some time hanging out with a bunch of Jehovah's Witnesses. I always avoided conversations about my godlessness with others. It's an unaccepted belief. People have to believe in something to make their existence worthwhile. I had no right to judge the hopes and dreams of others; their god would be their judge.

"And that's what you believe? I thought you told me you were agnostic or something."

"Agnostic means I believe in something, a higher power. That's twelve-step bullshit. I believe in nothing. Nothing, get it? I refuse to believe in anything. We are nothing more than the mess we create." I met her gaze full on. "Take a look around, Monica. I'm sure that kid who got shot the fuck up last week on the corner went to church every Sunday. He said his prayers. The church is the most crowded building in this town. Which religion won out in his life, huh? I'll tell you which one: the religion of gangs, the religion that assured him protection and survival. And you know what? I don't think religion is wrong. I just see the world in a different way than you. It sucks for me, because in all of the bloody wars fought in the name of religion all of the sworn enemies agree on one thing—my religion, none, is the worst one. Their gods can fight each other until the end of time. Mine wasn't even invited to the pre-bout."

"Then you're an atheist."

"I'm nothing. I don't deserve even to be classified. I'm nothing."

"Well, if that's what you believe, I feel sorry for you. Without hope, you'll never be anything but alone."

"Don't be mad, Monica, I envy you and your ability to see a light, a promise of something coming from the sky or wherever. All I've ever seen or felt has been taken from me."

"Is that why you throw up?" she asked, trying to understand.

I shook my head and sucked into the filter of my smoke. "No, I don't think so. I just pity everyone. I haven't had a miserable life, but whenever I internalize—like I am now—I just feel rotten. No matter how much I wish I could pray, I know it wouldn't save me from catching a bullet. I think that's why I run. I'm always running, escaping from something. I care about you, Monica. I care about you so much, but I know that your god has even less time to be your bodyguard than I do."

"Who's *your* bodyguard? I mean, who watches you, D?"

"You do."

Months went by, and although I didn't stay true to my many promises to Monica, she thought I had and I guess that was all that really mattered. Whether she knew that I continued or not, she hadn't questioned me about it. Most likely, she ignored it. In June, her birthday rolled around and I had a surprise for her. It wouldn't make her forget my problems, but it would help. After several frightening months in the Art District, I'd managed to secure a loan through the Denny Donnelly Publishing Credit Union. It was enough money to put a security deposit down on a new place. It wasn't by any stretch of the imagination a place for the two of us to grow old together, but the place I'd found would keep us alive. Just outside of the confines of Kingdom Cum, the place wasn't a mansion that I had stumbled on or inherited from an uncle I didn't even know existed. Ridiculous stories like those were for the fantasy world. Nobody who lived in Kingdom Cum would have a nephew of my low standards.

Nestled on a cove under a highway, the place I rented was a pretty rundown two-bedroom, two-story house. Not a special home, but it was quiet and it had blinds on all of the windows. In the front yard, one of the straggler palm trees that didn't make the call for security in Kingdom Cum stood proudly. He was a carpetbagger like Monica and me.

About that same time, I was promoted to senior editor of *Thruster*. With Monica and I both working, we would be able to afford it. I didn't want to worry about Monica's portion of the security deposit. She was having trouble juggling school, her bartending job, and her credit card bills. Instead, I paid the initial move-in and divvied up the rent so that I would be paying two-thirds and she would pay the rest.

The house had no backyard to speak of, but the front had a five-foot fence that would allow Ripken to run around and shit at his leisure. Most of the grass was dead, so I decided that I might lay down some mulch or something. The general was always mulching useless little tree beds around the yard when I was a kid. My decision to rely on mulch of all things was one of those habits that were passed down. I was quite sure that Ripken would spread it all over the place and turn it into a complete mess while chasing the shadows of anything that drove by or flew overhead. But at least I would be showing Monica that I could do adult-type things. Things that didn't take place in the bathroom.

Like I said, the one palm tree wasn't as grand or noble as the guards of Kingdom Cum. Unfortunately, it also grew extremely close to one of the windows. When I was looking at the house, the landlord told me that it bumped against the window during windy nights, but then also promised me that none of the windows in the house had ever been broken since it was erected in the fifties. Nearly fifty years was a long time for the original windows to still be intact. Rather than curse myself for defacing a historical landmark, I figured that it was time for a little change. Ripken had become unusually hyper and he was at the age where chasing motorcycles was kid's stuff. He had moved onto bigger and better things, like cars and buses.

That night, Monica had class and then she had to work a few hours at the bar. Before she got home, I had planned to do something nice for her and then surprise her with the house after she was already content with the perfect birthday. As part of our cleaning regime, we traded dishes and vacuuming according to a list that she had semi-prepared on my computer. That day, her birthday, was her day to clean. In my preparation for what was to be the best birthday of her life, I remembered that she yearned for the day when she could return home and have a bath drawn up for her. I went one step further.

She called from her bartending job. "I'll probably be out of here in about in hour," she began. "The bar is pretty dead."

"You'd better hurry up; the house reeks. Remember the pizza crusts you fed Ripken last night?"

"Yeah, why?"

"Well, they came out the other end in the form of diarrhea all over the bathroom floor."

"So clean it up. Do you have polio?"

"I would clean it up, but your little cleaning list on the fridge clearly states that it's your day to clean."

"It's my birthday, jerk."

"Tough shit," I said sternly. "You made the list, and you also thought it was a good idea to feed the woolly mammoth pizza. You know his stomach can't handle it." I wanted to laugh, but if I was going to surprise her, she had to truly believe in her heart that I was the heartless asshole that Snif had told her I was.

"Whatever, D. Do you have any plans for tonight?"

"Not really. I figured we would just sit around and get drunk. Maybe we could watch basketball." She hated basketball. With a detectable bit of anger in her voice, she said good-bye. I got to work. Using a cookbook of her father's recipes that had been collecting dust since she moved in, I prepared a Swiss dish. It was Zürcher Eintopf, the meal that she'd recommended I order the first night I met her at her parents' restaurant. I knew it wouldn't be as good as anything her father cooked, but it would suffice.

With some of the leftover money from the loan, I bought a shitload of flowers and candles to strategically flood the outside of the tub. Sure, it might have been a little gay, but on this one day, I really wanted the chance to thank her for coming into my lonely life. Even though the sentiment of flowers is somewhat void in the eyes of someone who looks at them as a peace offering to a shitty world, I knew how important they were to her. From what she had told me about her childhood, not only had she never gotten flowers from anyone, but her parents usually handed her a stack of cash and sent her off in a cab to the nearest toy store. She needed to know what it felt like to be pampered and desired. She needed to know how miserable I was without her.

On the side of the tub, next to a rose and a card, I placed a glass of Captain Morgan's and Sprite with a bucket next to it that contained two full bottles of each beverage. It wasn't poetic. It was my way of offering my unconditional love.

"Did you clean it up?" she said as she entered the shitbox. After a full day of schooling and bartending, Ripken's mess was the last thing that she wanted to think about.

"No." I shook my head, hiding the corners of my lips inching into a smirk. "I already told you that it's your job."

"Why is the bath water running?"

"You know that new dress that you left on the bathroom floor?" She nodded and her face became pale. "He shit all over that, too." She looked over at Ripken. He was on the coach gnawing on a planted copy of what I wanted her to think was her favorite movie, *Urban Cowboy*.

"Ripken!" she screamed. "Come here." As always, whenever she commanded him to do something, he promptly responded. He pushed the phony tape to the side and ran over to lean on her waist. He couldn't tell the difference between anger and sympathy in a human's voice. As far as he knew, she was going to rub his belly. When he reached her, she grabbed him by the collar and escorted him to the mess. She marched through the kitchenette, and as planned, ignored the unfamiliar smell of cooking in the unused pots and pans.

She was furious. She was on fire. Cappy said it best; "she was a live one." In seconds after she opened the door to the bathroom, she realized that she had been fooled. Candles lit up in her eyes and she bent over to pick up one of the fifty flowers that lined the linoleum floor. That night was Monica's first real birthday.

As the two of us mowed down my "almost-as-good-as-her-father's" dinner, she told me that she had no idea that I could even cook. Ignoring my intuition to make a remark like "Wait until you try the seconds," I decided to turn off my habit of running to the bathroom. I didn't even think about the barfarama. Like I had told Sandler at Prophecy, it can be turned off and on. Respecting the work and feelings of others seemed sometimes to be more important than one meal.

"What do you want to do now?" she asked as she whispered in my ear and stroked my ribs.

"We can go out to a bar," I suggested. "I heard about this new lounge-type place across town."

"Baby, you've already spent enough money on me. Let's just stay in."

"Money is not an issue tonight, Monica. It's your day, and I want it to be as perfect as possible."

"Okay, D. Let's only go for a few drinks though. I have to wake up early tomorrow."

"So do I. That's cool. And don't worry about babysitting me tonight; I'm driving."

"Another first! I'm impressed."

"This is a night of many firsts, Monica. It's almost like being a grown up."

"Shut up, old man. Let's go."

I acted lost as we pulled up under the highway. I snatched the scribbled faux directions to the bar from my pocket, and acted as if I needed a decoder ring to understand them.

"Who gave you those directions, anyway? Who the hell told you about this bar? Do you even know what it's called?"

"I can't remember." I acted confused. "Some guy at work."

"Great. You're taking me to a tit bar."

"Give me a break. You know I hate those places."

"Let me see those directions." She grabbed the crumpled and soiled note from me and tried to read it. At first I could tell that she didn't understand the message. However, as soon as she saw the "rented" sign on the fence in the front yard, it was easy for her to put two and two together.

"Welcome to your new home, Monica. I love you," the note said.

Tears streamed down her face.

"I miss my home. I miss my friends. I miss my parents. I cry every day, D, and I don't know why. It's not about you. I can't even get to school on time in the morning because I have to pull over for an hour. Every time I get in my car, I have an emotional breakdown." The loneliness in her voice reflected what I had felt before she came into my life. It was as if I passed on my fears to her.

"I don't understand."

"I miss my parents." She rubbed at her face with her forearm, trying to keep her sadness from me. Was she was ashamed of herself? "It isn't you, D. I love you, and I know that you're trying, but I don't have any girlfriends out here, and our relationship is more like a relationship of two best friends. We don't have sex anymore, really, and that's partly my fault."

I shot back; frustrated with the way my surprise had backfired. "I don't have any friends either." I chose to confuse her melancholy with dissatisfaction. All I could hear in her voice was rejection. I had hesitated to return home, to Kudzutown, for so long that I actually forgot what it felt like to miss somebody.

"My parents have worked their whole lives to make me happy and this is how I repaid them—by running away, chasing unrealistic dreams. You're lucky, D; you know what you want to do with your life."

"Do I?" I jammed the car into park and lit a cigarette. I couldn't look at her. "I don't even know when or where my life began. I buried myself a long time ago."

"I know they want to retire soon, D. They have worked their entire lives as slaves to that restaurant and that fucking school. Something in my head keeps telling me that they need me now."

I was angry and I wanted to strike. I didn't have the right to judge her. Bad experiences in life are easier to forget, if you don't talk about them.

"I know that this house isn't much, Monica. I just wanted us to be safe together. I did this for us."

She grabbed my hand, but didn't look me in the eyes. "D,

how long do you think you're going to live? I mean, your body isn't going to be able to handle the way you treat it forever."

"What does that have to do with anything?"

"It's just that you say all the time how much you want us to be together."

"I mean that."

She beat her palm on the windshield. "How long?"

"I don't fucking know. Do you think that I've got the answers to everything? Do you think that I've come close to terms with who I am? I've done this shit for so long that I just figured that my body would have adjusted to it by now."

"Get the fuck out of here. You're killing yourself, D. Don't you think that it hurts me whenever you complain about your heart? Don't you think that it grosses me out when I feel your back and all I can feel are sharp bones? Don't you think that it hurts me when we have sex and your hip bones bruise my body?"

"I thought that the cushion from my gut prevented that."

"It's not funny. I hate seeing the way that your body collapses whenever you drink. I keep telling myself that it's going to change. How long is it going to be before you fall down and never get up again? I know you still do the barfarama. You haven't gained any weight since you promised me you'd stop. With the amount of beer you drink, it doesn't make any sense. How long is it going to be before you fall down?"

"I don't understand. I'm trying to do all of this for you."

"Why don't you do something for *yourself*? I'm not the one who needs help. What's going to happen when your body doesn't listen to you anymore? It sickens me to think about it. The more I try to forget about it, the more I see you crashing off of a barstool or running to the bathroom after you eat. Don't you believe that what you're doing is wrong? God didn't intend for you to do those things to your body."

Although the comfort and safety of her parents were the initial conversation, the focus had changed to the protection that I could never give Monica. "I don't believe in God, Monica," I answered, humiliated.

"If there is no God, who's going to watch over you if something did happen to me?"

"I'm a big boy."

"Bullshit. You're irresponsible. You have no clue what's

going on. You blindly look around at the world and figure that it is so horrible that you would rather hide and not exist. You ignore the responsibilities that any normal person your age has chosen to accept."

"And you're different, um, how?" I fired back in my defense. "You run away, too. For years you've ignored the things that your parents have provided you with and pursued anything that's different from that. Then, a few months down the road, you quit when you realize that you might have made a mistake. You always question your ability to follow your own dreams because you don't know what they are. You question whether or not there is something better for you than being a bartender who sells her integrity nightly to a bunch of dirty college kids."

"Maybe that's all I am." She sniffed.

"You know that's not true. You mean so much more to me than you could even imagine. You just haven't found what it is you're looking for. Big deal. I haven't found what I'm looking for, either. I want answers to who I am. I want to know why I act the way I do. Do you think I enjoy destroying myself? I know I say I love it, and that it's my euphoria. But the older I get, the more I realize that justifying my problems just perpetuates them. I've never thought I was depressed. I know when I'm around you I'm not."

"That's just it, D. I think that we do each other more harm than good."

I took one last look at the palm tree that proved even a seed planted in concrete could blossom, and I realized that my attempt to provide Monica with a new home, a new life, was a mistake. She was lonely because I couldn't give her what she really wanted. She wanted me.

Whenever the phone rang late at night, I didn't answer it. Usually it turned out to be an old friend who was drunk and thinking about me. Every once and a while though, it was bad news. I had a cut off time of eleven o'clock, especially on the weeknights. Instead of answering, I would stubbornly torture myself until morning before I retrieved the message. It sucked to not know what pain waited for me when the sun came up, but it gave me a chance to come up with solutions to all of life's little dilemmas. It was the way I was. For instance, I hated ripping off Band-aids in one quick motion. The thought of instant and quick pain didn't appeal to me at all. Monica was the opposite of me.

That day, she and I started packing to move into our new house under the highway. Luckily, she calmed down after her birthday passed, and I comforted her once again with a handful of false promises. As a team we tried to come to terms with the things that bothered us about each other. In an ultimatum situation, I promised her that my health would be considered before every drink and every meal. In return, she promised that she would continue to search for her niche, her dream.

I really put in an honest effort to heal my wounds, even though I lacked any real answers. She, on the other hand, found solace in shutting herself out of my world by placing phone calls to her friends and family more regularly. I was more concerned by the comments her friends and family made to her about finding her dreams than I was about our absurdly expensive phone bill. I didn't blame them; they missed her just as much as I knew I would if she left. I just wished they'd given her a chance before they assumed that she only belonged behind a bar. Maybe searching for your dreams in a city like Los Angeles is worthless, but her schooling was a step in the right direction. She never spoke about me as her boyfriend though, and it bothered me a little. She always told me that her friends and family weren't interested, that they had other issues to deal with and didn't care. As far as they knew, I was either an imaginary friend or her pimp.

Monica wasn't like me when it came to ignoring late-night callers. The way she looked at it, any conversation, even if it was a drunken ex-boyfriend, was better than involving her in my problems. As nobly as we tried, our conversations almost always ended up on the question of my health or her lack of friends. Other than that, our other conversations were usually reduced to nonsense chatter performed in her parents' European accents. Since her birthday, we didn't have much to talk about, but anything that would make us laugh or smile, no matter how insignificant, was better than crying.

Sexually, we weren't active at all. She'd heard my sex issues before, and although I had successfully managed to climax quite a few times with her in my pursuit of stability, she suffered from a similar sex drive, or lack thereof. One time she even told me that her mom thought she was a lesbian because she wasn't banging guys all the time. It didn't bother me, but it had gotten so far off our radar that it became uncomfortable for me to even touch her. I couldn't remember how to touch her in a way that would make her smile. Whenever I purposely rolled over in bed to put my arm around her while she was sleeping, she had no reaction. I still had hope for us, though.

As soon as we escaped from the Art District, our lives would change. I knew that. After all, our problems had to be the result of our environment and our fear for our lives. That controlled our lack of sentiment. Better yet, when I proved to the motherfuckers in Kingdom Cum that I was worthy, the sex would come as regularly as it had when we first fell in love. By that time, I wouldn't have to worry about alcoholism or bulimia, because money would make those things go away. That kind of thinking seemed to justify all of the things I knew were wrong with me. Blame someone or something else.

"Hello," she said as she surrendered to the rings of the late night caller. Her face immediately transformed from an expression of anticipation to a stunned and lifeless mask. "How did it happen?" Like they had so many times recently, the waterworks began as the fists clenched. I knew from my experiences with late-night callers that this wasn't a drunken friend. The call wasn't going to be good for either of us. I reached my hand out to comfort her, but she shrugged it away.

I wanted to run. I wanted to seek the shelter of Nazareth for the first time in more years that I could count. I wasn't making her sad this time. I wanted to comfort her. I wanted to hold her like I used to and tell her that everything would get better. I couldn't remember how.

I still had no idea what the conversation was about. She was choked up, and the only things that she kept repeating were, "where," "when," and "how."

I couldn't hide. I couldn't help. I had already managed to fuck things up between us so badly. I wanted to promise that this time, it would be different. I wanted to feel her body and make her smile. I wanted to go back to the first day we were together. I wanted to win the lottery and heal the wounds. I wanted to build her a mansion in Kingdom Cum. I wanted to feel her breath on my neck as I slept. I wanted to live.

Goddamit, I wanted to live.

For her. For me.

I love you so much, my head squealed. I love you so fucking much. Please don't leave me alone. Please don't leave me here alone. I don't want to run anymore. I want to be in you. I can't be alone. Please don't leave me. You are the only thing that I have ever had. I can't be alone. I'll stop. I'll stop being crazy. I'll stop being sad. Please don't cry. Don't leave me, Monica. I love you so fucking much. I'll be better. I'll be good. I'll stop. Please don't go. Please let me make it right. Please give me another chance to show you. I can do it. Don't leave me. I love you so fucking much. Please don't let me *stop*.

She hung up the phone and collapsed onto the couch, onto Ripken. He licked furiously at her tears to make them go away as he whimpered. The Library, the only thing that her parents had ever owned, had burned to the ground, trapping several drunken Palmbrook students inside. Her only home was gone, and her parents' dreams had disappeared with smoke in the night.

I've never felt so helpless in my life.

If only I had tried harder. If only I had given her something to ensure that she could one day find a dream of her own. If I had, maybe our journey would have taken a different course. Instead, I'd shut her out forever. I knew she was right, whenever she questioned my future health. She would never have me.

I wanted to say something, to tell her what I felt, but I'd vomit away the words.

After two weeks of little-to-no conversation following that late night call, my angel disappeared.

CHAPTER FOUR

"*Raerwl*," I heard Ripken squealing from outside. I rushed out to see what was going on. To my surprise, Cappy had him rolled over on his back, begging for something.

"What are you doing?" I asked. I snapped my fingers and called Ripken to my side. He ignored me.

"Ha! What does it look like?"

"What are you feeding him?" I snapped my fingers again. No response.

"I'm feedin' him hot dogs and rat poison. What else would I be feedin' this animal, Booger?"

I clapped my hand furiously. "Ripken, get your ass over here!"

He rolled over in response and thought about it. He snarled at me and returned to his back.

"You really should have let Cappy train this dog, Booger."

"Ripken, get your ass over here!"

"What's wrong with you, Booger? I'm just playin' with him."

"Ripken!" I screamed as he snarled again. He wanted whatever obscure food Cappy dangled over the fence. If it had been me holding the food, Ripken would have bitten through my hand to get it. Then, Cappy dropped it.

"She left you, huh, Booger?"

I didn't want to look at him. I didn't want to look into the eyes of my neighbor I knew I'd be living next door to for a much longer period.

"What's wrong, Booger?" He sneered. "Never had a woman leave you before? You didn't just lose your woman Boog, you lost your voice."

As much as I hated it, he was right. Monica was my voice. She was my balls.

"Looks like you got no one to protect you now, Boog. That dumb old dog of yours ain't gonna cut it." He raised his hand and cupped his mouth emulating a megaphone. "You hear that, niggers? Booger's house is open for business. The witch is gone. The witch is gone."

"Fuck you, Cappy." A voice, I had a voice without Monica. Like he had done many times before, he wrapped his big hands firmly around the fence.

"What did you say, Booger?"

"I told you to fuck off. All you do every day is think of little ways to scare the shit out of me and let me know how worthless I am. Take a look at yourself. You're the one who's worthless. All you do is sit back here, fiddle about in your fucking junk and scribble in old *TV Guides* and yell at me for doing shit I never did. If you and your gang want to come rob my ass, then so be it. Get it the fuck over with."

"What are you, Booger? Ha! What the fuck are you? What right do you have to tell me to fuck off? Oh, I forgot, you're some kinda artist."

"Don't tell me who I am." I spat at him. "I know who I am."

"Do you? You think all that time you spend in that house makin' yourself sick and pissin' off your woman is 'knowin' who you are?'"

"And you know who *you*. You know, when you're pissing yourself drunk and firing your gun into the night. Yeah Cappy, I've seen your bad gangster ass out here." His eyes cringed as the aluminum fence bent in his grip. His nipple started to bleed because he had been scratching it so hard.

"You don't know anythin' about my life, Booger. You have no right to say anythin' to me. I know who you are because I've seen your shit come and go. You think you're a real bad artist because you can come into our town and survive for a couple of months. Then what are you gonna do? I'll tell you what you're gonna do. You're gonna sell your life experiences in what you think is a fucking hood to a bunch of pussies like yourself in Hollywood. Don't you dare tell me who I am!" Cappy smacked his hands together and dust puffed in front of his face. A vein on his head bulged and grew across his hairline.

"I know where I live. It's my life. It ain't prison for me. It's my life. Do you think I sit back here and fuck with your little ass so you will leave my life? You bet your ass, boy. I want you outta here so bad I can taste it. It's not because I'm a fuckin' bigot, it's because if you stay, you're gonna bring bad shit to my life. I know you're runnin', and living back up in here, counting the gunshots like a clock until you can get out, is not a life lesson for you. You ain't foolin' nobody with your green hair and your big dog and your woman with the big-assed mouth. The only person you're foolin' is you. You know you don't belong here and you hate it here. What will eventually follow you hates you even more."

"For the last time." I walked toward Ripken, avoiding contact with Cappy's eyes. "I'm not here because I'm a fucking pussy artist like those assholes who hang out down at the coffeehouse. I didn't move here because I had a choice. I live here because I have no money, no life, no anything. You're right. I don't have much without Monica. She was indeed my voice. She was my everything. She was my misery and my fucking happiness." With my head down, I grabbed Ripken by the collar and dragged him inside.

My shitbox was cold without Ripken to sleep on my feet. Earlier in the week, my landlord had come over to measure some wall in the house, like he was ever going to renovate or sell it. He saw a portion of the door that Ripken had gnawed away and sentenced the hound to a life outside. I had to make do. Every day that passed was another step closer to my escape from the Art District. I was so close that I could taste it. As the second hand flipped back and forth on my broken clock, the reality of being stuck—even for a little bit longer—rang all too profoundly every time a bullet nailed another churchgoer outside.

That night marked two months since Monica had left me. Although my attempt at getting my shit together to "show her" was in vain, I was close to reaching one of my original long-term goals. I was close to moving on. I hadn't sprouted from the corrupt soil or cracked cement. I hadn't flowered or grown. I'd depended too heavily on Monica and the things she taught me. In her absence, I was gone as well. Take two steps forward and then plunge backward into regret.

If only I had told her that I would try. I'd lied to her and myself. I wasn't who I aspired to be any longer. I wasn't even what anyone wanted me to be. I was a fraud, a criminal, and an asshole. Remembering her tears, the proof that maybe she did care too much for me to stand by my side as I crumbled, I wanted to touch her, let her know that I was there, tell her I wasn't bad. But I was grasping toward the past with no possible way of making amends. Of all the things left unsaid, this was the one I regretted the most.

Like any other night, I stayed awake counting and scribbling on a notepad, trying to think of ways to tell her that I needed her. I wrote half-assed poetry that made no sense because it was phony, coming from me. All that it said to her was "You're glad you left, I hope your life is great." On that night, I fell asleep without sorrow. I fell asleep knowing that there was no revenge, no tears, and no excuses that could have gotten her back. What I neglected to remember was that I had played a small part in her retreat from the Art District. Her parents needed her. I wasn't willing to give us a chance for her to stay.

At the end of reading my pages upon pages of bullshit, I decided to let it die. All I had written was offensive catch phrases and second-hand greeting card sympathies. The words were everything that I never wanted to be. Neither heroic nor heartfelt, it was a book of lies; shitty little lies about things changing, kindred spirits, and my heart. I needed sleep. Even if I had to wake up and take Cappy's shit for the next two weeks before I moved, I knew it would be another voice that I could place a face to other than memories. I dozed. Not thinking of anything in particular or a flowered pasture at the end of a rainbow, I dozed because I was worn out. She was right about one thing; years of treating my body like shit couldn't be cured with one week of health. I slept. I was ready to begin again, like I had months earlier, and forget the feeling of remorse.

My brain dimmed into sleep.

SNAP!

A piece of chalk broke across my room. Before I had the chance to even fully wake up or wipe my glazed eyes, a dilapidated figure shuffled toward me at a powerful speed. He didn't talk, but there was no mistaking my visitor. Was I dreaming? He wasn't pastures. He wasn't flowers. He wasn't rainbows and saviors and fucking motherships. Worse, he wasn't gangs. He wasn't dreams.

With a cane, he unleashed bitterness, condensed and focused. First across the front of my face, breaking out my teeth and crumbling them into my eyes. Then he delivered several lashings to my head.

SNAP!

Before I could get up to defend myself, he was standing over me, dripping chalk dust in my face. He plunged his scepter deeply into my chest cavity and dug it around. Every time he pulled the cane out to deliver another crunch, he tugged away at parts of my ribcage. I howled for air. I felt my right lung collapse. A tingling alarm went off in my arm as if a fisherman were skinning it and letting loose an explosion of spaghetti and veins and blood.

I gasped for air as the newly cracked holes in my mouth whistled. I felt sharp edges of teeth poking through and cutting my face.

My lung felt like it was slipping down my body. My stomach convulsed inward and he had his way with my genitals. I swallowed teeth, and my tongue broke into reflexive seizures in an attempt to clear a passage. He pounded furiously away at my nuts with the handle of his cane. I felt the iron eight ball take aim and pound away at the thing that he hated most about me. I was running. I was a runner. How did he fucking find me? I had escaped. How did he find me?

SNAP!

He pounded away on my kneecaps. I bent my legs to soften

the blows, but they doubled over and become flaccid. He was relentless, and he wanted revenge. He grunted and groaned like a sow as I tried to block off more blows to my face with my arms. My forearms were no match for his cane. I gripped to make a fist, but the barrage continued every second. My fingers extended and shook. I felt blood dripping everywhere, inside and out, up and down. Sores formed on my body.

Just as I fell into shock, I remembered Monica's weekly mail in the small boxes. They were much like the ones we had used to deliver our drugs back at Palmbrook. Just as I was about to sign off, to lose myself in the blessed escape of sleep, another dark figure appeared in my shitbox. He held Ripken by the collar.

Sleep.

+ + +

When I finally woke, I shot up with a mechanic energy driven by the machines around me. I was surprised that I was still among the living. My tongue, cut and lumpy, gave the first sign that the experience wasn't a dream. I tried to get up, but my body lay bent in directions I had never imagined. From what I could see in the mirrorless room, I was badly bruised—mangled, damaged goods. It was the work of my old friend and co-worker, Wade Smith, Snif. In his mind, taking away from me what Reno had taken from him was his way of getting back at the gang. I was there; I saw it and I was guilty.

I looked around the room; he had spared my eyes from the thrashing. White walls. An overpowering aroma of bleach from cleansing made me shiver. Slings and tubes paraded around my body, each assigned to its own task. I noticed an I.V. in my left arm. With my right, I struggled furiously in my mummy wrapping sheets to free myself from it. I pulled at it with the right, trying to inch it out of my arm. It didn't work. If I had any energy, I would have just pulled it out. As I accepted my situation and pain, a police officer entered my room.

"How do you feel, son?" He looked surprised that I was awake and moving at all.

The insides of my cheeks elapsed around my broken molars

when I tried to answer. My lung wasn't performing so well, either.

"It's okay, take your time."

"How did I get here?" I managed to gasp out.

"The captain brought you down here three days ago. We got a call of an attack on the night of the break-in. You sure are lucky. If the captain hadn't gotten you here when he did, there's no tellin' where you'd be now."

"What happened to—" I inched out.

"The attacker? Don't worry. We've got him in an infirmary down at the state prison. He won't be bothering you anymore. Good thing you had that dog. He saved your life. I'm gonna tell my wife the second I get home to let the dog sleep inside. If he wasn't in the house, who knows?"

Inside, I thought. I remembered clearly that Ripken had been outside. I closed my eyes. "And the dog."

"I'm sorry, son, they had to take him to Animal Control. He nearly ripped the throat of," he looked at his report, "Wade Smith. That was your attacker, right? Did you know him?"

"Hey, let the boy get some rest." Someone else entered the room.

"Sorry, Captain. Just trying to figure what went on over there."

"Well, you'd better dry off them ears, son. This kid can barely speak." It was Cappy. The questioning officer left the room.

"Cappy, I don't understand."

"Understand what, Booger?"

"I thought—" I couldn't even begin to explain how I felt. I was a bigot, another Reno Lee who based all his hunches on stereotypes.

"You didn't think nothin'. Was that what you were runnin' from? I told you it would catch you."

"Why did you even come over?"

"Listen, Booger, I saw another white shithead comin' into my neighborhood, and I knew somethin' was wrong, especially when I saw him climbin' in your window. I didn't want to see you sent home to your parents dead with that stupid-assed green hair."

"And you're a cop?"

"Captain James Dill. But not any more, Booger. All I do is help out where I can. I retired a few years ago. You see, Boog, the reason I gave you all them news articles was I knew you'd wind up dead if you didn't know the difference between what is really going on in the world and what you see in the town circle during an art festival."

"What about Ripken?"

"I got him. I told them they had to put him down. No need for paperwork. They have no reason not to believe me."

"He's yours, Captain Dill. He always belonged to you."

"He saved your life, Booger." He paused. "They always catch you, Booger. I told you that. You can run and hide. You can even hide in a place where most people would never want to go. They always find you. The thing about escape is that the rest of the world doesn't vanish. They'll either keep lookin' or caring until they are positive that you're gone."

"Why did you care?"

"You're a dumb kid. I really don't care about you; I just don't like seein' dumb kids with dreams get killed. Where I come from, where you live, people get shot up all the time. They think it's for some kind of loyalty to their neighborhood, their life, but it's all bullshit. Havin' a gun doesn't mean having a God."

"Do you believe in God?"

"I hope so." He nodded. "Hope and my wife are the only two things that I have left. Without my hope, I can only say that I was put on this earth to save dumb kids. Most of them, I couldn't do anythin' about. You get to be my age, Boog, and you'll understand. There comes a point in a person's life where the thought of not existin', not passin' anythin' on, really gets you down. Do you ever feel it? Feel like it's all gonna end for you, and that you're gonna just be nothing more than someone else's memory?"

The only thing I could think about was Monica. I didn't want to be her memory.

"I see the way you look, Boog, the way you act. I know things about you. You're already someone's memory, because you don't want to know why you act this way, why you can't think of a reason to be alive. My God might not be your God, but I know I have to believe in somethin'. Even if it is a fantasy, I have to believe."

"I'm not the memory," I began. "I'm the carrier of bad memories. I can't shake them. They follow me through life.

I'm sorry, Cappy, I can't have God because the things I've seen, the things that I've felt, won't let me."

"Then you're always gonna be runnin' from somethin', Boog. If you're runnin' from belief because it hasn't jumped out at you and kissed your ass, then you'll be runnin' forever. Until you know what other reasons you're running, you're not even alive. I'm not a guardian angel or a prophet. I've looked up at the sky many times and shot my God the finger. When I got into my house, though, I said my prayers and hoped he wasn't lookin'. Oh, by the way Boog, I saw some other white kids creepin' around the neighborhood earlier. Your house was cleaned out."

"I figured as much. Damn white bastards. What about Wade? What did he say?"

"Well, he couldn't really say nothin'. Griffey ripped most of his throat out."

"Griffey?"

"You don't honestly think I'm gonna go home and have a dog named Ripken, do you?"

"No." We said our final good-byes, and Cappy dropped Freddy's Monte Blanc pen into the front pocket of my hospital gown.

"I've been watchin' this for you. You should've learned about tolerance before you moved next door to me, D." He walked away.

CHAPTER FIVE

The general flew through a yellow stoplight decorated with a swirl of kudzu and Christmas lights. I shuddered. Home at last.

"It's good to see you again, son. It's been a long time," he said, clutching my shoulder at the airport.

My mother teared up. "There's this great publishing house here, now. You don't have to live all the way out there," she said. Something in her voice, the unease, made me realize that even though I'd been running away all those years, the trip home was long overdue. I hadn't returned for any spell since high school, and when I'd last been in the vicinity, I'd been in Sisters of Prophecy Hospital.

I returned home with a mission. I had a fear of not getting that final chance to grip my parents and tell them I loved them before they passed. It was a mistake I had made too many times and it wasn't going to happen again. I returned home to come clean. I needed to right all of my wrongs.

"Get in check! Resurrect!"

That's what the sign promised with its gaudy neon catch phrase. It hovered, watched, and foretold the transformations that took place in the once-Kudzu-diseased town where I grew up. The billboarded gospel spoke loudly to townspeople willing to accept anything beyond the lives that they had lived and known for so long. It was the promise of Reverend Jackson

Christopher and the Resurrection Ministry.

From what I had seen of Christopher when channel-surfing while struggling with insomnia, he had become quite a powerful man. A sharply dressed former lawyer, he owned twelve all-day, all-night modern religious cable franchises. He had a popular syndicated radio show. He had an empire of glossy publications that fixated on our country's disregard for the Bible and God. Like any businessman, he put a spin on his brand—his many alleged encounters with God—by making it fashionable. "Get in check. Resurrect," was just one of the catch phrases his disciples screamed out in unison. His testament replaced the Hail Mary with the high five, the body of Christ with Doritos, and the cloth with a knotted silk scarf.

The rest of Christopher's ministry looked like a talent photo for an à la mode talk radio station. I hadn't seen all of the pay-to-play preachers; I had only been back in Kudzutown for two days. From what I saw on the billboards that seemed to be on every street corner in town, I guessed they were pretty unorthodox.

One of the preachers I did recognize: an ex-rapper named B9 (get it? Benign.). The alleged "streets of Chicago" native spent about a year on the charts. He collected a nice pocketful of change and then blew it on hookers, crack, and an entourage. Luckily for him, and Christopher as well, he found God. God pays people that defeated misfits easily recognize. Christopher was just the cashier in the whole process.

I had seen footage of B9 finding God on TV. He walked on stage during one of Reverend Christopher's convincing special effects shows with an Uzi, obviously a squirt gun, and threatened Christopher, saying that he was at wit's end. The show played out masterfully with strobe lights and pyrotechnics as the valiant priest walked toward his new follower, channeling the word of God, thereby showing lost B9 the way. I joked with a friend about how much God charged in licensing for his gospel. With Jackson Christopher's clutch on the misplaced, I'm sure he could afford whatever that fee might have been.

There was no way to avoid the sign from my parent's window. If Christopher and his team of ravenous lawyers hadn't moved in and taken the town, the general would have firebombed that thing the second they put it up. However, the general was a religious man. He found God whenever he was down on his luck. The facelift that the Resurrection Ministry had made to Kudzutown made the annoying rays of the sign bearable. Christopher had made the town where my parents lived and worked safe.

Instead burning it with an overgrowth of filth, the creeping kudzu cradled the renovated town. All of a sudden, new brown brick buildings, shopping malls and businesses sprang forth, empowered by the vine. The buildings were modern, but they gave off a rustic appeal because the overgrowth had actually carried a lot of history with it. It was no longer ugly as it threaded through the town. It was a promise of growth and a reflective memoir of a stale purgatory that had finally seen a light.

In the center of town, where the kudzu grew in tandem with the thriving industry of God, a repaired Norman Rockwell piece was outlined and ready for public viewing. Hometown businesses returned to their owners and out of the bank cellar, residents walked the streets proudly rather than lived on them, and a wind of relief brushed consumers with confidence. They had the money to spend and the places to buy the things that had once seemed always one town away. The closing of the paper mill and the toll it took for so many years was now just something for the little Christian soldiers to read about in Christopher's revisionist history pamphlet. This so-called history was taught at "Resurrection University," a small college that Christopher provided to the community members for free. It was free, at least, with the promise that the students would join his crusade and work for him.

I tried not to think much about the past. I managed to wash the pain off of my face, but I couldn't deny that if Christopher and his band had populated Kudzutown when I was in high school, maybe Freddy and Lori would still be alive.

Even my high school thrived. Test scores were up, the danger of gun-toting students dissipated, and, believe it or not, the school's football team, under the guidance of community college graduate Jim "Launch" Lonchar, had won two homecoming games in a row. Lonchar, a dedicated young coach, had even erected a memorial to Freddy Brubaker behind the home team goalpost on the new Resurrection Field. "The Team's Greatest Fan." I saw it briefly, but it seemed trivial to someone who knew Freddy. I was there. I remembered the price of being a fan. I remembered wiping away blood smeared in the home-team colors. I remembered.

Built, literally, from the ashes of the town, the Resurrection Ministry was conceived after the old paper mill was gutted. Reverend Christopher was lucky enough to get all the surrounding land, except for the land on the bank of the swamp where they built the new courthouse, for pennies. On these acres of land, the preacher built the ministry, the university, his television studio, and his many other businesses. The fact that he managed to populate most of the land in such a short period of time was nothing less than an actual miracle. I'd thought the soil and the buildings that were left after the paper mill had not only been condemned but also permanently retired. Apparently not.

The empire was self-funded by Christopher from the money he had made from solid investments over a ten-year period and the popularity of his first, and still highly rated show, *Get in Check. Resurrect!* The compound kept a watchful eye on the town because it was erected in such a way that it could be seen no matter where I was standing. I guess product placement, brainwashing, and billboards were not enough. The general told me on our drive in from the airport, that he (non-sacrilegiously of course) and his buddies jokingly nicknamed the superstructure Fort God.

Even in a perfectly harmonious world, there were problems. To begin with, if you didn't work for, attend school at, or dedicate your life to the church, you were either forced out of town or forced to prove your value to the town. Sure, you could be a Jew as long as you owned a successful business and had no skeletons in your closet. The reverend's power over Kudzutown was unquestionable. He was the closest thing to a Messiah that these poor fucks would ever get a chance to shake hands with. Although I'm sure Christopher could have had some of his special effects people rig something up, I could clearly see that this asshole's hands didn't bleed. The only thing that bled was the townspeople's pockets.

I admired the bridge Christopher built to join Church and State. Originally a lawyer by craft, he purposely built the ministry right next to the courthouse. No pun intended, the jury is still out on whether he funded the courthouse or not.

One casualty of the booming Kudzutown was the general.

He was diagnosed with bone cancer, and his intolerance to the Resurrection Ministry was not the best stance to take. He was still consulting when he had the strength to make it to work. What sucked about freelance consulting was that he no longer had the medical insurance that fulltime employment provided. With my mother's job at the courthouse, though, things were partially taken care of. Don't get me wrong; he wasn't some lifeless shell of his former self, he was just as powerful as ever physically. He just seemed more tolerant of the idiosyncrasies of the world. It wasn't about controlling and conquering for him anymore, it was more like self-control and sympathy. He had learned to deal with what his god had dealt him and accept it. Two fucked up children, for example. Too proud to admit his mistakes and too humbled to step on those draft dodgers he called "boss" or "sir." In his new state, he probably wouldn't have fought so strongly if the phone company misspelled his name on a bill.

My father had a new way about him. Although his form spoke differently, his demeanor was no longer one of kill-or-be-killed. He was more compassionate. He held my mother's hand and complimented her like I'm sure he did on the day when he carried her over the threshold away from her hateful father and into his life. He stood tall, but doubled over at times to cough. He closed his eyes in between thoughts to remind himself that he was human. Still a solider that frightened those who crossed him or his country, he wore his Purple Heart in a new way, with memory rather than with defiant pride. No one, especially Reverend Christopher, could ever take away his past and his dignity.

Would he understand the lame-by-comparison wars that I had fought? Did he really need to know? Probably not. I think that he rested much easier not knowing. If I didn't tell him, though, I knew something in my past would continue asking the questions for which I needed closure.

Do I know who I am?
I mean, really know who I am?
Do I know where I come from?
Do I know where I'm going?

My mother had gone to sleep, and I stayed awake with

the general trying to muster the courage to come clean. The general slept in his chair. I outlined the story and tried to make it plausible to someone who could never understand. I reached out every couple of minutes in an attempt to shake his knee and begin. Every time, I pulled away. In his restful state, in his sleep, did I have the right to use him as a receptacle for my sins, my pointless self-induced misery? As I fumbled through excuses and reasons, I remembered high school, Palmbrook, and what I had just left in Los Angeles: my real world, my third strike.

Get in Check. Resurrect!

What I had run from so many years ago, home, was now a safe house from the real world that sucker punched me as I stared at it blindly, star-struck. Great, this is fucking reality. This is what I condemned others for ignoring.

Get in Check. Resurrect!

On that Christmas Eve, that shitty sign was the only thing that I could see as it singed the blinds of my parent's house.

Get in check. Resurrect!

I licked the bridge inside my mouth that had replaced my front teeth as the end credits for Dickens's *Christmas Carol* rolled on what was already a draining night. It was time for me to resurrect the remains of my life. I finally found the guts to wake up the general and come clean about everything.

It was a tradition for the both of us to watch the Dickens masterpiece. My love for the film had nothing to do with religion or Christmas at all; I just liked it. I don't believe that the general ever stayed awake for more than the first ten minutes.

"Hey, Dad," I whispered as I nudged his knee. Nothing. Maybe I should have waited a little longer. I mean I had waited that long to say something, anyway; another day wasn't going to kill anybody. Almost everyone who was going to die was already dead. Ah, fuck it, I decided.

"Hey, Dad, wake up," I said a little louder. He sprung from his duck-print chair with his right eye open and a squirt of sleep juice on his chin. As his left hand slowly cranked itself ajar, he looked at his watch, then at the TV. When he had finally come to the conclusion that the film was over, he fell back into his chair and lit a butt.

"Movie's over, huh? It's a good one."

"Yeah. I wonder if you've ever seen it before."

"Don't have to; I read the book." He winked at me as he rolled the creaks out of his neck and ashed the cigarette that was quickly half finished. "What version were we watching anyway?"

"You know, the one where Tiny Tim got the operation," I joked. Even if Scrooge had given Tim this so-called miracle operation to help his problem he would still have been fucked up. Wait a minute; what the fuck was wrong with that kid, anyway? All I remember is that he was short, had a high-pitched voice, and scrambled around on a makeshift crutch. Could it be that Bob and his family pulled a fast one on Ebenezer?

"Your mother was really happy that you came home this Christmas," the general began, changing gears. "She and I really miss you. It is kind of strange not being able to see you son very much for ten years. We really wish that you'd move back here and be with us."

"Yeah, I know. But this isn't the place for me. I don't know what it is or why I didn't notice it when I was a kid, but I fucking hate it here. All I thought about on my flight over here was how much I wished the plane would crash into the old paper mill and engulf this shit in one big boom."

Was it that I regretted returning to Kudzutown? No, it was the horrible feeling that something bad might happen to my parents. Their ageing made saying anything about my mess more difficult. They weren't going to live forever. Maybe it would be better if they passed on still thinking of me as angel. Yeah, that would work. The way the general looked at it though, I knew that he would want to know everything. They would never quit loving me.

"The paper mill is gone. I know you don't like it here, son. There are times when I regret living here, too, but with the new courthouse working effectively, the police actually putting the dirtbags behind bars, and the new television station catching national attention, the businesses seem to be back on track. My consulting business is doing great." Television station. That's a laugh. The land Reverend Jackson Christopher had bought was filled with so much evil that even if every person in Kudzutown pissed holy water, they couldn't cleanse the rusted plumbing.

I swallowed and took a breath. If I was ever going to talk to the general, I had to do it now.

"Dad, listen, I wasn't completely honest with you about why Monica isn't with me any more. I didn't tell you why she moved home to be with her parents rather than me." I swallowed again. "I mean, she *did* go back to be by their sides. I would have done it if you and mom lost everything."

"I know, son. It's been hard for you." His head nodded back and forth as he began to fall back into the abyss of Christmas night. If I was going to drop a bomb, I sure as hell had to quit pulling on my dick and get down to business.

"It's more than that, Dad."

His head reluctantly sprung back up, as if he wished he had played possum and smoked his last cigarette of the night after I turned in.

"I came here to visit you this Christmas for a reason. I'm here to come clean about everything that I've kept from you. I want us to be right, because Monica and I never will be."

He arched his back, yawned, and cracked his neck again with his elbows and fists. Then the general popped up his mass with the arms of the chair and stood at attention. He shuffled toward the kitchen with his head down. "You want some coffee, son?" he grunted.

"Nah, I don't drink that mud. Maybe a glass of wine will do the trick."

With a half-grimace on his face he shot me a profile. "Since when do you drink wine?"

"I don't. But I figured since it's a holiday and all that I would show a tad of class."

"That's strange."

"Isn't it, though? People say and do the strangest things when they're scared. You'd better bring me the entire bottle."

He laughed. I knew comments like that ate him up, though.

"This is going to be pretty intense, isn't it, son?"

"That depends on whether or not you'll still respect me after you hear what I have to say." He lit another True Blue, fired up the coffeepot, and shrugged. I calmed down and readied myself for a court martial. It had been a long time coming. I finally came clean. I did. I told him everything.

+ + +

Stunned, amazed, and confused. Those were the emotions I read on my father's face. He didn't know what to say. Since I had hammered my way through about two bottles of wine, I didn't want to talk. The general was always a fair man. Sure, he played by his rules, but it was always his house. In the house of God, you play by those rules or you get your ass kicked.

"Why did you keep these things from us, son?" He placed his forehead in his hand.

I shrugged. "Why would I tell you? I'm not proud of it. I thought that it would have all come out in therapy."

"But son, your mother and I love you. We never want to see you in pain. Jesus Christ! It's not like we beat your brother to death when we found out he was dealing drugs. We *helped* him. All we ever wanted was to help you succeed and be a normal kid. I don't understand where all of this angst comes from." He paused in a revealing way, as if he did know something. He quickly covered his tracks. "What can your mother and I do to stop this? What can I do to make this right?" He wasn't disappointed in me and he didn't dig in to me with stories of Project Phoenix and how I've had it easy. I would never compare my modern pathetic experiences to what he had gone through; being in war is much worse than domestic and internal character flaws. For this one time, however, he didn't feel the need to judge me on what I hadn't done with my life compared to what he had done.

"I don't think that there is anything you can do, Dad. I don't blame you. I don't blame anyone. It's all about me. It's about these ridiculously childish fantasies that I have managed to convince myself are a reality. It's this gross life that I try to dismiss. I know nobody in Ethiopia is making themselves vomit or drinking themselves to death. I'm a joke. In this shithole we call home we have plenty of food, plenty of guns, and plenty of booze and drugs. Our over consumption automatically leads me to abuse anything I can get my hands on. You and Mom can't help me."

Tears streamed down his face. I think he understood my

pathetic attempt at being a scholar. He reached over to the couch with his superhuman hands and gripped my shoulder. "No, there is something." I felt his regret. There was something. My epitaph. "There is something more. Your mother and I never, ever wanted to tell you this." His voice grew cold and hesitant as if he were having flashbacks to a losing front on the battlefield. The church service choir pounding from the TV became louder. I couldn't control it. The general always held the remote between his legs, even if he was asleep. I had to watch what he was dreaming.

"What is it, Dad?"

"There is more to this story, more to your problems, than you have been led to believe. Since you were a kid, I guess we figured—your mother and me—that you would most likely forget all about it."

My heart went still in my chest. "What is it?" I shuddered and blinked. Did I want to hear this? Or did I already know? "Just tell me what it is. It can't be any worse than what I've already told you I've seen and done over the past ten years." For too long a moment, he didn't answer. "I mean, fuck, Dad, I haven't grown or learned anything except how to become angrier about everything, toward life. The only ability I have is pushing away people who love me, by treating them like shit because I don't have any answers for them."

I could feel myself slipping, tears slipping, and anger growing. The faces of my friends, the bitter end with Monica, it was all there. The general's face began to show signs of engine shutdown as the sides twitched and his lips triggered a flash of just one tooth underneath. He tried to hide his emotions by covering his face in his palms. He tried pushing it back together.

"Dad! Tell me!" I screamed. "Is it going to be okay? How's it going to end?"

He cleared his throat and took his face from the trenches and continued the epitaph. "Although I'm going against your mother's wishes, it is clear to me that this can't continue."

I shivered, breathing like a boar. My confused heart roamed around my chest; my stomach howled; my head filled with magnificent snowflakes and fuzzy rain. This time, it wasn't so enjoyable. I felt bodies hovering over me like limp marionettes, or like the multitude of ghosts, floating around with their chains in *A Chrismas Carol.* Freddy, bleeding and dripping with the face paint carved into his skin by the speed freak killer. Lori drenched and rung out by the strings of her puppet master, Rick Conroy. Mariah covered in parasites, dissipating and crumbling like a fossil under the foot of her father. In his father's hands, More-ganja smoking and burning into waste.

Horror stories.

"Not well, I'm afraid. For many years I have lied to you and kept something from you. I had hoped that by not telling you that you'd be able to live a normal life, a good life. You always had friends. You seemed well adapted in any situation. You never complain. I wanted to protect you. I never had any clear answers. D, I too am human. I too am a product of society. I fought in a war that I knew I couldn't win, but I believed I could, anyway. I did what I still believe was the right thing to do. In your case, you have fought something quite different—yourself. You have fought to find answers to your puzzle, and no matter how hard you tried to complete that journey, to get around the barriers, you still don't know what you're making because there is one piece still missing."

I composed myself and looked to his hand for guidance. "You know the final chapter. You have that final piece, Dad. Do I want to know?"

"No, you don't. But the time has come. If you hadn't woken me up tonight and told me everything about your experiences, I probably wouldn't have told you anything. I would have let everything work itself out." He sucked in one last breath and exhaled my greatest fear. "You were abused, D."

"By you?"

He was delirious. "No." He paused. "When you were young, a neighborhood teen, Tommy Horton. He raped you repeatedly. You were really young, five or so, and he was probably just starting his deviance."

"But I thought he only pissed on me under the porch." I kept trying to sidestep, hide. It was my way.

"Which is true. He did that, son, because he told you if you ever told anyone about it he would urinate on you for the rest of your life." The general didn't look up. "One day, your mother was on the porch, and she heard the entire thing. That night, when your mother told me, I went over to the Horton's house crying bloody murder and assaulted his father. The only thing we could do was keep our mouths shut and let them move away, or I would have faced criminal charges for pistol-whipping him with my Beretta. I acted like a machine. I was a trained killing machine. It was wrong." The tears had created a bib of water on the general's shirt.

"It wasn't wrong. You were protecting your family. You were protecting me. Where did it happen, Dad?"

"At the Horton's house, I kicked the door off the hinges and stormed in to kill that fucking little bastard. I wanted to kill a kid. His father jumped in and caught my fury while his mother drove him away."

"No, not that. Where did *it* happen?"

"One of your friends' mothers told Mom that they found you one day hidden and bleeding. You were over by the old paper mill."

"Hidden where, Dad?"

"I can't remember."

"Bullshit!"

"Underneath that old tree. The one that sat on the bank of the swamp." He closed his eyes and muttered, "That old tree."

"'Denial ain't just a river in Egypt'," I said, quoting Twain.

"I don't understand," the general returned, lifting an eyebrow and looking at me.

"I've always known something was wrong, Dad. I just wanted someone to say it."

"Maybe you should come back here and live for a while."

As the new reality of me came to light, the sign, Get in check. Resurrect! flickered out and all I could think about was my high school homecoming, and Rick Conroy at AutoRx wiping his cum into an oil rag.

EPILOGUE

I don't know if I'd been walking backwards or walking in circles since Freddy and Lori died. I wasn't walking straight, that's for sure. On Christmas day, I ventured back to my past. I decided to go back to Nazareth while the general informed my mom that their secret was out.

There was a lot more to the story than being ass fucked in a creek in front of a tree. I honestly have no recollection of the ass fucking, the touching, or the pissing events. So who knows why I wanted to go back. Who knows why I kept going back there in high school. Was it more for self-pity than catharsis? Most likely. I sure didn't want even a flicker of some neighborhood delinquent breathing close to me, whispering shit like, "If you tell your parents, you'll get spanked" and then dropping his juice all over my ass. Fuck that. I prefer making myself vomit to reliving that nightmare. Anyone who tells you that making yourself puke is a horrid and painful experience is a liar. When I puked I was in control and it was the only thing I could depend on. It was better than ejaculation, better than drugs, and better than companionship.

The winter wonderland of the Resurrection Ministry's park was draped in a foot of snow. The Rockwellian perfection reminded me of a torn up couch disguised with a silk sheet. Complete bullshit. There was no more bog. No more pollution. No more me. Now I was the carcass standing in the way of

Kudzutown's progress.

Icicles laced bush after bush and shimmering decorations guarded a path leading straight to the front door of Fort God. I supposed the path was meant to be a walking route for the health conscious. The path's final destination was a dead-end street for the higher-power conscious. Taking advice from Robert Frost, I walked through the snow.

I looked at the marble monument outlining the grave of Nazareth. The dedication on the monument read: "In the memory of Old Brother. Your watchful eye over our town will be greatly missed. Your power will carry on in the souls and hearts of us all. Amen."

Old Brother?

No one ever called the tree that. No one even knew it existed.

Below the metal plaque was the symbol for the Resurrection Ministry. They owned all the land now and they'd torn the fucking tree down. I looked up from the Reverend Jackson Christopher's historic masturbation, the erasing of my past. Inside an enclosed area, two small trees that I imagine some hippie planted grew from the once-dead soil. Little Christmas decorations of the Virgin Mary, Joseph, the Three Wise Man, the Baby Jesus, and most importantly, Santa Claus hung from the limbs.

"Hey, mister," said a small voice behind me. "Can you help me get my airplane off the lake?"

Lake. Don't you mean the pond that I used to shit and piss in when I was drunk? Don't you mean the watery grave where I buried my friends? I felt like someone shined the sun on my Dark Ages and melted away my life. All that was left was this. Perfection.

"Fuck off, kid," I snapped without looking at him.

"I'm telling my parents," the kid whimpered.

"Good. Tell them to fuck off, too." My eyes fastened on a painting of Nazareth centered between the new seedlings. The tree in the painting may have looked something like Nazareth, but the new man-made lake sparkled in the foreground and the ministry's main chapel blazed in the background. Abusing his artistic license, the painter portrayed the chapel's steeple breaking into the clouds and added the quote, "Kiss the Sky!" to the bottom of the painting.

"What the fuck?" I giggled.

FWAP!

A snowball pounded me in the back of the head. I spun around and caught a glimpse of my assailant standing on a mound a few yards away, packing a second snowball.

"Pretty nice, huh? A lot different from when you used to come here, D."

"Barry?" My eyes welled up. "What are you doing here?" With my knitted gloves, I wiped away my quick moment of weakness while getting the snowball remains off of my head.

Dressed in a police uniform was my former comrade, the Rastafarian football hero, Barry Denn.

"Umm. That would be, Detective Denn." He pointed to his badge. "I heard you were back, D. I come here all the time. I have been for years. Since I always used to see you here. I started coming here after—"

Silence befell both of us. "Yeah. After," I finally added. "What happened to the dreads?" I bent down to pack a snowball. "What happened to the Jamaican accent?"

Barry started jogging long to get a pass. "I stopped all that shit a long time ago."

"But what about being the descendant of Marcus Garvey, or whatever? What about that ring you had?" I threw the snowball about fifty yards downfield to Barry. He faked right and headed left. After the catch, he spiked the ball on an imaginary goal line. He hadn't lost a step.

"I bought that at a head shop," he yelled back.

"Kind of funny, huh, Barry?"

"What's that, D?"

"You know. That you used to work in a doughnut shop and now you're a cop."

"Yeah, D," Barry scoffed. "I haven't heard that one before."

I knew what I had to do. Like I had done the previous night with my father, I had to come clean to Barry. "You know I'm glad you're here." I took a deep breath and walked toward him. "I have something to tell you." I bent over to pack another snowball. "I know what else was found on Lori Conroy's car the night she died."

"Oh yeah." He nudged his head to the side. "What was

that?" He started sprinting out for a long pass. "Think you can throw this far, D?"

"It was a poem." I yelled.

"You wrote it, didn't you?" It wasn't really a question.

I nodded. Barry continued to go out for his pass. "I was there the night she died, Barry." I threw the snowball as hard as I could in his direction. I'd been running too long, but the words had followed me. It was time to free them. The general had made his confession. I had to make mine. Rather than food, I vomited the words out. "I pushed her off the Bay Bridge. She couldn't kill herself."

Barry stopped dead in his tracks. The snowball pegged him in the chest and dropped.

CARRRRUUNCH!

My head shot around. The ice in the middle of the lake had given way and the kid who asked me to help him retrieve his toy plane was being sucked under.

I turned back to Barry, who snapped into motion. "Holy fuck, D! Holy fuck!"

I took one last look at Barry. And then, one last look at Nazareth's grave. *It* wasn't going to happen again. I zipped up the front of my coat and dove chest first into the thin and breaking ice. I froze for a second and then began pawing around like a dog with one arm. My other arm furiously swiped about under the water, trying to grab on to the kid.

"D! Get the fuck out of there." Barry threw off his police belt, his holster and his cell phone and dove in behind me as soon as he reached the shoreline. He, too, froze on impact.

"It's not gonna happen again, Barry," I shivered. "God fucking dammit! I'm not gonna let it happen again!"

My right arm went completely numb. I continued to thrash around with the left. If I bumped into the kid, I doubt that I would even be able to feel him.

I turned around. Barry's face was bright blue and his lip quivered.

I got sucked under. As I went down a shard of ice cut into my head and pulled my beanie off.

"D! D!" Barry yelled.

I can't really remember how long I was under. Seconds felt

like eternity and my face froze as hard as a rock. I popped my head up.

Barry gained ground as quickly as he could. I propped my arm on a stable piece of ice. I gasped for air, but icy water filled my throat. I wanted to vomit but the only thing coming out poured from my nose. I sucked in. I sucked in again. I found something.

"D! D! You've got him." Barry was on top of me. "Help me pull him up."

With what I had left in my arm, I lifted as Barry bent the kid over his shoulder.

"It's not gonna happen again, Barry," I exhaled. Blood from my skull dripped into my eyes and congealed onto my eyebrows, my eyelashes, and my entire face. I felt faint and the flurries of my mind danced around as I faded in and out. Cold and numb.

"Come on, D!" Barry screeched. "I've got the kid!"

I pushed forward, eyeing the shore. It was just a few feet away. Barry tossed the kid on land and dragged himself out of the water. I faded out. A tree limb smacked me in the head, agitating the wound caused by the ice. Blood spurted out and somehow found its way into my mouth.

With the last bit of energy I had left, I grabbed onto the limb and Barry towed me in.

I faded again.

Coughed snot and water jolted me back to life seconds later. I looked next to me to see Barry cocooning the kid. The kid shivered and his eyes rolled around in his head.

"I only wanted my plane," he coughed.

"I know," Barry began. He looked over at me. "You okay, D?"

"The kid?"

"He's okay." Barry coughed. I did too. He patted around the snow for his cell phone. He found it and brought it to his mouth. "We have an emergency in Old Brother Park. A ten-year-old white male fell into the ice. Please send backup immediately."

"I found it hard to breathe and harder to talk. I forced the words out anyway. "I still need to talk to you," I started.

He looked back at me. "Don't tell them anything, D."

"What are you talking about, Barry?"

"I'm," he gasped for air, as if it were the last chance he had to speak. "I'm not the only one who knows you were on the Bay Bridge the night Lori died."

DREW STEPEK

Born in Royal Oak, Michigan on October 21st, 1970, the 35-year-old Drew Stepek has worked as a writer in all areas of the entertainment industry, including television, print and the Internet. After moving to LA in 1993, Drew began his career as a writer for Larry Flynt and eventually moved on to work for major shows writing, producing and directing online initiatives for *The Tonight Show with Jay Leno, Late Night with Conan O'Brien, Saturday Night Live, Buffy the Vampire Slayer, The Profiler, The Pretender,* TNBC and ESPN. He earned a BA degree in English/ Anthropology from Rollins College in Winter Park, Florida.

Throughout his amazing career as an illuminating and creative writer, Drew has been struggling with the effects of bulimia for more than 17 years and decided to attack the issue of addiction from an entirely new perspective. Using his painstaking explorations and personal observations, he has written a novel that takes readers on an intense journey of what lies beneath, behind and beyond addiction. His first novel, *GODLESS,* which is realizing huge success based on 100% word of mouth, comes after his short story "Nazareth," published in Joe Firmage's book The Truth in 1998. Several million intrigued readers were shocked by Drew's realistic portrait of the world. Now, in *GODLESS,* Drew paints a portrait of a character named D, who views reality in a confused world. Attempting to come to terms with a dilemma that most would be terrified to face, the primary character in *GODLESS* makes an agonizing attempt at overcoming a vicious struggle with bulimia, alcoholism and drug abuse. While some take offense at Drew's distinctive openness in sharing his truth, through his desire to deal with a very painful addiction, Drew's readers cannot help but to be drawn into an unknown and unspoken territory that affects countless individuals.

What is the essence of Drew Stepek's message? His underground success communicates emotions, truth and the pain of addiction, in a way that makes one stop and take notice. Giving his readers an invaluable resource, the plain and simple truth is that Drew is a writer that makes you live his words. Drew is currently working on the first of four sequels to *GODLESS* titled *MARTYR*. To learn more about Drew, check out www.godless.com.

Very special thanks and love to Laurie.

www.ingramcontent.com/pod-product-compliance
Lightning Source LLC
Chambersburg PA
CBHW020257030826
48979CB00026B/1382/J

* 9 7 8 0 9 7 8 6 0 2 4 9 9 *